Lawrence Block is the author of twelve Matthew Scudder mysteries, including *A Dance at the Slaughterhouse*. He is the winner of three Edgar Allan Poe Awards, four Shamus Awards, a Nero Wolfe Award, and two Maltese Falcon Awards. He lives in New York City.

THE MATTHEW SCUDDER NOVELS
BY LAWRENCE BLOCK

The Sins of the Fathers
Time to Murder and Create
In the Midst of Death
A Stab in the Dark
Eight Million Ways to Die
When the Sacred Ginmill Closes
Out on the Cutting Edge
A Ticket to the Boneyard
A Dance at the Slaughterhouse
A Walk Among the Tombstones
The Devil Knows You're Dead
A Long Line of Dead Men

The Matthew Scudder series

'Scudder is one of the most appealing series characters around' *LA Times*

'It's well plotted, well written and very, very nasty'
Washington Sunday Times

'Pitch perfect . . . Scudder's evolution in Block's series is as convincing as real life' *Publishers Weekly*

'Outstanding . . . excellent . . . smoothly paced, deftly plotted, brightly phrased study of perversity'
Chicago Tribune

'One of the very best writers now working the beat . . . Block has done something new and remarkable with the private-eye novel' *Wall Street Journal*

'Absolutely riveting . . . Block is terrific'
Washington Post

A Walk
Among the Tombstones

LAWRENCE BLOCK

PHŒNIX

A PHOENIX PAPERBACK

First published in Great Britain by Orion in 1993
This paperback edition published in 1994 by Phoenix,
a division of Orion Books Ltd,
Orion House, 5 Upper St Martin's Lane,
London WC2H 9EA

Reissued 1996

Copyright © 1992 by Lawrence Block

Published by arrangement with William Morrow & Co, Inc.

A CIP catalogue record for this book is available from the
British Library.

ISBN: 1 85799 302 0

Printed and bound in Great Britain by
The Guernsey Press Co. Ltd, Guernsey, C.I.

for LYNNE

Acknowledgments

I am pleased to acknowledge the substantial contributions of the Writers Room, where much of the preliminary work on this book was done, and of the Ragdale Foundation, where it was written. Thanks, too, to George Cabanas and Eddie Lama, and also to Jack Hitt and Paul Tough, who introduced me to the Kongs. And, finally, to Sarah Elizabeth Miles, who swears she'll do anything—anything!—to get her name in a book.

Baby, baby, naughty baby
Hush, you squalling thing, I say
Peace this moment, peace, or maybe
Bonaparte will pass this way

Baby, baby, he's a giant
Tall and black as Monmouth steeple
And he breakfasts, dines and suppers
Every day on naughty people

Baby, baby, if he hears you
As he gallops past the house
Limb from limb at once he'll tear you
Just as pussy tears a mouse

And he'll beat you, beat you, beat you
And he'll beat you all to pap
And he'll eat you, eat you, eat you
Every morsel snap snap snap!

                              English Lullaby

1

On the last Thursday in March, somewhere between ten-thirty and eleven in the morning, Francine Khoury told her husband she was going out for a while, she had marketing to do.

"Take my car," he suggested. "I'm not going anywhere."

"It's too big," she said. "Time I took it, I felt like I was steering a boat."

"Whatever you say," he said.

The cars, his Buick Park Avenue and her Toyota Camry, shared the garage behind their house, a mock-Tudor structure of half-timbered stucco on Colonial Road between Seventy-eighth and Seventy-ninth streets, in the Bay Ridge section of Brooklyn. She started up the Camry, backed out of the garage, triggered the remote unit to close the garage door, then backed all the way out to the street. At the first red light she popped a classical cassette into the tape deck. Beethoven, one of the late quartets. She listened to jazz at home, it was Kenan's favorite music, but classical chamber music was what she played when she drove.

She was an attractive woman, five-six, 115 pounds, built

large on top, narrow at the waist, trim in the hips. Dark hair, lustrous and curly, combed back off her face. Dark eyes, an aquiline nose, a generous, full-lipped mouth.

The mouth is always closed in photographs. She had, I understand, prominent upper incisors and a substantial overbite, and anxiety over this feature kept her from smiling much. In her wedding pictures she is beaming and radiant, but her teeth remain invisible.

Her complexion was olive, and her skin tanned deeply and readily. She already had a start on the summer's tan; she and Kenan had spent the last week of February on the beach at Negril, in Jamaica. She'd have been darker, but Kenan made her use sunscreen and limited her hours of exposure. "It's not good for you," he told her. "Too dark's not attractive. Lying in the sun's what turns a plum into a prune." What was so good about plums, she wanted to know. They're ripe and juicy, he told her.

When she had driven half a block from her driveway, about the time she reached the corner of Seventy-eighth and Colonial, the driver of a blue panel truck started his engine. He gave her another half-block lead, then pulled out from the curb and followed after her.

She turned right at Bay Ridge Avenue, then left again at Fourth Avenue, heading north. She slowed when she reached the D'Agostino's at the corner of Sixty-third Street, and eased the Camry into a parking space half a block past it.

The blue panel truck passed the Camry, circled the block, and parked at a fire hydrant right in front of the supermarket.

When Francine Khoury left her house, I was still having breakfast.

I'd been up late the previous night. Elaine and I had had dinner at one of the Indian joints on East Sixth Street, then caught a revival of *Mother Courage* at the Public Theater on Lafayette. Our seats weren't great and it was hard to hear some of the actors. We would have left at intermission, but one of the actors was the boyfriend of one of Elaine's neighbors, and we wanted to go backstage after the final curtain and assure him that he was wonderful. We wound up joining him for a drink at a bar around the corner that was absolutely packed for no reason I could fathom.

"That was great," I told her when we got out of there. "For three hours I couldn't hear him onstage, and for the past hour I couldn't hear him across the table. I wonder if he's got a voice."

"The play didn't last three hours," she said. "More like two and a half."

"It seemed like three hours."

"It seemed like five," she said. "Let's go home."

We went to her place. She made coffee for me and a cup of tea for herself and we watched CNN for half an hour and talked through the commercials. Then we went to bed, and after an hour or so I got up and dressed in the dark. I was on my way out of the bedroom when she asked me where I was going.

"Sorry," I said. "I didn't mean to wake you."

"That's all right. Can't you sleep?"

"Evidently not. I feel wired. I don't know why."

"Read in the living room. Or put the TV on, it won't bother me."

"No," I said. "I'm too restless. The walk across town might do me good."

Elaine's apartment is on Fifty-first between First and Second. My hotel, the Northwestern, is on Fifty-seventh between Eighth and Ninth. It was cold enough out that at first I thought I might take a cab, but by the time I'd walked a block I wasn't feeling it.

Waiting for a light to change, I happened to catch a glimpse of the moon between a couple of tall buildings. It was just about full, and that didn't come as a surprise. The night had a full-moon feel to it, stirring tides in the blood. I felt like doing something and couldn't think what.

If Mick Ballou had been in town I might have gone over to his saloon looking for him. But he was out of the country, and a saloon of any sort was no place for me, as restless as I was feeling. I went home and picked up a book, and somewhere around four I turned the light off and went to sleep.

By ten o'clock I was around the corner at the Flame. I had a light breakfast and read a newspaper, giving most of my attention to the local crime stories and the sports pages. Globally we were between crises, so I wasn't paying much attention to the bigger picture. The shit really has to hit the fan before I take an interest in national and international issues. Otherwise they seem too remote and my mind refuses to come to grips with them.

God knows I had time for all the news, and the want ads and legals, too. I'd had three days' work the previous week at Reliable, a big detective agency with offices in the Flatiron Building, but they'd had nothing for me since, and the last work I'd done on my own hook had been ages ago. I was all right for money so I didn't have to work, and I've always been able to find ways to get through the days, but I would have been glad of something to do. The restlessness I'd felt the night before hadn't passed with the setting of the moon. It was still there, a low-grade fever in the blood, an itch somewhere down beneath the skin, where you couldn't scratch it.

Francine Khoury spent half an hour in D'Agostino's, filling a shopping cart in the process. She paid cash for her groceries. A bag boy loaded her three shopping bags back into her cart and followed her out of the store and down the street to where her car was parked.

The blue panel truck was still parked at the hydrant. Its rear doors were open, and two men had emerged from it and were on the sidewalk, apparently studying something on a clipboard one of them was holding. When Francine passed them, accompanied by the bag boy, they glanced in her direction. By the time she had opened the trunk of the Camry, they were back in the truck with the doors closed.

The boy put the bags in the trunk. Francine gave him two dollars, which was twice what most people gave him, to say nothing of the surprisingly high percentage of shoppers who didn't tip him at all. Kenan had taught her to tip well, not ostentatiously but generously. "We can always afford to be generous," he had told her.

The boy wheeled the cart back to the market. Francine got behind the wheel, started the engine, headed north on Fourth Avenue.

The blue panel truck stayed half a block behind.

I don't know precisely what route Francine took to get from D'Agostino's to the imported-foods store on Atlantic Avenue. She could have stayed on Fourth Avenue all the way to Atlantic, could have taken the Gowanus Expressway into South Brooklyn. There's no way to know, and it doesn't much matter. One way or another she drove the Camry to the corner of Atlantic Avenue and Clinton Street. There is a Syrian restaurant called Aleppo on the southwest corner, and next to it, on Atlantic, is a food market, a large delicatessen, really, called The Arabian Gourmet. (Francine never called it that. Like most of the people who shopped there, she called the store Ayoub's, after the former owner who had sold out and moved to San Diego ten years ago.)

Francine parked at a metered spot on the north side of Atlantic, almost directly across the street from The Arabian Gourmet. She walked to the corner, waited for the light to turn, then crossed the street. By the time she entered the food store, the blue panel truck was parked in a loading zone in front of the Aleppo restaurant, and just next door to The Arabian Gourmet.

She was not in the store long. She only bought a few things, and she didn't need any help carrying them. She left the store at approximately 12:20. She was wearing a camel-hair car coat over charcoal-gray slacks and two sweaters, a beige cable-knit cardigan over a chocolate turtleneck. She had her purse over her shoulder, and was carrying a plastic shopping bag in one hand and her car keys in the other.

The back doors of the panel truck were open, and the two men who had gotten out of it earlier were on the sidewalk once again. When Francine emerged from the store, they moved up on either side of her. At the same time, a third man, the driver of the truck, started his engine.

One of the men said, "Mrs. Khoury?" She turned, and he flipped his wallet open and shut, giving her a quick peek at a badge, or at nothing at all. The second man said, "You'll have to come with us."

"Who are you?" she said. "What's this about, what do you want?"

They each took hold of an arm. Before she could have known what was happening they had hurried her across the sidewalk and up into the open back of the truck. Within seconds they were inside the truck with her and the doors were shut and the truck was pulling away from the curb and into the stream of traffic.

Although it was the middle of the day, and although the abduction took place on a busy commercial street, hardly anyone was in a position to see what happened, and the few people who did witness it had no clear idea what they were seeing. Everything must have happened very quickly.

If Francine had stepped back and cried out at their first approach...

But she didn't. Before she could do anything she was in the truck with the doors shut. She may have screamed then, or struggled, or tried to. But by then it was too late.

I know exactly where I was when they snatched her. I went to the noon meeting of the Fireside group, which runs from 12:30 to 1:30 weekdays at the Y on West Sixty-third Street. I got there early, so I was almost certainly sitting with a cup of coffee when the two of them hustled Francine across the sidewalk and into the back of the panel truck.

I don't remember any of the details of the meeting. For several years now I've been going to AA meetings on a surprisingly regular basis. I don't go to quite so many as I did when I first got sober, but I still must average somewhere around five a week. This meeting would have followed the group's usual format, with a speaker telling his or her own story for fifteen or twenty minutes and the rest of the hour given over to general discussion. I don't think I spoke up during the discussion period. I'd be likely to remember it if I had. I'm sure there were interesting things said, and funny things. There always are, but I can't remember anything specific.

After the meeting I had lunch somewhere, and after lunch I called Elaine. Her answering machine picked up, which meant either that she was out or that she had company. Elaine is a call girl, and having company is what she does for a living.

I met Elaine a couple of lives ago, when I was a hard-drinking cop with a new gold shield in my pocket and a wife and two sons out on Long Island. For a couple of years we had a relationship that served us both very well. I was her friend on the job, there to steer her through hassles, and once called upon to pilot a dead client from her bed to an alley down in the financial district. And she was the dream mistress, beautiful, bright, funny, professionally adept, and throughout it all as agreeable and undemanding as only a whore can be. Who could have asked for anything more?

After I left my home and my family and my job, Elaine and I pretty much lost touch with one another. Then a monster from out of our shared past turned up to threaten us both, and we were thrown together by circumstance. And, remarkably, we stayed together.

She had her apartment and I had my hotel room. Two or three or four nights a week we would see each other. Generally those nights would end at her apartment, and more often than not I would stay over. Occasionally we left the city together for a week or a weekend. On the days when we didn't see each other, we almost always spoke on the phone, sometimes more than once.

Although we hadn't said anything about forsaking all others, we had essentially done so. I wasn't seeing anybody else, and neither was she—with the singular exception of clients. Periodically she would trot off to a hotel room, or have someone up to her apartment. This had never bothered me in the early days of our relationship—it had probably been, truth to tell, part of the attraction—so I didn't see why it should bother me now.

If it did bother me, I could always ask her to stop. She had earned good money over the years and had saved most of it, putting the bulk of it in income-producing real estate. She could quit the life without having to change her lifestyle.

Something kept me from asking her. I suppose I was reluctant to admit to either of us that it bothered me. And I was at least as reluctant to do anything that would change any of the elements of our relationship. It wasn't broke, and I didn't want to fix it.

Things change, though. They can't do otherwise. If nothing else, they are altered by the sheer fact of their not changing.

We avoided using the L-word, although love is surely what I felt for her, and she for me. We avoided discussing the possibility of getting married, or living together, although I know I thought about it and had no doubt that she did. But we didn't talk about it. It was the thing we didn't talk about, except when we were not talking about love, or about what she did for a living.

Sooner or later, of course, we would have to think about these things, and talk about them, and even deal with them. Meanwhile we took it all one day at a time, which was how I had been taught to take all of life ever since I stopped trying to drink whiskey faster than they could distill it. As someone pointed out, you might as well take the whole business a day at a time. That, after all, is how the world hands it to you.

At a quarter to four that same Thursday afternoon the telephone rang at the Khoury house on Colonial Road. When Kenan Khoury answered it a male voice said, "Hey, Khoury. She never came home, did she?"

"Who is this?"

"None of your fuckin' business is who it is. We got your wife, you Arab fuck. You want her back or what?"

"Where is she? Let me talk to her."

"Hey, fuck you, Khoury," the man said, and broke the connection.

Khoury stood there for a moment, shouting "hello" into a dead phone and trying to figure out what to do next. He ran outside, went to the garage, established that his Buick was there and her Camry was not. He ran the length of the driveway to the street, looked in either direction, returned to the house, and picked up the phone. He listened to the dial tone and tried to think of someone to call.

"Jesus Christ," he said out loud. He put the phone down and yelled "*Francey!*"

He dashed upstairs and burst into their bedroom, calling her name. Of course she wasn't there, but he couldn't help himself, he had to check every room. It was a big house and he ran in and out of every room in it, shouting her name, at once the spectator and the participant in his own panic. Finally he was back in the living room and he saw that he had left the phone off the hook. That was brilliant. If they were trying to reach him, they couldn't get through. He hung up the phone and willed it to ring, and almost immediately it did.

It was a different male voice this time, calmer, more cultured. He said, "Mr. Khoury, I've been trying to reach you and getting a busy signal. Who were you talking to?"

"Nobody. I had the phone off the hook."

"I hope you didn't call the police."

"I didn't call anybody," Khoury said. "I made a mistake, I thought I hung up the phone, but I set it down alongside it. Where's my wife? Let me talk to my wife."

"You shouldn't leave the phone off the hook. And you shouldn't call anyone."

"I didn't."

"And certainly not the police."

"What do you want?"

"I want to help you get your wife back. If you want her back, that is. Do you want her back?"

"Jesus, what are you—"

"Answer the question, Mr. Khoury."

"Yes, I want her back. Of course I want her back."

"And I want to help you. Keep the line open, Mr. Khoury. I'll be in touch."

"Hello?" he said. "Hello?"

But the line was dead.

For ten minutes he paced the floor, waiting for the phone to ring. Then an icy calm settled over him and he relaxed into

21

it. He stopped walking the floor and sat in a chair next to the phone. When it rang he picked it up but said nothing.

"Khoury?" The first man again, the crude one.

"What do you want?"

"What do I want? What the fuck you think I want?"

He didn't respond.

"Money," the man said after a moment. "We want money."

"How much?"

"You fuckin' sand nigger, where do you get off askin' the questions? You want to tell me that?"

He waited.

"A million dollars. How's that strike you, asshole?"

"That's ridiculous," he said. "Look, I can't talk with you. Have your friend call me, maybe I can talk with him."

"Hey, you raghead fuck, what are you tryin' to—"

This time it was Khoury who broke the connection.

It seemed to him that it was about control.

Trying to control a situation like this, that was what made you crazy. Because you couldn't do it. They had all the cards.

But if you let go of the need to control it, you could at least quit dancing to their music, shuffling around like a trained bear in a Bulgarian circus.

He went into the kitchen and made himself a cup of thick sweet coffee, preparing it in the long-handled brass pot. While it cooled he got a bottle of vodka from the freezer and poured himself two ounces, drank it down in a single swallow, and felt the icy calm taking him over entirely. He carried his coffee into the other room, and he was just finishing it when the phone rang again.

It was the second man, the nice one. "You upset my friend, Mr. Khoury," he said. "He's difficult to deal with when he's upset."

"I think it would be better if you made the calls from now on."

"I don't see—"

"Because that way we can get this handled instead of getting all hung up in drama," he said. "He mentioned a million dollars. That's out of the question."

"Don't you think she's worth it?"

"She's worth any amount," he said, "but—"

"What does she weigh, Mr. Khoury? One-ten, one-twenty, somewhere in that neighborhood?"

"I don't—"

"Something like fifty kilograms, we might say."

Cute.

"Fifty keys at twenty a key, well, run the numbers for me, why don't you, Mr. Khoury? Comes to a mil, doesn't it?"

"What's the point?"

"The point is you'd pay a million for her if she was product, Mr. Khoury. You'd pay that if she was powder. Isn't she worth as much in flesh and blood?"

"I can't pay what I don't have."

"You have plenty."

"I don't have a million."

"What do you have?"

He'd had time to think of the answer. "Four hundred."

"Four hundred thousand."

"Yes."

"That's less than half."

"It's four hundred thousand," he said. "It's less than some things and it's more than others. It's what I've got."

"You could get the rest."

"I don't see how. I could probably make some promises and call in some favors and raise a little that way, but not that much. And it would take at least a few days, probably more like a week."

"You assume we're in a hurry?"

"*I'm* in a hurry," he said. "I want my wife back and I want you out of my life, and I'm in a big hurry as far as those two things are concerned."

"Five hundred thousand."

See? There were elements he could control after all. "No," he said. "I'm not bargaining, not where my wife's life is concerned. I gave you the top figure right away. Four."

A pause, then a sigh. "Ah, well. Silly of me to think I could get the better of one of your kind in a business deal. You people have been playing this game for years, haven't you? You're as bad as the Jews."

He didn't know how to answer that, so he left it alone.

"Four it is," the man said. "How long will it take you to get it ready?"

Fifteen minutes, he thought. "A couple of hours," he said.

"We can do it tonight."

"All right."

"Get it ready. Don't call anyone."

"Who would I call?"

Half an hour later he was sitting at the kitchen table looking at four hundred thousand dollars. He had a safe in the basement, a big old Mosler that weighed over a ton, itself set in the wall and screened by pine paneling and protected by a burglar alarm along with its own lock system. The bills were all hundreds, fifty in each banded stack, eighty stacks each containing five thousand dollars. He'd counted them out and tossed three and four stacks at a time into a woven plastic bushel basket Francine used for laundry.

She didn't have to do the laundry herself, for God's sake. She could hire all the help she needed, he'd told her that often enough. But she liked that, she was old-fashioned, she liked cooking and cleaning and keeping house.

He picked up the phone, held the receiver at arm's length, then dropped it in its cradle. Don't call anyone, the man had said. Who would I call? he'd demanded.

Who had done this to him? Set him up, stolen his wife away from him. Who would do something like that?

Well, maybe a lot of people would. Maybe anybody would, if they thought they could get away with it.

He picked up the phone again. It was clean, untapped. The whole house was free of bugs, as far as that went. He had two devices, both of them supposed to be state of the art, ought to be for what they cost him. One was a telephone-tap alert, installed in the phone line. Any change in the voltage, resistance, or capacitance anywhere on the line and he'd know it. The other was a Track-Lock, automatically scanning the radio spectrum for hidden microphones. Five, six grand he'd paid for the two units, something like that, and it was worth it if it kept his private conversations private.

Almost a shame there hadn't been cops listening the past couple of hours. Cops to trace the caller, come down on the kidnappers, bring Francey back to him—

No, last thing he needed. Cops would just fuck up the whole thing beyond recognition. He had the money. He'd pay it, and he'd either get her back or he wouldn't. Things you can control and things you can't—he could control paying the money, control how that went to some degree, but he couldn't control what happened afterward.

Don't call anyone.

Who would I call?

He picked up the phone one more time and dialed a number he didn't have to look up. His brother answered on the third ring.

He said, "Petey, I need you out here. Jump in a cab, I'll pay for it, but get out here right away, you hear me?"

A pause. Then, "Babe, I'd do anything for you, you know that—"

"So jump in a cab, man!"

"—but I can't be in anything has to do with your business. I just can't, babe."

"It's not business."

"What is it?"

"It's Francine."

"Jesus, what's the matter? Never mind, you'll tell me when I get out there. You're at home, right?"

"Yeah, I'm at home."

"I'll get a cab. I'll be right out."

While Peter Khoury was looking for a cabdriver willing to take him to his brother's house in Brooklyn, I was watching a group of reporters on ESPN discussing the likelihood of a cap on players' salaries. It didn't break my heart when the phone rang. It was Mick Ballou, calling from the town of Castlebar in County Mayo. The line was clear as a bell; he might have been calling from the back room at Grogan's.

"It's grand here," he said. "If you think the Irish are crazy in New York you should meet them on their own home ground. Every other storefront's a pub, and no one's out the door before closing hour."

"They close early, don't they?"

"Too bloody early by half. In your hotel, though, they have to serve drink at any hour to any registered guest that wants it. Now that's the mark of a civilized country, don't you think?"

"Absolutely."

"They all smoke, though. They're forever lighting cigarettes and offering the pack around. The French are even worse that way. When I was over there visiting my father's people they were peeved with me for not smoking. I believe Americans are the only people in the world who've had the sense to give it up."

"You'll still find a few smokers in this country, Mick."

"Good luck to them, then, suffering through plane rides and films and all the rules against it in public places." He told a long story about a man and woman he'd met a few nights before. It was funny and we both laughed, and then he asked about me and I said I was all right. "Are you, then," he said.

"A little restless, maybe. I've had time on my hands lately. And the moon's full."

"Is it," he said. "Here, too."

"What a coincidence."

"But then it's always full over Ireland. Good job it's always raining so you don't have to look at it all the time. Matt, I've an idea. Get on a plane and come over here."

"What?"

"I'll bet you've never been to Ireland."

"I've never been out of the country," I said. "Wait a minute, that's not true, I've been to Canada a couple of times and Mexico once, but—"

"You've never been to Europe?"

"No."

"Well, for Jesus' sake, get on a plane and come over. Bring herself if you want"—meaning Elaine—"or come alone, it makes no matter. I talked to Rosenstein and he says I'd best stay out of the country awhile yet. He says he can get it all straightened out but they've got this fucking federal task force and he doesn't want me on American soil until the all clear's sounded. I could be stuck in this fucking pesthole another month or more. What's so funny?"

"I thought you loved the place, and now it's a pest-hole."

"Anywhere's a pesthole when you haven't your friends about you. Come on over, man. What do you say?"

Peter Khoury got to his brother's house just after Kenan had had still another conversation with the gentler of the kidnappers. The man had seemed rather less gentle this time, especially toward the end of the conversation when Khoury tried to demand some evidence that Francine was alive and well. The conversation went something like this:

KHOURY: I want to talk with my wife.

KIDNAPPER: That's impossible. She's at a safe house. I'm at a pay phone.

KHOURY: How do I know she's all right?

KIDNAPPER: Because we've had every reason to take good care of her. Look how much she's worth to us.

KHOURY: Jesus, how do I even know you've got her in the first place?

KIDNAPPER: Are you familiar with her breasts?

KHOURY: Huh?

KIDNAPPER: Would you recognize one of them? That would be the simplest way. I'll cut off one of her tits and leave it on your doorstep, and that will put your mind at rest.

KHOURY: Jesus, don't say that. Don't even say that.

KIDNAPPER: Then let's not talk about proof, shall we? We have to trust each other, Mr. Khoury. Believe me, trust is everything in this business.

That was the whole thing, Kenan told Peter. He had to trust them, and how could he do that? He didn't even know who they were.

"I tried to think who I could call," he said. "You know, people in the business. Someone to stand by me, back me up. Anybody I can think of, for all I know, they're in on it. How can I rule anybody out? Somebody set this up."

"How did they—"

"I don't know. I don't know anything, all I know is she went shopping and she never came back. She went out, took the car, and five hours later the phone rings."

"Five hours?"

"I don't know, something like that. Petey, I don't know what I'm doing here, I got no experience in this shit."

"You do deals all the time, babe."

"A dope deal's completely different. You structure that so everybody's safe, everybody's covered. This case—"

"People get killed in dope deals all the time."

"Yeah, but there's generally a reason. Number one, dealing with people you don't know. That's the killer. It looks good and it turns into a rip-off. Number two, or maybe it's number one and a half, dealing with people you think you know but you don't really. And the other thing, whatever number you want to give it, people get in trouble because they try to chisel. They try to do the deal without the money, figure they'll make it good afterward. They get in over their heads, they get away with it, and then one time they don't. You know where that comes from nine times out of ten, it's people who get into their own product and their judgment goes down the toilet."

"Or they do everything right and then six Jamaicans kick the door in and shoot everybody."

"Well, that happens," Kenan said. "It doesn't have to be Jamokes. What was I reading the other day, Laotians in San Francisco. Every week there's some new ethnic group looking to kill you." He shook his head. "The thing is, in a righteous dope deal you can walk away from anything that doesn't look right. You never have to do the deal. If you've got the money, you can spend it somewhere else. If you've got the product, you can sell it to somebody else. You're only in the deal for as long as it works, and you can back yourself up, build in safeguards along the way, and from the jump you know the people and whether or not you can trust them."

"Whereas here—"

"Whereas here we got nothing. We got our thumb up our ass, that's what we got. I said we'll bring the money and you bring my wife, they said no. They said that's not the way it works. What am I gonna say, keep my wife? Sell her to somebody else, you don't like the way I do business? I can't do that."

"No."

"Except I could. He said a million, I said four hundred thousand. I said fuck you, that's all there is, and he bought it. Suppose I said—"

The phone rang. Kenan talked for a few minutes, making notes on a scratch pad. "I'm not coming alone," he said at one point. "I got my brother here, he's coming with me. No arguments." He listened some more and was about to say something else when the phone clicked in his ear.

"We gotta roll," he said. "They want the money in two Hefty bags. That's easy enough. Why two, I wonder? Maybe they don't know what four hundred large is, how much space it takes up."

"Maybe the doctor told them no heavy lifting."

"Maybe. We're supposed to go to the corner of Ocean Avenue and Farragut Road."

"That's in Flatbush, isn't it?"

"I think so."

"Sure, Farragut Road, that's a couple of blocks from Brooklyn College. What's there?"

"A phone booth." When they had the money divided up and packed in a pair of garbage bags, Kenan handed Peter a gun, a 9-mm automatic. "Take it," he insisted. "We don't want to walk into this unarmed."

"We don't want to walk into it at all. What good's a gun gonna do me?"

"I don't know. Take it anyway."

On the way out the door Peter grabbed his brother's arm. "You forgot to set the alarm," he said.

"So? They got Francey and we're carrying the money. What's left to steal?"

"You got the alarm, you might as well set it. It can't be any less useful than the goddamn guns."

"Yeah, you're right," he said, and ducked into the house. When he emerged he said, "State-of-the-art security system. You can't break into my house, can't tap my phones, can't bug the premises. All you can do is snatch my wife and make me run around the city with trash bags full of hundred-dollar bills."

"What's the best way, babe? I was thinking Bay Ridge Parkway and then Kings Highway to Ocean."

"Yeah, I guess. There's a dozen ways you could go, but that's as good as any. You want to drive, Petey?"

"You want me to?"

"Yeah, why don't you. I'd probably rear-end a cop car, the way I am now. Or run over a nun."

They were supposed to be at the Farragut Road pay phone at eight-thirty. They got there three minutes early, according to Peter's watch. He stayed in the car while Kenan went over to the phone and stood there waiting for it to ring. Earlier, Peter had wedged the gun under his belt in the small of his back. He'd been conscious of the pressure of it while he was driving, and now he took it out and held it in his lap.

The phone rang and Kenan answered it. Eight-thirty, Peter's watch said. Were they doing this by the clock or were they eyeballing the whole operation, somebody sitting in a window in one of the buildings across the street, watching it all happen?

Kenan trotted back to the car, leaned against it. "Veterans Avenue," he said.

"Never heard of it."

"It's somewhere between Flatlands and Mill Basin, that area. He gave me directions. Farragut to Flatbush and Flatbush to Avenue N and that runs you right into Veterans Avenue."

"And then what happens?"

"Another pay phone at the corner of Veterans and East Sixty-sixth Street."

"Why the running around, do you have any idea?"

"Make us crazy. Make sure we don't have a backup. I don't know, Petey. Maybe they're just trying to break our balls."

"It's working." Kenan went around to the passenger side, got in. Peter said, "Farragut to Flatbush, Flatbush to N. That'd be a right on Flatbush and then I guess a left turn on N?"

"Right. I mean yes, right on Flatbush and left on N."

"How much time have we got?"

"They didn't say. I don't think they said a time. They said to hurry."

"I guess we won't stop for coffee."

"No," Kenan said. "I guess not."

The drill was the same at the corner of Veterans and Sixty-sixth. Peter waited in the car. Kenan went to the phone, and it rang almost immediately.

The kidnapper said, "Very good. That didn't take long."

"Now what?"

"Where's the money?"

"In the backseat. In two Hefty bags, just like you said."

"Good. Now I want you and your brother to walk up Sixty-sixth Street to Avenue M."

"You want us to walk there?"

"Yes."

"With the money?"

"No, leave the money right where it is."

"In the backseat of the car."

"Yes. And leave the car unlocked."

"We leave the money in an unlocked car and walk a block—"

"Two blocks, actually."

"And then what?"

"Wait on the corner of Avenue M for five minutes. Then get in your car and go home."

"What about my wife?"

"Your wife is fine."

"How do I—"

"She'll be in the car waiting for you."

"She better be."

"What was that?"

"Nothing. Look, there's one thing bothers me, that's leaving the money unattended in an unlocked car. What I'm worried, somebody grabbing it before you get to it."

"Not to worry," the man said. "This is a good neighborhood."

They left the car unlocked, left the money in it, walked one short block and one long block to Avenue M. They waited five minutes by Peter's watch. Then they headed back toward the Buick.

I don't think I ever described them, did I? They looked like brothers, Kenan and Peter. Kenan stood five-ten, which made him a scant inch taller than his brother. They were both built like rangy middleweights, although Peter was beginning to thicken just the least bit at the waist. Both had olive skin tones and straight dark hair, parted on the left and combed back neatly. At thirty-three, Kenan was starting to develop a slightly higher forehead as his hairline receded. Peter, two years older, still had all his hair.

They were handsome men, with long straight noses and dark eyes set deep under prominent brows. Peter had a mustache, neatly trimmed. Kenan was cleanshaven.

If you were going by appearances, and if you were up against the two of them, you would take Kenan out first. Or try to, anyway. There was something about him that suggested he was the more dangerous of the two, that his responses would be more sudden and more certain.

That's how they looked, then, walking rapidly but not too rapidly back to the corner where Kenan's car was parked. It was still there, and still unlocked. The bags of money were no longer in the backseat. Francine Khoury wasn't there, either.

Kenan said, "Fuck this shit, man."

"The trunk?"

He opened the glove box, triggered the trunk release. He went around and lifted the lid. There was nothing in the trunk but the spare tire and the jack. He had just closed the trunk lid when the pay phone rang a dozen yards away.

He ran to it, grabbed it.

"Go home," the man said. "She'll probably get there before you do."

I went to my usual evening meeting around the corner from my hotel at St. Paul the Apostle, but I left on the break. I returned to my room and called Elaine and told her about the conversation with Mick.

"I think you should go," she said. "I think that's a great idea."

"Suppose we both go."

"Oh, I don't know, Matt. It would mean missing classes."

She was taking a course Thursday evenings at Hunter, in fact she'd just got back from it when I called. "Indian Art and Architecture Under the Moghuls." "We'd just go for a week or ten days," I said. "You'd miss one class."

"One class isn't such a big deal."

"Exactly, so—"

"So I guess what it comes down to is I don't really want to go. I'd be a fifth wheel, wouldn't I? I have this picture in my mind of you and Mick rocketing around the countryside and teaching the Irish how to raise hell."

"That's some picture."

"But what I mean is it'd be a sort of boys' night out, wouldn't it, and who needs a girl along? Seriously, I don't particularly want to go, and I know you're restless and I think it would do you a world of good. You've never been anywhere in Europe?"

"Never."

"How long has Mick been gone? A month?"

"Just about."

"I think you should go."

"Maybe," I said. "I'll think about it."

She wasn't there.

Nowhere in the house. Kenan went compulsively from room to room, knowing it was senseless, knowing she couldn't have gotten past the alarm system without either setting it off or disarming it. When he ran out of rooms he went back to the kitchen where Peter was making coffee.

He said, "Petey, this really sucks."

"I know it, babe."

"You're making coffee? I don't think I want any. Bother you if I have a drink?"

"Bother me if *I* have a drink. Not if you do."

"I just thought—never mind. I don't even want one."

"That's where we differ, babe."

"Yeah, I guess." He spun around. "Why the fuck are they jerking me around like this, Petey? They say she's gonna be in the car and then she's not. They say she'll be here and she isn't. What the fuck's going on?"

"Maybe they got stuck in traffic."

"Man, what happens now? We fucking sit here and wait? I don't even know what we're waiting for. They got the money and we got what? Fucked is what we got. I don't know who they are or where they are, I don't know zip, and—Petey, what do we do?"

"I don't know."

"I think she's dead," he said.

Peter was silent.

"Because why wouldn't they, the fucks? She could identify them. Safer to kill her than to give her back. Kill her, bury her, and that's the end of it. Case closed. That's what I would do, I was them."

"No you wouldn't."

"I said if I was them. I'm not, I wouldn't kidnap some woman in the first place, innocent gentle lady who never did anybody any harm, never had an unkind *thought*—"

"Easy, babe."

They would fall silent and then the conversation would begin again, because what else was there to do? After half an hour of this the phone rang and Kenan jumped for it.

"Mr. Khoury."

"Where is she?"

"My apologies. There was a slight change in plans."

"Where *is* she?"

"Just around the corner from you, on, uh, Seventy-ninth

34

Street, I believe it's the south side of the street, three or four houses from the corner—"

"What?"

"There's a car parked illegally at a fire hydrant. A gray Ford Tempo. Your wife is in it."

"She's in the car?"

"In the trunk."

"You put her in the trunk?"

"There's plenty of air. But it's cold out tonight so you'll want to get her out of there as soon as possible."

"Is there a key? How do I—"

"The lock's broken. You won't need a key."

Running down the street and around the corner, he said to Peter, "What did he mean, the lock's broken? If the trunk's not locked why can't she just crawl out? What's he talking about?"

"I don't know, babe."

"Maybe she's tied up. Tape, handcuffs, something so she can't move."

"Maybe."

"Oh, Jesus, Petey—"

The car was where it was supposed to be, a battered Tempo several years old, its windshield starred and the passenger door deeply dented. The trunk lock was missing altogether. Kenan flung the lid open.

No one in there. Just packages, bundles of some sort. Bundles of various sizes wrapped in black plastic and secured with freezer tape.

"No," Kenan said.

He stood there, saying "No, no, no." After a moment Peter took one of the parcels from the trunk, got a jackknife from his pocket, and cut away the tape. He unwound the length of black plastic—it was not unlike the Hefty bags in which the money had been delivered—and drew out a human foot, severed a couple of inches above the ankle. Three toenails showed circles of red polish. The other two toes were missing.

Kenan put his head back and howled like a dog.

2

That was Thursday. Monday I got back from lunch and there was a message for me at the desk. Call Peter Curry, it said, and there was a number and the 718 area code, which meant Brooklyn or Queens. I didn't think I knew a Peter Curry in Brooklyn or Queens, or anywhere else for that matter, but it's not unheard-of for me to get calls from people I don't know. I went up to my room and called the number on the slip, and when a man answered I said, "Mr. Curry?"

"Yes?"

"My name's Matthew Scudder, I got a message to call you."

"You got a message to call me?"

"That's right. It says here you called at twelve-fifteen."

"What was the name again?" I gave it to him again, and he said, "Oh, wait a minute, you're the detective, right? My brother called you, my brother Peter."

"It says Peter Curry."

"Hold on."

I held on, and after a moment another voice, close to the

36

first but a note deeper, a little bit softer, said, "Matt, this is Pete."

"Pete," I said. "Do I know you, Pete?"

"Yeah, we know each other, but you wouldn't necessarily know my name. I'm pretty regular at St. Paul's, I led a meeting there, oh, five or six weeks ago."

"Peter Curry," I said.

"It's Khoury," he said. "I'm of Lebanese descent, lemme see how to describe myself. I'm sober about a year and a half, I'm in a rooming house way west on Fifty-fifth Street, I've been working as a messenger and delivery boy but my field is film editing, only I don't know if I'll be able to get back into it—"

"Lot of drugs in your story."

"That's right, but it was alcohol really stuck it to me at the end. You've got me placed?"

"Uh-huh. I was there the night you spoke. I just never knew your last name."

"Well, that's the program for you."

"What can I do for you, Pete?"

"I'd like it if you could come out and talk with me and my brother. You're a detective and I think that's what we need."

"Could you give me some idea what it's about?"

"Well—"

"Not over the phone?"

"Probably better not to, Matt. It's detective work and it's important, and we'll pay whatever you say."

"Well," I said, "I don't know that I'm open to work right now, Pete. As a matter of fact I've got a trip planned, I'll be going overseas the end of the week."

"Whereabouts?"

"Ireland."

"That sounds great," he said. "But look, Matt, couldn't you just come out here and let us lay it out for you? You listen, and if you decide you can't do anything for us, no hard feelings and we'll pay for your time and your cab out and back." In the background the brother said something I couldn't make out, and Pete said, "I'll tell him. Matt, Kenan says we could drive in and pick you up, but we'd have to come back here and I think it's quicker if you just jump in a taxi."

It struck me I was hearing a lot about cabs from somebody who was working as a messenger and delivery boy, and then his brother's name rang a bell. I said, "You have more than one brother, Pete?"

"Just the one."

"I think you mentioned him in your qualification, something about his occupation."

A pause. Then, "Matt, I'm just asking you to come out and listen."

"Where are you?"

"Do you know Brooklyn?"

"I'd have to be dead."

"How's that?"

"Nothing, I was just thinking out loud. A famous short story, 'Only the Dead Know Brooklyn.' I used to know parts of the borough reasonably well. Where are you in Brooklyn?"

"Bay Ridge. Colonial Road."

"That's easy."

He gave me the address and I wrote it down.

The R train, also known as the Broadway local of the BMT, runs all the way from 179th Street in Jamaica to within a few blocks of the Verrazano Bridge at the southwest corner of Brooklyn. I caught it at Fifty-seventh and Seventh and got off two stops from the end of the line.

There are those who hold that once you leave Manhattan you're out of the city. They're wrong, you're just in another part of the city, but there's no question that the difference is palpable. You could spot it with your eyes closed. The energy level is different, the air doesn't hum with the same urgent intensity.

I walked a block on Fourth Avenue, past a Chinese restaurant and a Korean greengrocer and an OTB parlor and a couple of Irish bars, then cut over to Colonial Road and found Kenan Khoury's house. It was one of a group of detached single-family homes, solid square structures that looked to have been built sometime between the wars. A tiny lawn, a half-flight of wooden steps leading to the front entrance. I climbed them and rang the bell.

Pete let me in and led me into the kitchen. He introduced me to his brother, who stood up to shake hands, then motioned for me to take a chair. He stayed on his feet, walked over to the stove, then turned to look at me.

"Appreciate your coming," he said. "You mind a couple of questions, Mr. Scudder? Before we get started?"

"Not at all."

"Something to drink first? Not a *drink* drink, I know you know Petey from AA, but there's coffee made or I can offer you a soft drink. The coffee's Lebanese style, which is the same general idea as Turkish coffee or Armenian coffee, very thick and strong. Or there's a jar of instant Yuban if you'd rather have that."

"The Lebanese coffee sounds good."

It tasted good, too. I took a sip and he said, "You're a detective, is that right?"

"Unlicensed."

"What's that mean?"

"That I have no official standing. I do per diem work for one of the big agencies occasionally, and on those occasions I'm operating on their license, but otherwise what I do is private and unofficial."

"And you used to be a cop."

"That's right. Some years ago."

"Uh-huh. Uniform or plainclothes or what?"

"I was a detective."

"Had a gold shield, huh?"

"That's right. I was attached to the Sixth Precinct in the Village for several years, and before that I was stationed for a little while in Brooklyn. That was the Seventy-eighth Precinct, that's Park Slope and just north of it, the area they're calling Boerum Hill."

"Yeah, I know where it is. I grew up in the Seventy-eighth Precinct. You know Bergen Street? Between Bond and Nevins?"

"Sure."

"That's where we grew up, me and Petey. You'll find a lot of people from the Middle East in that neighborhood, within a few blocks of Court and Atlantic. Lebanese, Syrians, Yemenites, Palestinians. My wife was Palestinian, her folks lived on President Street just off Henry. That's South Brooklyn, but I guess they're calling it Carroll Gardens now. That coffee all right?"

"It's fine."

"You want more, just speak up." He started to say something else, then turned to face his brother. "I don't know, man," he said. "I don't think this is going to work out."

"Tell him the situation, babe."

"I just don't know." He turned to me, spun a chair around, sat down straddling it. "Here's the deal, Matt. Okay to call you that?" I said it was. "Here's the deal. What I need to know is whether I can tell you something without worrying who you're gonna tell it to. I guess what I'm asking is to what extent you're still a cop."

It was a good question, and I'd often pondered it myself. I said, "I was a policeman for a lot of years. I've been a little less of one every year since I left the job. What you're asking is if what you tell me will stay confidential. Legally, I don't have the status of an attorney. What you tell me isn't privileged information. At the same time, I'm not an officer of the court, either, so I'm no more obliged than any other private citizen to report matters that come to my attention."

"What's the bottom line?"

"I don't know what the bottom line is. It seems to move around a lot. I can't offer you a lot in the way of reassurance, because I don't know what it is you're thinking about telling me. I came all the way out here because Pete didn't want to say anything over the phone, and now you don't seem to want to say anything here, either. Maybe I should go home."

"Maybe you should," he said.

"Babe—"

"No," he said, getting to his feet. "It was a good idea, man, but it's not working out. We'll find 'em ourselves." He took a roll of bills from his pocket and peeled off a hundred, extending

40

it across the table to me. "For your cabs out and back and for your time, Mr. Scudder. I'm sorry we dragged you all the way out here for nothing." When I didn't take the bill he said, "Maybe your time's worth more than I figured. Here, and no hard feelings, huh?" He added a second bill to the first and I still didn't reach for it.

I pushed back my chair and stood up. "You don't owe me anything," I said. "I don't know what my time's worth. Let's call it an even-up trade for the coffee."

"Take the money. For Christ's sake, the cab had to be twenty-five each way."

"I took the subway."

He stared at me. "You came out here on the subway? Didn't my brother tell you to take a cab? What do you want to save nickels and dimes for, especially when I'm paying for it?"

"Put your money away," I said. "I took the subway because it's simpler and faster. How I get from one place to another is my business, Mr. Khoury, and I run my business the way I want. You don't tell me how to get around town and I won't tell you how to sell crack to schoolchildren, how does that strike you?"

"Jesus," he said.

To Pete I said, "I'm sorry we wasted each other's time. Thanks for thinking of me." He asked me if I wanted a ride back to the city, or at least a lift to the subway stop. "No," I said, "I think I'd like to walk around Bay Ridge a little. I haven't been out here in years. I had a case that brought me to within a few blocks of here, right on Colonial Road but a little ways to the north. Right across from the park. Owl's Head Park, I think it is."

"That's eight, ten blocks from here," Kenan Khoury said.

"That sounds about right. The guy who hired me was charged with killing his wife, and the work I did for him helped get the charges dropped."

"And he was innocent?"

"No, he killed her," I said, remembering the whole thing. "I didn't know that. I found out after."

"When there was nothing you could do."

41

"Sure there was," I said. "Tommy Tillary, that was his name. I forget his wife's name, but his girlfriend was Carolyn Cheatham. When she died, he wound up going away for it."

"He killed her, too?"

"No, she killed herself. I fixed it so it looked like murder, and I fixed it so he would go away for it. I got him out of one scrape that he didn't deserve to get out of, so it seemed fitting to get him into another one."

"How much time did he do?"

"As much as he could. He died in prison. Somebody stuck a knife in him." I sighed. "I thought I'd go walk past his house, see if it brought back any memories, but they seem to have come back all by themselves."

"It bother you?"

"Remembering, you mean? Not particularly. I can think of a lot of things I've done that bother me more." I looked around for my coat, then remembered I hadn't worn one. It was spring outside, sport jacket weather, although it would be going down into the forties in the evening.

I started for the door and he said, "Hold it a minute, will you, Mr. Scudder?"

I looked at him.

"I was out of line," he said. "I apologize."

"You don't have to apologize."

"Yes I do. I flew off the handle. This is nothing. Earlier today I broke a phone, I got a busy signal and I flew into a rage and smashed the receiver against the wall until the housing splintered." He shook his head. "I never get like that. I've been under a strain."

"There's a lot of that going around."

"Yeah, I suppose there is. The other day some guys kidnapped my wife, cut her up in little pieces wrapped in plastic and sent her back to me in the trunk of a car. Maybe that's the same strain everybody else is under. I wouldn't know."

Pete said, "Easy, babe—"

"No, I'm all right," Kenan said. "Matt, sit down a minute. Let me just run the whole thing down for you, top to bottom, and then you decide if you want to walk or not. Forget what I

42

said before. I'm not worried, who you're gonna tell or not tell. I just don't want to say it out loud 'cause it makes it all real, but it's real already, isn't it?"

He took me through it, giving me the story essentially as I recounted it earlier. There were some details I supplied that came out later in my own investigation, but the Khoury brothers had already unearthed a certain amount of data on their own. Friday they had found the Toyota Camry where she'd parked it on Atlantic Avenue, and that had led them to The Arabian Gourmet, while the bags of groceries in the trunk had let them know about her stop at D'Agostino's.

When he was done telling it I declined the offer of another cup of coffee and accepted a glass of club soda. I said, "I have some questions."

"Go ahead."

"What did you do with the body?"

The brothers exchanged glances, and Pete gestured for Kenan to go ahead. He took a breath and said, "I have this cousin, he's a veterinarian, has an animal hospital on—well, it doesn't matter where it is, it's in the old neighborhood. I called him and told him I needed private access to his place of business."

"When was this?"

"This was Friday afternoon that I called him and Friday night that I got the key from him and we went over there. He has a unit, I guess you would call it an oven, that he uses for cremating people's pets that he puts to sleep. We took the, uh, we took the—"

"Easy, babe."

He shook his head, impatient. "I'm all right, I just don't know how to say it. What do you call it? We took the pieces of, of Francine, and we cremated her."

"You unwrapped all of the, uh—"

"No, what for? The tape and plastic burned along with everything else."

"But you're sure it was her."

"Yeah. Yeah, we unwrapped enough to, uh, to be sure."

43

"I have to ask all this."

"I understand."

"The point is there's no corpse left, is that correct?"

He nodded. "Just ashes. Ashes and bone chips, is what it amounts to. You think cremation and you think you'll wind up with nothing but powdery ash, like what comes out of a furnace, but that's not how it works. There's an auxiliary unit he's got for pulverizing the bone segments so it's less obvious what you've got." He raised his eyes to meet mine. "When I was in high school I worked afternoons at Lou's place. I wasn't going to mention his name. Fuck it, what difference does it make? My father wanted me to become a doctor, he thought this would be good training. I don't know if it was or not, but I was familiar with the place, the equipment."

"Does your cousin know why you wanted to use his place?"

"People know what they want to know. He couldn't have figured I wanted to slip in there at night and give myself a rabies shot. We were there all night. The unit he has is pet size, we had to do several loads and let the unit cool down in between. Jesus, it's killing me to talk about it."

"I'm sorry."

"It's not your fault. Did Lou know I used the cooker? I figure he had to know. He has to have a pretty good idea what kind of business I'm in. He probably figures I killed a competitor and wanted to get rid of the evidence. People see all this shit on television and they think that's how the world works."

"And he didn't object?"

"He's family. He knew it was urgent and he knew it wasn't something we should talk about. And I gave him some money. He didn't want to take it, but the guy's got two kids in college so how can he not take it? It wasn't that much."

"How much?"

"Two grand. That's pretty low-budget for a funeral, isn't it? I mean you can spend more than that on a casket." He shook his head. "I got the ashes in a tin can in the safe downstairs. I don't know what to do with them. No idea what she would have wanted. We never discussed it. Jesus, she was twenty-four years old. Nine years younger than me, nine years less a month. We were married two years."

"No children."

"No. We were gonna wait one more year and then—oh, Jesus, this is terrible. It bother you if I have a drink?"

"No."

"Petey says the same. Fuck it, I'm not having one. I had one pop Thursday afternoon after I talked on the phone with them and I haven't had anything since. I get the urge and I just push it away. You know why?"

"Why?"

"Because I want to feel this. You think I did the wrong thing? Taking her to Lou's place, cremating her. You think that was wrong?"

"I think it was unlawful."

"Yeah, well, I wasn't too worried about that aspect of it."

"I know you weren't. You were just trying to do what was decent. But in the process you destroyed evidence. Dead bodies hold a great deal of information for someone who knows what to look for. When you reduce a body to ashes and bone chips, all that information is lost."

"Does it matter?"

"It might be helpful to know how she died."

"I don't care how. All I want to know is who."

"One might lead to the other."

"So you think I did the wrong thing. Jesus, I couldn't call the cops, hand them a sack full of cuts of meat, say, 'This is my wife, take good care of her.' I never call the cops, I'm in a business where you don't, but if I had opened the trunk of the Tempo and she was there in one piece, dead but intact, maybe, maybe, I'd have reported it. But this way—"

"I understand."

"But you think I did the wrong thing."

"You did what you had to do," Peter said.

Isn't that what everybody always does? I said, "I don't know a lot about right and wrong. I probably would have done the same thing, if I'd had a cousin with a crematorium in his back room. But what I would have done is beside the point. You did

45

what you did. The question is where do you go from here."

"Where?"

"That's the question."

It wasn't the only question. I asked a great many questions, and I asked most of them more than once. I took them both back and forth over their story, and I wrote down a lot of notes in my notebook. It began to look as though the segmented remains of Francine Khoury constituted the only piece of tangible evidence in the entire affair, and they had gone up in smoke.

When I finally closed my notebook the two Khoury brothers sat waiting for a word from me. "On the face of it," I said, "they look pretty safe. They made their play and carried it off without giving you a clue who they are. If they left tracks anywhere, they haven't shown up yet. It's possible someone at the supermarket or the place on Atlantic Avenue recognized one of them or caught a license number, and it's worth an intensive investigation to try to turn up such a witness, but he's no more than hypothetical at this point. The odds are that there won't be a witness, or that what he saw won't lead anywhere."

"You're saying we got no chance."

"No," I said. "That's not what I'm saying at all. I'm saying an investigation has to do something besides work with the clues they left behind. One starting point lies in the fact that they got away with almost half a million dollars. There's two things they could do, and either one could spotlight them."

Kenan thought about it. "Spend it's one of them," he said. "What's the other?"

"Talk about it. Crooks talk all the time, especially when they've got something to brag about, and sometimes they talk to people who'll happily sell them out. The trick is to get the word out so those people know who the buyer is."

"You've got an idea how to do that?"

"I've got a lot of ideas," I admitted. "Earlier you wanted to know to what extent I was still a cop. I don't know, but I still approach this kind of problem the way I did when I carried a badge, turning it this way and that until I can get some kind of grip on it. In a case like this one I can immediately see several different lines of investigation to pursue. There's every chance in the world that none of them will lead anywhere, but they're still the approaches that ought to be tried."

"So you want to give it a shot?"

I looked down at my notebook. I said, "Well, I have two problems. The first one I think I mentioned to Pete on the phone. I'm supposed to go to Ireland the end of the week."

"On business?"

"Pleasure. I just made the arrangements this morning."

"You could cancel."

"I could."

"You lose any money canceling, your fee from me'd make that up to you. What's the other problem?"

"The other problem's what use you'll make of whatever I might turn up."

"Well, you know the answer to that."

I nodded. "That's the problem."

"Because you can't make a case against them, prosecute them for kidnapping and homicide. There's no evidence of any crime committed, there's just a woman who disappeared."

"That's right."

"So you must know what I want, what the point of all this is. You want me to say it?"

"You might as well."

"I want those fuckers dead. I want to be there, I want to do it, I want to see them die." He said this calmly, levelly, in a voice with no emotion in it. "That's what I want," he said. "Right now I want it so bad I don't want anything else, I can't imagine ever wanting anything else. That about what you figured?"

"Just about."

"People who'd do something like this, take an innocent woman and turn her into cutlets, does it bother you what happens to them?"

I thought about it, but not for very long. "No," I said.

"We'll do what has to be done, me and my brother. You won't have a part of that."

"In other words I'd just be sentencing them to death."

He shook his head. "They sentenced themselves," he said. "By what they did. You're just helping play out the hand. What do you say?"

I hesitated.

He said, "You've got another problem, don't you? My profession."

"It's a factor," I said.

"That line about selling crack to schoolchildren. I don't, uh, set up shop in the schoolyard."

"I didn't figure you did."

"Properly speaking, I'm not a dealer. I'm what they call a trafficker. You understand the distinction?"

"Sure," I said. "You're the big fish that manages to stay out of the nets."

He laughed. "I don't know that I'm big particularly. In certain respects the middle-level distributors are the biggest, do the most volume. I deal in weight, meaning I either bring product in in quantity or I buy it from the person who brings it in and turn it over to someone who sells smaller amounts. My customer probably does more business than I do because he's buying and selling all the time, where I may only do two or three deals a year."

"But you make out all right."

"I make out. It's hazardous, you've got the law to worry about and you've got people looking to rip you off. Where the risks are high the rewards are generally high also. And the business is there. People want the product."

"By product you mean cocaine."

"Actually I don't do much with coke. Most of my business is heroin. Some hash, but mostly heroin the past couple years. Look, I'll tell you right out, I'm not gonna apologize for it. People take it, they get hooked, they rob their mother's purse, they break into houses, they OD and die with needles in their arms, they share needles and get AIDS. I know the whole story. There's people who make guns, people who distill liquor, people who grow tobacco. How many people a year die of liquor and tobacco compared to the number die from drugs?"

"Alcohol and tobacco are legal."

"What difference does that make?"

"It makes some kind of difference. I'm not sure how much."

"Maybe. I don't see it myself. Either case, the product is dirty. It kills people, or it's the substance they use to kill themselves or each other. One thing in my favor, I don't advertise what I sell, I don't have lobbyists in Congress, I don't hire PR people to tell the public the shit I sell is good for them. The day people stop wanting drugs is the day I find something else to buy and sell, and I won't whine about it and look for the government to give me a federal subsidy, either."

Peter said, "It's still not lollipops you're selling, babe."

"No, it's not. The product's dirty. I never said it wasn't. But what I do I do clean. I don't screw people, I don't kill people, I deal fair and I'm careful who I deal with. That's why I'm alive and that's why I'm not in jail."

"Have you ever been?"

"No. I've never been arrested. So if that's a consideration, how it would look, you working for a known dope dealer—"

"That's not a consideration."

"Well, from an official standpoint, I'm not a known dealer. I won't say there's nobody in the Narcotics Squad or the DEA who knows who I am, but I don't have a record, I've never to my knowledge been the official subject of an investigation. My house isn't bugged and my phone's not tapped. I'd know if it was, I told you about that."

"Yes."

"Sit still a minute, I want to show you something." He went into another room and came back with a picture, a five-by-seven color shot in a silver frame. "That's at our wedding," he said. "That's two years ago, not quite two years, be two years in May."

He was in a tuxedo and she was all in white. He was smiling hugely, while she was not smiling, as I think I mentioned earlier. She was beaming, though, and you could see that she was radiant with happiness.

I didn't know what to say.

"I don't know what they did to her," he said. "That's one of the things I won't let myself think about. But they killed her and they butchered her, they made some kind of dirty joke out of her, and I have to do something about it because I'll die if I don't. I'd do it all myself if I could. In fact we tried, me and Petey, but we don't know what to do, we don't have the knowledge, we don't know the moves. The questions you asked before, the approach you took, if nothing else it showed me that this is an area where I don't know what I'm doing. So I want your help and I can pay you whatever I have to, money's not a problem, I've got plenty of money and I'll spend whatever I have to. And if you say no I'll either find someone else or try to do it myself because what the hell else am I gonna do?" He reached across the table and took the picture away from me and looked at it. "Jesus, what a perfect day that was," he said, "and all the days since, and then it all turned to shit." He looked at me. He said, "Yes, I'm a trafficker, a dope dealer, whatever you want to call it, and yes, it's my intention to kill these fucks. So that's all out on the table. What do you say? Are you in or out?"

My best friend, the man I'd planned to join in Ireland, was a career criminal. According to legend, he had one night walked the streets of Hell's Kitchen carrying a bowler's bag from which he displayed the severed head of an enemy. I couldn't swear it happened, but more recently I'd been at his side in a cellar in Maspeth when he severed a man's hand with one blow of a cleaver. I'd had a gun in my hand that night, and I'd used it.

So if I was still very much a cop in some respects, in other ways I had undergone considerable change. I'd long since swallowed the camel; why strain at the gnat?

"I'm in," I said.

3

I got back to my hotel a little after nine. I'd had a long session with Kenan Khoury, filling pages of my notebook with names of friends and associates and family members. I'd gone to the garage to inspect the Toyota, and found the Beethoven cassette still in the tape deck. If there were any other clues in Francine's car, I couldn't spot them.

The other car, the gray Tempo used to deliver her segmented remains, was not available for inspection. The kidnappers had parked it illegally, and sometime in the course of the weekend a tow truck from Traffic had showed up to haul it away. I could have attempted to track it down, but what was the point? It had surely been stolen for the occasion, and had probably been previously abandoned, given the condition of it. A police lab crew might have turned up something in the trunk or interior, stains or fibers or markings of some sort, that would point out a profitable line of investigation. But I didn't have the resources for that kind of inspection. I'd be running all over Brooklyn to look at a car that wouldn't tell me a thing.

In the Buick the three of us traced a long circuitous course, past the D'Agostino's and the Arabian market on Atlantic Avenue, then south to the first pay phone at Ocean and Farragut, then south on Flatbush and east on N to the second booth on Veterans Avenue. I didn't really have to see these sights, there's not a tremendous amount of information you can glean by staring at a public telephone, but I've always found it worthwhile to put in time on the scene, to walk the pavements and climb the stairs and see it all firsthand. It helps make it real.

It also gave me a way to take the Khourys through it again. In a police investigation, witnesses almost always complain about having to relate the same story over and over to a host of different people. It seems pointless to them, but there's a point to it. If you tell it enough times to enough different people, maybe you'll come up with something you've previously left out, or maybe one person will hear something that sailed past everybody else.

Somewhere in the course of things we stopped at the Apollo, a coffee shop on Flatbush. We all ordered the souvlaki. It was good, but Kenan hardly touched his. In the car afterward he said, "I should have ordered eggs or something. Ever since the other night I got no taste for meat. I can't eat it, it turns my stomach. I'm sure I'll get over it, but for the time being I've got to remember to order something else. It makes no sense, ordering something and then you can't bring yourself to eat it."

Peter drove me home in the Camry. He was staying at Colonial Road, he'd been there since the kidnapping, sleeping on the couch in the living room, and he needed to stop by his room to pick up clothes.

Otherwise I'd have called a livery service and taken a taxi. I'm comfortable enough on the subway, I rarely feel unsafe on it, but it seemed a false economy to stint on cab fare with ten thousand dollars in my pocket. I'd have felt pretty silly if I ran into a mugger.

That was my retainer, two banded stacks of hundreds with

fifty bills in each, two packets of bills indistinguishable from the eighty packets paid to ransom Francine Khoury. I've always had trouble putting a price on my services, but in this case I'd been spared the decision. Kenan had dropped the two stacks on the table and asked if that was enough to start with. I told him it was on the high side.

"I can afford it," he said. "I've got plenty of money. They didn't tap me out, they didn't come close."

"Could you have paid the million?"

"Not without leaving the country. I've got an account in the Caymans with half a mil in it. I had just under seven hundred large in the safe here. Actually I probably could have raised the other three here in town, if I made a few phone calls. I wonder."

"What?"

"Oh, crazy thinking. Like suppose I paid the mil, would they have returned her alive? Suppose I never pressed on the phone, suppose I was polite, kissed their asses and all."

"They'd have killed her anyway."

"That's what I tell myself, but how do I know? I can't keep myself from wondering if there was something I could have done. Suppose I played hardball all the way, not a penny paid unless they showed me proof she was alive."

"She was probably already dead when they called you."

"I pray you're right," he said, "but I don't know. I keep thinking there must have been some way I could have saved her. I keep figuring it was my fault."

We took expressways back to Manhattan, the Shore Parkway and the Gowanus into the tunnel. Traffic was light at that hour but Pete took it slow, rarely pushing the Camry past forty miles an hour. We didn't talk much at first, and the silences tended to stretch.

"It's been some couple of days," he said finally. I asked him how he was holding up. "Oh, I'm all right," he said.

"Have you been getting to meetings?"

"I'm pretty regular." After a moment he said, "I haven't

had a chance to get to a meeting since this shit started. I've been, you know, pretty busy."

"You're no good to your brother unless you stay sober."

"I know that."

"There are meetings in Bay Ridge. You wouldn't have to come into the city."

"I know. I was gonna go to one last night, but I didn't get to it." His fingers drummed the steering wheel. "I thought maybe we'd get back in time to get over to St. Paul's tonight, but we missed it. It's gonna be way past nine by the time we get there."

"There's a ten o'clock meeting on Houston Street."

"Oh, I don't know," he said. "By the time I get to my room, pick up what I need—"

"If you miss the ten there's a midnight meeting. Same place, Houston between Sixth and Varick."

"I know where it is."

Something in his tone did not invite further suggestion. After a moment he said, "I know I shouldn't let my meetings slide. I'll try to make the ten o'clock. The midnight, I don't know about that. I don't want to leave Kenan alone for that long."

"Maybe you'll catch a Brooklyn meeting tomorrow during the day."

"Maybe."

"What about your job? You're letting that slide?"

"For the time being. I called in sick Friday and today, but if they wind up letting me go it's no big deal. Job like that's not hard to come by."

"What is it, messenger work?"

"Delivering lunches, actually. For the deli on Fifty-seventh and Ninth."

"It must be hard, working a get-well job like that while your brother's raking it in."

He was silent for a moment. Then he said, "I have to keep all that separate, you know? Kenan wanted me to work for him, with him, whatever you want to call it. I can't be in that business and stay sober. It's not that you're around drugs all the time, because actually you're not, there's not that much physical contact with the product. It's the whole attitude, the mind-set, you know what I mean?"

"Sure."

"You were right, what you said about meetings. I've been wanting to drink ever since I found out about Francey. I mean about her being kidnapped, before they did what they did. I haven't come close or anything but it's hard keeping the thought out of my mind. I push it away and it comes right back."

"Have you been in touch with your sponsor?"

"I don't exactly have one. They gave me an interim sponsor when I first got sober, and I called him fairly regularly at first but we more or less drifted apart. He's hard to get on the phone, anyway. I should find a regular sponsor, but for some reason I never got around to it."

"One of these days—"

"I know. Do you have a sponsor?"

I nodded. "We got together just last night. We generally have dinner Sunday, go over the week together."

"Does he give you advice?"

"Sometimes," I said. "And then I go ahead and do what I want."

When I got back to my hotel room, the first call I made was to Jim Faber. "I was just talking about you," I told him. "A fellow asked if my sponsor gives me advice, and I told him how I always do exactly what you suggest."

"You're lucky God didn't strike you dead on the spot."

"I know. But I've decided not to go to Ireland."

"Oh? You seemed determined last night. Did it look different to you after a night's sleep?"

"No," I admitted. "It looked about the same, and this morning I went to a travel agent and managed to get a cheap seat on a flight leaving Friday evening."

"Oh?"

"And then this afternoon somebody offered me a job and I said yes. You want to go to Ireland for three weeks? I don't think I can get my money back for the ticket."

"Are you sure? It's a shame to lose the money."

"Well, they told me it was nonrefundable, and I already paid for it. It's all right, I'm making enough on the job so that I can write off a couple hundred. But I did want to let you know that I wasn't on my way to the land of Sodom and Begorrah."

"It sounded like you were setting yourself up," he said. "That's why I was concerned. You've managed to hang out with your friend in his saloon and still stay sober—"

"He does the drinking for both of us."

"Well, one way or another it seems to work. But on the other side of the ocean with your usual support system thousands of miles away, and with you restless to begin with—"

"I know. But you can rest easy now."

"Even if I can't take the credit."

"Oh, I don't know," I said. "Maybe it's your doing. God works in mysterious ways, His wonders to perform."

"Yeah," he said. "Doesn't He just."

Elaine thought it was too bad I wouldn't be going to Ireland after all. "I don't suppose there was any possibility of postponing the job," she said.

"No."

"Or that you'll be done by Friday."

"I'll barely be started by Friday."

"It's too bad. But you don't sound disappointed."

"I guess I'm not. At least I didn't call Mick, so that saves having to call again and tell him I changed my mind. To tell you the truth, I'm glad I've got the work."

"Something to sink your teeth into."

"That's right. That's what I really need, more than I need a vacation."

"And it's a good case?"

I hadn't told her anything about it. I thought for a moment and said, "It's a terrible case."

"Oh?"

"Jesus, the things people do to each other. You'd think I'd get used to it, but I never do."

"You want to talk about it?"

"When I see you. Are we on for tomorrow night?"

"Unless your work gets in the way."

"I don't see why it should. I'll come by for you around seven. If I'm going to be later than that I'll call."

I had a hot bath and a good night's sleep, and in the morning I went to the bank and added seventy $100 bills to the stash in my safe-deposit box. I deposited two thousand dollars to my checking account and kept the remaining thousand in my hip pocket.

There was a time when I would have rushed to give it away. I used to spend a lot of idle hours in empty churches, and I tithed religiously, so to speak, stuffing a precise ten percent of the cash I received into the next poor box I passed. This quaint custom had faded away in sobriety. I don't know why I stopped doing it, but then I couldn't tell you why I ever started doing it in the first place.

I could have stuffed my Aer Lingus ticket in the nearest poor box, for all the good I was going to get out of it. I stopped at the travel agent's and confirmed what I had already suspected, that my ticket was indeed nonrefundable. "Ordinarily I'd say get a doctor to write a letter saying you had to cancel for medical reasons," he said, "but that wouldn't work here because it's not the airline you're dealing with, it's an outfit that buys space wholesale from the airlines and offers it at a deep discount." He offered to try to resell it for me, and I left it with him and walked to the subway.

I spent the whole day in Brooklyn. I'd taken a picture of Francine Khoury when I left the house on Colonial Road, and I showed it around at the Fourth Avenue D'Agostino's and at The Arabian Gourmet on Atlantic Avenue. I was working a colder trail than I would have liked—it was Tuesday now, and the abduction had taken place on Thursday—but there was nothing I could do about that now. It would have been nice if Pete had called me on Friday instead of waiting until the weekend had passed, but they'd had other things to do.

Along with the picture, I showed around a card from Reliable with my name on it. I was investigating in connection with an insurance claim, I explained. My client's car had been clipped by another vehicle, which had sped off without stopping, and it would expedite the processing of her claim if we could identify the other party.

At D'Agostino's I talked with a cashier, who remembered Francine as a regular customer who always paid cash, a memorable trait in our society but par for the course in dope-dealing circles. "And I can tell you something else about her," the woman said. "I bet she's a good cook." I must have looked mystified. "No prepared foods, no frozen this and that. Always fresh ingredients. Young as she is, you don't find many that are into cooking. But you never see any TV dinners in her cart."

The bag boy remembered her, too, and volunteered the information that she was always a two-dollar tipper. I asked about a truck, and he remembered a blue panel truck that had been parked out front and moved off after her. He hadn't noticed the make of the truck or the license plate but was reasonably certain of the color, and he thought there was something about TV repair painted on the side.

They remembered more on Atlantic Avenue because there had been more to notice. The woman behind the counter recognized the picture immediately and was able to tell me just what Francine had bought—olive oil, sesame tahini, foul madamas, and some other terms I didn't recognize. She hadn't seen the actual abduction, though, because she'd been waiting on another customer. She knew something curious had happened, because a customer had come in with some story about two men and a woman running from the store and leaping into the back of a truck. The customer had been concerned that they might have robbed the store and were making a getaway.

I managed a few more interviews before noon, at which time I thought I'd go next door for lunch. Instead I remembered the advice I'd been so quick to hand out to Peter Khoury. I hadn't been to a meeting myself since Saturday, and here it was Tuesday and I'd be spending the evening with Elaine. I called the Intergroup office and learned that there was a twelve-thirty meeting about ten minutes away in Brooklyn Heights. The speaker was a little old lady, as prim and proper in appearance as could be, and her story made it clear that she had not been ever thus. She'd been a bag lady, evidently, sleeping in doorways and never bathing or changing her clothes, and she kept stressing how filthy she had been, how foul she had smelled. It was hard to square the story with the person at the head of the table.

After the meeting I went back to Atlantic Avenue and picked up where I'd left off. I bought a sandwich and a can of cream soda at a deli and interviewed the proprietor while I was there. I ate my lunch standing up outside, then talked to the clerk and a couple of customers at a corner newsstand. I went into Aleppo and talked to the cashier and two of the waiters. I went back to Ayoub's—I'd taken to thinking of The Arabian Gourmet by that name, since I kept talking to people who were calling it that. I went back there, and by this time the woman had been able to come up with the name of the customer who'd been afraid the men in the blue van had robbed the place. I found the man listed in the phone book, but no one answered when I rang the number.

I had dropped the insurance-investigation story when I got to Atlantic Avenue because it didn't seem likely to jibe with what people would have seen. On the other hand, I didn't want to leave the impression that anything on the scale of kidnapping and homicide had taken place, or someone might deem it his civic duty to report the matter to the police. The story I put together, and it tended to vary somewhat depending upon my audience of the moment, went more or less along these lines:

My client had a sister who was considering an arranged marriage to an illegal alien who was hoping to stay in the country. The prospective groom had a girlfriend whose family was bitterly opposed to the marriage. Two men, relatives of the girlfriend, had been harassing my client for days in an attempt to enlist her aid to stop the marriage. She was sympathetic to their position but didn't really want to get involved.

They had been dogging her steps on Thursday, and followed her to Ayoub's. When she left they got her into the back of their truck on a pretext and drove around with her, trying to convince her. By the time they let her out she was slightly hysterical, and in the course of getting away from them she lost not only the groceries (olive oil, tahini, and so on) but also her purse, which at the time contained a rather valuable bracelet. She didn't know the name of these men, or how to get in touch with them, and—

I don't suppose it made much sense, but I wasn't pitching it to the networks for a TV pilot, I was just using it to reassure some reasonably solid citizens that it was both safe and noble to be as helpful as possible. I got a lot of gratuitous advice— "Those marriages are a bad thing, she should tell her sister it's not worth it," for instance. But I also got a fair amount of information.

I knocked off a little after four and caught a train to Columbus Circle, beating the rush hour by a few minutes. There was mail for me at the desk, most of it junk. I ordered something from a catalog once and now I get dozens of them every month. I live in one small room and wouldn't have room for the catalogs themselves, let alone the products they want me to buy.

Upstairs, I tossed everything but the phone bill and two message slips, both informing me that "Ken Curry" had called, once at 2:30, again at 3:45. I didn't call him right away. I was exhausted.

The day had taken it out of me. I hadn't done that much physically, hadn't spent eight hours hefting sacks of cement, but all those conversations with all those people had taken their toll. You have to concentrate hard, and the process is especially demanding when you're running a story of your own. Unless you're a pathological liar, a fiction is more arduous to utter than the truth; that's the principle on which the lie detector is based, and my own experience tends to bear it out. A full day of lying and role-playing takes it out of you, especially if you're on your feet for most of it.

I took a shower and touched up my shave, then put the TV news on and listened to fifteen minutes of it with my feet up and my eyes closed. Around five-thirty I called Kenan Khoury and told him I'd made some progress, although I didn't have anything specific to report. He wanted to know if there was anything he could do.

"Not just yet," I said. "I'll be going back to Atlantic Avenue tomorrow to see if the picture fills in a little more. When I'm done there I'll come out to your place. Will you be there?"

"Sure," he said. "I got no place to go."

I set the alarm and closed my eyes again, and the clock snatched me out of a dream at half past six. I put on a suit and tie and went over to Elaine's. She poured coffee for me and Perrier for herself, and then we caught a cab uptown to the Asia Society, where they had recently opened an exhibit that centered on the Taj Mahal, and thus tied right in with the course she was taking at Hunter. After we'd walked through the three exhibit rooms and made the appropriate noises we followed the crowd into another room, where we sat in folding chairs and listened to a soloist perform on the sitar. I have no idea whether he was any good or not. I don't know how you could tell, or how he himself would know if his instrument was out of tune.

Afterward there was a wine-and-cheese reception. "This need not detain us long," Elaine murmured, and after a few minutes of smiling and mumbling we were on the street.

"You loved every minute of it," she said.

"It was all right."

"Oh boy," she said. "The things a man will put himself through in the hope of getting laid."

"Come on," I said. "It wasn't that bad. It's the same music they play at Indian restaurants."

"But there you don't have to listen to it."

"Who listened?"

We went to an Italian restaurant, and over espresso I told her about Kenan Khoury and what had happened to his wife. When I was finished she sat for a moment looking down at the tablecloth in front of her as if there were something written on it. Then she raised her eyes slowly to meet mine. She is a resourceful woman, and a durable one, but just then she looked touchingly vulnerable.

"Dear God," she said.

"The things people do."

"There's just no end, is there? No bottom to it." She took a sip of water. "The cruelty of it, the utter sadism. Why would anyone—well, why ask why."

"I figure it has to be pleasure," I said. "They must have gotten off on it, not just on the killing but on rubbing his nose in it, jerking him around, telling him she'll be in the car, she'll be home when he gets there, then finally letting him find her in pieces in the trunk of the Ford. They wouldn't have to be sadists to kill her. They could see it as safer that way than to leave a witness who could identify them. But there was no practical advantage in twisting the knife the way they did. They went to a lot of trouble dismembering the body. I'm sorry, this is great table talk, isn't it?"

"That's nothing compared to what a great pre-bedtime story it makes."

"Puts you right in the mood, huh?"

"Nothing like it to get the juices flowing. No, really, I don't mind it. I mean I mind, of course I mind, but I'm not squeamish. It's gross, cutting somebody up, but that's really the least of it, isn't it? The real shock is that there's that kind of evil in the world and it can come from out of nowhere and zap you for no good reason at all. That's what's awful, and it's just as bad on an empty stomach as on a full one."

We went back to her apartment and she put on a Cedar Walton solo piano album that we both liked, and we sat together on the couch, not saying much. When the record ended she turned it over, and halfway through Side Two we went into the bedroom and made love with a curious intensity. Afterward neither of us spoke for a long time, until she said, "I'll tell you, kiddo. If we keep on like this, one of these days we're gonna get good at it."

"You think so, huh?"

"It wouldn't surprise me. Matt? Stay over tonight."

I kissed her. "I was planning to."

"Mmmm. Good plan. I don't want to be alone."

Neither did I.

4

I stayed for breakfast, and by the time I got out to Atlantic Avenue it was almost eleven. I spent five hours there, most of it on the street and in shops but some of it in a branch library and on the phone. A little after four I walked a couple of blocks and caught a bus to Bay Ridge.

When I'd seen him last he'd been rumpled and unshaven, but now Kenan Khoury looked cool and composed in gray gabardine slacks and a muted plaid shirt. I followed him into the kitchen and he told me his brother had gone to work in Manhattan that morning. "Petey said he'd stay here, he didn't care about work, but how many times are we gonna have the same conversation? I made him take the Toyota so he's got that to get back and forth. How about you, Matt? You getting anywhere?"

I said, "Two men about my size took your wife off the street in front of The Arabian Gourmet and hustled her into a dark blue panel truck or van. A similar truck, probably the same one, was tailing her when she left D'Agostino's. The truck had lettering on the doors, white lettering according to one witness. TV Sales & Service, with the company name composed of indeterminate initials. B & L, H & M, different people saw different things. Two people remembered an address in Queens and one specifically recalled it as Long Island City."

"Is there such a firm?"

"The description's vague enough so that there are a dozen or more firms that would fit. A couple of initials, TV repair, a Queens address. I called six or eight outfits and couldn't come up with anybody who runs dark blue trucks or who had a vehicle stolen recently. I didn't expect to."

"Why not?"

"I don't think the truck was stolen. My guess is that they had your house staked out Thursday morning hoping your wife would go out by herself. When she did they followed her. It probably wasn't the first time they tailed her, waiting for an opportunity to make their play. They wouldn't want to steal a truck each time and ride around all day in something that's liable to show up any hour on the hot-car sheet."

"You think it was their truck?"

"Most likely. I think they painted a phony company name and address on the doors, and once they completed the snatch they painted the old name out and a new name in. By now I wouldn't be surprised if the whole body's repainted some color other than blue."

"What about the license plate?"

"It had probably been switched for the occasion, but it hardly matters because nobody got the plate number. One witness thought the three of them had just knocked over the food market, that they were robbers, but all he wanted to do was get inside the store and make sure everybody was all right. Another man thought something funny was going on and he did take a look at the plate, but all he remembered was that it had a nine in it."

"That's helpful."

"Very. The men were dressed alike, dark pants and matching work shirts, matching blue windbreakers. They looked to be in uniform, and, between that and the commercial vehicle they were driving, they appeared legitimate. I learned years ago that you can walk in almost anywhere if you're carrying a clipboard because it looks as though you're doing your job. They had that edge going for them. Two different people told me they thought they were watching two undercover guys from INS taking an illegal alien off the street. That's one reason nobody interfered, that and the fact that it was over and done with before anyone had time to react."

"Pretty slick," he said.

"The uniform dress did something else, too. It made them invisible, because all people saw was their clothing, and all they remembered was that both of them looked the same. Did I mention that they had caps on, too? The witnesses described the caps and the jackets, things they put on for the job and got rid of afterward."

"So we don't really have anything."

"That's not really true," I said. "We don't have anything that leads directly to them, but we've got something. We know what they did and how they did it, that they're resourceful, that they planned their approach. How do you figure they picked you?"

He shrugged. "They knew I was a trafficker. That was mentioned. That makes you a good target. They know you've got money and they know you're not going to call the police."

"What else did they know about you?"

"My ethnic background. The one guy, the first one, he called me some names."

"I think you mentioned that."

"Raghead, sand nigger. That's a nice one, huh? Sand nigger. He left out camel jockey, that's one I used to hear from the Italian kids at St. Ignatius. 'Hey, Khoury, ya fuckin' camel jockey!' Only camel I ever saw was on a cigarette pack."

"You think being an Arab made you a target?"

"It never occurred to me. There's a certain amount of prejudice, no question about it, but I'm not usually that conscious of it. Francine's people are Palestinian, did I mention that?"

"Yes."

"They have it tougher. I know Palestinians who say they're

66

Lebanese or Syrian just to avoid hassles. 'Oh, you're Palestinian, you must be a terrorist.' That kind of ignorant remark, and there are people who have bigoted ideas about Arabs in general." He rolled his eyes. "My father, for instance."

"Your father?"

"I wouldn't say he was anti-Arab, but he had this whole theory that we weren't actually Arabs. Our family's Christian, see."

"I wondered what you were doing at St. Ignatius."

"There were times I wondered myself. No, we were Maronite Christians, and according to my old man we were Phoenicians. You ever hear of the Phoenicians?"

"Back in biblical times, weren't they? Traders and explorers, something like that?"

"You got it. Great sailors, they sailed all around Africa, they colonized Spain, they probably reached Britain. They founded Carthage in North Africa, and there were a lot of Carthaginian coins dug up in England. They were the first people to discover Polaris, that's the North Star, I mean to discover that it was always in the same spot and could be used for navigation. They developed an alphabet that served as the basis for the Greek alphabet." He broke off, slightly embarrassed. "My old man talked about them all the time. I guess some of it must have soaked in."

"It looks like it."

"He wasn't a lunatic on the subject, but he knew a lot about it. That's where my name comes from. The Phoenicians called themselves the Kena'ani, or Canaanites. My name should be pronounced Keh-*nahn*, but everyone's always said *Kee*-nan."

"'Ken Curry' is the message I got yesterday."

"Yeah, that's typical. I've ordered things on the phone and they turn up addressed to Keane & Curry, it sounds like a couple of Irish lawyers. Anyway, according to my father the Phoenicians were a completely different people from the Arabs. They were the Canaanites, they were already a people at the time of Abraham. Whereas the Arabs were descended from Abraham."

"I thought the Jews were descendants of Abraham."

"Right, through Isaac, who was the legitimate son of Abraham and Sarah. Meanwhile the Arabs were the sons of Ishmael, who was the son Abraham fathered with Hagar. Jesus, here's something I haven't thought of in a long time. When I was a kid my father had this mild feud with this grocer around the block on Dean Street, and he used to refer to him as 'that Ishmaelite bastard.' God, what a character he was."

"Is he still living?"

"No, he died three years ago. He was diabetic, and over the years it weakened his heart. When I'm down on myself I tell myself he died of a broken heart because of how his sons turned out. He was hoping for an architect and a doctor and instead he got a drunk and a dope dealer. But that's not what killed him. His diet killed him. He was diabetic and he was fifty pounds overweight. Me and Petey could have turned out to be Jonas Salk and Frank Lloyd Wright and it wouldn't have done him any good."

Around six Kenan made the first of a series of phone calls after the two of us had worked out an approach. He dialed a number, waited for a tone, then punched in his own number and hung up. "Now we wait," he said, but we didn't have to wait very long. In less than five minutes the phone rang.

He said, "Hey, Phil, how's it going? Great. Here's the deal. I don't know if you ever met my wife. The thing is, we had this kidnap threat, I had to send her out of the country. I don't know what it's about but I think it has to do with the business, you follow me? So what I'm doing, I've got a guy checking it out for me, like a professional. And I wanted, you know, to pass the word, because the sense I got is these people are serious about this and my impression is they're stone killers. Right. Yeah, that's the thing, man, we sit here and we're easy marks, we got plenty of cash and we can't holler for the law, and that makes us the perfect target for home invasions and every goddam thing... Right. So all I'm saying is be careful, you know, and keep an eye and an ear open. And pass the word around, you know, to whoever you think ought to hear it. And if any shit comes down, man, call me, you understand? Right."

He hung up and turned to me. "I don't know," he said. "I think all I did was convince him I'm getting paranoid in my old age. 'Why'd you send her out of the country, man? Why not just buy a dog, hire a bodyguard?' Because she's dead, you dumb fuck, but I didn't want to tell him that. If the word gets around it's got to mean problems. Shit."

"What's the matter?"

"What do I tell Francine's family? Every time the phone rings I'm afraid it's one of her cousins. Her parents are separated and her mother moved back to Jordan, but her father's still in the old neighborhood and she's got relatives all over Brooklyn. What do I tell them?"

"I don't know."

"I'll have to fill them in sooner or later. Time being, I'll say she went on a cruise, something like that. You know what they'll figure?"

"Marital problems."

"That's it. We're just back from Negril, so why's she going on a cruise? Must be trouble between the Khourys. Well, they can think whatever they want. Truth of the matter is we never had a cross word, we never had a bad day. Jesus." He picked up the phone, punched in a number, keyed in his own number at the tone. He hung up and drummed the tabletop impatiently, and when the phone rang he picked it up and said, "Hey, man, how's it going? Oh, yeah? No shit. Hey, here's the deal...."

5

I went to the eight-thirty meeting at St. Paul's. On the way over it had crossed my mind that I might run into Pete Khoury there, but he didn't show up. Afterward I helped fold chairs, then joined a group of people for coffee at the Flame. I didn't stay there long, though, because by eleven I was at Poogan's Pub on West Seventy-second Street, one of the two places where Danny Boy Bell could generally be found between the hours of 9:00 P.M. and 4:00 A.M. The rest of the time you couldn't count on finding him anywhere.

His other place is a jazz club called Mother Goose on Amsterdam. Poogan's was closer, so I tried it first. Danny Boy was at his usual table in back, deep in conversation with a dark-skinned black man with a pointed chin and a button nose. He was wearing wraparound sunglasses with mirrored lenses and a powder-blue suit with more in the shoulders than God or Gold's Gym could have put there. A little cocoa-brown straw hat perched on top of his head, adorned with a flamingo-pink hatband.

I had a Coke at the bar and waited while he finished his

business with Danny Boy. After five minutes or so he uncoiled himself from his chair, clapped Danny Boy on the shoulder, laughed heartily, and headed for the street. I turned around to get my change from the bar, and when I turned back again his place had been taken by a balding white man with a brushy mustache and a belly straining at his shirtfront. I hadn't recognized the first fellow, other than generically, but I knew this man. His name was Selig Wolf and he owned a couple of parking lots and took bets on sporting events. I had arrested him once ages ago on an assault charge, but the complainant had decided not to press it.

When Wolf left I took my second Coke with me and sat down. "Busy evening," I said.

"I know," Danny Boy said. "Pick a number and wait, it's getting as bad as Zabar's. It's good to see you, Matthew. I saw you before but I had to suffer through the hour of the Wolf. You must know Selig."

"Sure, but I didn't know the other fellow. He's head of fund-raising for the United Negro College Fund, right?"

"A mind is a terrible thing to waste," he said solemnly. "To think you would waste yours judging by appearances. The gentleman was wearing a sartorial classic, Matthew, known as the zoot suit. That's a zoot suit, you know, with a drape shape and a reet pleat. My father had one in his closet, a souvenir of his flaming youth. Every now and then he would take it out and threaten to wear it, and my mother would roll her eyes."

"Good for her."

"His name is Nicholson James," Danny Boy said. "It should have been James Nicholson, but the names were reversed on some official document early on and he decided it had more style that way. You might say it goes with his retro fashion statement. Mr. James is a pimp."

"Go figure. I never would have guessed."

Danny Boy poured himself some vodka. His own fashion statement was one of quiet elegance, a tailored dark suit and tie, a boldly patterned red-and-black vest. He is a very short, slightly built albino African-American—it would be way off the mark to call him black, since he's anything but. He spends his

71

nights in saloons, and he's partial to dim lighting and low noise levels. He's as rigid as Dracula about not venturing out in daylight, and rarely answers the phone or the door during those hours. Every night, though, he's in Poogan's or Mother Goose, listening to people and telling them things.

"Eiaine's not with you," he said.

"Not tonight."

"Give her my love."

"I will," I said. "I brought you something, Danny Boy."

"Oh?"

I palmed him a pair of hundreds. He looked at the money without flashing it, then glanced at me with his eyebrows elevated.

"I have a prosperous client," I said. "He wants me to take cabs."

"Did you want me to call you one?"

"No, but I thought I ought to spread a little of his dough around. All you have to spread is the word."

"What word is that?"

I ran through the official story without mentioning Kenan Khoury's name. Danny Boy listened, frowning occasionally in concentration. When I was finished he took out a cigarette, looked at it for a moment, then put it back in the pack.

"A question arises," he said.

"Go."

"Your client's wife is out of the country, and presumably safe from those who would harm her. So he assumes they'll direct their attention at someone else."

"Right."

"Well, why should he care? I love the idea of a public-spirited dope dealer, like all those marijuana growers in Oregon who make huge anonymous cash donations to Earth First and the eco-saboteurs. Well, when I was growing up I liked Robin Hood, as far as that goes. But what difference does it make to your man if the bad guys snatch somebody else's sweetie? They get the ransom and that just leaves one of his competitors in a negative cash-flow situation, that's all. Or they screw up and that's the end of them. As long as his own wife's out of the picture—"

"Jesus, it was a perfectly good story until I told it to you, Danny Boy."

"Sorry."

"His wife didn't make it out of the country. They snatched her and they killed her."

"He tried to stonewall? Wouldn't pay the ransom?"

"He paid four hundred large. They killed her anyway." His eyes widened. "Your ears only," I added. "The death isn't being reported, so that part of it shouldn't get out on the street."

"I understand. Well, that makes his motive easier to grasp. He wants to get even. Any idea who they are?"

"No."

"But you figure they'll do it again."

"Why quit on a winning roll?"

"Nobody ever does." He helped himself to more vodka. At both of his regular places they bring him the bottle in an ice bucket, and he drinks great quantities of it without paying much attention to it, just drinking it down like water. I don't know where he puts it, or how his body processes it.

He said, "How many bad guys?"

"Minimum of three."

"Splitting four tenths of a mil. They might be taking cabs a lot themselves, don't you think?"

"I had that thought myself."

"So if somebody's throwing a lot of money around, that would be useful information."

"It might."

"And the drug dealers, especially the major players, should get the word that they're at risk for kidnapping. They might just as easily grab a dealer, don't you think? It wouldn't have to be a woman."

"I'm not sure about that."

"Why's that?"

"I think they enjoyed the killing. I think they got off on it. I think they used her sexually, and I think they tortured her, and then when the novelty wore off they killed her."

"The body showed signs of torture?"

"The body came back in twenty or thirty pieces, individually wrapped. And that's not for the street, either. I hadn't planned on mentioning it."

"I'd just as soon you hadn't, to tell you the truth. Matthew, is it my imagination or is the world turning nastier?"

"It doesn't seem to be lightening up."

"It doesn't, does it? Remember the Harmonic Convergence, all the planets lining up like soldiers? Wasn't that supposed to signal the dawn of some kind of New Age?"

"I'm not holding my breath."

"Well, they say it's always darkest before the dawn. I see what you mean, though. If killing's part of the fun, and if they're into rape and torture, well, they won't pick some raggedy-ass dope dealer with a beer gut and a five o'clock shadow. Nothing queer about these fellows."

"No."

He thought for a moment. "They'll have to do it again," he said. "They could hardly be expected to quit after a score like that. I wonder, though."

"If they've done it before? I was wondering the same thing myself."

"And?"

"They were pretty slick," I said. "I get the feeling they had some practice."

First thing after breakfast the next morning I walked over to the Midtown North station house on West Fifty-fourth. I caught Joe Durkin at his desk, and he caught me off balance by complimenting me on my appearance. "You're dressing better these days," he said. "I think it's that woman's doing. Elaine, right?"

"That's right."

"Well, I think she's a good influence on you."

"I'm sure she is," I said, "but what the hell are you talking about?"

"That's a nice-looking jacket, that's all."

"This blazer? It must be ten years old."

"Well, you never wear it."

"I wear it all the time."

"Maybe it's the tie."

"What's so special about the tie?"

"Jesus Christ," he said. "Did anybody ever tell you you're a difficult son of a bitch? I tell you you look nice and the next thing I know I'm on the fucking witness stand. How about we start over? 'Hello, Matt, it's great to see you. You look like shit. Have a seat.' Is that better?"

"Much better."

"I'm glad. Sit down. What brings you here?"

"I had the urge to commit a felony."

"I know the feeling. There's hardly a day goes by that I don't get the same urge myself. You got any particular felony in mind?"

"I was thinking of a class D felony."

"Well, we got lots of those. Criminal possession of forgery devices is a class D felony, and you're probably committing that one at this very minute. You got a pen in your pocket?"

"Two pens and a pencil."

"Gee, it sounds as though I better Mirandize you and get you booked and printed. But I don't suppose that's the class D felony you had in mind."

I shook my head. "I was thinking of violating Section Two Hundred Point Zero Zero of the Criminal Code."

"Two Hundred Point Zero Zero. You're gonna make me look that up, aren't you?"

"Why not?"

He gave me a look, then reached for a black looseleaf binder and flipped through it. "It's a familiar number," he said. "Oh, right, here we are. 'Two Hundred Point Zero Zero. Bribery in the third degree. A person is guilty of bribery in the third degree when he confers, or offers or agrees to confer, any benefit upon a public servant upon an agreement or understanding that such public servant's vote, opinion, judgment, action, decision or exercise of discretion as a public servant will thereby be influenced. Bribery in the third degree is a class D felony.'" He went on reading silently for a moment, then said, "Are you sure you wouldn't prefer to violate Section Two Hundred Point Zero Three?"

"What's that?"

"That's bribery in the second degree. It's the same as the other only it's a class C felony. To qualify for Bribery Two, the benefit you confer or offer or agree to confer, Jesus, don't you love the way they word these things, the benefit has to be in excess of ten thousand dollars."

"Ah," I said. "I think class D is my limit."

"I was afraid of that. Can I ask you something? Before you commit your class D felony? How many years has it been since you were on the job?"

"It's been a while."

"So how'd you remember the class of felony, let alone the article number?"

"I've got that kind of memory."

"Bullshit. They've renumbered the sections over the years, they've changed half the book at one time or another. I just want to know how you did it."

"You really want to know?"

"Yes."

"I looked it up in Andreotti's book on my way up here."

"Just to break my balls, right?"

"Just to keep you on your toes."

"Only my best interests at heart."

"Absolutely," I said. I'd set aside a bill in my jacket pocket earlier, and I palmed it now and tucked it into the pocket where he keeps his cigarettes, except during those intervals when he swears off and smokes other people's. "Buy yourself a suit," I told him.

We were all alone in the office, so he took the bill out and examined it. "We'll have to update the terminology. A hat's twenty-five dollars, a suit's a hundred. I don't know what a decent hat costs these days, I can't remember the last time I bought one. But I don't know where you'd get a suit for a hundred bucks outside of a thrift shop. 'Here's a hundred bucks, take your wife to dinner.' What's this for, anyway?"

"I need a favor."

"Oh?"

"There was a case I read about," I said. "Had to be six months ago and it could have been as much as a year. Couple of guys grabbed a woman off the street, rode off with her in a truck. She turned up a few days later in the park."

"Dead, I'm assuming."

"Dead."

" 'Police suspect foul play.' Can't say it rings a bell. It wasn't one of our cases, was it?"

"It wasn't even Manhattan. I seem to remember that she turned up on a golf course in Queens, but it could as easily have been somewhere in Brooklyn. I didn't pay any attention at the time, it was just an item I read while I drank a second cup of coffee."

"And what do you want now?"

"I want my memory refreshed."

He looked at me. "You're getting pretty free with a buck, aren't you? Why make a donation to my wardrobe fund when you could go to the library, look it up in the *Times Index*?"

"Under what? I don't know where or when it happened or any of the names. I'd have to scan every issue for the last year, and I don't even know what paper I read it in. It may not have made the *Times*."

"Be easier if I made a couple of phone calls."

"That's what I was thinking."

"Why don't you take a walk? Have yourself a cup of coffee. Get yourself a table at the Greek place on Eighth Avenue. I'll probably drop in there an hour from now, have myself some coffee and a piece of Danish."

Forty minutes later he came to my table in the coffee shop at Eighth and Fifty-third. "Just over a year ago," he said. "Woman named Marie Gotteskind. What's that mean, God is kind?"

"I think it means 'child of God.' "

"That's better, because God wasn't kind to Marie. She was reported abducted in broad daylight while shopping on Jamaica Avenue in Woodhaven. Two men drove off with her in a truck, and three days later a couple of kids walking across Forest Park Golf Course came upon her body. Sexual assault, multiple stab wounds. The One-Oh-Four caught the case and bounced it back to the One-Twelve once they ID'd her, because that was where the original abduction took place."

"They get anywhere?"

He shook his head. "Guy I talked to remembered the case well enough. It had people in the neighborhood pretty shook up for a couple of weeks there. Respectable woman walks down the street, couple of clowns grab her, it's like getting struck by lightning, you know what I mean? If it can happen to her it can happen to anybody, and you're not even safe in your own home. They were afraid there'd be more of the same, gang rape on wheels, the whole serial-killer bit. What was that case in L.A., they made a miniseries out of it?"

"I don't know."

"Two Italian guys, I think they were cousins. They were doing hookers and leaving them up in the hills. Hillside Strangler, that's what they called it. Stranglers, it should have been, but I guess the media named the case before they knew it was more than one person."

"The woman in Woodhaven," I said.

"Right. They were afraid she was the first of a series, but then there weren't any more and everybody relaxed. They still put a lot of effort into the case but nothing led anywhere. It's an open file now, and the thinking is that the only way they'll break it is if the perps get caught doing it again. He asked if we had anything tied into it. Do we?"

"No. What did the woman's husband do, did you happen to notice?"

"I don't think she was married. I think she was a school-teacher. Why?"

"She live alone?"

"What difference does it make?"

"I'd love to see the file, Joe."

"You would, huh? Whyntcha ride out to the One-Twelve and ask them to show it to you."

"I don't think that would work."

"You don't, huh? You mean there are cops in this town won't go out of their way to do a favor for a private license? Jesus, I'm shocked."

"I'd appreciate it."

"A phone call or two's one thing," he said. "I didn't have to commit a flagrant breach of departmental regulations and neither did the guy on the job in Queens. But you're asking for disclosure of confidential materials. That file's not supposed to leave the office."

"It doesn't have to. All he has to do is take five minutes to fax it."

"You want the whole file? Full-scale homicide investigation, there's got to be twenty, thirty pages in that file."

"The department can afford the fax charges."

"I don't know," he said. "The mayor keeps telling us the city's going broke. What's your interest in it, anyway?"

"I can't say."

"Well, Jesus Christ, Matt. You want it all flowing in one direction, don't you?"

"It's a confidential matter."

"No shit. It's confidential, but departmental files are an open book, is that it?" He lit a cigarette and coughed. He said, "This wouldn't have anything to do with a friend of yours, would it?"

"I don't follow you."

"Your buddy Ballou. This got anything to do with him?"

"Of course not."

"You sure of that?"

"He's out of the country," I said. "He's been gone for over a month and I don't know when he's coming back. And he's never been big on raping women and leaving them in the middle of the fairway."

"I know, he's a gentleman, he replaces all divots. They're looking to put together a RICO case against him, but I suppose you already knew that."

"I heard something about it."

"I hope they make it stick, tuck him away in a federal joint for the next twenty years. But I suppose you feel differently."

"He's a friend of mine."

"Yeah, so I've been told."

"Anyway, he's got nothing to do with this matter." He just looked at me, and I said, "I have a client whose wife disappeared. The MO looks similar to the Woodhaven incident."

"She was abducted?"

"It looks that way."

"He report it?"

"No."

"Why not?"

"I guess he has his reasons."

"That's not good enough, Matt."

"Suppose he's in the country illegally."

"Half the city's in the country illegally. You think we catch a kidnap case, the first thing we do is turn the victim over to the INS? And who is this guy, he can't swing a green card but he's got the money for a private investigator? Sounds to me like he's got to be dirty."

"Whatever you say."

"Whatever I say, huh?" He put out his cigarette and frowned at me. "The woman dead?"

"It's beginning to look that way. If it's the same people—"

"Yeah, but why would it be the same people? What's the connection, the MO of the abduction?" When I didn't say anything he picked up the check, glanced at it, and tossed it across the table to me. "Here," he said. "Your treat. You still at the same number? I'll call you this afternoon."

"Thanks, Joe."

"No, don't thank me. I have to go figure out if there's any way this is going to come back and haunt me. If not I'll make the call. Otherwise forget it."

I went to the noon meeting at Fireside, then back to my room. There was nothing from Durkin, but a message slip indicated that I'd had a call from TJ. Just that—no number, no further message. I crumpled the slip and tossed it.

TJ is a black teenager I met about a year and a half ago

on Times Square. That's his street name, and if he has another name he's kept it to himself. I'd found him breezy and saucy and irreverent, a breath of fresh air in the fetid swamp of Forty-second Street, and the two of us had hit it off together. I let him do some minor legwork on a case a little later on with a Times Square handle to it, and since then he'd kept in infrequent contact. Every couple of weeks there would be a call or a series of calls from him. He never left a number and I had no way of getting in touch with him, so his messages were just a way of letting me know he was thinking of me. If he really wanted to contact me he'd keep calling until he caught me at home.

When he did, we sometimes talked until his quarter ran out, or sometimes we would meet in his neighborhood or mine and I would buy him a meal. Twice I'd given him little jobs to do in connection with cases I was working, and he seemed to get a kick out of the work that couldn't be explained by the small sums I paid him.

I went up to my room and called Elaine. "Danny Boy says hello," I said. "And Joe Durkin says you're a good influence on me."

"Of course I am," she said. "But how does he know?"

"He says I'm better dressed since we started keeping company."

"I told you that new suit is special."

"That's not what I was wearing."

"Oh."

"I was wearing my blazer. I've had the damn thing forever."

"Well, it still looks nice. Gray slacks with it? Which shirt and tie?" I told her, and she said, "Well, that's a nice outfit."

"Pretty ordinary, though. I saw a zoot suit last night."

"Honestly?"

"With a drape shape and a reet pleat, according to Danny Boy."

"Danny Boy wasn't wearing a zoot suit."

"No, it was an associate of his named—well, it doesn't matter what his name was. He was also wearing a straw hat with a shocking-pink band. Now if I'd worn something like that to Durkin's office—"

"He would have been impressed. Maybe it's something in your stance, honey, maybe it's an attitude thing that Durkin's picking up on. You're wearing your clothes with more authority."

"Because my heart is pure."

"That must be it."

We kibitzed a little more. She had a class that night and we talked about getting together afterward but decided against it. "Tomorrow's better," she said. "Maybe a movie? Except I hate to go on the weekend, everything decent is mobbed. I know, maybe an afternoon movie and dinner after it, assuming you're not working." I told her that sounded good.

I hung up and the man on the desk rang to say I'd had a call while I was on the phone with Elaine. They've changed the phone system a few times since I've been at the Northwestern. Originally all calls had to go through the switchboard. Then they fixed it so you could dial out directly, but incoming calls were still routed through the board. Now I have a direct line for making or receiving calls, but if I don't pick up after four rings it gets transferred downstairs. I get my own bill from NYNEX, the hotel doesn't impose any charges, and I come out of it with a free answering service.

The call was from Durkin, and I rang him back. "You left something here," he said. "You want to pick it up or should I toss it?"

I said I'd be right over.

He was on the phone when I got to the squad room. He had his chair tilted back and he was smoking a cigarette while another one burned up in the ashtray. At the desk next to his, a detective named Bellamy was peering over the tops of his eyeglasses at the screen of his computer.

Joe covered the mouthpiece of the phone and said, "I think that's your envelope there, it's got your name on it. You left it when you were here earlier."

Without waiting for a reply he went back to his conversation. I reached over his shoulder and picked up a nine-by-twelve manila clasp envelope with my name on it. Behind me, Bellamy told the computer, "Well, that makes no fucking sense at all."

I didn't argue the point.

6

Back in my room I spread a sheaf of curling fax copies on my bed. They had evidently faxed the whole file, thirty-six pages of it. Some of them only had a few lines on them, but others were densely packed with information.

Shuffling through them, it struck me what a different proposition all this would have been in my own cop days. We didn't have copying machines, let alone fax. The only way to see Marie Gotteskind's file would have required traipsing out to Queens and going through it on the spot, with some anxious cop looking over your shoulder and trying to hurry you along.

Nowadays you just fed everything into a fax transmitter and it came out by sheer magic five or ten miles away—or on the other side of the world, for that matter. The original file never left the office where it was kept, and no unauthorized person snuck in for a peek at it, so nobody had to get uptight about a breach in security.

And I had all the time I needed to pore over the Gotteskind file.

It's just as well I did because I had no clear idea what I

was looking for. One thing that hasn't changed a bit since I got out of the Police Academy is the amount of paperwork the job entails. Whatever kind of cop you are, you spend less time doing things than you do establishing a record on paper of what you've done. Some of this is the usual bureaucratic horseshit and some comes under the general heading of covering your ass, but much of it is probably inescapable. Police work is a collective effort, with a variety of people contributing to even the simpler sort of investigation, and if it's not all written down somewhere nobody can get an overview of it and figure out what it amounts to.

I read everything, and when I got to the end I went back and pulled a few pieces of paper for a second look. One thing that became evident early on was the extraordinary similarity between the Gotteskind abduction and the way Francine Khoury was taken in Brooklyn. I noted the following points of similarity:

1. Both women were abducted from commercial streets.
2. Both women had parked cars nearby and were shopping on foot.
3. Both were seized by a pair of men.
4. In both instances, the men were described as being similar in height and weight, and w re dressed alike. The Gotteskind kidnappers had worn khaki trousers and navy windbreakers.
5. Both women were carried off in trucks. The truck used in Woodhaven was described by several witnesses as a light blue van. One witness identified it specifically as a Ford, and supplied a partial plate number, but it hadn't led anywhere.
6. Several witnesses agreed that the body of the truck was lettered with the name of a household appliance firm. They variously identified the firm as P J Home Appliance, B & J Household Appliance, and variations on the foregoing. A second line read SALES AND SERVICE. There was no address, but witnesses reported that there was a phone number, although no one could supply it.

A thorough investigation had failed to link the truck to any of the innumerable companies in the borough that sold and serviced home appliances, and the conclusion seemed warranted that the firm's name, like the plate number, was spurious.

7. Marie Gotteskind was twenty-eight years old and employed as a substitute teacher in the New York City primary schools. For three days, including the day of her abduction, she had filled in for a fourth-grade teacher in Ridgewood. She was about the same height as Francine Khoury and within a few pounds of her in weight, blond and light-complected where Francine was dark-haired and olive-skinned. There was no photograph in the file except for those taken at the scene in Forest Park, but testimony from acquaintances indicated that she was considered attractive.

There were differences. Marie Gotteskind was unmarried. She had had a few dates with a male teacher whom she'd met on an earlier substitute assignment, but their relationship does not seem to have amounted to much and his alibi for the time of her death was in any case unassailable.

Marie lived at home with her parents. Her father, a former steamfitter with a disability pension for a job-related injury, operated a small mail-order business from his home. Her mother helped him with the business and also served as a part-time bookkeeper for several neighborhood enterprises. Neither Marie nor either of her parents had any demonstrable connection to the drug subculture. Nor were they Arabs, or Phoenicians.

The medical examination had been detailed, of course, and there was a lot to report. Death had come as a result of multiple stab wounds to the chest and abdomen, any of several of which would have been fatal. There was evidence of repeated sexual assault, with traces of semen in her anus, her vagina, and her mouth, as well as in one of the knife wounds. Forensic measurements indicated that at least two different knives had been used on her, and suggested that both could be kitchen knives, with one having a longer and wider blade than the other. An analysis of the semen indicated the presence of at least two assailants.

In addition to the knife wounds, the nude body showed multiple bruises, indicating that the victim had been subjected to a beating.

Finally, and I missed this on first reading, the medical examiner's report supplied the information that the thumb and index finger of the victim's left hand had been severed. The two digits had been recovered, the index finger from her vagina, the thumb from her rectum.

Cute.

Reading the file had a numbing, deadening effect on me. That's very likely why I missed the thumb-and-finger item first time through. The report of the woman's injuries and the image they conjured up of her last moments was more than the mind wanted to take in. Other entries in the file, interviews with parents and coworkers, had painted a picture of the living Marie Gotteskind, and the medical report took that living person and turned her into dead and grossly mistreated flesh.

I was sitting there, feeling drained and exhausted by what I had just read, when the phone rang. I answered it and a voice I knew said, "So where's it at, Matt?"

"Hey, TJ."

"How you doin'? You a hard man to reach. Be out all the time, goin' places, doin' things."

"I got your message but you didn't leave a number."

"Don't have a number. I was a drug dealer I might could have a beeper. You like it better that way?"

"If you were a dealer you'd have a cellular phone."

"Now you talkin'. Have me a long car with a phone in it, and just be sittin' in it thinkin' long thoughts and doin' long things. Man, I got to say it again, you *hard* to reach."

"Did you call more than once, TJ? I only got the one message."

"Well, see, I don't always like to waste the quarter."

"What do you mean?"

"Well, you know, I got your phone figured. It's like those answering machines, how they pick up after three or four rings, whatever it is? Dude on the desk, he always lets your phone ring four times before he cuts in. And you just got the one room, so it ain't about to take you more than three rings to get to the phone, 'less you be in the bathroom or something."

"So you hang up after three rings."

"And get my quarter back. 'Less I want to leave a message, but why leave a message when I already left one? You come home an' there's a whole stack of messages, you think to yourself, 'This TJ, he musta tapped a parking meter, he got all these quarters he don't know what to do with.' "

I laughed.

"So you workin'?"

"As a matter of fact I am."

"Big job?"

"Fairly big."

"Any room in it for TJ?"

"Not as far as I can see."

"Man, you not lookin' hard enough! Must be something I could do, make up for some of the quarters I burn up callin' you. What kind of job is it, anyway? You not up against the Mafia, are you?"

"I'm afraid not."

"Glad to hear it, because those cats are bad, Tad. You see *GoodFellas*? Man, they nasty. Oh, damn, my quarter be runnin' out."

A recorded voice cut in, demanding five cents for a minute's worth of phone time.

I said, "Give me the number and I'll call you back."

"Can't."

"The number of the phone you're talking on."

"Can't," he said again. "Ain't no number on it. They takin' 'em off all the pay phones so the players can't get calls back on 'em. No problem, I got some change." The phone chimed as he dropped a coin in. "The dealers, they got certain pay phones where they know the number whether it shows there or not.

So it still business as usual, only somebody like you wants to call somebody like me back, ain't no way to do it."

"It's a great system."

"It's cool. We still talkin', ain't we? Nobody stoppin' us doin' what we want to do. They just forcin' us to be resourceful."

"By putting in another quarter?"

"You got it, Matt. I be drawin' on my resources. That's what you call bein' resourceful."

"Where are you going to be tomorrow, TJ?"

"Where I be? Oh, I dunno. Maybe I fly to Paris on the Concorde. I ain't made up my mind yet." It struck me that he could take my ticket and go to Ireland, but he wasn't likely to have a passport. Nor did it seem probable that Ireland was ready for him, or he for Ireland. "Where I be," he said heavily. "I be on the fuckin' Deuce, man. Where else I gonna be?"

"I thought maybe we could get something to eat."

"What time?"

"Oh, I don't know. Say around twelve, twelve-thirty?"

"Which?"

"Twelve-thirty."

"That's twelve-thirty in the daytime or in the night?"

"Daytime. We'll have some lunch."

"Ain't no time of the day or night you can't have lunch," he said. "You want me to come by your hotel?"

"No," I said, "because there's a chance I'll have to cancel and I wouldn't have any way to let you know. So I don't want to hang you up. Pick a place on the Deuce and if I don't show up we'll make it another time."

"That's cool," he said. "You know the video arcade? Uptown side of the street, two, three doors from Eighth Avenue? There's the store with the switchknives in the window, man, I don't know how they get away with that—"

"They're sold in kit form."

"Yeah, an' they use it for an IQ test. You can't put the kit together, you have to go back an' do first grade all over again. You know the store I mean."

"Sure."

"Right next to it there's the entrance to the subway, and before you go down the stairs there's an entranceway to the video arcade. You know where it's at?"

"I have a hunch I can find it."

"Say twelve-thirty?"

"It's a date, Kate."

"Hey," he said. "You know somethin'? You learnin'."

I felt better when I got off the phone with TJ. He usually had that effect on me. I made a note of our lunch date, then picked up the Gotteskind material again.

It was the same perpetrators. Had to be. The similarity of MO was too great to be coincidental, and the amputation and insertion of the thumb and forefinger looked like a rehearsal for the more extensive butchery they'd practiced on Francine Khoury.

But what did they do, go into hibernation? Lie low for a year?

It seemed unlikely. Sex-linked violence—serial rape, lust murder—seems to be addictive, like any strong drug that releases you momentarily from the prison of self. Marie Gotteskind's killers had pulled off a perfectly orchestrated abduction, only to repeat it a year later with very minor variations and, of course, a substantial profit motive. Why wait so long? What were they doing in the meantime?

Could there have been other abductions without anyone drawing a connection to the Gotteskind case? It was possible. The murder rate in the five boroughs is now over seven a day, and most of them don't get a lot of play in the media. Still, if you take a woman off a street in front of a bunch of witnesses, it makes the papers. If you've got a similar case sitting in an open file, you probably hear about it. And you almost have to draw a connection.

On the other hand, Francine Khoury had been snatched off the street in front of witnesses, and nobody in the press or the One-Twelve knew the first thing about it.

Maybe they really had lain low for a year. Maybe one or more of them had been in jail for all or part of that year, maybe a predilection for rape and murder had led to still worse crimes, like writing bad checks.

Or maybe they'd been active, but in a way that hadn't drawn any attention.

Either way, I knew something now that I had previously only suspected. They had done this before, for pleasure if not for profit. That lowered the odds against finding them, and at the same time it raised the stakes.

Because they'd do it again.

7

Friday I spent the morning at the library, then walked over Forty-second Street to meet TJ in the video arcade. Together we watched a kid with a ponytail and a wispy blond mustache run up the score on a game called Freeze!!! It had the same premise as most of the games—i.e., that there were hostile forces in the universe, apt to leap out at you without warning at any moment, bound on doing you harm. If you were quick enough you could survive for a while, but sooner or later one of them would do you in. I couldn't argue with that.

We left when the boy finally crapped out. On the street TJ told me the player's name was Socks because his own never matched. I hadn't noticed. According to TJ, Socks was about the best on the Deuce at what he did, often able to play for hours on a single quarter. There had been other players as good or better, but they didn't come around much anymore. For a moment my mind spun with visions of a previously unknown motive for serial homicide, video-game aces rubbed out by an arcade proprietor because they were eating up his profits, but that wasn't it. You got to a certain level, he explained, and then you couldn't get any better, and eventually you lost interest.

We had lunch at a Mexican place on Ninth Avenue and he tried to get me to talk about the case I was working on. I left out the details, but I probably wound up telling him more than I intended to.

"What you need," he said, "you need me workin' for you."

"Doing what?"

"Anything you say! You don't want to be runnin' all over town, see this, check that. What you want to do is send me. You don't think I can find things out? Man, I'm down here on the Deuce every day findin' things out. It's what I do."

"So I gave him something," I told Elaine. We'd met at the Baronet on Third Avenue to catch a four o'clock movie, then went to a new place she'd heard about where they served English tea with scones and clotted cream. "He'd said something earlier that added another item to my list of things to find out, so I figured it was only fair to let him run it down for me."

"What was that?"

"The pay phones," I said. "When Kenan and his brother delivered the ransom, they were sent to a pay phone. They got a call there, and the caller sent them to still another pay phone, where they got a call telling them to leave the money and take a hike."

"I remember."

"Well, yesterday TJ called me and talked until his quarter dropped, and when I wanted to call him back I couldn't, because the number wasn't posted on the phone he was calling from. I walked around the neighborhood on my way to the library this morning, and most of the phones are like that."

"You mean the little slips are missing? I know people will steal absolutely anything, but that's the stupidest thing I ever heard of."

"The phone company removes them," I said, "to discourage drug dealers. They beep each other from pay phones, you know how it works, and now they can't do that."

"And that's why all the drug dealers are going out of business," she said.

"Well, I'm sure it looked good on paper. Anyway, I got to thinking about those pay phones in Brooklyn, and I wondered if their numbers were posted."

"What difference does it make?"

"I don't know," I said. "Probably somewhere between not much and none at all, which is why I didn't chase out to Brooklyn myself. But I can't see where it would hurt me to have the information, so I gave TJ a couple of dollars and sent him to Brooklyn."

"Does he know his way around Brooklyn?"

"He will by the time he gets back. The first phone's a few blocks from the last stop on the Flatbush IRT, so that's fairly easy to find, but I don't know how the hell he's going to get to Veterans Avenue. A bus out Flatbush, I suppose, and then a long hike."

"What kind of neighborhood is it?"

"It looked all right when I drove through it with the Khourys. I didn't pay a whole lot of attention. A basic white working-class neighborhood, as far as I could tell. Why?"

"You mean like Bensonhurst or Howard Beach? What I mean is will TJ stand out like a dark thumb?"

"I never even thought of that."

"Because there are parts of Brooklyn where they get funny when a black kid walks down the street, even if he is conservatively dressed in high-top sneakers and a Raiders jacket, and I just know he has one of those haircuts."

"He's got a sort of geometric design cut into the hair on the back of his neck."

"I thought he might. I hope he comes back alive."

"He'll be all right."

Later in the evening she said, "Matt, you were just making work for him, weren't you? TJ, I mean."

"No, he's saving me a trip. I would have had to run out there myself sooner or later, or catch a ride with one of the Khourys."

"Why? Couldn't you use your old cop tricks to wheedle the number out of the operator? Or look it up in a reverse directory?"

"You have to know a number to look it up in a reverse directory. A reverse directory has phones listed numerically, and you look up the number and it tells you the location."

"Oh."

"But there is a book that lists pay phones by location, yes. And yes, I could call an operator and pass myself off as a police officer in order to obtain a number."

"So you were just being nice to TJ."

"Nice? According to you I was sending him to his death. No, I wasn't just being nice. Looking in the book or conning the operator would give me the number of the pay phone, but it wouldn't tell me if the number's posted on the phone. That's what I'm trying to find out."

"Oh," she said. And, a few minutes later, "Why?"

"Why what?"

"Why do you care if the number's posted on the phone? What difference does it make?"

"I don't know that it does make a difference. But the kidnappers knew to call those phones. If the number's posted, well, then there was nothing special about their knowledge. If not, they found out one way or another."

"By conning the operator or looking in the book."

"Which would mean that they know how to con an operator, or where to find a list of pay phones. I don't know what it would mean. Probably nothing. Maybe I want to get the information because it's the only thing about the phones I can find out."

"What do you mean?"

"It's been nagging at me," I said. "Not what I sent TJ for, that's easy enough to find out with or without his help. But I was sitting up last night and it struck me that the only contact with the kidnappers was phone contact. That was the only trace they left of themselves. The abduction itself was clean as a whistle. A few people saw them, and even more people saw them take that schoolteacher off Jamaica Avenue, but they didn't leave anything you could use to reel them in. But they did make some phone calls. They made four or five calls to Khoury's house in Bay Ridge."

"There's no way to trace them, is there? After the connection is broken?"

"There ought to be," I said. "I was on the phone yesterday for over an hour with different phone-company personnel. I found out a lot of things about how the phones work. Every call you make is logged."

"Even local calls?"

"Uh-huh. That's how they know how many message units you use in each billing period. It's not like a gas meter where they're just keeping track of the running total. Each call gets recorded and charged to your account."

"How long do they keep that data?"

"Sixty days."

"So you could get a list—"

"Of all the calls made from a particular number. That's how the data is organized. Say I'm Kenan Khoury. I call up, I say I need to know what calls were made from my phone on a given day, and they can give me a printout with the date and time and duration of every call I made."

"But that's not what you want."

"No, it's not. What I want is the calls made *to* Khoury's phone, but that's not how they log them, because there's no point. They've got the technology to tell you what number's calling you before you even pick up the phone. They can mount a little LED gadget on your phone that'll display the number of the calling party and you can decide whether or not you want to talk."

"That's not available yet, is it?"

"No, not in New York, and it's controversial. It would probably cut down on nuisance calls and put a lot of telephone perverts out of business, but the police are afraid it'd keep a lot of people from phoning in anonymous tips, because they'd suddenly be a lot less anonymous."

"If it were available now, and if Khoury had had it on his phone—"

"Then we'd know what phones the kidnappers called from. They probably used pay phones, they've been professional enough in other respects, but at least we'd know which pay phones."

"Is that important?"

"I don't know," I admitted. "I don't know what's important. But it doesn't matter because I can't get the information. It seems to me that if the calls are logged somewhere in the computer there ought to be some way to sort them by the called number, but everyone I talked to said it was impossible. That's not the way they're stored, so they can't be accessed that way."

"I don't know anything about computers."

"Neither do I, and it's a pain in the ass. I try to talk to people and I don't understand half the words they use."

"I know what you mean," she said. "That's how I feel when we watch football."

I stayed over that night, and in the morning I used up some of her message units while she was at the gym. I called a lot of police officers and I told a lot of lies.

Mostly I claimed to be a journalist doing a roundup piece on criminal abductions for a true-crime magazine. I got a lot of cops who had nothing to say or were too busy to talk to me, and I got a fair number who were happy to cooperate but wanted to talk about cases that were years old or ones in which the criminals had been spectacularly stupid, or had been caught through some particularly clever police work. What I wanted— well, that was the problem, I didn't really know what I wanted. I was fishing.

Ideally, I would have loved to hook a live one, somebody who had been abducted and survived. It was conceivable that they had worked their way up to murder, that there had been earlier exploits, joint or individual, in which the victim had been released alive. It was also possible that a victim could have somehow escaped. There was a world of difference, though, between postulating the existence of such a woman and finding her.

My pose as a free-lance crime reporter wouldn't do me any good in my search for a live witness. The system is pretty good about shielding rape victims—at least until they get to court, where the defendant's attorney gets to violate them all over again in front of God and everybody. Nobody was going to give out the names of rape victims over the phone.

So my pitch changed for the sex-crimes units. I became a private investigator again, Matthew Scudder, retained by a film producer who was making a TV movie of the week about abduction and rape. The actress selected for the lead—I wasn't authorized to disclose her name at the present time—wanted an opportunity to research the role in depth, specifically by meeting one-on-one with women who had themselves been through this ordeal. She wanted, essentially, to learn as much as she could about the experience short of undergoing it herself, and the women who assisted her would be compensated as technical advisers and could be listed as such in the credits or not, as they preferred.

Naturally I didn't want names or numbers, and had no intention of attempting to initiate contact myself. My thought was that perhaps someone from the unit, possibly a woman who had done victim counseling, could make contact with whatever victims struck her as likely prospects. The woman in *our* scenario, I explained, was abducted by a pair of sadistic rapists who forced her into a truck, brutalized her, and threatened her with grievous physical harm, threatened specifically to maim her. Obviously someone whose experience was in any way parallel to our fictional narrative would be just what we were looking for. If such a woman was interested in helping us out, and perhaps in helping in some small way other women who might be exposed to such treatment in the future, or who had already gone through it, and might find it a cathartic, even a therapeutic, experience to coach a Hollywood actress in what could be a showcase role—

The whole thing played surprisingly well. Even in New York, where you're always coming upon film crews shooting location sequences on the street, the mere mention of the movie business tends to turn people's heads. "Just have anyone who's interested give me a call," I wound up, leaving my name and number. "They don't have to give their names. They can remain anonymous throughout the entire process, if they want."

Elaine walked in just as I was finishing my pitch to a woman in the Manhattan Sex Crimes Unit. When I got off the phone she said, "How are you going to get all of these calls at your hotel? You're never there."

"They'll take messages at the desk."

"From people who don't want to leave a name or number? Look, give them my number. I'm usually here, and if I'm not they'll at least get an answering machine with a woman's voice on it. I'll be your assistant, I can certainly screen the calls and get names and addresses from the ones who are willing to give them. What's wrong with that?"

"Nothing," I said. "Are you sure you want to do it?"

"Sure."

"Well, I'm delighted. That was the Manhattan unit I was just talking to, and I called the Bronx earlier. I was saving Brooklyn and Queens for last, since we know they've operated there. I wanted to work the bugs out of my routine before I called them."

"Is it bug-free now? And I don't want to horn in, but is there any advantage in my making the calls? You sounded low-key and sympathetic as could be, but it seems to me that whenever a man talks about rape there's the undercurrent of suspicion that he's getting off on the whole thing."

"I know."

"I mean, all you have to do is say 'movie of the week' and the subtext a woman gets is that sisterhood is going to be violated yet again in another tacky exploitation drama. Whereas if I say it the subliminal message is that the whole thing's under the sponsorship of NOW."

"You're right. I think it went reasonably well, especially on the Manhattan call, but there was a lot of resistance there."

"You sounded terrific, honey. But can I try?"

We went over the premise first to make sure she had it down, and then I got through to the Sex Crimes Unit at the Queens County DA's office and gave her the phone. She was on the phone for almost ten minutes, at once earnest and polished and professional, and when she rang off I felt like applauding.

"What do you think?" she asked. "A little too sincere?"

"I thought you were perfect."

"Really?"

"Uh-huh. It's almost scary to see what a slick liar you are."

"I know. When I was listening to you I thought, he's so honest, where did he learn to lie like that?"

"I never knew a good cop who wasn't a good liar," I said. "You're playing a part all the time, creating an attitude to fit the person you're dealing with. The same skill's even more important when you work private, because you're constantly asking for information you've got no legal right to. So if I'm good at it, you can say it's part of the job description."

"For me, too," she said. "Now that I come to think of it. I'm always acting, it's what I do."

"That was great acting last night, incidentally."

She gave me a look. "It's tiring, though, isn't it? Lying, I mean."

"You want to quit?"

"Screw that, I'm just getting warmed up. Who else do I do, Brooklyn and Staten Island?"

"Forget Staten Island."

"Why? No sex crimes in Staten Island?"

"All sex is a crime in Staten Island."

"Har har."

"No, they could have a unit, for all I know, although the incidence there is nothing compared to the other boroughs. But I can't see our three men in a van zooming across the Verrazano Bridge bent on rape and mayhem."

"So I've only got one more call to make?"

"Well," I said, "there are also sex-crime units in the various police-department borough commands, and there are frequently rape specialists in individual precincts. You just ask the desk officer to route the call to the appropriate person. I could make a list, but I don't know how much time you've got for this."

She gave me a come-hither look. "If you've got the money, honey," she said archly, "I've got the time."

"As a matter of fact, there's no reason why you shouldn't get paid for this. There's no reason you shouldn't be on Khoury's payroll."

"Oh, please," she said. "Whenever I find something I like somebody tries to get me to take money for it. No, seriously, I don't want to get paid. When this is all but a memory you can take me out for a really extravagant dinner somewhere, okay?"

"Whatever you say."

"And afterward," she said, "you can slip me a hundred for cab fare."

8

I stayed around while she charmed the daylights out of a staffer in the Brooklyn DA's Office, then left her with a list of people to call and walked to the library. There was no need for me to supervise her. She was a natural.

In the library I did what I'd started doing the previous morning, working my way through six months' worth of *The New York Times* on microfilm. I wasn't looking for abductions because I didn't really expect to find any reported as such. Instead I was assuming that they had occasionally snatched someone off the street without anyone witnessing the act, or at least without their reporting it. I was looking for victims who turned up dead in parks or alleys, especially victims who'd been sexually assaulted and mutilated, specifically dismembered.

A problem lay in the fact that touches of that sort weren't very likely to make the papers. It's standard police policy to withhold specific details of mutilation in order to spare themselves a variety of aggravations—phony confessions, copycat offenders, false witnesses. For their part, newspapers tend to spare their readers the more graphic details. By the time the

102

news gets to the reader, it's hard to tell what happened.

Some years ago there was a sex criminal who was killing young boys on the Lower East Side. He lured them onto rooftops, stabbed or strangled them, and amputated and carried off their penises. He was at it long enough for cops on the case to come up with a name for him. They called him Charlie Chopoff.

Naturally enough, the police reporters called him the same thing—but not in print. There was no way any New York newspaper was going to provide that little detail for their readers, and there was no way to use the nickname without the reader having a pretty fair idea as to just what was chopped off. So they didn't call him anything, and reported only that the killer had mutilated or disfigured his victims, which could cover anything from ritual disembowelment to a lousy haircut.

Nowadays they might be less restrained.

Once I got the hang of it, I was able to go through the weeks with fair speed. I didn't have to scan an entire paper, just the Metropolitan section where the local crime news was concentrated. The biggest time waster was the same one I always have in a library, which is a tendency to get sidetracked by something interesting that has nothing to do with what brought me there. Fortunately they don't carry comics in the *Times*. Otherwise I'd have had to wrestle with the temptation to wallow in six months' worth of *Doonesbury*.

By the time I got out of there I had half a dozen possible cases jotted down in my notebook. One was particularly likely, the victim an accounting major at Brooklyn College who went missing three days before a birdwatcher encountered her one morning in Green-Wood Cemetery. The story said that she'd been subjected to sexual assault and sexual mutilation, which suggested to me that someone had done a job on her with a carving knife. Evidence at the scene indicated that she had been killed elsewhere and dumped at the cemetery, and police had drawn a similar conclusion about Marie Gotteskind, that she had already been dead when her killers discarded her body on the Forest Park Golf Course.

* * *

I got back to my hotel around six. There were messages from Elaine and both Khourys, along with three slips announcing simply that TJ had called.

I called Elaine first and she reported that she'd made all the calls. "By the end I was beginning to believe my own cover story," she said. "I was thinking to myself, This is fun, but it'll be even more fun when we make the movie. Except there's not going to be a movie."

"I think somebody already made it."

"I wonder if anybody will actually call."

I got Kenan Khoury and he wanted to know how things were coming along. I told him I had managed to open up several lines of inquiry, but that I didn't expect quick results.

"But you think we got a shot," he said.

"Definitely."

"Good," he said. "Listen, why I called, I'm going to be out of the country on business for a couple of days. I have to go to Europe. I'm flying out tomorrow from JFK and I'll be coming back Thursday or Friday. Anything comes up, just call my brother. You've got his phone number, don't you?"

I had it on a message slip right in front of me, and I called it after I got off the phone with Kenan. Peter sounded groggy when he answered and I apologized for waking him. He said, "No, that's okay, I'm glad you did. I was watching basketball and I dozed off in front of the set. I hate when that happens, I always wind up with a stiff neck. Reason I called, I was wondering if you were planning to go to a meeting tonight."

"I thought I would, yes."

"Well, how about if I pick you up and we go together? There's a Saturday night meeting in Chelsea I got in the habit of going to, nice little group, meets at eight o'clock in the Spanish church on Nineteenth Street."

"I don't think I know it."

"It's a little out of the way, but when I first got sober I was in an outpatient program in that neighborhood and this became my regular Saturday meeting. I don't get down there as much these days but having the car and all, you know I've got Francine's Toyota—"

"Yes."

"So suppose I pick you up in front of your hotel around seven-thirty? That sound good?"

I said it sounded fine, and when I left the hotel at seven-thirty he was parked out in front. I was just as glad I didn't have to walk anywhere. It had been drizzling on and off during the afternoon, and now it was coming down steadily.

On the way to the meeting we talked about sports. The baseball teams were a month into spring training, with the season opener less than a month away. I'd been having a little trouble getting interested this spring, although I would probably get caught up in it once they got going. For the time being, though, most of the news was about contract negotiations, with one player sulking because he knew he was worth more than $83 million a year. I don't know, maybe he's worth it, maybe they're all worth it, but it makes it hard for me to give a damn whether they win or lose.

"I think Darryl's finally ready to dig in and play," Peter said. "He's been hitting a ton the past few weeks."

"Now that we don't have him anymore."

"Always the way it is, huh? Years we spend waiting for him to reach his full potential, and we got to see him do it in a Dodger uniform."

We parked on Twentieth Street and walked around the block to the church. It was Pentecostal, and held services in both Spanish and English. The meeting was in the basement, with perhaps forty people in attendance. I saw a few faces I recognized from other meetings around town, and Pete said hello to quite a few people, one of whom said she hadn't seen him in a while. He said he'd been going to other meetings.

The format was one you didn't encounter that often in New York. After the speaker told his story, the meeting broke up into small groups, with seven to ten people sitting around each of five tables. There was a table for beginners, one for general discussion, one to discuss one of the Twelve Steps, and I forget what else. Pete and I both wound up at the general discussion table, where people tended to talk about what was going on in their lives at the moment and how they were managing to stay sober. I usually seem to get more out of that than discussion that centers around a topic, or on one of the philosophical underpinnings of the program.

One woman had recently started work as an alcoholism counselor, and she talked about how it was difficult for her to retain her enthusiasm for meetings after spending eight hours dealing with the same issues at her job. "It's hard to keep it separate," she said. A man talked about the fact that he had just been diagnosed as HIV-positive, and how he was dealing with that. I talked about the cyclical nature of my work, and how I grew restless when I went too long between jobs and put myself under too much pressure when a job did come along. "It was easy to balance things out when I drank," I said, "but I can't do that anymore. Meetings help."

Pete talked when it was his turn, mostly commenting on some points other people had made. He didn't say much about himself.

At ten o'clock we stood in a big circle and held hands and said the prayer. Outside, the rain had softened some. We walked to the Camry and he asked if I was hungry. I realized that I was. I hadn't had dinner, just a slice of pizza on the way home from the library.

"You like Middle Eastern food, Matt? I don't mean your hole-in-the-wall felafel stand, I mean the real thing. Because there's a place in the Village that's really good." I said it sounded fine. "Or you know what we could do, we could take a run out to the old neighborhood. Unless you spent so much time on Atlantic Avenue lately that you're sick of it."

"It's out of the way, isn't it?"

"Hey, we got a car, right? We got it, we might as well get some use out of it."

He took the Brooklyn Bridge. I was thinking that it was beautiful in the rain, and he said, "I love this bridge. I was reading the other day how all the bridges are deteriorating.

You can't just leave a bridge alone, you got to maintain it, and the city does, but not sufficiently."

"There's no money."

"How did that happen? For years the city could afford to do whatever it had to do, and now all the time there's no money. Why is that, do you happen to know?"

I shook my head. "I don't think it's just New York. It's the same story everywhere."

"Is it? Because all I see is New York, and it's like the city is crumbling. The whadayacallit, the infrastructure? Is that the word I want?"

"I guess."

"The infrastructure's falling apart. There was another water-main break last month. What it is, the system is old and everything's wearing out. Who ever heard of water mains bursting ten, twenty years ago? Do you remember that sort of thing happening?"

"No, but that doesn't mean it didn't happen. Lots of things happened that I didn't notice."

"Yeah, well, you got a point. That would go for me, too. Lots of things still happen that I don't notice."

The restaurant he chose was on Court half a block from Atlantic. At his suggestion I had the spinach pie appetizer, which he assured me would be entirely different from the *spanakopita* they served in Greek coffee shops. He was right. The main course, a casserole of cracked wheat and sauteed chopped meat and onions, was also excellent, but too much for me to finish.

"So you can take it home," he said. "You like this place? Nothing fancy, but you can't beat the food."

"I'm surprised they're open this late."

"Saturday night? They'll be serving until midnight, probably later." He leaned back in his chair. "Now the way to cap off the meal, if you were to do it right. You ever had something called arak?"

"Is that anything like ouzo?"

"Sort of like ouzo. There's a difference, but yeah, it's sort of like it. You like ouzo?"

107

"I wouldn't say I liked it. There used to be a bar on the corner of Fifty-seventh and Ninth called Antares and Spiro's, a Greek joint—"

"No kidding, with that name."

"—and sometimes I'd drop in after a long night drinking bourbon at Jimmy Armstrong's and have a glass or two of ouzo for a nightcap."

"Ouzo on top of bourbon, huh?"

"As a digestive," I said. "To settle the stomach."

"Settle it once and for all, from the sound of it." He caught the waiter's eye, signaled for more coffee. "I really wanted to drink the other day," he said.

"But you didn't."

"No."

"That's the important thing, Pete. Wanting to is normal. This isn't the first time you wanted to drink since you got sober, is it?"

"No," he said. The waiter came and filled our cups. When he'd walked away Pete said, "But it's the first time I considered it."

"Seriously considered it?"

"Yeah, I would say seriously. I would say so."

"But you didn't do it."

"No," he said. He was looking down into his coffee cup. "What I almost did, I almost copped."

"Drugs?"

He nodded. "Smack," he said. "You ever have any experience with heroin?"

"None."

"Never even tried it?"

"Never even considered the possibility. Never even knew anybody who used it, not in the days when I was drinking. Except for the kind of people I had occasion to arrest."

"Smack was strictly for lowlife types, then."

"That's how I always saw it."

He smiled gently. "You probably knew some people who used it. They just didn't let you know it."

"That's possible."

"I always liked it," he said. "I never shot it, I only snorted. I was afraid of needles, which was lucky, because otherwise I'd probably be dead of AIDS by now. You know, you don't have to shoot to develop a jones."

"So I understand."

"I got dopesick a couple of times and it scared me. I kicked it with the help of booze, and then, well, you know the rest of the story. I kicked junk on my own, but I had to go to a rehab to stop drinking. So it was alcohol that really kicked my ass, but in my heart I'm a junkie as much as I'm a drunk."

He took a sip of coffee. "And the thing is," he said, "it's a different city out there when you can see it through a junkie's eyes. I mean, you were a cop and all, and you've got street smarts, but if the two of us walk down the street together I'm going to see more dealers than you are. I'm gonna see them and they're gonna see me and we're gonna recognize each other. I go anywhere in this city and it wouldn't take me more than five minutes to find somebody happy to sell me a bag of dope."

"So? I walk past bars all day, and so do you. It's the same thing, isn't it?"

"I guess. Heroin's been looking real good lately."

"Nobody ever said it was going to be easy, Pete."

"It was easy for a while. It's harder now."

In the car he took up the theme again. "I think, why bother? Or I go to a meeting and I'm like, who *are* these people? Where are they coming from? All this shit about turning everything over to a Higher Power and then life's a piece of cake. You believe in that?"

"That life's a piece of cake? Not quite."

"More like a shit sandwich. No, do you believe in God?"

"It depends when you ask me."

"Well, today. That's when I'm asking you. Do you believe in God?" I didn't say anything at first, and he said, "Never mind, I got no right to pry. Sorry."

"No, I was just trying to come up with an answer. I guess the reason I'm having trouble is I don't think the question's important."

"It's not important whether there's a God or not?"

"Well, what difference does it make? Either way I've got the day to get through. God or no God, I'm an alcoholic who can't drink safely. What's the difference?"

"The program's all about a Higher Power."

"Yes, but it works the same whether He exists or not, and whether I believe in Him or not."

"How can you turn over your will to something you don't believe in?"

"By letting go. By not trying to control things. By taking appropriate action and letting things work out the way God wants them to."

"Whether He exists or not."

"Right."

He thought about it for a moment. "I don't know," he said. "I grew up believing in God. I went to parochial school, I learned what they teach you. I never questioned it. I got sober, they said get a Higher Power, okay, no problem. Then when those fuckers send Francey back in pieces, man, what kind of a God lets something like that happen?"

"Shit happens."

"You never knew her, man. She was a really good woman. Sweet, decent, innocent. A beautiful human being. Being around her made you want to be a better human being yourself. More than that. It made you feel like you could." He braked at a red light, looked both ways, went on through it. "Got a ticket like that once. Middle of the night, I stop, there's no one for miles in either direction, so what kind of idiot stands there waiting for the light to change? Fucking cop's lying doggo halfway down the block with his lights out, gives me a ticket."

"I think we got away with it this time."

"Looks like it. Kenan uses smack now and then. I don't know if you knew that."

"How would I know it?"

"I didn't figure you did. Maybe once a month he'll snort up a bag. Maybe less than that. It's recreational with him, he'll go to a jazz club and do up a bag in the john so that he can get into the music better. The thing is, he didn't let Francey know.

He was sure she wouldn't approve, and he didn't want to do anything that would lower him in her eyes."

"Did she know he trafficked in it?"

"That was different. That was business, that was what he did. And he wasn't going to stay in it forever. A few years and out, that's his plan."

"That's everybody's plan."

"I see what you're saying. Anyway, she was cool about it. It was something he did, it was his business, it was off to one side in a separate world. But he didn't want her to know he used sometimes." He was silent for a beat. Then he said, "He was stoned the other day. I called him on it and he denied it. I mean, fuck, man, he's gonna deceive a junkie on the subject of dope? Man's obviously high and swears he's not. I guess it's because I'm clean and sober, he don't want to put temptation in front of me, but give me credit for some basic intelligence, huh?"

"Does it bother you that he can get high and you can't?"

"Does it bother me? Of course it fucking bothers me. He's going to Europe tomorrow."

"He told me."

"Like he's got to do a deal right away, build up the cash. That's a good way to get arrested, rushing into deals. Or worse than arrested."

"Are you worried about him?"

"Jesus," he said. "I'm worried about all of us."

On the bridge back to Manhattan he said, "When I was a kid I loved bridges. I collected pictures of them. My old man got it into his head that I should be an architect."

"You still could, you know."

He laughed. "What, go back to school? No, see, I never wanted that for myself. I didn't have an inclination to build bridges. I just liked to look at 'em. I ever get the urge to pack it in, maybe I'll do a Brodie off the Brooklyn Bridge. Be something to change your mind halfway down, wouldn't it?"

"I heard a guy qualify once. He came out of a blackout on

one of the bridges, I think it was this one, on the other side of the railing and with one foot in space."

"Seriously?"

"He sounded pretty serious to me. No memory of having gone there, just whammo, there he is with one hand on the rail and one foot in the air. He climbed back and went home."

"And had a drink, probably."

"I would think so. But imagine if he came to five seconds later."

"You mean after he took another step? Be a horrible feeling, wouldn't it? Only good thing about it is it wouldn't last long. Oh, shit, I should have got in the other lane. That's all right, we'll go a few blocks out of our way. I like it down here, anyway. You get down here much, Matt?"

We were driving around the South Street Seaport, a restored area around the Fulton Street fish market. "Last summer," I said. "My girlfriend and I spent the afternoon, walked around the shops, ate at one of the restaurants."

"It's a little yuppied up, but I like it. Not in the summer, though. You know when it's nicest? On a night like this when it's cold and empty and you've got a light rain falling. That's when it's really beautiful down here." He laughed. "Now that," he said, "is a stone junkie talking, man. Show him the Garden of Eden and he'll say he wants it dark and cold and miserable. An' he wants to be the only one there."

In front of my hotel he said, "Thanks, Matt."

"For what? I was planning on going to a meeting. I should be thanking you for the ride."

"Yeah, well, thanks for the company. Before you go, one thing I've been meaning to ask you all night. This job you're doing for Kenan. You think you got much of a chance of getting anyplace with it?"

"I'm not just going through the motions."

"No, I realize you're giving it your best shot. I just wondered if you figured there was much chance it would pay off."

"There's *a* chance," I said. "I don't know how good it is. I didn't start out with a lot to work with."

"I realize that. You started with next to nothing, the way it looked to me. Of course you're looking at it from a professional standpoint, you're going to see it differently."

"A lot depends on whether some of the actions I'm taking lead anywhere, Pete. And their actions in the future are a factor, too, and they're impossible to foresee. Am I optimistic? It depends when you ask me."

"Same as your Higher Power, huh? The thing is, if you come to the conclusion that it's hopeless, don't be in a rush to tell my brother, huh? Stay on it an extra week or two. So he'll think he did everything he can."

I didn't say anything.

"What I mean—"

"I know what you mean," I said. "The thing is, it's not something I have to be told. I've always been a stubborn son of a bitch. When I start something I have a hell of a time letting go of it. I think that's the main way I solve things, to tell you the truth. I don't do it by being brilliant. I just hang on like a bulldog until something shakes loose."

"And sooner or later something does? I know they used to say nobody gets away with murder."

"Is that what they used to say? They don't say it much anymore. People get away with murder all the time." I got out of the car, then leaned in to finish the thought. "That's in one sense," I said, "but in another sense they don't. I don't honestly think anybody ever gets away with anything."

9

I was up late that night. I tried sleeping and couldn't, tried reading and couldn't, and wound up sitting in the dark at my window, looking out at the rain falling through the light of the streetlamps. I sat and thought long thoughts. "The thoughts of youth are long, long thoughts." I read that line in a poem once, but you can think long thoughts at any age, if you can't sleep and there's a light rain falling.

I was still in bed when the phone rang around ten. TJ said, "You got a pen, Glenn? You want to get one, write this down." He reeled off a pair of seven-digit numbers. "Better write down seven-one-eight, too, 'cause you got to dial that first."

"Who will I get if I do?"

"Woulda got me, was you home first time I called you. Man, you harder to get than lucky! Called you Friday afternoon, called you Friday night, called you yesterday all day and all night up until midnight. You a hard man to reach."

"I was out."

"Well, I more or less 'stablished that. Man, that was some trip you sent me on. Ol' Brooklyn, it go on for days."

"There's a lot of it," I agreed.

"More than you'd have a need for. First place I went, rode to the end of the line. Train came up above ground and I got to see some pretty houses. Looked like an old-time town in a movie, not like New York at all. Got to the first phone, called you. Nobody home. Went chasin' out to the next phone, and man, that was a trip. I went down some streets that the people looked at me like, nigger, what you doin' here? Didn't nobody say anything, but you didn't have to listen real hard to hear what they thinkin'."

"But you didn't have any trouble."

"Man, I never have trouble. What I do, I make it a point to see trouble 'fore trouble sees me. I found the second telephone, called you a second time. Didn't get you 'cause you wasn't there to be got. So I thinkin', hey, maybe I'm closer to some other subway, on account of I am miles from where I get off the last one. So I go into this candy store, say, like, 'Can you tell me where the nearest subway station is?' I say it like that, you know, you woulda thought you was hearin' an announcer on TV. Man looks at me, says, 'Subway?' Like it not just a word he don't know, it a whole concept he can't get his mind around. So I just went back the way I came, man, back to the end of the Flatbush line, 'cause at least I knew how to do that."

"I think that was probably the closest station anyway."

"I think you right, 'cause I looked at a subway map later an' I couldn't see one closer. One more reason to stay in Manhattan, man. You never far from a train."

"I'll keep it in mind."

"I sure was hopin' you be there when I called. Had it all set, I run the number by you, say, 'Call it right now.' You dial, I pick up an' say, 'Here I am.' Tellin' you about it now it don't seem all that cool, but I couldn't wait to do it."

"I gather the phones had the numbers posted."

"Oh, right! *That's* what I left out. Second one, the one way to hell an' gone out Veterans Avenue? Where everybody look at you real strange? That phone did have the number posted. The other one, Flatbush an' Farragut, it didn't."

"Then how'd you get it?"

"Well, I resourceful. Told you that, didn't I?"

"More than once."

"What I did, I call the operator. Say, 'Hey, girl, somebody screwed up, ain't no number here on the phone, so how do I know where I callin' from?' An' she say how she got no way to tell what the number is of the phone I'm at, so she can't help me."

"That seems unlikely."

"Thought so myself. Thought they got all that equipment, you ask them a number at Information an' they can say it about as fast as you can ask it, so how come they can't give you the number of your own phone? An' I thought, TJ, you fool, they took out the numbers to fuck up dope dealers, an' here you go soundin' just like one. So I dial *0* again, on account of you can call the operator all day long an' never spend no quarter, it a free call. An' you know you get somebody different every time you call. So I got some other chick, an' this time I took all the street out of my voice, I said, 'Perhaps you can help me, miss. I'm at a pay phone and I have to leave the number with my office for a call back, and someone defaced the phone with spray-painted graffiti in such a way that the number is impossible to make out. I wonder if you could possibly check the line and supply it for me.' An' I ain't even through sayin' it when she's readin' off the number for me. Matt? Oh, shit."

The recording had cut in to ask for more money.

"Quarter ran out," he said. "I got to feed in another one."

"Give me the number, I'll call you."

"Can't. I ain't in Brooklyn now, I didn't happen to con nobody out of the number for this particular phone." The phone chimed as his coin dropped. "There, we be all right now. Pretty slick, though, way I got the other number. You there? How come you ain't sayin' nothin'?"

"I'm stunned," I said. "I didn't know you could talk like that."

"What, you mean talk straight? 'Course I can. Just because I street don't mean I be ignorant. They two different languages, man, and you talkin' to a cat's bilingual."

"Well, I'm impressed."

"Yeah? I figured you'd be impressed I got to Brooklyn an' back. What you got for me to do next?"

"Nothing right now."

"Nothin'? Sheee, ought to be somethin' I can do. I did good on this, didn't I?"

"You did great."

"I mean, man didn't have to be a rocket scientist to find his way to Brooklyn an' back. But it was cool how I got the number out of that operator, wasn't it?"

"Definitely."

"I was bein' resourceful."

"Very resourceful."

"But you still ain't got nothin' for me today."

"I'm afraid not," I said. "Check with me in a day or two."

"Check with you," he said. "Man, I'd check with you any-time you say if only you was there to be checked with. You know who oughta have a beeper? Man, *you* oughta have a bee-per. I could beep you, you'd say to yourself, 'Must be TJ tryin' to get hold of me, must be important.' What's so funny?"

"Nothing."

"Then how come you laughin'? I be checkin' with you every day, my man, because I think you *need* me workin' for you. An' that is final, Lionel."

"Hey, I like that."

"Thought you would," he said. "Been savin' it up for you."

It rained all day Sunday and I spent most of the day in my room. I had the TV on and switched back and forth between tennis on ESPN and golf on one of the networks. There are days when I can get caught up in a tennis match but this wasn't one of them. I can never get caught up in golf, but the scenery is pretty and the announcers aren't as relentlessly chatty as they are in most other sports, so it's not a bad thing to have going on while I sit thinking about something else.

Jim Faber called in the middle of the afternoon to cancel our standing dinner date. A cousin of his wife's had died and they had to go put in an appearance. "We could meet someplace now for a cup of coffee," he said, "except it's such a lousy day outside."

We spent ten minutes on the phone instead. I mentioned that I was a little worried about Peter Khoury, that he might pick up a drink or a drug. "The way he talked about heroin," I said, "he had me wanting some myself."

"I noticed that about junkies," he said. "They get this wistful quality, like an old man talking about his lost youth. You know you can't keep him sober."

"I know."

"You're not sponsoring him, are you?"

"No, but neither is anybody else. And last night he was using me like a sponsor."

"Be just as well if he didn't formally ask you to be his sponsor. You've already got a professional relationship with his brother, and to an extent with him."

"I thought of that."

"But even if he did, that still doesn't make him your responsibility. You know what constitutes being a successful sponsor? Staying sober yourself."

"It seems to me I've heard that."

"From me, probably. But nobody can keep anybody else sober. I'm your sponsor. Do I keep you sober?"

"No," I said. "I stay sober in spite of you."

"In spite of me or to spite me?"

"Maybe a little of both."

"What's Peter's problem, anyway? Feeling sorry for himself because he can't drink or shoot up?"

"Snort."

"Huh?"

"He stayed away from needles. But yeah, that's most of it. And he's pissed off at God."

"Shit, who isn't?"

"Because what kind of a God would let something like that happen to a wonderful person like his sister-in-law?"

"God pulls that kind of shit all the time."

"I know."

"And maybe He had a reason. Maybe Jesus wants her for a sunbeam. Remember that song?"

"I don't think I ever heard it."

"Well, I hope to God you never hear it from me, because I'd have to be drunk to sing it. Do you figure he was fucking her?"

"Do I figure who was fucking who?"

"Whom. Do you figure Peter was fucking the sister-in-law?"

"Jesus," I said. "Why would I think that? You've got a hell of a mind, you know that?"

"It's the people I hang around with."

"It must be. No, I don't think he was. I think he's just feeling sad, and I think he wants to drink and take dope, and I hope he doesn't. That's all."

I called Elaine and told her I was free for dinner, but she'd already made arrangements for her friend Monica to come over. She said they were going to order Chinese food in, and I was welcome to come over, that way they could order more dishes. I said I would pass.

"You're afraid it'll be an evening of girl talk," she said. "And you're probably right."

Mick Ballou called while I was watching *60 Minutes* and we talked for ten or twelve of them. I told him in the same breath that I had booked a trip to Ireland and that I'd had to cancel it. He was sorry I wasn't coming over but glad I'd found something to keep me busy.

I told him a little about what I was doing, but not the sort of person I was working for. He had no sympathy for drug dealers, and occasionally supplemented his income by invading their homes and taking their cash.

He asked about the weather and I said it had been raining all day. He said it was always raining there, that he was finding it hard to recall what the sun looked like. Oh, and had I heard? They'd come up with evidence that Our Lord was Irish.

"Is that so?"

"It is," he said. "Consider the facts. He lived with his parents until He was twenty-nine years old. He went out drinking with the lads the last night of His life. He thought His mother was a virgin, and herself, the good woman, she thought He was God."

The week started slowly. I hammered away at the Khoury case, if you want to call it that. I managed to get the name of one of the officers who'd caught the Leila Alvarez homicide. She was the Brooklyn College student who'd been dumped in Green-Wood Cemetery, and the case belonged not to the Seventy-second Precinct but to Brooklyn Homicide. A Detective John Kelly had headed the investigation, but I had trouble reaching him and was reluctant to leave a name and number.

I saw Elaine Monday and she was disappointed that her phone hadn't been ringing off the hook with calls from rape victims. I told her she might not get any response, that it was like that sometimes, that you had to throw a lot of baited hooks in the water and sometimes you went a long time without a bite. And it was early, I said. It was unlikely the people she spoke to would have made any calls until the weekend was over.

"It was over today," she reminded me. I said if they did make calls it might take them a while to reach people, and it might take the victims a couple of days to make up their minds to call.

"Or not to call," she said.

She was more discouraged when Tuesday passed without a call. When I spoke to her Wednesday evening she was excited. The good news was that three women had called her. The bad news was that none of the calls looked to have anything to do with the men who had killed Francine Khoury.

One was a woman who had been ambushed by a solitary assailant in the hallway of her apartment house. He had raped her and stolen her purse. Another had accepted a ride home from school with someone she took to be another student; he had shown her a knife and ordered her into the backseat, but she had been able to escape.

"He was a skinny kid and he was alone," Elaine said, "so I thought it was stretching it to figure him as a possibility. And the third call was date rape. Or pickup rape, I don't know what you'd call it. According to her, she and her girlfriend picked up these two guys in a bar in Sunnyside. They went for a ride in the guys' car and her girlfriend got carsick so they stopped the car so she could get out and vomit. And then they drove off and left her there. Can you believe that?"

"Well, it's not very considerate," I said, "but I don't think I'd call it rape."

"Funny. Anyway, they drove around for a while and then they went back to her house and they wanted to have sex with her, and she said nothing doing, what kind of a girl do you think I am, blah blah blah, and finally she agreed that she'd fuck one of them, the one she'd been more or less partnered with, and the other one would wait in the living room. Except he didn't, he walked in while they were getting it on and watched, which did little to cool his ardor, as you might have figured."

"And?"

"And afterward he said please please please, and she said no no no, and finally she gave him a blow-job because that was the only way to get rid of him."

"She told you this?"

"In more ladylike terms, but yeah, that's what happened. Then she brushed her teeth and called the cops."

"And reported it as rape?"

"Well, I'd be willing to call it that. It escalated from please please please to Get me off or I'll kick your teeth down your throat, so I'd say that qualifies as rape."

"Oh, sure, if it was that forceful."

"But it doesn't sound like our guys."

"No, not at all."

"I got their numbers just in case you want to follow up on them, and I told them we'd call if the producer decided to pursue it, that the whole project was kind of iffy just now. Was that right?"

"Definitely."

"So I didn't come up with anything helpful, but it's encouraging that I got three calls, don't you think? And there'll probably be more tomorrow."

There was one call Thursday, and it had seemed promising

121

early on. A woman in her early thirties taking graduate courses at St. John's University, abducted at knifepoint by three men as she was unlocking her parked car in one of the campus parking lots. They piled into the car with her and drove to Cunningham Park, where they had oral and vaginal sex with her, menaced her throughout with one or more knives, threatened various forms of mutilation, and did in fact cut her on one arm, although the wound may have been inflicted accidentally. When they were done with her they left her there and escaped in her car, which had still not been recovered almost seven months after the incident.

"But it can't be them," Elaine said, "because the guys were black. The ones on Atlantic Avenue were white, weren't they?"

"Yeah, that's one thing everybody agrees on."

"Well, these men were black. I kept, you know, returning to that point, and she must have thought I was a racist or something, or that I suspected her of being a racist, or I don't know what. Because why should I keep pounding away at the color of the rapists? But of course it was all-important from my point of view, because it means that she's out of the picture for our purposes. Unless sometime between now and last August they figured out how to change color."

"If they worked that out," I said, "it'd be worth a lot more than four hundred thousand to them."

"Nice. Anyway, I felt like an idiot, but I took her name and number and said we'd call her if we got a green light on the project. You want to hear something funny? She said whether it leads to anything or not she's glad she called, because it did her good to talk about it. She talked about it a lot right after it happened and she had some counseling but she hasn't talked about it lately, and it helped."

"That must have made you feel good."

"It did, because up to then I'd been feeling guilty for putting her through it under false pretenses. She said I was very easy to talk to."

"Well, that comes as no surprise to this reporter."

"She thought I was a counselor. I think she was leading up to asking if she could come in once a week for therapy. I told her I was an assistant to a producer, and that you needed pretty much the same skills."

That same day, I finally managed to get hold of Detective John Kelly of Brooklyn Homicide. He remembered the Leila Alvarez case and said it was a terrible thing. She'd been a pretty girl and, according to everyone who knew her, a nice kid and a serious student.

I said I was doing a piece on bodies abandoned in unusual locations, and I asked if there had been anything unusual about the condition of the body when it was found. He said there'd been some mutilation and I asked if he could give me a little more detail and he said he thought he'd better not. Partly because they were keeping certain aspects of the case confidential, and partly to spare the feelings of the girl's family.

"I'm sure you can understand," he said.

I tried a couple of other approaches and kept running up against the same wall. I thanked him and I was going to hang up, but something made me ask him if he'd ever worked out of the Seven-eight. He asked why I wanted to know.

"Because I knew a John Kelly who did," I said, "except I don't see how you could be the same man, because he would have to be well past retirement age by now."

"That was my dad," he said. "You say your name's Scudder? What were you, a reporter?"

"No, I was on the job myself. I was at the Seven-eight for a while, and then I was at the Six in Manhattan when I made detective."

"Oh, you made detective? And now you're a writer? My dad talked about writing a book, but that's all it ever was, talk. He retired, oh, it must be eight years now, he's down in Florida growing grapefruit in his backyard. Lot of cops I know are working on a book, or say they are. Or say they're thinking about it, but you're actually doing it, huh?"

It was time to shift gears. "No," I said.

"I beg your pardon?"

"That was crap," I admitted. "I'm working private, it's what I've been doing since I left the department."

"So what do you want to know about Alvarez?"

"I want to know the nature of the mutilation."

"Why?"

"I want to know if it involved amputation."

There was a pause, long enough for me to regret the whole line of questioning. Then he said, "You know what I want to know, mister? I want to know just where the fuck you're coming from."

"There was a case in Queens a little over a year ago," I said. "Three men took a woman off Jamaica Avenue in Woodhaven and left her on a golf course in Forest Park. Along with a lot of other brutality, they cut off two of her fingers and stuck them in, uh, bodily openings."

"You got a reason to think it was the same people did both women?"

"No, but I have reason to believe that whoever did Gotteskind didn't stop at one."

"That was her name in Queens? Gotteskind?"

"Marie Gotteskind, yes. I've been trying to match her killers to other cases, and Alvarez looked possible, but all I know about it is what wound up in the papers."

"Alvarez had a finger up her ass."

"Same with Gotteskind. She also had one in front."

"In her—"

"Yeah."

"You're like me, you don't like to use the words when it's a dead person. I don't know, you hang around the MEs, they're the most irreverent bastards on earth. I guess it's to insulate themselves from feeling it."

"Probably."

"But it seems disrespectful to me. These poor people, what else can they hope for but a little respect after they're dead? They didn't get any from the person who took their life."

"No."

"She had a breast missing."

"I beg your pardon?"

"Alvarez. They cut off a breast. From the bleeding, they say she was alive when it happened."

"Dear God."

"I want to get these fucks, you know? Working Homicide you want to get everybody because there's no such thing as a little murder, but some of them get to you and this was one that got to me. We really worked it, we checked her movements, we talked to everybody who knew her, but you know how it is. When there's no connection between the victim and the killer and not much in the way of physical evidence, you can only take it so far. There was very little on-scene evidence because they did her somewhere else, then dumped her in the cemetery."

"That was in the paper."

"Same thing with Gotteskind?"

"Yes."

"If I'd known about Gotteskind—you say over a year ago?" I gave him the date. "So it's been sitting in a file in Queens and how am I supposed to know about it? Two corpses with fingers, uh, removed and reinserted, and here I am with my thumb up my ass, and I didn't mean to say that. Jesus."

"I hope it helps."

"You hope it helps. What else have you got?"

"Nothing."

"If you're holding out—"

"All I know about Gotteskind is what's in her file. And all I know about Alvarez is what you just told me."

"And what's your connection? Your own personal connection?"

"I just told you I—"

"No, no, no. Why the interest?"

"That's confidential."

"The hell it is. You got no right to hold out."

"I'm not."

"Well, what do you call it, then?"

I took a breath. I said, "I think I've said as much as I have to. I have no special knowledge of either homicide, Gotteskind or Alvarez. I read the one's file and you told me about the other and that's the extent of my knowledge."

"What made you read the file in the first place?"

"A newspaper story a year ago, and I called you on the basis of another newspaper story. That's it."

"You got some client you're covering for."

"If I've got a client, he's certainly not the perpetrator, and I can't see how he's anything but my own business. Wouldn't you rather compare the two cases yourself and see if that gives you a wedge into them?"

"Yeah, of course I'm gonna do that, but I wish I knew your angle."

"It's not important."

"I could tell you to come in. Or have you picked up, if you'd rather play it that way."

"You could," I agreed. "But you wouldn't get a damn thing more than I already told you. You could cost me some time, but you'd be wasting time of your own."

"You got your fucking nerve, I'll say that for you."

"Hey, come on," I said. "You've got something now that you didn't before I called. If you want to cop a resentment I suppose you can hang on to one, but what's the point?"

"What am I supposed to say, thank you?" It wouldn't hurt, I thought, but kept the thought to myself. "The hell with it," he said. "But I think you'd better let me have your address and phone, just in case I need to get in touch with you."

The mistake had been in letting him have my name. I could find out if he was enough of a detective to look me up in the Manhattan book, but why? I gave him my address and phone and told him I was sorry I wasn't able to answer all his questions, but I had certain responsibilities to a client of mine. "That would have pissed me off when I was on the job," I said, "so I can understand why it would have the same effect on you. But I have to do what I have to do."

"Yeah, that's a line I've heard before. Well, maybe it's the same people in both cases, and maybe something'll break if we put 'em side by side. That'd be nice."

That was as close to "thank you" as we were going to get, and I was happy to settle for it. I said it would be very nice, and wished him luck. I asked to be remembered to his father.

10

That night I went to a meeting and Elaine attended her class, and afterward we both took cabs and met at Mother Goose and listened to the music. Danny Boy turned up around eleven-thirty and joined us. He had a girl with him, very tall, very thin, very black and very strange. He introduced her as Kali. She acknowledged the introductions with a nod but didn't say a word or appear to hear anything anyone else said for a good half hour, at which point she leaned forward, stared hard at Elaine, and said, "Your aura is teal blue and very pure, very beautiful."

"Thank you," Elaine said.

"You have a very old soul," Kali said, and that was the last thing she said, and the last sign she gave that she was aware of our presence.

Danny Boy didn't have anything much to report, and we mostly just enjoyed the music, chatting about nothing important between sets. It was fairly late when we left. In the cab to her place I said, "You have a very old soul and a teal-blue aura and a cute little ass."

"She's very perceptive," Elaine said. "Most people don't notice my teal-blue aura until the second or third meeting."

"Not to mention your old soul."

"Actually, it would be a good idea not to mention my old soul. You can say what you want about my cute little ass. Where does he find them?"

"I don't know."

"If they were all stock bimbettes from Central Casting it would be one thing, but his girls don't run to type. This one, Kali—what do you figure she was on?"

"No idea."

"Because she certainly seemed to be traveling in another realm. Do people still use psychedelics? She was probably on magic mushrooms, or some hallucinogenic fungus that grows only on decaying leather. I'll tell you one thing, she could make good money as a dominatrix."

"Not if her leather's decaying. And not unless she could keep her mind on her work."

"You know what I mean. She's got the looks for it, and the presence. Can't you see yourself groveling at her feet and loving every minute of it?"

"No."

"Well, you," she said. "The Marquis de Suave himself. Remember the time I tied you up?"

The driver was working hard at hiding his amusement. "Would you please shut up," I said.

"Remember? You fell asleep."

"That shows how safe I felt in your presence," I said. "Will you *please* shut up?"

"I will wrap myself in my teal-blue aura," she said, "and I will be very quiet."

Before I left the following morning she told me she had a good feeling about the calls from rape victims. "Today's the day," she said.

But she turned out to be wrong, teal-blue aura or not. There were no calls at all. When I talked to her that night she was glum about it. "I guess that's it," she said. "Three Wednesday, one yesterday, and now nothing. I thought I was going to be a hero, come up with something significant."

"Ninety-eight percent of an investigation is insignificant," I said. "You do everything you can think of because you don't know what will be useful. You must have been sensational on the phone because you got a very big response, but it's pointless to feel like a failure because you didn't turn up a living victim of the three stooges. You were looking for a needle in a haystack, and it's probably a haystack that didn't have a needle in it in the first place."

"What do you mean?"

"I mean they probably didn't leave any witnesses. They probably killed every woman they victimized, so you were probably trying to find a woman who doesn't exist."

"Well, if she doesn't exist," she said, "then I say to hell with her."

TJ was calling in every day, sometimes more than once a day. I had given him fifty dollars to check out the two Brooklyn phones, and he couldn't have come out very far ahead on the deal, because what he hadn't spent on subways and buses he was sinking into telephone calls. He got a better return on his time shilling for monte dealers or assisting a street peddler or doing any of the other street chores that combined to give him an income. But he still kept pestering me for work.

Saturday I wrote out a check for my rent and paid the other monthly bills that had come in—the phone bill, my credit card. Looking at the telephone bill made me think again of the calls made to Kenan Khoury's phone. I had made another attempt a few days before to find a phone-company employee who could figure out a way to supply that data, and had been told once again that it was unobtainable.

So that was on my mind when TJ called around ten-thirty. "Give me some more phones to check out," he pleaded. "The Bronx, Staten Island, anywhere."

"I'll tell you what you can do for me," I said. "I'll give you a number and you tell me who called it."

"Say what?"

"Oh, nothing."

"No, you said somethin', man. Tell me what it was."

"Maybe you could do it at that," I said. "Remember how you sweet-talked the operator out of the phone number on Farragut Road?"

"You mean with my Brooks Brothers voice?"

"That's it. Maybe you could use the same voice to find some phone company vice president who can figure out how to come up with a listing of calls to a certain number in Bay Ridge." He asked a few more questions and I explained what I was looking for and why I was unable to find it.

"Hang on," he said. "You sayin' they won't give it to you?"

"They don't have it to give. They've got all the calls logged but there's no way to sort them."

"Shit," he said. "First operator I call up, she tell me ain't no way she can tell me my number. Can't believe everything they tell you, man."

"No, I—"

"You somethin'," he said. "Call you up every damn day, say what you got for TJ, an' all the time you ain't got nothin'. How come you never tell me 'bout this before? You been silly, Willie!"

"What do you mean?"

"I mean if you don't tell me what you want, how I gonna give it to you? Told you that the first time I met you, walkin' around the Deuce not sayin' nothin' to nobody. Told you right then, said, tell me what you jonesin' on, I help you find it."

"I remember."

"So why you be dickin' around with the telephone company when you could be comin' to TJ?"

"You mean you know how to get the numbers from the phone company?"

"No, man. But I know how to get the Kongs."

"The Kongs," he said. "Jimmy and David."

"They're brothers?"

"Ain't no family resemblance far as I can see. Jimmy Hong

is Chinese and David King is Jewish. Least his father is Jewish. I think his mother might be Rican."

"Why are they the Kongs?"

"Jimmy Hong and David King? Hong Kong and King Kong?"

"Oh."

"Plus their favorite game used to be Donkey Kong."

"What's that, a video game?"

He nodded. "Pretty good one."

We were at a snack bar in the bus terminal, where he'd insisted I meet him. I was drinking a cup of bad coffee and he was eating a hot dog and drinking a Pepsi. He said, "Remember that dude Socks, we was watchin' him at the arcade? He 'bout the best there is, but he ain't nothin' next to the Kongs. You know how a player is always tryin' to keep up with the machine? Kongs didn't have to keep up with it. They was always out ahead of it."

"You brought me down here to meet a couple of pinball wizards?"

"Big difference between pinball and video games, man."

"Well, I suppose there is, but—"

"But it ain't nothin' compared to the difference between video games an' where the Kongs is at now. I told you what happens to guys hang around the arcade, how you can get so good an' then there ain't no better for you to get? So you lose interest."

"So you said."

"What some dudes get interested in is computers. What I heard, the Kongs was into computers all along, fact they used a computer to stay ahead of the video games, know what the machine was gonna do before it could do it. You play chess?"

"I know the moves."

"You an' me'll play a game sometime, see if you any good. You know those stone tables they got down by Washington Square? People bring their time clocks, study chess books while they waitin' to play? I play there sometimes."

"You must be good."

He shook his head. "Some of those dudes," he said, "you play against them, it's like you tryin' to run a footrace standin' in water up to your waist. You can't get nowhere, 'cause they always five, six moves ahead of you in their mind."

"Sometimes it feels like that in my line of work."

"Yeah? Well, that's how video games got for the Kongs, they was five or six moves out in front. So they into computers, they what you call hackers. You know what that is?"

"I've heard the term."

"Man, you want something from the phone company, you don't call no operator. Don't mess with no vice president, either. You call the Kongs. They get in the phones and crawl around in there, like the phone company's a monster and they swimmin' in its bloodstream. You know that picture, whatchacallit, *Fantastic Voyage*? They take a voyage in the phones."

"I don't know," I said. "If an executive at the company can't figure out how to extract that data—"

"Man, ain't you listenin'?" He sighed, then sucked hard on his straw and drained the last of his Pepsi. "You want to know what's happenin' on the streets, what's goin' down on the Deuce or in the Barrio or in Harlem, who do you go and ask? The fuckin' mayor?"

"Oh," I said.

"You see what I sayin'? They hangin' out on the streets of the phone company. You know Ma Bell? The Kongs be lookin' up her skirt."

"Where are we going to find them? The arcade?"

"Told you. They lost interest some time ago. They come by once in a while just to see what's shakin', but they don't hang out there no more. We ain't gonna find them. They gonna find us. I told 'em we'd be here."

"How did you reach them?"

"How you think? Beeped 'em. Kongs ain't never too far from a phone. You know, that hot dog was good. You wouldn't think you'd get anything decent, place like this, but they give you a good hot dog."

"Does that mean you want another?"

"Might as well. Take 'em some time to get here, and then they want to look you over before they come an' meet you. Want to satisfy themselves that you alone and that they can split in a hot second if they scared of you."

"Why would they be scared of me?"

"'Cause you might be some kind of cop workin' for the phone company. Man, the Kongs is outlaws! Ma Bell ever gets her hands on them, she gone whip their ass."

"The thing is," Jimmy Hong said, "we have to be careful. People in suits are convinced that hackers are the biggest threat to corporate America since the Yellow Peril. The media is always running stories about what hackers could do to the system if we wanted to."

"Destroying data," David King said. "Altering records. Wiping out circuitry."

"It makes a good story, but they lose sight of the fact that we never pull that shit. They think we're going to put dynamite on the railroad tracks when all we're doing is hitching a free ride."

"Oh, every once in a while some nitwit introduces a virus—"

"But most of that isn't hackers, it's some jerk with a grudge against a company or somebody introducing a glitch into the system by using bootleg software."

"The point is," David said, "Jimmy's too old to take chances."

"Turned eighteen last month," Jimmy Hong said.

"So if they catch us he'll be tried as an adult. That's if they go by chronological age, but if they take emotional maturity into account—"

"Then David would go scot-free," Jimmy said, "because he hasn't reached the age of reason."

"Which came between the Stone Age and the Iron Age."

Once they decided they trusted you, you couldn't get them to shut up. Jimmy Hong was around six-two, long and lean, with straight black hair and a long, saturnine face. He wore aviator sunglasses with amber lenses, and after we'd been sitting together for ten or fifteen minutes he changed them for a pair of horn-rimmed glasses with round untinted lenses, altering his appearance from hip to studious.

David King was no more than five-seven, with a round face and red hair and a lot of freckles. Both of them wore Mets warm-up jackets and chinos and Reeboks, but the similarity of dress wasn't enough to make them look like twins.

If you closed your eyes, though, you might have been fooled. Their voices were close and their speech patterns were very similar and they finished each other's sentences a lot.

They liked the idea of playing a role in a murder case—I hadn't gone into a great deal of detail—and they were amused at the response I'd received from various functionaries at the telephone company. "That's beautiful," Jimmy Hong said. "Saying it can't be done. Meaning most likely that he couldn't figure out how to do it."

"It's their system," David King said, "and you'd think they would at least understand it."

"But they don't."

"And they *hate* us, because we understand it better than they do."

"And they think we'd hurt the system—"

"—when actually we happen to *love* the system. Because if you're going to do any serious hacking, NYNEX is where it's at."

"It's a beautiful system."

"Unbelievably complex."

"Wheels within wheels."

"Labyrinths within labyrinths."

"The ultimate video game, and the ultimate Dungeons and Dragons, all rolled into one."

"Cosmic."

I said, "But it can be done?"

"What can? Oh, the numbers? Phone calls placed on a specific day to a specific number?"

"Right."

"Be a problem," David King said.

"An interesting problem, he means."

"Right, very interesting. A problem with a solution for sure, a solvable problem."

"But a tricky one."

"Because of the amount of data."

"Tons of data," Jimmy Hong said. "Millions and millions of pieces of data."

"By data he means phone calls."

"Billions of phone calls. Untold billions of phone calls."

"Which you have to process."

"But before you even start to do that—"

"You have to get in."

"Which used to be easy."

"Used to be a cinch."

"They would leave the door open."

"Now they close it."

"Nail it shut, you could say."

I said, "If you need to buy special equipment—"

"Oh, no. Not really."

"We already got everything we need."

"Doesn't take much. Halfway decent laptop, a modem, an acoustic coupler—"

"Whole package won't run more than twelve hundred dollars."

"Unless you went crazy and bought a high-priced laptop, but you don't have to."

"The one we use cost seven-fifty, and it's got everything you need."

"So you could do it?"

They exchanged glances, then looked at me. Jimmy Hong said, "Sure, we could do it."

"Be interesting, actually."

"Have to pull an all-nighter."

"Can't be tonight, either."

"No, tonight's out. How soon would it have to be?"

"Well—"

"Tomorrow's Sunday. Sunday night all right with you, Matt?"

"It's fine with me."

"You, Mr. King?"

"Works for me, Mr. Hong."

"TJ? You figuring to be there?"

"Tomorrow night?" It was the first he'd said anything since introducing me to the Kongs. "Lessee, tomorrow night. What did I have planned for tomorrow night? Was that the press reception at Gracie Mansion or was I supposed to have dinner with Henry Kissinger at Windows on the World?" He mimed paging through a date book, then looked up bright-eyed. "What do you know? I be free."

Jimmy Hong said, "There'll be some expenses, Matt. We'll need a hotel room."

"I have a room."

"You mean where you live?" They grinned at each other, amused at my naïveté. "No, what you want is someplace anonymous. See, we're going to be deep inside NYNEX—"

"Crawling around inside the belly of the beast, you could say—"

"—and we might leave footprints."

"Or fingerprints, if you prefer."

"Even voiceprints, speaking metaphorically, of course."

"So you don't want to do this from a phone that could be traced to anybody. What you want to do is rent a hotel room under a false name and pay cash for it."

"A reasonably decent one."

"It doesn't have to be ritzy."

"Just so it has direct-dial phones."

"Which most of them do nowadays. And push-button, it should be push-button."

"Not the old rotary dial."

"Well, that's easy enough," I said. "Is that what you usually do? Rent a hotel room?"

They exchanged glances again.

"Because if there's a hotel you prefer—"

David said, "The thing is, Matt, when we want to hack we don't generally have a hundred or a hundred and fifty bucks to spend on a decent hotel room."

"Or even seventy-five dollars for a crummy hotel room."

136

"Or fifty for a disgusting hotel room. So what we'll do—"

"We find a bank of pay phones where there's not much traffic, like in the Grand Central waiting room over by the commuter lines—"

"—because there's not many commuter trains leaving in the middle of the night—"

"—or in an office building, anything like that."

"Or one time we sort of let ourselves into an office—"

"Which was stupid, man, and I never want to do that again."

"We just did it to use the phone."

"And can you feature telling that to the cops? 'It's not burglary, Officer, we just dropped in to use the phones.'"

"Well, it was exciting, but we wouldn't do it again. The thing is, see, we'll probably have to spend hours and hours on this—"

"And you wouldn't want anybody walking in, or having to switch phones when we're all hooked up."

"No problem," I said. "We'll get a decent hotel room. What else?"

"Coke."

"Or Pepsi."

"Coke's better."

"Or Jolt. 'All the sugar and twice the caffeine.'"

"Maybe some junk food. Maybe some Doritos."

"Get the ranch flavor, not the barbecue."

"Potato chips, Cheez Doodles—"

"Oh, man, not Cheez Doodles!"

"I *like* Cheez Doodles."

"Man, that has got to be the lamest junk food there is. I challenge you to name anything edible that is stupider than Cheez Doodles."

"Pringles."

"No fair! Pringles aren't food. Matt, you got to judge this one. What do you say? Are Pringles food?"

"Well—"

"They're not! Hong, you are so sick. Pringles are tiny Frisbees that warped, that's all they are. They're not *food*."

* * *

137

When Kenan Khoury didn't answer I tried his brother. Peter's voice was thick with sleep and I apologized for waking him. "I keep doing that," I said. "Sorry."

"My own fault, nodding out in the middle of the afternoon. My sleep schedule got all turned around lately. What's up?"

"Not much. I was trying to reach Kenan."

"Still in Europe. He called me last night."

"Oh."

"Coming back Monday. Why, you got some good news to report?"

"Not yet. I've got some cabs I have to take."

"Huh?"

"Expenses," I said. "I'll have to shell out close to two thousand dollars tomorrow. I wanted to clear it with him."

"Hey, no problem. I'm sure he'll say yes. He said he'd cover your expenses, didn't he?"

"Yes."

"So lay it out. He'll pay you back."

"That's the problem," I said. "My money's in the bank and it's Saturday."

"Can't you use an ATM?"

"Not for a safe-deposit box. I can't get it all out of my checking account because I just paid the bills the other day."

"So write a check and cover it Monday."

"This isn't the kind of expense where the people will take a check."

"Oh, right." There was a pause. "I don't know what to tell you, Matt. I could come up with a couple of hundred, but I haven't got anything like two grand."

"Doesn't Kenan have it in the safe?"

"Probably a lot more than that, but I can't get in there. You don't give a junkie the combination to your safe, not even if he's your brother. Not unless you're crazy."

I didn't say anything.

"I'm not bitter," he said. "I'm just stating a fact. No reason on earth for me to have the combination to the safe. I got to tell you, I'm glad I don't have it. I wouldn't trust myself with it."

"You're clean and sober now, Pete. What's it been, a year and a half?"

"I'm still a drunk and a junkie, man. You know the difference between the two? A drunk will steal your wallet."

"And a junkie?"

"Oh, a junkie'll steal your wallet, too. And then he'll help you look for it."

I almost asked Pete if he wanted to go to that Chelsea meeting again, but something made me let the moment pass. Maybe I remembered that I wasn't his sponsor, and that it was not a position for which I wanted to volunteer.

I called Elaine and asked her how she was fixed for cash. "Come on over," she said. "I've got a house full of money."

She had fifteen hundred in fifties and hundreds and said she could get more from the ATM, but no more than $500 a day. I took twelve hundred so I wouldn't leave her broke. That, added to what I had in my wallet and what I could get from my own ATM, would be plenty.

I told her what I needed the money for and she thought the whole thing was fascinating. "But is it safe?" she wanted to know. "It's obviously illegal, but how illegal is it?"

"It's worse than jaywalking. Computer trespass is a felony, and so is computer tampering, and I have a feeling the Kongs will be committing both of them tomorrow night. I'll be aiding and abetting them, and I've already committed criminal solicitation. I'll tell you, you can't turn around these days without trampling all over the penal law."

"But you think it's worth it?"

"I think so."

"Because they're just kids. You wouldn't want to get them in trouble."

"I wouldn't want to get myself in trouble, either. And they run this particular risk all the time. At least they're getting paid for it."

"How much are you going to give them?"

"Five hundred apiece."

She whistled. "That's not bad for a night's work."

"No, it's not, and if they'd come up with a figure it would probably have been a lot less. They went blank when I asked them how much they wanted, so I suggested five hundred each. That seemed fine to them. They're middle-class kids, I don't think they're hurting for money. I have a feeling I could have talked them into doing the job for free."

"By appealing to their better nature."

"And their desire to be in on something exciting. But I didn't want to do that. Why shouldn't they have the dough? I'd have been willing to pay more than that to some phone-company employee if I could have figured out who to bribe. But I couldn't find anybody who'd admit what I wanted was technologically possible. Why not give it to the Kongs? It's not my money, and Kenan Khoury says you can always afford to be generous."

"And if he decides to bail out?"

"That doesn't seem likely."

"Unless, of course, he gets arrested going through customs wearing a vest full of powder."

"I guess something like that could happen," I said, "but that would just mean I'd be out of pocket to the tune of a little under two grand, and I started out by taking ten thousand dollars from him a couple of weeks ago. That's almost how long it's been. It'll be two weeks Monday."

"What's the matter?"

"Well, I haven't accomplished very much in that amount of time. It seems as though—well, the hell with it, I'm doing what I can. Anyway, the point is that I can afford to take the chance that I won't get reimbursed."

"I suppose so." She frowned. "How do you get two thousand dollars? Say one-fifty for a hotel room, and a thousand for the two Kongs. How much Coca-Cola can two kids drink?"

"I drink Coke, too. And don't forget TJ."

"He drinks a lot of Coke?"

"All he wants. And he gets five hundred dollars."

"For introducing you to the Kongs. I didn't even think of that."

"For introducing me to the Kongs, and for thinking of introducing me to the Kongs. They're the perfect way to spirit information out of the phone company, and I never would have thought of looking for someone like that."

"Well, you hear about computer hackers," she said, "but how would you find one? They don't list them in the Yellow Pages. Matt, how old is TJ?"

"I don't know."

"You never asked him?"

"I never got a straight answer. I'd say fifteen or sixteen, and I don't think I could be off by more than a year either way."

"And he lives on the street? Where does he sleep?"

"He says he's got a place. He's never said where or with whom. One thing you learn on the street, you don't want to be too quick to tell your business to people."

"Or even your name. Does he know how much he's getting?"

I shook my head. "We haven't discussed it."

"He won't be expecting that much, will he?"

"No, but why shouldn't he have it?"

"I'm not disagreeing with you. I just wonder what he's going to do with five hundred dollars."

"Whatever he wants. At a quarter a shot, he could call me up two thousand times."

"I guess," she said. "God, when I think of the different people we know. Danny Boy, Kali. Mick. TJ, the Kongs. Matt? Let's not ever leave New York, okay?"

11

On Sundays Jim Faber and I usually have our weekly dinner at a Chinese restaurant, although we occasionally go somewhere else. I met him at six-thirty at our regular place, and a few minutes after seven he asked me if I had a train to catch. "Because that's the third time in the past fifteen minutes you looked at your watch."

"I'm sorry," I said. "I didn't realize it."

"You anxious about something?"

"Well, there's something I have to do later," I said, "but there's plenty of time. I don't have to be anywhere until eight-thirty."

"I'll be going to a meeting myself at eight-thirty, but I don't suppose that's what you've got scheduled."

"No. I went to one this afternoon because I knew I wouldn't be able to fit one in tonight."

"This appointment of yours," he said. "You're not nervous because you're gonna be around booze, are you?"

"God, no. There won't be anything stronger than Coca-Cola. Unless somebody picks up some Jolt."

"Is that a new drug I don't know about?"

"It's a cola drink. Like Coke, but twice as much caffeine."

"I don't know if you can handle it."

"I don't know that I'm going to try. You want to know where I'm going after I leave here? I'm going to check into a hotel under a phony name and then I'm going to have three teenage boys up to my room."

"Don't tell me any more."

"I won't, because I wouldn't want you to have foreknowledge of a felony."

"You're planning on committing a felony with these kids?"

"They're the ones who'll be committing a felony. I'm just going to watch."

"Have some more of the sea bass," he said. "It's especially good tonight."

By nine o'clock all four of us were assembled in a $160-a-night corner room in the Frontenac, a 1,200-room hotel built a few years ago with Japanese money and since sold to a Dutch conglomerate. The hotel was on the corner of Seventh Avenue and Fifty-third Street, and from our room on the twenty-eighth floor you could get a glimpse of the Hudson. Or you could have, if we hadn't drawn the shades.

There was a spread of snack food laid out on the top of the dresser, including Cheez Doodles but not including Pringles. The little refrigerator held three varieties of cola, a six-pack of each. The telephone had been relocated from the bedside table to the desk, with something called an acoustic coupler attached to its earpiece and something else called a modem plugged into its rear. It shared the desk with the Kongs' laptop computer.

I had signed the register as John J. Gunderman and gave an address on Hillcrest Avenue, in Skokie, Illinois. I paid cash, along with the fifty-dollar deposit required of cash customers who wanted access to the telephone and mini-bar. I didn't care about the mini-bar, but we damn well needed the phone. That was why we were in the room.

Jimmy Hong was seated at the desk, his fingers flashing on

the computer's keyboard, then punching numbers on the phone. David King had drawn up another chair but was standing, looking over Jimmy's shoulder at the computer screen. Earlier he had tried to explain to me how the modem allowed the computer to hook into other computers through the telephone lines, but it was a little like trying to explain the fundamentals of non-Euclidean geometry to a field mouse. Even when I understood the words he used, I still didn't know what the hell he was talking about.

The Kongs had worn suits and ties, but only to get through the hotel lobby; their ties and jackets were on the bed now, and they had their sleeves rolled up. TJ was in his usual costume, but they hadn't hassled him at the desk. He'd come lugging two sacks of groceries, disguised as a delivery boy.

Jimmy said, "We're in."

"All right!"

"Well, we're into NYNEX but that's like being inside the hotel lobby when you need to be in a room on the fortieth floor. Okay, let's try something."

His fingers danced and combinations of numbers and letters popped up on the screen. After a while he said, "Bastards keep changing the password. You know the amount of effort they spend just trying to keep people like us out?"

"As if they could."

"If they put the same energy into improving the system—"

"Stupid."

More letters, more numbers. "Damn," Jimmy said, and reached for his can of Coke. "You know what?"

"Time for our people-to-people program," David said.

"That's what I was thinking. You feel like refining your human-contact skills?"

David nodded and took the phone. "Some people call this 'social engineering,'" he told me. "It's hardest with NYNEX because they warn their people about us. Good thing for us that most of the people who work there are morons." He dialed a telephone number, and after a moment he said, "Hi, this is Ralph Wilkes, I'm troubleshooting your line. You've been having trouble getting into COSMOS, right?"

"They always do," Jimmy Hong murmured. "So it's a safe question."

"Yeah, right," David was saying. There was a lot of jargon I couldn't follow, and then he said, "Now how do you log in? What's your access code? No, right, don't tell me, you're not supposed to tell me, it's security." He rolled his eyes. "Yeah, I know, they give us grief about the same thing. Look, don't tell me the code, just punch it in on your keyboard." Numbers and letters appeared on our screen and Jimmy's fingers were quick to enter them on our keyboard. "Fine," David said. "Now can you do the same thing with your password for COSMOS? Don't tell me what it is, just enter it. Uh-huh."

"Beautiful," Jimmy said softly as the number came up on our screen. He punched it in.

"That ought to do it," David told whoever he was talking to. "I don't think you should have any problems from here on in." He broke the connection and let out a huge sigh. "I don't think we should have any problems, either. 'Don't tell me the number, just enter it. Don't tell me, darling, just tell my computer.'"

"Hot damn," Jimmy said.

"We're in?"

"We're in."

"Yay!"

"Matt, what's your phone number?"

"Don't call me," I said. "I'm not home."

"I don't want to call you. I want to check your line. What's the number? Never mind, don't tell me, see if I care. 'Scudder, Matthew.' West Fifty-seventh Street, right? That look familiar?"

I looked at the screen. "That's my phone number," I said.

"Uh-huh. You happy with it? You want me to change it, give you something easier to remember?"

"If you call the phone company to get your number changed," David said, "it takes them a week or so to run it through channels. But we can do it on the spot."

"I think I'll keep the number I've got," I said.

"Suit yourself. Uh-huh. You've got pretty basic service, haven't you? No Call Forwarding, no Call Waiting. You're at a hotel, you've got the switchboard backing you up, so maybe you don't need Call Waiting, but you ought to have Call Forwarding anyhow. Suppose you stay over at somebody's house? You could get your calls routed there automatically."

"I don't know if I'd use it enough to make it worthwhile."

"Doesn't cost anything."

"I thought there was a monthly charge for it."

He grinned and his fingers were busy on the keypad. "No charge for you," he said, "because you have influential friends. As of this moment you've got Call Forwarding, compliments of the Kongs. We're in COSMOS now, that's the particular system we invaded, so that's where I'm entering changes in your account. The system that figures your billing won't know about the change, so it won't cost you anything."

"Whatever you say."

"I see you use AT&T for your long-distance calls. You didn't select Sprint or MCI."

"No, I didn't figure I would save that much."

"Well, I'm giving you Sprint," he said. "It's going to save you a fortune."

"Really?"

"Uh-huh, because NYNEX is going to route your long-distance calls to Sprint, but Sprint's not going to know about it."

"So you won't get billed," David said.

"I don't know," I said.

"Trust me."

"Oh, I don't doubt what you said. I just don't know how I feel about it. It's theft of services."

Jimmy looked at me. "We're talking about the phone company," he said.

"I realize that."

"You think they're gonna miss it?"

"No, but—"

"Matt, when you make a call from a pay phone and the call goes through but the quarter comes back anyway, what do you do? Keep it or put it back in the slot?"

"Or send it to them in stamps," David suggested.

"I see your point," I said.

146

"Because we all know what happens when the phone eats your quarter and doesn't put the call through. Face it, none of us are way out in front of the game when we're dealing with Mother Bell."

"I suppose."

"So you've got free long distance and free Call Forwarding. There's a code you have to enter to forward your calls, but just ring them up and tell them you lost the slip and they'll explain it to you. Nothing to it. TJ, what's your phone number?"

"Ain't got one."

"Well, your favorite pay phone."

"Favorite? I don't know. Don't know the number of any of 'em, anyhow."

"Well, pick one out and give me the location."

"There be a bank of three of 'em in Port Authority that I use some."

"No good. Too many phones there, it's impossible to know if we're talking about the same one. How about one on a street corner?"

He shrugged. "Say Eighth and Forty-third."

"Uptown, downtown?"

"Uptown, east side of the street."

"Okay, let's just . . . there, got it. You want to write down the number?"

"Just change it," David suggested.

"Good idea. Make it an easy one to remember. How about TJ-5-4321?"

"Like it's my own phone number? Hey, I like that!"

"Let's just see if it's available. Nope, somebody's got it. So why don't we take the other direction? TJ-5-6789. No problem, so let's make it all yours. So ordered."

"You can just do that?" I wondered. "Aren't different three-number prefixes specifically linked to different areas?"

"Used to be. And there's still exchanges, but that works for the particular line number, and that has nothing to do with what you dial. See, the number you dial, like the one I just gave TJ, is the same as the PIN code you use to get money out of your ATM at the bank. It's just a recognition code, really."

"Well, it's an access code," David said. "But it accesses the line, and that's what routes the call."

"Let's fix the phone for you, TJ. It's a pay phone, right?"

"Right."

"Wrong. It was a pay phone. Now it's a free phone."

"Just like that?"

"Just like that. Some idiot'll probably report it in a week or two, but until then you can save yourself a few quarters. Remember when we played Robin Hood?"

"Oh, that was fun," David said. "We were down at the World Trade Center one night making calls from a pay phone, and of course the first thing we did was convert it, make it free—"

"—or otherwise we'd be dropping quarters in all night long, which is pretty ridiculous—"

"—and Hong here says pay phones should be free for everybody, same as the subways ought to be free, they ought to eliminate the turnstiles—"

"—or make them turn with or without a token, which you could do if they were computerized, but they're mechanical—"

"—which is pretty primitive, when you stop and think about it—"

"—but with pay phones we're in a position to do something, so for I think it was two hours—"

"—more like an hour and a half—"

"—we're hopping through COSMOS, or maybe it was MIZAR—"

"—no, it was COSMOS—"

"—and we're changing one pay phone after another, liberating it, setting it free—"

"—and Hong's really getting into it, like 'Power to the People' and everything—"

"—and I don't know how many phones we switched by the time we were done." He looked up. "You know something? Sometimes I can see why NYNEX wants to nail our hides to the wall. If you look at it in a certain way, we're sort of a major pain in the ass to them."

"So?"

"So you've got to see their point of view, that's all."

"No you don't," David King said. "The last thing you have to do is see their point of view. That's about as smart as playing Pac-Man and feeling sorry for the blue meanies."

Jimmy Hong argued the point, and while they kicked it back and forth I cracked a fresh Coke. When I got back where the action was Jimmy said, "All right, we're in the Brooklyn circuits. Give me that number again."

I looked it up and read it off and he fed it to the computer. More letters and numbers, meaningless to me, appeared on the screen. His fingers danced on the keys, and my client's name and address showed up.

"That your friend?" Jimmy wanted to know. I said it was. "He's not talking on the phone," he said.

"You can tell that?"

"Sure. We could listen in if he was. You can just drop in and listen to anybody."

"Except it's so boring."

"Yeah, we used to do it sometimes. You think maybe you'll hear something hot, or people talking about a crime or spy stuff. But all you really get to hear is this remarkably tedious crap. 'Pick up a quart of milk on your way home, darling.' Really boring."

"And so many people are so inartic late. They just stutter and stammer along, and you want to tell 'em to spit it out or forget about it."

"Of course there's always phone sex."

"Don't remind me."

"That's King's favorite. Three dollars a minute billed to your home phone, but if you've got a pay phone that you taught not to be a pay phone, then it's free."

"It feels creepy, though. What we did once, though, we just dropped in and listened on some of those lines."

"And then cut in and made comments, which really freaked this one guy. He was paying to talk one-on-one to this woman with this incredible voice—"

"—who probably had a face like Godzilla, but nobody could tell—"

149

"—and here's King dropping in on him in the middle of a sentence and trashing his fantasy."

"The girl was freaking, too."

"Girl, she was probably a grandmother."

"She's going, like, 'Who said that? Where are you? How did you get on this line?'"

Throughout this exchange Jimmy Hong had been participating in another dialogue as well, this one with the computer. Now he held up a hand for silence and hit keys with the other. "Okay," he said. "Gimme the date. It was in March, right?"

"The twenty-eighth."

"Month three, date two-eight. And we want calls to 04-053-904."

"No, his number is—"

"That's his line number, Matt. Remember the difference? Uh, what I figured. Data not available."

"What does that mean?"

"Means we were smart to bring in a lot of food. Could somebody bring me some of those Doritos? We're going to be here awhile, that's all. You interested in calls he made from his phone, while we're in this part of the system? Seems a shame to waste it."

"Might as well."

"See what we get. Look at that, it doesn't want to tell me a thing. Okay, let's try this. Uh-huh. Okay, now—"

Then the system began spitting out a record of calls, reeling them off chronologically starting a few minutes after midnight. There were two calls before one in the morning, then nothing until 8:47, when the system logged a thirty-second call to a 212 number. There was one other call in the morning and several in the early afternoon, and none at all between 2:51 and 5:18, when he had been on the phone for a minute and a half with his brother. I recognized Peter Khoury's number.

Then nothing else that night.

"Anything you want to copy, Matt?"

"No."

"Okay," he said. "Now for the hard part."

* * *

150

I couldn't tell you what it was that they did. A little after eleven they switched and David took over the controls, while Jimmy paced the floor and yawned and stretched and went to the bathroom and came back and polished off a package of Hostess cupcakes. At twelve-thirty they switched again and David went into the bathroom and took a shower. By this time TJ was sound asleep on the bed, lying fully clothed on the bedspread, shoes and all, and clutching one of the pillows as if the world were trying to get it away from him.

At one-thirty Jimmy said, "God damn it, I can't believe there's no way into NPSN."

"Give me the phone," David said. He dialed a number, snarled, broke the connection, dialed again, and on the third try got through to somebody. "Yo," he said. "Who'm I talkin' to? Great. Listen, Rita, this is Taylor Fielding at NICNAC Central an' I got a Code Five emergency coming down. I need your NPSN access code and your password before the whole thing backs up clear to Cleveland. That's Code Five, did you hear me?" He listened intently, then reached out a hand for the computer keyboard. "Rita," he said, "you're beautiful. You saved my life, no joke. Can you believe I had two people in a row didn't know a Code Five takes precedence? Yeah, well, that's 'cause you pay attention. Listen, if you get any static on this, I'll take full responsibility. Yeah, you too. 'Bye."

"You take full responsibility," Jimmy said. "I like that."

"Well, it seemed only right."

"What the hell is a Code Five, will you tell me that?"

"I don't know. What's NICNAC Central? Who's Taylor Feldman?"

"You said Fielding."

"Well, it was Feldman before he changed it. I don't know, man. I just made it all up but it sure impressed Rita."

"You sounded so desperate."

"Well, why shouldn't I be? Half-past one in the morning and we're not even into NPSN yet."

"We are now."

"And how sweet it is. I'll tell you, Hong, you can't beat that Code Five. It really cuts through all the bureaucratic bullshit, you know what I mean. 'I got a Code Five emergency coming down.' Man, that just about blew her doors off."

"'Rita, you're beautiful.'"

"Man, I was falling in love, I have to say it. And by the time we were through we'd sort of established a relationship, you know?"

"You gonna call her again?"

"I bet I can get a password off her anytime, unless something tips her that she just gave away the store. Otherwise next time I call her we're gonna be old friends."

"Call her sometime," I said, "and don't try to get a password or an access code or anything else."

"You mean just ring her up to chat?"

"That's the idea. Maybe give her some information, but don't try to get anything out of her."

"Far out," David said.

"And then later on—"

"Got it," Jimmy said. "Matt, I don't know if you've got either the digital dexterity or the hand-eye coordination, and you don't really know a thing about the technology, but I have to tell you something. You've got the heart and soul of a hacker."

According to the Kongs, the whole process really got interesting after they got into NPSN, whatever that meant. "This is the part that's fascinating from a technical standpoint," David explained, "because here's where we try retrieving information the NYNEX people claimed wasn't available. They'll say that just to brush you off, but some of them were telling the truth, or what they thought was the truth, because the fact of the matter is they wouldn't know how to go about finding it. So it's almost as though we have to invent our own program and feed it into their system so it'll spit out the data we want."

"But," Jimmy said, "if you're not into the technical side of it, there's really nothing there to keep you on the edge of your chair."

TJ, awake now, was standing behind David's chair and watching the computer screen as if hypnotized. Jimmy went over to the refrigerator for a can of Jolt. I dropped into the one easy chair, and David was right, there was nothing to keep me on the edge of it. I sank back into the cushions, and the next thing I knew TJ was shaking me gently by the shoulder, saying my name.

I opened my eyes. "I must have been sleeping."

"Yeah, you sleepin', all right. You was snorin' some earlier."

"What time is it?"

"Almost four. The calls is comin' up now."

"Can they just get a printout?"

TJ turned and relayed the request, and the Kongs started giggling. David got control of himself and reminded me that we didn't have a printer with us. My sponsor was a printer, I almost said. Instead I said, "No, of course not. I'm sorry, I'm still half-asleep."

"Stay where you are. We'll copy it all down for you."

"I'll get you some Jolt," TJ offered. I told him not to bother but he brought me a can of it anyway. I took a sip of it but it really wasn't what I wanted, nor was I entirely certain what I did want. I got to my feet and tried to stretch some of the stiffness out of my back and shoulders, then walked over to the desk where David King was working the computer while Jimmy Hong copied down the information on the screen.

"There they are," I said.

They were coming right up on the screen, starting with the first call at 3:38 to tell Kenan Khoury his wife was missing. Then three calls at roughly twenty-minute intervals, the last one logged at 4:54. Kenan had called his brother at 5:18, and the next call he'd received came in at 6:04, which must have been just before Peter got to the Colonial Road house.

Then there was a sixth call at 8:01. That would have been the one ordering them to Farragut Road, where they received the call that sent them chasing out to Veterans Avenue. And then they'd come home, having been assured that Francine would be delivered there, and then they waited in an empty house until 10:04, when the last call came, the one that sent them around the corner to the Ford Tempo with the parcels in its trunk.

"Wow," David was saying. "This has been, like, the most

amazing education. Because we had to keep at it, you know? There was data you needed, so we couldn't quit. When you're just hacking you can only take so much boredom before you go and do something else, but we had to stay with it until we crashed through the boredom and got to what was on the other side of it."

"Which was more boredom," Jimmy said.

"But you learn a lot, you really do. If we had to do this same operation again—"

"God forbid."

"Yeah, but if we did, we could do it in half the time. Less, because the whole speed-search option gets double-timed when you cut back into the—"

What he said after that was even less comprehensible to me, and I'd stopped listening anyway because Jimmy Hong was handing me a sheet of all calls into the Khoury house on the twenty-eighth of March. "I should have told you," I said. "The early ones don't matter, just the seven starting at three-thirty-eight." I studied the list. He'd copied everything: time of the call, the line number of the caller, the phone number you'd dial in order to reach that phone, and the duration of the call. That, too, was more than I needed, but there was no reason to tell him that.

"Seven calls, each from a different phone," I said. "No, I'm wrong. They used one phone twice, for calls two and seven."

"Is it what you wanted?"

I nodded. "How much it gives me is something else again. It could be a lot or a little. I won't know until I get hold of a reverse directory and find out who those phones belong to."

They stared at me. I still didn't get it until Jimmy Hong took off his glasses and blinked at me. "A reverse directory? You've got the two of us here, with everything buried in the deep inner recesses of NPSN, and you think you need a reverse directory?"

"Because we're talking child's play here," David King said. He sat down at the keyboard again. "Okay," he said. "Give me the first number."

* * *

They were all pay phones.

I'd been afraid of that. They had been professionally cautious throughout, and there was no reason to suppose that they wouldn't have taken care to use phones that couldn't be linked to them.

But a different pay phone each time? That was harder to figure, but one of the Kongs came up with a theory that made sense. They were guarding against the possibility that Kenan Khoury had alerted someone who was in a position to tap in on the line and identify the phone at the other end. By keeping the calls short they could be sure of being away from the scene before anyone who traced the call could get there; by never returning to the same phone, they were covered even if Khoury had the call traced and the telephone staked out.

"Because tracing a call is instantaneous now," Jimmy told me. "You don't really trace it, not if you're hooked into it with a setup like this. You just look on the screen and read it off."

Why the lapse in security on the last call? By then they'd obviously known there was no need for it. Khoury had done everything the way he was supposed to, had made no attempt to interfere with the ransom pickup, and was no longer worth such elaborate precautions. That was the time they could have felt safe enough to use a phone in their own house or apartment, and if only they'd done so I would have had the bastards. If it had started raining, if there'd been some compelling reason to stay inside. If nobody had wanted to leave the other two with the ransom money.

It was too bad. It would have been nice to get lucky for a change.

On the other hand, the night's work and the seventeen hundred and change it was costing me were by no means wasted. I had learned something, and not just that the three men I was after were very careful planners for a trio of psychopathic sex killers.

The addresses were all in Brooklyn. And they were all in a far more compact area than the whole Khoury case covered. The kidnap and ransom delivery had begun in Bay Ridge, moved to Atlantic Avenue in Cobble Hill, ranged to Flatbush and Farragut and then way over to Veterans Avenue, and then swung back to the drop-off of the remains in Bay Ridge again. That covered a fair chunk of the borough, while their previous activities were spread all over Brooklyn and Queens. Their home base could be anywhere.

But the pay phones weren't that far apart. I would have to sit down with the list and a map to plot their positions precisely, but I could tell already that they were all in the same general area, on the west side of Brooklyn, north of Khoury's house in Bay Ridge and south of Green-Wood Cemetery.

Where they'd dumped Leila Alvarez.

One phone was on Sixtieth Street, another on New Utrecht at Forty-first, so it's not as though they were within walking distance of each other. They had left the house and driven around to make those calls. But it stood to reason that home base was somewhere in that neighborhood, and probably not too far from the one phone they'd used a second time. It was all over, they were all done, all that remained was to rub salt in Kenan Khoury's wounds, so why drive ten blocks out of the way if you didn't have to? Why not use the handiest pay phone of the lot?

Which happened to be on Fifth Avenue between Forty-ninth and Fiftieth streets.

I didn't go into all of that with the boys, and indeed a lot of my own ruminations had to wait until later on. I gave the Kongs five hundred dollars each and told them how much I appreciated what they'd done. They insisted it was fun, even the boring part. Jimmy said he had a headache and a bad case of hacker's wrist, but that it was worth it.

"You two go down first," I said. "Put your ties and jackets on and just nonchalant your way out the front door. I'll want to make sure there's nothing traceable in the room, and I guess I'll have to stop at the desk and settle up what I owe for the phone. I left a fifty-dollar deposit but we were hooked into it for over seven hours, and I don't have any idea what the charges are going to be."

"Oh, my," David said. "He just doesn't get it."

156

"It's amazing," Jimmy said.

"Huh? What don't I get?"

"You don't get to pay any phone charges," Jimmy said. "First thing I did once we were hooked up was bypass the desk. We could have called Shanghai and there wouldn't be any record of it at the desk." He grinned. "You might as well let them keep the deposit, though. Because King had about thirty dollars' worth of macadamia nuts from the mini-bar."

"Which means thirty macadamia nuts at a dollar each," David said.

"But if I were you," Jimmy said, "I'd just go home."

After they left I paid TJ. He fanned the sheaf of bills I handed him, looked at me, looked at them again, at me again, and said, "This here for me?"

"Would have been no game without you. You brought the bat and the ball."

"I figured a hundred," he said. "I didn't do much, just sat around, but you was payin' out a lot of bread and I figured you wasn't about to leave me out. How much I got here?"

"Five," I said.

"I knew this'd pay off," he said. "Me an' you. I like this detectin' business. I be resourceful, I good at it, and I like it."

"It doesn't usually pay this well."

"Don't make no difference. Man, what other line of work I gone find lets me use all the shit I know?"

"So you want to be a detective when you grow up, TJ?"

"Ain't gonna wait that long," he said. "Gonna be one now. And that's where it's at, Matt."

I told him his first assignment was to get out of the hotel without drawing the wrong kind of attention from the hotel staff. "It would be easier if you were dressed like the Kongs," I said, "but we work with what we've got. I think you and I should walk out together."

"White guy your age and a black teenager? You know what they be thinking."

"Uh-huh, and they can shake their heads over it all they want. But if you walk out by yourself they'll think you've been burgling the rooms, and they might not let you walk."

"Yeah, you right," he said, "but you not lookin' at all the possibilities. Room's all paid for, right? Checkout time's like noon. An' I seen where you live, man, and I don't mean to be dissin' you, but your room ain't this nice."

"No, it's not. It doesn't cost me a hundred and sixty dollars a night, either."

"Well, this room ain't gonna cost me a dime, Simon, an' I gonna take me a hot shower an' dry myself on three towels an' get in that bed an' sleep six or seven hours. 'Cause this room ain't just better than where you live, it's like ten times better than where *I* live."

"Oh."

"So I gone hang the 'Do Not Disturb' sign on the knob and kick back an' be undisturbed, like. Then noon comes an' I walk outta here an' nobody look at me twice, nice young man like me, musta just come an' delivered somebody's lunch. Hey, Matt? You think I can call downstairs an' they'll gimme a wake-up call at half-past eleven?"

"I think you can count on it," I said.

12

I stopped at an all-night coffee shop on Broadway. Someone had left an early edition of the *Times* in the booth, and I read it along with my eggs and coffee, but nothing much registered. I was too groggy, and what little mental acuity I had insisted on centering itself on the locations of the six pay phones in Sunset Park. I kept yanking the list out of my pocket and studying it, as if the order and precise locations of the phones held a secret message if one only possessed the key. There ought to be someone I could call, claiming a Code Five emergency. "Give me your access code," I would demand. "Tell me the password."

The sky was bright with dawn by the time I got back to my hotel. I showered and went to bed, and after an hour or so I gave up and turned on the television set. I watched the morning news program on one of the networks. The secretary of state had just come back from a tour of the Middle East, and they had him on, and followed him with a Palestinian spokesman commenting on the possibilities for a lasting peace in the region.

That brought my client to mind, if he'd ever been far from my thoughts, and when the next interview was with a recent

Academy Award winner I hit the Mute button and called Kenan Khoury.

He didn't answer, but I kept trying, calling every half hour or so until I got him around ten-thirty. "Just walked in the door," he said. "Scariest part of the trip was just now in the cab coming back from JFK. Driver was this maniac from Ghana with a diamond in his tooth and tribal scars on both cheeks, drove like dying in a traffic accident guaranteed you priority entry to heaven, green card included."

"I think I had him once myself."

"You? I didn't think you ever rode in cabs. I thought you were partial to the subway."

"I took cabs all last night," I said. "Really ran up the meter."

"Oh?"

"In a manner of speaking. I turned up a couple of computer outlaws who found a way to dig some data out of the phone company's records that the company said didn't exist." I gave him an abbreviated version of what we'd done and what I'd learned from it. "I couldn't reach you for authorization and I didn't want to wait on this, so I laid it out."

He asked what it came to and I told him. "No problem," he said. "What did you do, front the expense money yourself? You shoulda asked Pete for it."

"I didn't mind fronting it. I did ask your brother, as a matter of fact, because I couldn't get to my own cash over the weekend. But he didn't have it either."

"No?"

"But he said to go ahead, that you wouldn't want me to wait."

"Well, he was right about that. When'd you talk to him? I called him the minute I walked in the door but there was no answer."

"Saturday," I said. "Saturday afternoon."

"I tried him before I got on the plane, wanted him to meet my flight, save me from the Ghanaian Flash. Couldn't get him. What did you do, stall those guys on the cash?"

"I got a friend to lend me enough to cover."

"Well, you want to pick up your dough? I'm beat, I've been

on more planes in the past week than Whatsisname, just got back from the Middle East himself. The secretary of state."

"He was just on television."

"We were in and out of some of the same airports, but I can't say we crossed paths. I wonder what he does with his Frequent Flyer miles. I ought to be eligible for a free trip to the moon by now. You want to come over? I'm wiped out and jet-lagged but I'm not gonna be able to sleep now anyway."

"I think I could," I said. "In fact I think I'd better. I'm not used to pulling all-nighters, as my partners in crime called it. They took it in stride, but they're a few years younger than I am."

"Age makes a difference. I never used to believe there was such a thing as jet lag, and now I could be the poster boy if they got up a national campaign against it. I think I'll try to get some sleep myself, maybe take a pill to help me get under. Sunset Park, huh? I'm trying to think who I know there."

"I don't think it's going to be anyone you know."

"You don't, huh?"

"They've done this before," I said. "But strictly as amateurs. I know a few things about them I didn't know a week ago."

"We getting close, Matt?"

"I don't know how close we're getting," I said. "But we're getting somewhere."

I called downstairs and told Jacob I was taking my phone off the hook. "I don't want to be disturbed," I said. "Tell anybody who calls that they can reach me after five."

I set the clock for that hour and got in bed. I closed my eyes and tried to visualize the map of Brooklyn, but before I could even begin to focus in on Sunset Park I was gone.

Traffic noises roused me slightly at one point, and I told myself I could open my eyes and check the clock, but instead I drifted off into a complicated dream involving clocks and computers and telephones, the source of which was not terribly difficult to guess. We were in a hotel room and someone was banging on the door. In the dream I went to the door and opened it. Nobody was there, but the noise continued, and then

I was out of the dream and awake and somebody was pounding on my door.

It was Jacob, saying that Miss Mardell was on the phone and said it was urgent. "I know you wanted to sleep till five," he said, "and I told her that, and she said wake you no matter what you said. She sounded like she meant it."

I hung up the phone and he went back downstairs and put the call through. I was anxious waiting for it to ring. The last time she'd called up and said it was urgent, a man turned up determined to kill us both. I snatched the phone when it rang, and she said, "Matt, I hated waking you, but it really couldn't wait."

"What's the matter?"

"It turns out there was a needle in the haystack after all. I just got off the phone with a woman named Pam. She's on her way over here."

"So?"

"She's the one we're looking for. She met those men, she got in the truck with them."

"And lived to tell the tale?"

"Barely. One of the counselors I pitched the movie story to called her right away, and she spent the past week working up the courage to call. I heard enough over the phone to know not to let this one get away. I told her I could guarantee her a thousand dollars if she'd come over and run through her story in person. Was that all right?"

"Of course."

"But I don't have the cash. I gave you all my cash Saturday."

I looked at my watch. I had time to stop at the bank if I hurried. "I'll get cash," I told her. "I'll be right over."

13

"Come on in," Elaine said. "She's already here. Pam, this is Mr. Scudder, Matthew Scudder. Matt, I'd like you to meet Pam."

She had been sitting on the couch and she arose at our approach, a slender woman, about five-three, with short dark hair and intensely blue eyes. She was wearing a dark gray skirt and a pale blue angora sweater. Lipstick, eye shadow. High-heeled shoes. I sensed she'd chosen her outfit for our meeting, and that she wasn't sure she'd made the right choices.

Elaine, looking cool and competent in slacks and a silk blouse, said, "Sit down, Matt. Take the chair." She joined Pam on the couch and said, "I just finished telling Pam that I got her here under false pretenses. She's not going to meet Debra Winger."

"I asked who the star was gonna be," Pam said, "and she said Debra Winger, and I'm like, wow, Debra Winger is gonna do a movie of the week? I didn't think she would do TV." She shrugged. "But I guess there's not gonna be a movie, so what difference does it make who the star is?"

"But the thousand dollars is real," Elaine said.

"Yeah, well, that's good," Pam said, "because I can use the money. But I didn't come for the money."

"I know that, dear."

"Not just for the money."

I had the money, a thousand for her and the twelve hundred I owed Elaine and some walking-around money for myself, three thousand dollars total from my safe-deposit box.

"She said you're a detective," Pam said.

"That's right."

"And you're going after those guys. I talked a lot with the cops, I must of talked with three, four different cops—"

"When was that?"

"Right after it happened."

"And that was—?"

"Oh, I didn't realize you didn't know. It was in July, this past July."

"And you reported it to the police?"

"Jesus," she said. "What choice did I have? I had to go to the hospital, didn't I? The doctors are like, wow, who did this to you, and what am I gonna say, I slipped? I cut myself? So they called the police, naturally. I mean, even if I didn't say anything, they would of called the police."

I propped open my notebook. I said, "Pam, I don't think I got your last name."

"I didn't give it. Well, no reason not to, is there? It's Cassidy."

"And how old are you?"

"Twenty-four."

"You were twenty-three when the incident took place?"

"No, twenty-four. My birthday's the end of May."

"And what sort of work do you do, Pam?"

"Receptionist. I'm out of work at the moment, that's why I said I could use the money. I guess anybody could always use a thousand dollars, but especially now, being out of work."

"Where do you live?"

"Twenty-seventh between Third and Lex."

"Is that where you were living at the time of the incident?"

"Incident," she said, as if trying out the word. "Oh, yeah,

I been there for almost three years now. Ever since I came to New York."

"Where did you come from?"

"Canton, Ohio. If you ever heard of it I can guess what for. The Pro Football Hall of Fame."

"I almost went for a visit once," I said. "I was in Massillon on business."

"Massillon! Oh, sure, I used to go there all the time. I knew a ton of people in Massillon."

"Well, I probably never met any of them," I said. "What's the address on Twenty-seventh Street, Pam?"

"One fifty-one."

"That's a nice block," Elaine said.

"Yeah, I like it okay. The only thing, it's silly, but the neighborhood doesn't have a name. It's west of Kips Bay, it's below Murray Hill, it's above Gramercy, and of course it's way east of Chelsea. Some people started calling it Curry Hill, you know, because of all the Indian restaurants."

"You're single, Pam?" A nod. "You live alone?"

"Except for my dog. He's just a little dog but a lot of people won't break into a place if there's a dog, no matter what size he is. They're just scared of dogs, period."

"Would you like to tell me what happened, Pam?"

"The incident, you mean."

"Right."

"Yeah," she said. "I guess. That's what we're here for, right?"

It was on a summery evening in the middle of the week. She was two blocks from her house, standing on the corner of Park and Twenty-sixth waiting for the light to change, and this truck pulled up and this guy called her over wanting directions to some place, she couldn't catch the name.

He got out of the truck, explaining that maybe he had the name of the place wrong, that it was on the invoice, and she went around with him to the rear of the truck. He opened the back of the truck, and there was another man inside, and they both had knives. They made her get in the back of the truck with the second man, and the driver got back in the truck and drove off.

At this point I interrupted her, wanting to know why she had been so obliging about getting in the truck. Had there been people around? Had anyone witnessed the abduction?

"I'm a little hazy on the details," she said.

"That's all right."

"It happened so quick."

Elaine said, "Pam, could I ask you a question?"

"Sure."

"You're in the game, aren't you, dear?"

I thought, Jesus, how did I miss that?

"I don't know what you mean," Pam said.

"You were working that night, weren't you?"

"How did you know?"

Elaine took the girl's hand. "It's all right," she said. "Nobody's going to hurt you, nobody's here to judge you. It's all right."

"But how did you—"

"Well, it's a popular stroll, isn't it, that stretch of Park Avenue South? But I guess I knew earlier. Honey, I was never on the pavement, but I've been in the game myself for almost twenty years."

"No!"

"Honestly. Right in this apartment, which I bought when it went co-op. I've learned to call them clients instead of tricks, and when I'm around squares I sometimes say I'm an art historian, and I've been real smart about saving my pennies over the years, but I'm in the life the same as you, dear. So you can tell it to us the way it really happened."

"God," she said. "Actually, you know something? It's a relief. Because I didn't want to come here and tell you a story, you know? But I didn't think I had any choice."

"Because you thought we'd disapprove of you?"

"I guess. And because of what I told the cops."

"The cops didn't know you were hooking?" I asked.

"No."

"They never even brought it up? With the pickup taking place right on the stroll?"

"They were Queens cops," she said.

"Why would Queens cops catch the case?"

"Because of where I wound up. I was in Elmhurst General Hospital, that's in Queens, so that's where the cops were from. What do they know about Park Avenue South?"

"Why did you wind up at Elmhurst General? Never mind, you'll get to that. Why don't you start over from the beginning?"

"Sure," she said.

It was a summery evening in the middle of the week. She was two blocks from her house, standing on the corner of Park and Twenty-sixth waiting for someone to hit on her, and this truck pulled up and a guy motioned for her to come over. She walked around and got in on the passenger side and he drove a block or two and turned on one of the side streets and parked at a hydrant.

She thought it would be a quick blow-job while he sat behind the wheel, twenty or twenty-five for maybe five minutes. The guys in cars almost always wanted head and they wanted to be done right there in their cars. Sometimes they wanted it while the car was moving, which seemed crazy to her, but go figure. The johns who came around on foot would generally spring for a hotel room, and the Elton at Twenty-sixth and Park was reasonable and convenient for that. There was always her apartment, but she almost never took anybody back there unless she was desperate, because she didn't believe it was safe. Besides, who wanted to trick in the bed you slept in?

She never saw the guy in the back until the truck was parked. Never even knew he was there until his arm came around her neck and his hand clapped over her mouth.

He said, "Surprise, Pammy!"

God, she was scared. She just froze while the driver laughed and reached into her blouse and started feeling her tits. She had big tits and she'd learned to dress to show them on the street, in a halter top or a revealing blouse, because guys who went for tits really went for them, so you might as well show the merchandise. He went right for the nipple and tweaked it and it hurt and she knew these two were going to be rough.

"We'll all get in back," the driver said. "More privacy, room to stretch out. We might as well be comfortable, right, Pammy?"

She hated the way they said her name. She had introduced herself as Pam, not Pammy, and they said it in a mocking way, a very nasty way.

When the guy in back let go of her mouth she said, "Look, nothing rough, huh? Whatever you want, and I'll give you a real good time, but no rough stuff, okay?"

"You on drugs, Pammy?"

She said no, because she wasn't. She didn't care for drugs much. She would smoke a joint if somebody handed it to her, and coke was nice but she never yet actually bought any. Sometimes guys would lay out lines for her, and they got insulted if you weren't interested, and anyway she liked it well enough. Maybe they thought it got her hot, made her more into it, like sometimes you would get a guy who would put a dab of coke on his dick, like that would be such a treat for you when you went down on him that he'd get extra good head on account of it.

"You a junkie, Pammy? Where do you fix, up your nose? Between your toes? You know any big drug dealers? You got a boyfriend deals junk, maybe?"

Really stupid questions. Like there was no purpose to them, like they more or less got off on asking the questions. The one did, anyway. The driver. He was the one all hipped on the subject of drugs. The other one was more into calling her names. "You dirty cunt, you fucking piece-of-shit bitch," like that. Sickening if you let it get to you but actually a lot of guys were like that, especially when they got excited. One guy, she must have done him four, five times, always in his car, and he was always very polite before and after, very considerate, never rough, but it was always the same story when she was copping his joint and he was getting close to getting off. "Oh, you cunt, you cunt, I wish you were dead. Oh, I wish you would die, I wish you were dead, you fucking cunt." Horrible, just horrible, but except for that he was a perfect gentleman and he paid fifty dollars each time and never took long to come, so what was the big deal if he had a nasty mouth? Sticks and stones, right?

They went in the back of the truck and it was all fixed up with a mattress, which made it comfortable, actually, or it would have been comfortable if she could have relaxed, but you couldn't, not with these guys, because they were too weird. How could you relax?

They made her take everything off, every stitch, which was a pain in the ass but she knew not to argue. And then, well, they fucked her, taking turns, first the driver, then the other one. That part was pretty much routine, except of course that there were the two of them, and when the second man was doing her the driver pinched her nipples. That hurt, but she knew better than to say anything, and anyway she knew he was aware that it hurt. That was why he was doing it.

They both did her and they both got off, which was encouraging, because it was when a guy couldn't get it up or couldn't finish that you were sometimes in danger, because they got mad at you, like it was your fault. After the second one groaned and rolled off of her she said, "Hey, that was great. You guys are all right. Let me get dressed, huh?"

That was when they showed her the knife.

A switchblade, a big one, really skanky-looking. The second man, the one with the dirty mouth, had the knife, and he said, "You ain't going nowhere, you fucking cunt."

And Ray said, "We're all going somewhere, we're going for a little ride, Pammy."

That was his name, Ray. The other one called him Ray, that's how she knew it. The other one's name, if she heard it then it never registered, because she didn't have a clue. But the driver was Ray.

Except they switched, so he wasn't the driver now. The other one climbed over the seat and got behind the wheel and Ray stayed in back with her, and he kept the knife, and of course he didn't let her put on her clothes.

This was where it started getting really hard to remember. She was in the back of the truck and it was dark and she couldn't see out and they drove and drove and she didn't have any idea where they were or where they were going. Ray asked her about drugs again, he was hipped on the subject, he told her junkies were just looking to die, that it was a death trip, and that they should all get what they were looking for.

He made her go down on him. That was better, at least he would shut up, and at least she was, like, *doing* something.

Then they were parked again, God knows where, and then there was a lot of sex. They took turns with her and they just did stuff for a long time, and she was like zoning in and out, like she wasn't really a hundred percent there for part of the time. She was pretty sure that neither of them came. They both got off the first time, on Twenty-fourth Street or wherever it was, but now it was like they didn't want to come because that would break up the party. They did it to her in, well, all the usual places, and they put other things inside her besides parts of themselves. She wasn't really too clear on what they used. Some of what they did hurt and some didn't and it was awful, it was all terrible, and then she remembered something, she hadn't remembered this before, but there was a point where she got really peaceful.

Because, see, she knew she was going to die. And it's not like she wanted to die, because she didn't, she definitely didn't, but the thought somehow came to her that that's what was going to happen, and that was all that was going to happen, and she thought, well, like I can handle that. Like I can live with it, almost, which was ridiculous because that was the point, she couldn't live, not if she died.

"Okay, I can handle that." Just like that, really.

And then, just as she had really come to terms with it, just as she was enjoying this feeling of peacefulness, Ray said, "You know what, Pammy? You're going to get a chance. We're going to let you live."

The two of them argued then, because the other man wanted to kill her, but Ray said they could let her go, that she was a whore, that nobody cared about whores.

But she wasn't just any whore, he said. She had the best

set of tits on the street. He said, "Do you like 'em, Pammy? Are you proud of them?"

She didn't know what she was supposed to say.

"Which one's your favorite? Come on, eeny meeny miney mo, pick one, Pammy. Pam-mee"—singsong, like a taunting child—"pick a titty, Pammy. Which one's your favorite?"

And he had something in his hand, sort of a loop of wire, coppery in the dim light.

"Pick the one you want to keep, Pammy. One for you and one for me, that's fair, isn't it, Pam-mee? You can keep one and I'll take the other one, and it's your choice, Pam-mee, you have to choose, you hot little bitch, you have to pick one. It's Pammy's choice, you remember *Sophie's Choice,* but that was tots and this is *tits,* Pam-mee, and you better pick one or I'll take them both."

God, he was crazy, and what was she supposed to do, how could she pick one breast? There had to be a way to win this game but she couldn't think what it was.

"Look at that, look at that, I touch them and the nipples get hard, you get hot even when you're scared, even when you're crying, you little cunt, you. Pick one, Pammy. Which one will it be? This one? This one? What are you waiting for, Pammy? Are you trying to stall? Are you trying to make me angry? Come on, Pammy. Come on. Touch the one you want to keep."

God, what was she supposed to do?

"That one? Are you sure, Pammy?"

God—

"Well, I think it's a good choice, an excellent choice, so that one's yours and this one's mine and a deal's a deal and a trade's a trade and no trades back, Pam-mee."

The wire was a circle around her breast, and there was a wooden handle attached to each end of the wire, like the kind they slipped under the string of a package so you could carry it, and he held the handles and drew his hands apart, and—

And she was out of her body, just like that, floating without a body, up in the air above the truck and able to look down through the roof of the truck, watching, watching as the wire slipped through her flesh as if through a liquid, watching the breast slide slowly away from the rest of her, watching the blood seep.

Watching until the blood filled up the whole of her vision, watching it darken, darken, until the world went black.

14

Kelly was away from his desk. The man who answered his phone at Brooklyn Homicide said he could try to have him paged, if it was important. I said it was important.

When the phone rang Elaine answered it, said, "Just a minute," and nodded. I took the phone from her and said hello.

"My dad remembers you," he said. "Said you were real eager."

"Well, that was a while ago."

"So he said. What's so important they got to beep me in the middle of a meal?"

"I have a question about Leila Alvarez."

"You got a question. I thought you had something for me."

"About the surgery she had."

"'Surgery.' That what you want to call it?"

"Do you know what he used to sever the breast?"

"Yeah, a fucking guillotine. Where are you coming from with the questions, Scudder?"

"Could he have used a piece of wire? Piano wire, say, used almost like a garrote?"

173

There was a long pause, and I wondered if I'd pronounced the word incorrectly and he didn't know what I meant. Then, his voice tight, he said, "What the fuck are you sitting on?"

"I've been sitting on it for ten minutes, and I've spent five of them waiting for you to call back."

"God damn it, what have you got, mister?"

"Alvarez wasn't their only victim."

"So you said. Also Gotteskind. I read the file and I think you're right, but where did you get piano wire with Gotteskind?"

"There's another victim," I said. "Raped, tortured, a breast severed. The difference is she's alive. I figured you'd want to talk to her."

Drew Kaplan said, "*Pro bono,* huh? You like to tell me why those are the two Latin words everybody knows? By the time I got through Brooklyn Law I'd learned enough Latin to start my own church. *Res gestae, corpus juris, lex talionis.* Nobody ever says these words to me. Just *pro bono.* You know what it means, *pro bono?*"

"I'm sure you'll tell me."

"The full phrase is *pro bono publico.* For the public good. Which is why big corporate law firms use the phrase to refer to the minuscule amount of legal work which they deign to undertake for causes they believe in as a sop to their consciences, which are understandably troubled by virtue of the fact that they spend upwards of ninety percent of their time grinding the faces of the poor and billing upwards of two hundred dollars an hour for it. Why are you looking at me like that?"

"That's the longest sentence I've ever heard you speak."

"Is that right. Miss Cassidy, as your attorney it's my duty to caution you against associating with men like this gentleman. Matt, seriously, Miss Cassidy's a Manhattan resident, the victim of a crime which took place nine months ago in the borough of Queens. I'm a struggling lawyer with modest offices on Court Street in the borough of Brooklyn. So how, if you don't mind my asking, do I come into it?"

We were in his modest offices, and the banter was just his way of breaking the ice, because he already knew why Pam

Cassidy needed a Brooklyn lawyer to see her through inter-rogation by a Brooklyn homicide detective. I had gone over the situation with him at some length on the phone.

"I'm going to call you Pam," he said now. "Is that all right with you?"

"Oh, sure."

"Or do you prefer Pamela?"

"No, Pam's fine. Just so it's not Pammy."

The special significance of that would have been lost on Kaplan. He said, "It'll be Pam, then. Pam, before you and I go down to see Officer Kelly—it's Officer, Matt? Or Detective?"

"Detective John Kelly."

"Before we meet with the good detective, let's get our sig-nals straight. You're my client. That means I don't want you questioned by anyone unless I'm at your side. Do you under-stand?"

"Sure."

"That means from anyone, cops, press, TV reporters stick-ing microphones in your face. 'You'll have to speak with my attorney.' Let me hear you say that."

"You'll have to speak with my attorney."

"Perfect. Somebody calls you on the phone, asks you what the weather's like outside, what do you say?"

"You'll have to speak with my attorney."

"I think she's got it. One more. Guy calls you on the phone, says you've just won a free trip to Paradise Island in the Ba-hamas in connection with a special promotion they're running. What do you say?"

"You'll have to speak with my attorney."

"No, him you can tell to fuck off. Everybody else on the planet, however, they have to speak to your attorney. Now we'll go over some specifics, but generally speaking I only want you answering questions when I'm present, and only if they relate directly to the outrageous crime which was committed upon your person. Your background, your life before the incident, your life since the incident, none of that is anybody's business. If a line of questioning is introduced that I object to, I'll cut in and stop you from answering. If I don't say anything, but if for any reason whatsoever the question bothers you, you don't answer it. You say that you want to confer privately with your attorney. 'I want to confer privately with my attorney.' Let's hear you say that."

"I want to confer privately with my attorney."

"Excellent. The point is you're not charged with anything and you're not going to be charged with anything, so you're doing them a favor in the first place, which puts us in a very good position. Now let's just go over the background one time while we've got Matt here, and then you and I can go see Detective Kelly, Pam. Tell me how you happened to ask Matthew Scudder to try to track down the men who abducted and assaulted you?"

We had worked out the details before I'd called either John Kelly or Drew Kaplan. Pam needed a story that would make her the initiator of the investigation and leave Kenan Khoury out of it. She and Elaine and I batted it around, and this is what we came up with:

Pam, nine months after the incident, was trying to get on with her life. This was rendered more difficult by the dread she had that she would be victimized again by the same men. She had even thought of leaving New York to get away from them but felt the fear would remain with her no matter how far she fled.

Recently she had been with a man to whom she had told the story of the loss of her breast. This fellow, who was a respectable married man and whose name she would not under any circumstances divulge, was shocked and sympathetic. He told her she would not rest easy until the men were caught, and that even if it was impossible to find them it would almost certainly be helpful to her emotional recovery if she herself took some action toward their discovery and apprehension. Since the police had had ample time to investigate and had evidently accomplished nothing, it was his recommendation that she engage a private investigator who could concentrate wholeheartedly upon the case instead of practicing the sort of criminological triage required of policemen.

There was in fact a private operative he knew and trusted, because this nameless fellow had been a client of mine in the past. He had sent her to me, and in addition had agreed to cover my fee and expenses, with the understanding that his role in all of this would not be divulged to anyone under any circumstances.

A couple of interviews with Pam had suggested to me that the most effective way to approach the case was by assuming that she had not been their only victim. Indeed, the way they had discussed killing her seemed to indicate that they had in fact committed murder. I had accordingly tried multiple approaches designed to turn up evidence of crimes committed by the same two men either before or after the maiming of my client.

Library research had turned up two cases which I considered likely, Marie Gotteskind and Leila Alvarez. The Gotteskind case involved abduction by means of a truck, and by securing the Gotteskind file through unconventional channels I had confirmed that it had also involved an amputation. The Alvarez case looked like probable abduction, and was similar, too, in that the victim was abandoned in a cemetery. (Pam had been dropped in Mount Zion Cemetery, in Queens.) When I learned on Thursday that Alvarez's mutilation, unspecified in the newspaper account, had been identical to Pam's, it seemed self-evident to me that the same criminals were involved.

So why didn't I say anything to Kelly at the time? Most important, I couldn't ethically do so without my client's permission, and I had spent the weekend talking her into it and preparing her for what she would have to face. In addition, I wanted to see if any of the other hooks I had in the water would bring in a bite.

One of these was the movie-of-the-week pitch, which I'd had Elaine try on various sex-crime units around town in the hope of turning up a living victim. Several women had called, although none had proved even remote possibilities, but I'd wanted to wait until the weekend was over before giving up on that line of inquiry.

Amusingly enough, Pam herself had gotten a telephone

call from a woman at the Queens unit, suggesting that she might find it worth her while to contact this Miss Mardell and see what it was all about. At the time she'd had no idea we were trying this particular approach, so she'd been very uncertain with the woman on the phone, but then we all had a good laugh when she mentioned it to me and found out who this movie producer really was.

As of this afternoon, Monday, I couldn't see any justification for withholding information from the police, since our so doing would unquestionably hamper their investigation of the two homicides, and since I had no useful course to pursue on my own. I had managed to sell this argument to Pam, who was still more than a little wary of being interrogated again by police officers, but who was more sanguine about it when I told her she could have a lawyer looking after her interests.

And so they were on their way to see Kelly, and I was done chasing lust murderers, and that was that.

"I think it'll play," I told Elaine. "I think it covers everything, all the activities I've engaged in since the first call I got, except for anything that has to do with Khoury. I don't see how anything Pam might tell them could lead them toward the investigation I conducted on Atlantic Avenue or the computer games I watched the Kongs play last night. Pam doesn't know about any of that so she couldn't spill it even if she wanted to, she never heard the names of Francine or Kenan Khoury. Come to think of it, I'm not sure she knows why I got into the case in the first place. I think all she knows is her cover story."

"Maybe she believes it."

"She probably will by the time she's done telling it. Kaplan thought it sounded fine."

"Did you tell him the real story?"

"No, there was no reason to do that. He knows what he's got is incomplete, but he can be comfortable with it. The important thing is that he'll keep the cops from ganging up on her and paying more attention to my role in the case than to who did it."

"Would they do that?"

I shrugged. "I don't know what they'd do. There's a team of serial killers who've been doing their little number for over a year now and the NYPD doesn't even know they exist. It's going to put a lot of people's noses out of joint to have a private detective come up with what everybody else missed."

"So they'll kill the messenger."

"It wouldn't be the first time. Actually the cops didn't miss anything obvious. It's very easy to miss serial murder, especially when different precincts and boroughs get different cases and the unifying elements are the kind that don't make it into newspaper stories. But they could still hold it against Pam for showing them up, especially given that she's a hooker and that she didn't mention that little tidbit first time around."

"Is she going to mention it now?"

"She's going to mention now that she used to make ends meet by occasionally prostituting herself. We know they've got a sheet on her, she was booked a couple of times for prostitution and loitering with intent. They didn't find that out when they investigated her case because she was the victim, so there was no compelling need to determine whether she had a record."

"But you think they should have checked."

"Well, it was pretty sloppy," I said. "Hookers are targets for this all the time because they're so accessible. They could have checked. It should have been automatic."

"But she's going to tell them she stopped hooking after she got home from the hospital. That she was afraid to go back to it."

I nodded. She had quit for a while, scared to death at the thought of getting into a car with a stranger, but old habits die hard and she'd gone back to it. At first she limited herself to car dates, not wanting to risk disappointing or disgusting a man by taking off her shirt, but she'd found that most men didn't mind her deformity that much. Some found it an interesting peculiarity, while a small minority were extremely excited by it, and became regular clients.

But nobody had to know any of that. So she would be telling them that she had had a couple of jobs waitressing, working off the books in the neighborhood, and that she was being more or less kept by the anonymous benefactor who had referred her to me.

"And what about you?" Elaine wanted to know. "Aren't you going to have to see Kelly and give him a statement?"

"I suppose so, but there's no rush. I'll talk to him tomorrow and see if he needs anything formal from me. He may not. I don't have anything for him, really, because I didn't uncover any evidence. I just spotted some invisible links between three existing cases."

"So for you ze war is over, *mein Kapitän*?"

"Looks that way."

"I'll bet you're exhausted. Do you want to go in the other room and lie down?"

"I'd rather stay up so that I can get back on my normal schedule."

"Makes sense. Are you hungry? Oh my God, you haven't eaten anything since breakfast, have you? Sit there, I'll fix us something."

We had a tossed salad and a big bowl of butterfly pasta with oil and garlic. We ate at the kitchen table, and afterward she made tea for herself and coffee for me and we went into the living room and sat together on the couch. At one point she said something uncharacteristically coarse; when I laughed she asked me what was so funny.

I said, "I love it when you talk street."

"You think it's a pose, huh? You think I'm some sheltered hothouse blossom, don't you?"

"No, I think you're the rose of Spanish Harlem."

"I wonder if I could have made it on the street," she said thoughtfully. "I'm glad I never had to find out. I'll tell you one thing, though. When this is all over Little Miss Street Smarts is going to come in out of the cold. She can just bundle up her remaining tit and get the hell off the pavement."

"Are you planning on adopting her?"

"No, and we're damn well not going to be roommates and do each other's hair, either. But I can get her a place in a decent house or show her how to build a book and work out of her apartment. If she's smart you know what she'll do? Run a couple of ads in *Screw* letting the tit fanciers out there know they can now get one for the price of two. You're laughing again, was that street talk?"

"No, it was just funny."

"Then you're allowed to laugh. I don't know, maybe I should just butt out and let her live her life. But I liked her."

"So did I."

"I think she deserves better than the street."

"Everybody does," I said. "She may come out of this all right. If they get the guys and there's a trial, she could have her allotted fifteen minutes of fame. And she's got a lawyer who'll make sure that nobody gets her story without paying her for it."

"Maybe there'll be a TV movie."

"I wouldn't rule it out, although I don't think we can count on Debra Winger playing our friend."

"No, probably not. Oh, I got it. Are you with me on this? What you do, you get an actress to play her who's a post-mastectomy patient in real life. I mean, are we talking high concept here or what? You see what a statement we'd be making?" She winked. "That's my show-biz persona. I bet you like my street act better."

"I'd call it a toss-up."

"Fair enough. Matt? Does it bother you to work on a case like this and then hand it over to the police?"

"No."

"Really?"

"Why should it? I couldn't justify keeping it to myself. The NYPD has resources and manpower I don't have. I'd taken it as far as I could, that end of it, anyway. I'll still follow up the lead I got last night and see what I can turn up in Sunset Park."

"You're not telling the police about Sunset Park."

"No way to do that."

"No. Matt? I have a question."

"Go ahead."

"I don't know if you want to hear it, but I have to ask. Are you sure it's the same killers?"

"Has to be. A piece of wire used to amputate a breast? Once with Leila Alvarez, once with Pam Cassidy? Both victims dumped in cemeteries? Give me a break."

"I was assuming that the ones who did Pam also did the Alvarez girl. And the woman in Forest Park, the schoolteacher."

"Marie Gotteskind."

"But what about Francine Khoury? She was not dumped in a cemetery, she did not necessarily have a breast amputated with a garrote, and she was reportedly snatched by three men. If there was one thing Pam was positive of it was that there were only two men, Ray and the other one."

"There could have been just two with Khoury."

"You said—"

"I know what I said. Pam also said that they went from the driver's seat to the back of the truck and back again. Maybe it just looked as though there were three people because when you see two guys enter the back of a truck and then it pulls away you assume somebody was up front to drive it."

"Maybe."

"We know these guys did Gotteskind. Gotteskind and Alvarez are tied together by the business with the fingers, amputation and insertion, and Alvarez and Cassidy both had the breast cut off, so that means—"

"They're all three the same. All right, I follow that."

"Well, the Gotteskind eyewitnesses also said there were three men, two who did the snatching and one who drove. That could have been an illusion. Or they could have had three that day, and again the day they did Francine, but one guy was home with the flu the night they picked up Pam."

"Home jerking off," she said.

"Whatever. We could ask Pam if there were any references to another man. 'Mike would like her ass,' something like that."

"Maybe they took her breast home for Mike."

"'Hey, Mike, you should have seen the one that got away.'"

"Spare me, will you? Do you think they'll get a decent description out of her?"

"I couldn't." She'd said she didn't remember what the two men looked like, that when she tried to picture them she saw wholly undefined faces, as if they'd been wearing nylon stockings as masks. That had made the original investigation an exercise in futility when they gave her books full of sex-offender mug shots to pore over. She didn't know what faces she was looking for. They'd tried her with an Identi-Kit technician and that had been hopeless, too.

"When she was here," she said, "I kept thinking of Ray Galindez." He was an NYPD cop and an artist, with an uncanny ability to hook up with a witness and extract a remarkable likeness. Two of his sketches, matted and framed, were on Elaine's bathroom wall.

"I had the same thought," I said, "but I don't know what he could get out of her. If he'd worked with her a day or two after it happened he might have got somewhere. Now it's been too long."

"What about hypnosis?"

"It's possible. She must have blocked the memory, and a hypnotist could possibly unblock her. I don't know that much about it. Juries don't necessarily trust it, and I'm not sure I do either."

"Why not?"

"I think hypnotized witnesses can create memories out of their imaginations because of a desire to please. I'm suspicious of a lot of the incest memories I hear about in meetings, memories that suddenly surface twenty or thirty years after the event. I'm sure some of them are real, but I get the sense that more than a few of them are summoned up out of the whole cloth because the patient wants to make her therapist happy."

"Sometimes it's real."

"No question. But sometimes it's not."

"Maybe. I'll grant you it's the trauma *du jour* these days. Pretty soon women without incest memories are going to start worrying that their fathers thought they were ugly. You want to play I'm a naughty little girl and you're my daddy?"

"I don't think so."

"You're no fun. You want to play I'm a hip slick and cool street hooker and you're sitting behind the wheel of your car?"

"Would I have to go rent a car?"

"We could pretend the couch is a car, but that might be a stretch. What can we do that'll keep our relationship exciting and hot? I'd tie you up but I know you. You'd just go to sleep."

"Especially tonight."

"Uh-huh. We could pretend you're into deformities and I'm missing a breast."

"God forbid."

"Yeah, amen to that. I don't want to *beshrei* it, as my mother would say. You know from *beshrei*? I think it means inviting a Yiddish equivalent of hubris. 'Don't even say it, you might give God ideas.'"

"Well, don't."

"No. Honey? Do you want to just go to bed?"

"Now you're talking."

15

Tuesday I slept late, and Elaine was gone when I woke up. A note on the kitchen table told me to stay as long as I wanted. I helped myself to breakfast and watched CNN for a while. Then I went out and walked around for an hour or so, winding up at the Citicorp Building in time for the noon meeting. Afterward I went to a movie on Third Avenue, walked to the Frick and looked at the paintings, then took a bus down Lexington and caught a five-thirty meeting a block from Grand Central, commuters bracing themselves to pass up the club car.

The meeting was on the Eleventh Step, the one about seeking to know God's will through prayer and meditation, and most of the discussion was relentlessly spiritual. When I got out I decided to treat myself to a cab. Two sailed past me, and when a third one pulled up a woman in a tailored suit and flowing bow tie elbowed me out of the way and beat me to it. I hadn't done any praying or meditating, but I didn't have a whole lot of trouble figuring out God's will in the matter. He wanted me to go home by subway.

There were messages to call John Kelly, Drew Kaplan, and

Kenan Khoury. That struck me as an awful lot of people with the same last initial, and I hadn't even heard from the Kongs yet. There was a fourth message from someone who hadn't left a name, just a number; perversely, that was the call I returned first.

I dialed the number, and instead of ringing it responded with a tone. I decided I'd been disconnected and hung up, and then I got it and dialed again, and when the tone sounded I punched in my phone number and hung up.

Within five minutes my phone rang. I picked it up and TJ said, "Hey, Matt, my man. What's happenin'?"

"You got a beeper."

"Surprised you, huh? Man, I had five hundred dollars all at once. What you 'spect me to do, buy a savings bond? They was havin' a special, you got the beeper and the first three months' service for a hundred an' ninety-nine dollars. You want one, I'll go to the store with you, make sure they treat you right."

"I'll wait awhile. What happens after three months? They take the beeper back?"

"No, I own it, man. I just got to pay so much a month to keep it on-line. I stop payin', I still own it, but you call it an' nothin' happens."

"Not much point in owning it then."

"Lotta dudes got 'em, though. Wear 'em all the time an' you never hear 'em beep because they ain't paid to stay on-line."

"What's the monthly charge?"

"They told me but I forget. Don't matter. Way I figure, by the time the three months is up you'll be pickin' up the monthly tab for me just to have me at your beck an' call."

"Why would I do that?"

"Because I indispensable, man. I a key asset to your operation."

"Because you're resourceful."

"See? You're gettin' it."

* * *

186

I tried Drew but he wasn't at his office and I didn't want to bother him at home. I didn't call Kenan Khoury or John Kelly, figuring they could wait. I stopped around the corner for a slice of pizza and a Coke and went to St. Paul's for my third meeting of the day. I couldn't recall the last time I'd gone to that many, but it had certainly been a while.

It wasn't because I felt in danger of drinking. The thought of a drink had never been further from my mind. Nor did I feel beset by problems, or unable to reach a decision.

What I did feel, I realized, was a sense of depletion, of exhaustion. The all-nighter at the Frontenac had taken its toll, but its effects had been pretty much offset by a couple of good meals and nine hours of uninterrupted sleep. But I was still very much at the effect of the case itself. I had worked hard on it, letting it absorb me entirely, and now it was finished.

Except, of course, that it wasn't. The killers had not even been identified, let alone apprehended. I had done what I recognized as excellent detective work and it had produced significant results, but the case itself had not been brought to anything like a conclusion. So the exhaustion I felt wasn't part of a glorious feeling of completion. Tired or not, I had promises to keep. And miles to go.

So I was at another meeting, a safe and restful place. I talked with Jim Faber during the break, and walked out with him at the end of the meeting. He didn't have time to get a cup of coffee but I walked him most of the way to his apartment and we wound up standing on a street corner and talking for a few minutes. Then I went home and once again I didn't call Kenan Khoury, but I did call his brother. His name had come up in my conversation with Jim, and neither of us could remember having seen him in the past week. So I dialed Peter's number but there was no answer. I called Elaine and we talked for a few minutes. She mentioned that Pam Cassidy had called to say she wouldn't be calling—i.e., Drew had told her not to be in touch with me or Elaine for the time being, and she wanted to let Elaine know so she wouldn't worry.

I called Drew first thing the next morning and he said

everything had gone well enough and he'd found Kelly hard-nosed but not unreasonable. "If you want to wish for something," he suggested, "wish that the guy turns out to be rich."

"Kelly? You don't get rich in Homicide. There's no graft in it."

"Not Kelly, for God's sake. Ray."

"Who?"

"The killer," he said. "The one with the wire, for God's sake. Don't you listen to your own client?"

She wasn't my client, but he didn't know that. I asked him why on earth we would want Ray to turn out to be rich.

"So we can sue his ass off."

"I was hoping to see it locked up for the rest of his life."

"Yeah, I have the same hope," he said, "but we both know what can happen in criminal court. But one thing I damn well know is that if they so much as indict the son of a bitch I can get a civil judgment for every dime he's got. But that's only worth something if he's got a few bucks."

"You never know," I said. What I did know was that there weren't too many millionaires living in Sunset Park, but I didn't want to mention Sunset Park to Kaplan, and anyway I had no reason to assume that both of them, or all three of them if we were dealing with three, actually lived there. For all I knew, Ray had a suite at the Pierre.

"I know I'd like to find somebody to sue," he said. "Maybe the bastards used a company truck. I'd like to find some collateral defendant somewhere down the line so that I can at least get her a decent settlement. She deserves it after what she went through."

"And that way your *pro bono* work would turn out to be cost-effective, wouldn't it?"

"So? There's nothing wrong with that, but I've got to tell you that my end of this isn't my chief concern. Seriously."

"Okay."

"She's a damn good kid," he said. "Tough and gutsy, but there's a core of innocence about her, do you know what I mean?"

"I know."

"And those bastards really put her through it. Did she show you what they did to her?"

"She told me."

"She told me, too, but she also showed me. You think the knowledge prepares you, but believe me, the visual impact is staggering."

"No kidding," I said. "Did she also show you what she's got left, so you could appreciate the extent of her loss?"

"You've got a dirty mind, you know that?"

"I know," I said. "At least that's what everybody tells me."

I called John Kelly's office and was told he was in court. When I gave my name the cop I was talking to said, "Oh, he'll want to talk to you. Give me your number, I'll beep him for you." A little while later Kelly got back to me and we arranged to meet at a place called The Docket around the corner from Borough Hall. The place was new to me, but it felt just like places I knew in downtown Manhattan, bar-restaurants with a clientele that ran to cops and lawyers and a decor that featured a lot of brass and leather and dark wood.

Kelly and I had never met, a point we both overlooked when we set up the meeting, but as it turned out I had no trouble recognizing him. He looked just like his father.

"I been hearing that all my life," he said.

He picked up his beer from the bar and we took a table in back. Our waitress had a snub nose and infectious good humor, and she knew my companion. When he asked her about the pastrami she said, "It's not lean enough for you, Kelly. Take the roast beef." We had roast beef sandwiches on rye, the meat sliced thin and piled high, accompanied by crisp french fries and a horseradish sauce that would bring tears to the eyes of a statue.

"Good place," I said.

"Can't beat it. I eat here all the time."

He had a second bottle of Molson's with his sandwich. I ordered a cream soda, and when that got a headshake from the waitress I said I'd have a Coke. I saw this register with Kelly, although he didn't comment at the time. When she brought our drinks, though, he said, "You used to drink."

"Your father mentioned that? I wasn't hitting it all that heavy when I knew him."

"I didn't get it from him. I made a few calls, asked around. I hear you had your troubles with it and then you stopped."

"You could say that."

"AA, I heard. Great organization, everything I hear of it."

"It has its good points. But it's no place to be if you want a decent drink."

It took him a second to realize I was joking. He laughed, then said, "That where you know him from? The mysterious boyfriend?"

"I'm not going to answer that."

"You're not prepared to tell me anything about him."

"No."

"That's okay, I'm not about to give you a lot of grief on the subject. You got her to come in, I have to give you that. I don't exactly love it when a witness shows up holding hands with her lawyer, but under the circumstances I got to admit it's the right move for her. And Kaplan's not too much of a sleaze. He'll make you look like a monkey in court if he can, but what the hell, that's his job, and they're all like that. What are you going to do, hang the whole profession?"

"There are people who wouldn't think it was such a bad idea."

"You're talking about half the people in this room," he said, "and the other half are attorneys themselves. But what the hell. Kaplan and I agreed to keep this dark as far as the press is concerned. He said he was sure you'd go along."

"Of course."

"If we had a good sketch of the two perps it'd be different, but I put her together with an artist and the best we could come up with is they each got two eyes, a nose, and a mouth. She's not too sure about ears, thinks they had two apiece but doesn't want to commit herself. Be like running a picture of a smile button on page five of the *Daily News*: 'Have You Seen This Man?' What we got is linkage of three cases which we're now officially treating as serial homicide, but do you see any advantage in making it public? Besides scaring the shit out of people, what do you accomplish?"

We didn't linger over lunch. He had to be back by two to testify in the trial of a drug-related homicide, which was the sort of thing that kept him from ever getting his desk clear. "And it's hard to keep on giving a shit if they kill each other," he said, "or to break your back trying to nail them for it. I wish to hell they'd legalize all that shit, and I honest to Christ never thought I'd hear myself say that."

"I never thought I'd hear any cop say it."

"You hear it all the time now. Cops, DAs, everybody. There's still DEA guys playing the same old tune. 'We're winning the war on drugs. Give us the tools and we can do the job.' I don't know, maybe they believe it, but you're better off believing in the Tooth Fairy. Least that way you might wind up with a quarter under your pillow."

"How can you rationalize making crack legal?"

"I know, it's a pisser. My all-time favorite is angel dust. An ordinary peaceable guy'll go get himself dusted, and he goes straight into a blackout and acts out violently. Then he wakes up hours later and somebody's dead and he doesn't remember a thing, he can't even tell you if he enjoyed the high. Would I like to see them selling dust at the corner candy store? Jesus, I can't say I would, but would they move any more of it that way than they do right now, selling it on the street in front of the candy store?"

"I don't know."

"Neither does anybody else. As a matter of fact they're not selling that much angel dust these days, but it's not because people are going away for it. Crack's taking a lot of the dust market. So there's good news from the world of drugs, sports fans. Crack is helping us win that war."

We split the check, and on the sidewalk we shook hands. I agreed to get in touch if I thought of anything he ought to know about, and he said he'd keep me posted if they got any kind of a break in the case. "I can tell you there'll be some manpower on it," he said. "These are guys we really want to take off the street."

I had told Kenan Khoury I'd be out later that afternoon, so I headed in that direction. The Docket is on Joralemon Street, where Brooklyn Heights butts up against Cobble Hill. I walked east to Court Street and down Court to Atlantic, passing Drew Kaplan's law office and the Syrian place I'd gone to with Peter Khoury. I turned on Atlantic so that I could pass Ayoub's and visualize the kidnapping *in situ*, which was another Latin phrase Drew could put in the basket with *pro bono*. I thought I'd take a bus south, but when I got to Fourth Avenue a bus was just pulling away from the curb, and it was a beautiful spring day anyway and I was enjoying the walk.

I walked for a couple of hours. I never consciously planned on walking all the way to Bay Ridge, but that's what I wound up doing. At first I just thought I'd walk eight or ten blocks and then catch the first bus that came long. By the time I got to the first of the numbered streets I realized I was only about a mile from Green-Wood Cemetery. I cut over to Fifth Avenue and walked to the cemetery and went in, strolling for ten or fifteen minutes among the graves. The grass was bright the way it never is except in early spring, and there were a lot of spring bulbs in bloom around the headstones, along with other flowers that had been placed in urns.

The cemetery covers a vast expanse of ground and I had no idea in what section of it Leila Alvarez had been lost and found, although there may well have been some indication in the news story. If so I had long since forgotten, and what difference did it make, anyway? I wasn't going to psych out anything by tuning in to the vibrations emanating from the patch of grass on which she'd lain. I'm willing to believe that some people can operate that way, that they can use willow twigs to find lost objects and missing children, even that they can see auras that escape my vision (although I wasn't sure I'd grant such powers to Danny Boy's latest girlfriend). But I couldn't.

Still, just being in a place might jog a thought loose, allow a mental connection that might otherwise never be made. Who knows how the process works?

Maybe I went there looking for some kind of connection to the Alvarez girl. Maybe I just wanted to spend a few minutes walking on green grass, and looking at the flowers.

I entered the cemetery at Twenty-fifth Street and left it half a mile south at Thirty-fourth. By this point I had made my way through all of Park Slope and was on the northern edge of the Sunset Park section, and just a couple of blocks from the small park that gave the neighborhood its name.

I walked to the park, and across it. Then, one by one, I made my way to all six of the pay phones that had been used to call the Khoury house, starting with the one on New Utrecht Avenue at Forty-first Street. The one I was most interested in was on Fifth Avenue between Forty-ninth and Fiftieth. That was the phone they had used twice, the one that thus figured to be closest to their base of operations. Unlike the other phones, it was not located on the street but just inside the entrance of a twenty-four-hour laundromat.

There were two women in the place, both of them fat. One was folding laundry while the other sat in a chair tipped back against the concrete-block wall and read a copy of *People* magazine with Sandra Dee's picture on the cover. Neither of them paid any attention to the other, or to me. I dropped a quarter in the phone and called Elaine. When she picked up I said, "Do all laundromats have telephones? Is it a regular thing, are you always going to find a pay phone in a laundromat?"

"Do you have any idea how many years I've been waiting for you to ask me that?"

"Well?"

"It's flattering that you think I know everything, but I have to tell you something. I haven't set foot inside a laundromat in years. In fact I'm not sure I've ever been in one. We have machines in the basement. So I can't answer your question, but I can ask you one. Why?"

"Two of the calls to Khoury the night of the kidnapping came from a laundromat pay phone in Sunset Park."

193

"And you're there right now. You're calling me from that very phone."

"Right."

"And? Why does it matter if other laundromats have phones? Don't tell me, I'll figure it out for myself. I can't figure it out for myself. Why?"

"I was thinking they'd have to live very close for it to occur to them to use this phone. You can't see it from the street, so unless you lived within a block or two of it you wouldn't think of it when you needed to make a phone call. Unless every laundromat in the world has a phone."

"Well, I don't know about laundromats. There's no phone in our basement. What do you do about laundry?"

"Me? There's a laundry around the corner."

"They have a phone?"

"I don't know. I drop it off in the morning and pick it up at night, if I remember. They do everything. I give it to them dirty and it comes back clean."

"I bet they don't separate colors."

"Huh?"

"Never mind."

I left the laundromat and had a *café con leche* at the Cuban lunch counter at the corner. He'd talked on that phone, the son of a bitch. I was that close to him.

He had to live in the neighborhood. And not just in the general area, but almost certainly within a block or two of the laundromat. It wasn't hard for me to start believing I could feel his presence somewhere within a few hundred yards of where I was sitting. But that was a lot of crap. I didn't have to pick up vibrations, all I had to do was figure out what must have happened.

They picked her up when she left the house, tailed her to D'Agostino's, laid off when the bag boy walked her to her car, then tailed her again to Atlantic Avenue. They made the snatch when she came out of Ayoub's and drove off with her in the back of the truck. And headed where?

Any of dozens of places. Some side street in Red Hook. An alleyway behind a warehouse. A garage.

There was a gap of several hours between the kidnapping and the first phone call, and I figured they had spent a good portion of those hours doing to her what they had done to Pam Cassidy. After she was dead they'd have headed for home, parked in their own parking space if they weren't there already. The truck, which had borne lettering identifying it as the vehicle of a TV outfit in Queens, would get some cosmetic attention. They'd paint over the lettering—or just wash it off, if they'd applied washable paint to begin with. If they had the right setup in their garage, the truck might get a whole change of color.

Then what? A quick course in Meat-cutting for Beginners? They could have done that then, could have waited until afterward. It didn't matter.

Then, at 3:38, the first call. At 4:01, the second call—Ray's first call—from the laundromat. More calls, until at 8:01 the sixth call sent the Khourys off to deliver the money. Having made that call, Ray or another man would get in position to watch the pay phone at Flatbush and Farragut, dialing its number when Kenan approached.

Or was that necessary? They'd told Kenan to be there at eight-thirty. They could have called the phone at one-minute intervals starting a few minutes before the appointed hour; whenever Khoury arrived and answered the phone, he'd have the impression that they'd called when he and his brother drove up.

Immaterial. However they did it, they made the call and Kenan answered it and they went next to Veterans Avenue, where one or more of the kidnappers was probably already in place. Another call came in, probably coordinated with the Khourys' arrival because the kidnappers would in this instance want to be in position to watch the Khourys walk away from the money.

Once they did, once they were out of the way, once it was quite clear no one had hung back to watch the car, then Ray and his friend or friends grabbed the money and took off.

No.

At least one of them lingered in the area and watched the Khourys look in the car and fail to find Francine. Then a call to the pay phone telling them to go home, that she'd be back there before they were. And then, while the Khourys did in fact return to Colonial Road, the kidnappers returned to home base. Parked the truck, and—

No. No, the truck had stayed in the garage. They hadn't completely disguised it yet, and Francine Khoury's body was probably still in the back. They had used another vehicle to drive out to Veterans Avenue.

The Ford Tempo, stolen for the occasion? That was possible. Or a third car, with the Tempo stolen and stashed, to be used for one purpose only, the delivery of the remains.

So many possibilities...

One way or another, though, they tricked the Tempo out now with Francine's butchered body. Cut up the corpse, wrapped each segment in plastic, secured each parcel with tape. Broke the lock of the trunk, filled it up like a meat locker, drove in two cars to Colonial Road and around the corner to a parking spot. Parked the Tempo, and whoever drove it joined his buddy in the other car, and they went home.

To $400,000 and the satisfaction of having had their crime go off flawlessly.

Only one thing left to do. A phone call to send Khoury around the corner to the parked Ford. The job's all done, you're flushed with triumph, but you have to rub his nose in it. What a temptation to use your own phone, the one right there on the table. Khoury hadn't called the cops, he hadn't used any backup, he'd parted readily with the money, so how was he ever going to know where this last call was coming from?

What the hell...

But no, wait a minute, you've done everything right so far, you've been strictly professional about this, so why fuck it up now? What's the sense in that?

On the other hand, you don't have to be a fanatic. Up to now you've used a different phone for every call and made sure every phone you used was a minimum of half a dozen blocks from every other phone. Just in case there was a trace, just in case they staked out one of those phones.

But they didn't. That's clear now, they didn't do anything

of the sort, so there's no need now to use more caution than the circumstances require. Use a pay phone, yes, do that much, but use the most convenient one around, the one that was your first choice, that's why you made your own first call from it.

While you're at it, do your laundry. You've been doing bloody work, you got your clothes filthy, so why not throw a load of wash in the machine?

No, hardly that. Not with four hundred large sitting on the kitchen table. You wouldn't wash those clothes. You'd get rid of them and buy new.

I walked up and down every street within two blocks of the laundromat, working within the rectangle formed by Fourth and Sixth avenues and Forty-eighth and Fifty-second streets. I don't know that I was hunting for anything in particular, although I probably would have looked twice at blue panel trucks with homemade lettering on their sides. What I most wanted was to get a feel for the neighborhood and see if anything caught my eye.

The neighborhood was economically and ethnically diverse, with scattered houses crumbling from neglect and others being spruced up and converted for single-family occupancy by their new upscale owners. There were blocks of row houses, some still clad in a crazy quilt of aluminum and asphalt siding, others stripped of this improvement and their bricks repointed. There were blocks, too, of detached frame houses with little patches of lawn. Some of the lawns were used for parking, while some of the houses had driveways and garages. I saw a lot of street life throughout, a lot of mothers with small children, a lot of furiously energetic kids, a lot of men working on their cars or sitting on stoops, drinking from cans in brown paper bags.

By the time I finished tracing the lines of the grid, I didn't know that I'd accomplished anything. But I was reasonably certain I'd walked past the house where it happened.

A little later I was standing in front of another house where a murder had taken place.

After a visit to the southernmost pay phone at Sixtieth and Fifth, I went over to Fourth Avenue and walked past the D'Agostino's and into Bay Ridge. When I got to Senator Street it struck me that I was only a couple of blocks from where Tommy Tillary had murdered his wife. I wondered if I could find it after all these years, and at first I had trouble, looking for it on the wrong block. Once I realized my mistake I spotted it right away.

It was a little smaller than my memory had it, like the classrooms in your old grammar school, but otherwise it was as I remembered it to be. I stood out in front and looked up at the third-floor attic window. Tillary had stowed his wife up there, then brought her downstairs and killed her, making it look as though she'd been slain by burglars.

Margaret, that was her name. It had come back to me. Margaret, but Tommy called her Peg.

He killed her for money. That has always struck me as a poor reason to kill, but perhaps I hold money too cheaply, and life too dear. It is, I'll warrant you, a better motive than killing for the fun of it.

I'd met Drew Kaplan in the course of that case. He was Tommy Tillary's lawyer on the first murder charge. Later, after they'd cut him loose and picked him up again for killing his girlfriend, Kaplan encouraged him to get other representation.

The house looked in good shape. I wondered who owned it, and what he knew of its history. If it had changed hands a few times over the years, the present owner might have missed the story. But this was a pretty settled neighborhood. People tended to stay put.

I stood there for a few minutes, thinking about those drinking days. The people I'd known, the life I'd led.

Long time ago. Or not so long, depending how you counted.

16

Kenan said, "I didn't figure you'd do it that way. Take it to a certain point, then wrap it up and hand it to the cops."

I started to explain again that the decision had been very clear-cut for me, that I hadn't seen myself as having much choice. Things had reached a point where the police could pursue whole avenues of investigation far more effectively than I could, and I'd been able to give them most of what I'd uncovered without bringing my client or his dead wife into the picture.

"No, I got all that," he said. "I see why you did what you did. Why not get 'em to do some of the work? That's what they're for, isn't it? I just wasn't expecting it, that's all. I had us pictured tracking 'em down, then winding it up with a car chase and a shoot-out or some such shit like that. I don't know, maybe I spend too much time in front of the television set."

He looked as though he spent too much time on airplanes, too much time indoors, too much time drinking too much coffee in back rooms and kitchens. He was unshaven, and his hair was shaggy and needed cutting. He'd lost weight and muscle tone since I'd seen him last, and his handsome face was drawn, with dark circles under the dark eyes. He was wearing light-colored linen slacks and a bronze silk shirt and loafers with no socks, the sort of outfit in which his usual look was one of quiet elegance. But today he looked rumpled and the least bit seedy.

"Say the cops get 'em," he said. "Then what happens?"

"It depends what kind of a case they're able to make. Ideally you'll get a lot of solid physical evidence linking them to one or more of the murders. In the absence of that, you might see one of the criminals testify against the others in return for the opportunity to plead to a lesser charge."

"Rat 'em out, in other words."

"That's right."

"Why let one of 'em cop a plea? The girl's a witness, isn't she?"

"Only to the crime she was a victim of, and that's a lesser charge than murder. Rape and forcible sodomy are class B felonies, calling for an indeterminate sentence of six to twenty-five years. If you can charge them with Murder Two they're looking at a life sentence."

"What about cutting her breast off?"

"All that amounts to is first-degree assault, and that's a lesser charge than rape and sodomy. I think the max on it is fifteen years."

"That seems off to me," he said. "I'd have to say it's worse than murder, what they did to her. One person kills another person, well, maybe he couldn't help it, maybe he had cause. But to hurt a person like that for the fun of it—what kind of people act like that?"

"Sick ones or evil ones, take your pick."

"You know what's making me crazy is thinking what they did to Francey." He was on his feet, pacing, and he crossed the room and looked out the window. With his back to me he said, "I try not to think about it. I try to tell myself they killed her right away, she fought and they hit her to quiet her and hit her too hard and she died. Just like that, wham, gone." He turned around and his shoulders sagged. "What the fuck's the difference? Whatever they put her through, it's over now. She's done hurting. She's gone, she's ashes. Whatever's not ashes is with God, if that's how it works. Or at peace, or born again into a bird or a flower or who knows what. Or just gone. I don't know how it works, what happens to you after you die. Nobody does."

"No."

"You hear this shit, near-death experiences, going through a tunnel and meeting Jesus or your favorite uncle and seeing a picture of your whole life. Maybe it happens that way. I don't know. Maybe that only works with near-death experiences. Maybe real death is different. Who knows?"

"I don't."

"No, and who fucking cares? We'll worry about it when it happens to us. What's the most they can get for rape? You said twenty-five years?"

"According to the statute, yes."

"And sodomy, you said. What's that amount to legally, anal?"

"Anal or oral."

He frowned. "I gotta stop this. Everything we talk about I immediately translate in terms of Francine and I can't do that, I just make myself nuts. You can get twenty-five years for fucking a woman in the ass and a max of fifteen for hacking her tits off. There's something wrong there."

"It'll be tough changing the law."

"No, I'm just looking for a way to make it the system's fault, that's all. Twenty-five years isn't enough, anyway. Life's not enough. They're animals, they should be fucking dead."

"The law can't do that."

"No," he said. "That's all right. All the law has to do is find them. After that anything can happen. If they go to prison, well, it's not that hard to get at somebody in prison. There's a lot of guys in the joint don't mind turning a buck. Or say they beat it in court or they make bail awaiting trial, they're out in the open and easy to get at." He shook his head. "Listen to me, will you? Like I'm the Godfather sitting back and ordering hits. Who knows what's gonna happen? Maybe I'll lose some of this heat by then, maybe twenty-five years in a cell's gonna sound like enough by then. Who knows?"

I said, "We could get lucky and find them before the police do."

"How? By walking around Sunset Park not knowing who you're looking for?"

"And by using some of what the police come up with. One thing they'll do is send everything they have to the FBI office that draws up profiles of serial killers. Maybe our witness will fill in some of the holes in her memory and I'll have a picture to work with, or at least a decent physical description."

"So you want to stay with it."

"Definitely."

He considered this, nodded. "Tell me again what I owe you."

"I gave the girl a thousand. The lawyer's not charging her anything. The computer technicians who tapped the phone-company records got fifteen hundred, and the room we used cost a hundred and sixty, plus fifty dollars' deposit on the phone, which I didn't try to recover. Call it twenty-seven hundred even."

"Uh-huh."

"I've had other expenses, but it seemed reasonable to pay them out of my end. These were unusual expenses, and I didn't want to delay action until I could get your okay. If anything seems out of line, I'm prepared to discuss it."

"What's there to discuss?"

"I get the feeling something's bothering you."

He sighed heavily. "You do, huh? The first conversation we had when I got in the other day, seems to me you said something about asking my brother."

"That's right. He didn't have it, so I raised it myself. Why?"

"He didn't have it or he said wait until you got an okay from me?"

"He didn't have it. In fact he specifically said he was sure you would cover the expense, but that he didn't have any cash to speak of."

"You're sure about that."

"Absolutely. Why? What's the problem?"

"He didn't say he could let you have some of my dough? Nothing like that?"

"No. As a matter of fact—"

"Yeah? As a matter of fact what?"

"He said you undoubtedly had money around the house, but that he didn't have access to that. He said something ironic to the effect that you wouldn't give a junkie the combination to your safe, not even if he was your brother."

"He said that, huh."

"I don't know that he meant you personally," I said. "The sense of it was that nobody in his right mind would give that information to a drug addict because he couldn't be trusted."

"So he was speaking generally."

"That's how it seemed to me."

"It could have been personal," he said. "And he would have been correct. I wouldn't trust him with that kind of money. My big brother, I'd probably trust him with my life, but cash running into six figures? No, I wouldn't do it."

I didn't say anything.

He said, "I talked to Petey the other day. He was supposed to come out here. He never showed."

"Oh."

"Something else. Day I left he ran me out to the airport. I gave him five thousand dollars. Case he's got any emergencies. So when you asked him for twenty-seven hundred—"

"Less than that. I spoke to him Saturday afternoon and that was before I needed the thousand for the Cassidy girl. I don't know what figure I mentioned. Fifteen hundred or two thousand, most likely."

He shook his head. "Can you make sense out of this? Because I can't. You call him Saturday and he says I'm not coming back until Monday, but go ahead and lay out the money and you'll get it back from me. That's what he says?"

"Yes."

"Now why would he do that? I can see him not wanting to part with any of my dough if he thinks I might be opposed to it. And rather than turn you down and look like a hard case he'll just say he doesn't have it to give. But he's essentially okaying the expense at the same time that he's hanging on to the dough. Am I right?"

"Yes."

"Did you give the impression that you had plenty of cash?"

"No."

"Because I could see him figuring if you got it then you can lay it out. But otherwise . . . Matt, I don't like to say it but I got a bad feeling about this."

"So do I."

"I think he's using."

"It sounds like it."

"He's keeping his distance, he says he'll be over and he doesn't show up, I call him and he's not there. What does that sound like?"

"I haven't seen him at a meeting in a week and a half. Now we don't always go to the same meetings but—"

"But you expect to run into him now and then."

"Yes."

"I give him five grand in case something comes up, and the minute something comes up he says he doesn't have it. What did he spend it on? Or if he's lying, what's he saving it for? Two questions and one answer, way it looks to me. Jay-You-En-Kay. What else?"

"There could be another explanation."

"I'm willing to hear it." He picked up a phone, dialed a number, and stood there holding himself in check while the phone rang. It must have rung ten times before he gave up. "No answer, but it means nothing. When he used to hole up with a bottle he would go days without answering his phone. I asked him once why he didn't at least take it off the hook. Then I'd know he was there, he said. He's a devious bastard, my brother."

"It's the disease."

"The habit, you mean."

"We generally call it a disease. I guess it amounts to the same thing."

"He kicked junk, you know. He was hooked bad and he quit it, but then he got into the booze."

"So he said."

"How long was he sober? Over a year."

"A year and a half."

"You'd think if you could do it that long you could do it forever."

"A day is the most anybody can do it."

"Yeah," he said impatiently. "A day at a time. I know all that, I heard all the slogans. When he was first getting sober Petey was here all the time. Francey and I would sit with him and give him coffee and listen to him run off at the mouth. Everything he heard at a meeting he came back and filled our ears with it, but we didn't mind because he was starting to put his life back together again. Then one day he told me how he couldn't hang out with me so much anymore because it could undercut his sobriety. Now he's somewhere with a bag of dope and a bottle of whiskey and what the hell happened to his sobriety?"

"You don't know that, Kenan."

He turned on me. "What else, for Christ's sake? What's he doing with five grand, buying lottery tickets? I never should have given him that much money. It's too much temptation. Whatever happens to him, it's my fault."

"No," I said. "If you gave him a cigar box full of heroin and said 'Watch this for me until I get back,' then it'd be your fault. That's more temptation than anybody should have to handle. But he's been clean and dry for a year and a half and he knows how to be responsible for his own sobriety. If the money made him nervous he could put it in the bank, or ask somebody in the program to hold it for him. Maybe he went out and maybe he didn't, we don't know yet, but whatever he did you didn't make him do it."

"I made it easy."

"It's never hard. I don't know what a bag of dope costs these days, but you can still get a drink for a couple of dollars, and one's all it takes."

"One wouldn't hold you for very long, though. Still, five thousand dollars ought to keep him going for a hell of a run. What can you spend on liquor, twenty dollars a day if you drink it at home? Two, three times that if you buy it over the bar? Heroin's a more expensive proposition, but even so it's hard to put more than a couple hundred dollars a day in your arm, and it'd take him a while to build his habit back up. Even if he makes a pig of himself, it ought to take him a month to shoot up five grand."

"He didn't use a needle."

"He told you that, huh?"

"It's not true?"

He shook his head. "He told people that, and there was a period when all he did was snort, but he was a needle junkie for a while there. The lie made the habit sound less serious. Plus he was afraid if women knew he used to shoot dope they'd be afraid to go to bed with him. Not that he's been knocking them over like dominoes lately, but you don't want to make it harder on yourself. He figured they'd assume he shared needles and be afraid he was HIV-positive."

"But he didn't share needles?"

"Says he didn't. And he got tested, and he doesn't have the virus."

"What's the matter?"

"Well, I was just thinking. Maybe he did share needles, maybe he never went for the HIV test. He could lie about that, too."

"What about you?"

"What about me?"

"Do you use a needle? Or do you just snort?"

"I'm not a junkie."

"Peter told me you snort a bag of dope about once a month."

"When was this? On the phone Saturday?"

"A week before. We went to a meeting, then had a meal and hung out together."

"And he told you that, huh?"

"He said he was here at your house a few days before that

206

and you were high. He said he called you on it and you denied it."

He lowered his eyes for a moment, lowered his voice, too, when he spoke. "Yeah, it's true," he said. "He did call me on it, and I did deny it. I thought he bought it."

"He didn't."

"No, I guess not. It bothered me to lie about it. It didn't bother me that I did up the dope. I wouldn't do it in front of him and I wouldn't have done it just then if I'd known he was coming over, but it don't hurt anybody, least of all me, if I do up a bag of dope once in a blue moon."

"Whatever you say."

"He said once a month? To tell you the truth, I doubt if it's that much. My guess would be seven, eight, ten times a year. It's never been more than that. I shouldn't have lied to him. I should have said, 'Yeah, I been feeling like shit, so I got off, and so what?' Because I can do it a few times a year and it never comes to more than that, and if he has one little taste he's got the whole habit back and they're stealing his shoes when he nods out in the subway. That happened to him, he woke up on the D train in his socks."

"It's happened to a lot of people."

"Including you?"

"No, but it could have."

"You're an alcoholic, right? I had a drink before you came over here. If you asked me I'd say so, I wouldn't lie about it. Why did I lie about it to my brother?"

"He's your brother."

"Yeah, that's part of it. Oh, shit, man. I'm worried about him."

"Nothing you can do at this point."

"No, what am I gonna do, drive through the streets looking for him? We'll go out together. You look out one side of the car for the fuckers who killed my wife and I'll look out the other side for my brother. How's that for a plan?" He made a face. "In the meantime I owe you money. What did we say, twenty-seven hundred?" He had a roll of hundreds in his pocket and counted out twenty-seven of them, which pretty much depleted the roll. He handed the money to me and I found a place to put it. He said, "What now?"

"I'll stay with it," I said. "Some of what I try will depend on where the police investigation leads, but—"

"No," he cut in, "that's not what I mean. What do you do now? You got a date for dinner, you got something doing in the city, what?"

"Oh." I had to think. "I'll probably go back to my room. I've been on my feet all day, I want to take a shower and change my clothes."

"You plan to walk back? Or will you take the subway?"

"Well, I won't walk."

"Suppose I drive you."

"You don't have to do that."

He shrugged. "I have to do something," he said.

In the car he asked me the location of the famous laundromat and said he wanted to have a look at it. We drove there and he parked the Buick across the street from it and killed the engine. "So we're on a stakeout," he said. "That's what it's called, right? Or is that only on TV?"

"A stakeout generally goes on for hours," I said. "So I hope we're not on one at the moment."

"No, I just wanted to sit here for a minute. I wonder how many times I drove past this place. It never once occurred to me to stop and make a phone call. Matt, you're sure these guys are the same ones who killed the two women and cut the girl?"

"Yes."

"Because this was for profit and the others were strictly, uh, what's the word? Pleasure? Recreation?"

"I know. But the similarities are too specific and too striking. It has to be the same men."

"Why me?"

"What do you mean?"

"I mean why me?"

"Because a drug dealer makes an ideal target, lots of cash and a reason to steer clear of the police. We discussed that before. And one of the men had a thing about drugs. He kept asking Pam if she knew any dealers, if she took drugs. He was evidently obsessed with the subject."

"That's why a drug dealer. That's not why me." He leaned forward, propped his arms on the steering wheel. "Who even knows I'm a dealer? I haven't been arrested, haven't had my name in the papers. My phone's not tapped and my house isn't bugged. I'm positive my neighbors don't have a clue how I make my money. The DEA investigated me a year and a half ago and they dropped the whole thing because they weren't getting anyplace. The NYPD, I don't even think they know I'm alive. You're some degenerate, likes to kill women, wants to get rich knocking off a drug dealer, how do you even know of my existence? That's what I want to know. Why me?"

"I see what you mean."

"I started off thinking I'm the target. You know, that the whole thing begins with someone looking to hurt me and take me off. But that's not true, according to you. It starts with crazies who are getting off on rape and murder. Then they decide to make it pay, and then they decide to go after a drug dealer, and then I'm elected. So I can't get anywhere backtracking people I know professionally, somebody who maybe thinks I screwed him in a transaction and he sees a good way of getting even. I'm not saying there aren't any crazy people dealing in the product, but—"

"No, I follow you. And you're right. You're the target incidentally. They're looking for a dope dealer and you're one they know of."

"But how?" He hesitated. "There was a thought I had."

"Let's hear it."

"Well, I don't think it makes much sense. But I gather my brother tells his story at meetings, right? He sits up in front and tells everybody what he did and where it got him. And I assume he mentions how his brother makes his living. Am I right?"

"Well, I knew Pete had a brother who dealt drugs, but I didn't know your name or where you lived. I didn't even know Pete's last name."

"If you asked him he would have told you. And how hard

would it be to get the rest? 'I think I know your brother. He live in Bushwick?' 'No, Bay Ridge.' 'Oh, yeah? What street?' I don't know. I guess it's farfetched."

"It seems it to me," I said. "I grant you you'll find all kinds at an AA meeting, and there's nothing to stop a serial killer from walking in the doors. God knows a lot of the famous ones were alcoholic, and always under the influence when they did their killing. But I don't know of any of them that ever got sober in the program."

"But it's possible?"

"I suppose so. Most things are. Still, if our friends live here in Sunset Park and Peter went to Manhattan meetings—"

"Yeah, you're right. They live a mile and a half from me and I'm trying to have them chase into Manhattan in order to hear about me. Of course when I said what I said I didn't know they were from Brooklyn."

"When you said what?"

He looked at me, the pain stitched into his forehead. "When I told Petey he ought to stop running his mouth about my business at his meetings. When I said maybe that's how they got onto me, that's how they picked Francine." He turned to look out the window at the laundromat. "It was when he drove me to the airport. It was just a flare-up. He was giving me grief about something, I forget what, and I threw that in his face. He looked for a second as though I just kicked him in the pit of the stomach. Then he said something, you know, indicating it washed right over him, that he wasn't going to take it seriously, he knew I was just spouting out of anger."

He turned the key in the ignition. "Fuck this laundry," he said. "I don't see a lot of people lining up to make phone calls. Let's get out of here, huh?"

"Sure."

And, a block or two farther along: "Suppose he kept mulling it over, brooding on it. Suppose it stayed on his mind. Suppose he wondered if it was true." He darted a glance at me. "You think that's what sent him out looking to cop? 'Cause I'll tell you, if I was Petey, that just might do it."

* * *

Back in Manhattan he said, "I want to go by his place, knock on his door. You want to keep me company?"

The lock wasn't working on the rooming-house door. Kenan drew it open and said, "Great security here. Great place altogether." We entered and climbed two flights of stairs through that flophouse smell of mice and soiled linen. Kenan walked to a door and listened for a moment, knocked on it, called out his brother's name. There was no response. He repeated the process with the same result, tried the door and found it locked.

"I'm afraid what I'll find in there," he said, "and at the same time I'm afraid to walk away."

I found an expired Visa card in my wallet and loided the door with it. Kenan glanced at me with new respect.

The room was empty, and a mess. The bed linen was half on the floor, and clothing was piled in disarray on a wooden chair. I spotted the Big Book and a couple of AA pamphlets on the oak bureau. I didn't see any bottles or drug paraphernalia, but there was a water tumbler on the bedside table and Kenan picked it up and sniffed at it.

"I don't know," he said. "What do you think?"

The glass was dry inside, but I thought I could smell a residue of alcohol. Still, suggestion would account for it. It wouldn't be the first time I'd smelled alcohol when there wasn't any there.

"I don't like poking around his things," Kenan said. "What little he's got, he's entitled to his privacy. I just had this vision of him turning blue with the needle still in his arm, you know what I mean?"

Out on the street he said, "Well, he's got money. He won't have to steal. 'Less he gets into cocaine, that'll take whatever you got, but he never liked coke much. Petey likes the bass notes, likes to get down as deep as you can go."

"I can identify with that."

"Yeah. He runs out of dough, he can always sell Francey's Camry. He hasn't got the title, but it Blue Books at eight or nine grand, so he can probably find somebody'll give him a few hundred for it without papers. That's junkie economics, makes perfect sense."

I told him Peter's joke about the difference between a drunk and a junkie. They'd both steal your wallet, but the junkie would help you look for it.

"Yeah," he said, nodding. "Says it all."

17

Several things happened over the course of the next week or so.

I made three trips to Sunset Park, two of them alone, the third in the company of TJ. At loose ends one afternoon, I beeped him and got a call back almost immediately. We met in the Times Square subway station and rode out to Brooklyn together. We had lunch at a deli and *café con leche* at the Cuban place and walked around some. We talked a lot, and while I didn't learn a great deal about him, he learned a few things about me, assuming he was listening.

While we waited for our train back to the city he said, "Say, you don't have to pay me nothin' for today. On account of we didn't do nothin'."

"Your time has to be worth something."

"If I be workin', but all I was doin' was hangin' around. Man, I been doin' that for free all my life."

Another night I was just about to leave the house and head for a meeting when a call from Danny Boy sent me chasing out to an Italian restaurant in Corona, where three small-time louts had recently blossomed as big spenders. It seemed unlikely—

Corona is in northern Queens, and light years from Sunset Park—but I went anyway and drank San Pellegrino water at the bar and waited for three guys in silk suits to come in and throw their money around.

The TV was on, and at ten o'clock the Channel 5 newscast included a shot of three men who'd just been arrested for the recent robbing and pistol-whipping of a Forty-seventh Street diamond merchant. The bartender said, "Hey, would you look at that! Those assholes were in here the past three nights, spending money like they couldn't get rid of it fast enough. I had a kind of a feeling where it came from."

"They made it the old-fashioned way," the man next to me said. "They stole it."

I was only a few blocks from Shea Stadium, but that still left me hundreds of miles from the Mets, who had lost a close one to the Cubs that afternoon at Wrigley. The Yankees were at home against the Indians. I walked to the subway and went home.

Another time I got a call from Drew Kaplan, who said that Kelly and his colleagues at Brooklyn Homicide wanted Pam to go down to Washington and pay a call at the FBI's National Center for the Analysis of Violent Crime at Quantico. I asked when she was going.

"She's not," he said.

"She refused?"

"At her attorney's suggestion."

"I don't know about that," I said. "The public-relations department was always where the Feebies were strongest, but what I've heard about their division that profiles serial killers is fairly impressive. I think she should go."

"Well," he said, "it's too bad you're not her lawyer. It's her interests I've been engaged to protect, my friend. Anyway, the mountain's coming to Mohammed. They're sending a guy up tomorrow."

"Let me know how it goes," I said, "insofar as that coincides with what you deem to be the best interests of your client."

He laughed. "Don't get hinky, Matt. Why should she have to schlep down to DC? Let him come here."

After the meeting with the profiler he called again to say he was not blown away by the session. "He seemed a little non-chalant to me," Drew said. "Like someone who's only killed two women and slashed a third isn't worth his time. I gather the more of a string a killer puts together, the more it gives them to work with."

"That figures."

"Yeah, but it's small consolation to the people at the end of the string. They'd probably just as soon the cops caught the guy early on instead of letting him provide such interesting items for their data base. He was telling Kelly they've put together a really solid profile of some yutz out on the West Coast. They could tell you he collected stamps as a boy and how old he was when he got his first tattoo. But they still haven't apprehended the son of a bitch and I think he said the current count is forty-two, with four more probables."

"I can see why Ray and his friend seem small-time."

"He wasn't wild about the frequency, either. He said serial killers generally manifest a higher level of activity. That means they don't wait months between victims. He said either they hadn't hit their stride yet or they were infrequent visitors to New York and did the bulk of their killing elsewhere."

"No," I said. "They know the city too well for that."

"Why do you say that?"

"Huh?"

"How do you know how well they knew the city?"

Because they had sent the Khourys chasing all over Brooklyn, but I couldn't mention that. "They used two different outer-borough cemeteries for dumping grounds," I said, "and Forest Park. Who did you ever hear of from out of town who could pick up a girl on Lexington Avenue and wind up in a cemetery in Queens?"

"Anybody could," he said, "if he picked up the wrong girl. Let me think what else he said. He said they were probably in their early thirties, probably abused as children. He came up

Lawrence Block

with a lot of very general stuff. There was one other thing he
said that gave me a chill."

"What's that?"

"Well, this particular guy's been with the division twenty
years, just about since they started it up. He's coming up on
retirement pretty soon and he said he's just as glad."

"Because he's burned out?"

"More than that. He said the rate at which these incidents
are occurring has been increasing all along in a really nasty way.
But the way the curve's shaping up now, they think these cases
are really going to spike between now and the end of the cen-
tury. Sport-killing, he called it. Says they're looking for it to be
the leisure craze of the nineties."

They didn't do this when I first came around, but these
days at AA meetings they generally invite newcomers with less
than ninety days of sobriety to introduce themselves and give
their day count. At most meetings each of these announcements
gets a round of applause. Not at St. Paul's, though, because of
a former member who came every night for two months and
said before each meeting, "My name is Kevin and I'm an alcoholic and I've got one day back. I drank last night but I'm
sober today!" People got sick of applauding this statement, and
at the next business meeting we voted, after much debate, to
drop the applause altogether. "My name is Al," someone will
say, "and I've got eleven days." "Hi, Al," we say.

It was a Wednesday when I walked from Brooklyn Heights
clear out to Bay Ridge and collected my expense money from
Kenan Khoury, and it was the following Tuesday at the eight-
thirty meeting when a familiar voice at the back of the room
said, "My name is Peter and I'm an alcoholic and a drug addict
and I've got two days back."

"Hi, Peter," everybody said.

I had planned to catch up with him during the break but
I got caught up in a conversation with the woman sitting next
to me, and when I turned to look for him he was gone. I called
him from the hotel afterward but he didn't answer. I called his
brother's house.

"Peter's sober," I said. "At least he was an hour ago. I saw him at a meeting."

"I spoke to him earlier today. He said he had most of my money left and nothing bad happened to the car. I told him I didn't give a shit about the money or the car, I cared about him, and he said he was all right. How'd he look to you?"

"I didn't see him. I just heard him speak up, and when I went to look for him he was gone. I just called to let you know he was alive."

He said he appreciated it. Two nights later Kenan called and said he was downstairs in the lobby. "I'm double-parked out front," he said. "You had dinner yet? C'mon downstairs, meet me outside."

In the car he said, "You know Manhattan better than I do. Where do you want to go? Pick a place."

We went to Paris Green on Ninth Avenue. Bryce greeted me by name and gave us a window table, and Gary waved theatrically from the bar. Kenan ordered a glass of wine and I asked for a Perrier.

"Nice place," he said.

After we'd ordered dinner he said, "I don't know, man. I got no reason to be in the city. I just got in the car and drove around and I couldn't think of a single place to go. I used to do that all the time, just drive around, do my part for the oil shortage and the air pollution. You ever do that? Oh, how could you, you don't have a car. Suppose you want to get away for a weekend? What do you do?"

"Rent one."

"Yeah, sure," he said. "I didn't think of that. You do that much?"

"Fairly often when the weather's decent. My girlfriend and I go upstate, or over to Pennsylvania."

"Oh, you got a girlfriend, huh? I was wondering. Two of you been keeping company for a long time?"

"Not too long."

"What's she do, if you don't mind my asking."

"She's an art historian."

"Very good," he said. "Must be interesting."

217

Lawrence Block

"She seems to find it interesting."

"I mean she must be interesting. An interesting person."

"Very," I said.

He was looking better this evening, his hair barbered and his face shaved, but there was still an air of weariness about him, with a current of restlessness moving beneath it.

He said, "I don't know what to do with myself. I sit around the house and it just makes me nuts. My wife's dead, my brother's doing God knows what, my business is going to hell, and I don't know what to do."

"What's the matter with your business?"

"Maybe nothing, maybe everything. I set up something on this trip I just made. I got a shipment due sometime next week."

"Maybe you shouldn't tell me about it."

"You ever have opiated hash? If you were strictly a boozer you probably didn't."

"No."

"That's what I got coming in. Grown in eastern Turkey and coming our way via Cyprus, or so they tell me."

"What's the problem?"

"The problem is I should have walked away from the deal. There are people in it I got no reason to trust, and I went in on it for the worst possible reason. I did it to have something to do."

I said, "I can work for you in the matter of your wife's death. I can do that irrespective of how you make your living, and I can even break a few laws on your behalf. But I can't work for you or with you as far as your profession is concerned."

"Petey told me that working for me would lead him back to using. Is that a factor for you?"

"No."

"It's just something you wouldn't touch."

"I guess so, yes."

He thought for a moment, then nodded. "I can appreciate that," he said. "I can respect it. On the one hand, I'd like to have you with me because I'd be confident with you backing my play. And it's very lucrative. You know that."

"Of course."

218

"But it's dirty, isn't it? I'm aware of it. How could I not be? It's a dirty business."

"So get out of it."

"I'm thinking about it. I never figured to make it my life's work. I always figured another couple of years, a few more deals, a little more money in the offshore account. Familiar story, right? I wish they'd just legalize it, make it simple for everybody."

"A cop said the same thing just the other day."

"Never happen. Or maybe it will. I'll tell you, I'd welcome it."

"Then what would you do?"

"Sell something else." He laughed. "Guy I met this past trip, Lebanese like me, I hung out with him and his wife in Paris. 'Kenan,' he says, 'you got to get out of this business, it deadens your soul.' He wants me to throw in with him. You know what he does? He's an arms dealer, for Christ's sake, he sells weapons. 'Man,' I said, 'my customers just kill themselves with the product. Your customers kill other people.' 'Not the same,' he insisted. 'I deal with nice people, respectable people.' And he tells me all these important people he knows, CIA, secret services of other countries. So maybe I'll get out of the dope business and become a big-time merchant of death. You like that better?"

"Is that your only choice?"

"Seriously? No, of course not. I could buy and sell anything. I don't know, my old man may have been slightly full of shit with the Phoenician business, but there's no question our people are traders all over the world. When I dropped out of college, first thing I did was travel. I went visiting relatives. The Lebanese are scattered all over the planet, man. I got an aunt and uncle in Yucatán, I got cousins all through Central and South America. I went over to Africa, some relatives on my mother's side are in a country called Togo. I never heard of it until I went there. My relatives operate the black market for currency in Lomé, that's the capital of Togo. They've got this suite of offices in a building in downtown Lomé. No sign in the lobby and you got to walk up a flight of stairs, but it's pretty much out in the open. All day long people are coming in with money to change, dollars, pounds, francs, traveler's checks. Gold, they buy and sell gold, weigh it and figure the price.

"All day long the money goes back and forth over the long table they got there. I couldn't believe how much money they handled. I was a kid, I never saw a lot of cash, and I'm looking at tons of money. See, they only make like one or two percent on a transaction, but the volume is enormous.

"They lived in this walled compound on the edge of town. It had to be huge to accommodate all the servants. I'm a kid from Bergen Street, I grew up sharing a room with my brother, and here are these cousins of mine and they've got something like five servants for each member of the family. That's including children. No exaggeration. I was uncomfortable at first, I thought it was wasteful, but it was explained to me. If you were rich you had an obligation to employ a lot of people. You were creating jobs, you were doing something for the people.

"'Stay,' they told me. They wanted to take me into the business. If I didn't like Togo, they had in-laws with the same kind of operation in Mali. 'But Togo's nicer,' they said."

"Could you still go?"

"That's the sort of thing you do when you're twenty years old, start a new life in a new country."

"What are you, thirty-two?"

"Thirty-three. That's a little old for an entry-level slot."

"You might not have to start in the mailroom."

He shrugged. "Funny thing is Francine and I discussed it. She had a problem with it because she was afraid of blacks. The idea of being one of a handful of white people in a black nation was frightening to her. She said, like, suppose they decide to take over? I said, honey, what's to take over? It's their country. They already own it. But she was not completely rational on the subject." His voice hardened. "And look who she got in a truck with, look who killed her. White guys. All your life you fear one thing and something else sneaks up on you." His eyes locked with mine. "It's like they didn't just kill her, they obliterated her. She ceased to exist. I didn't even see a body, I saw parts, chunks. I went to my cousin's clinic in the middle of the night and turned the chunks into ashes. She's gone and there's this hole in my life and I don't know what to put in it."

"They say time takes time," I said.

"It can take some of mine. I got time I don't know what to do with. I'm alone in the house all day and I find myself talking to myself. Out loud, I mean."

"People do that when they're used to having somebody around. You'll get over it."

"Well, if I don't, so what? If I'm talking to myself who's gonna hear me, right?" He sipped from his water glass. "Then there's sex," he said. "I don't know what the hell to do about sex. I have the desire, you know? I'm a young guy, it's natural."

"A minute ago you were too old to start a new life in Africa."

"You know what I mean. I have desires and I not only don't know what to do about them, I don't feel right about *having* them. It feels disloyal to want to go to bed with a woman whether I actually do it or not. And who would I go to bed with if I wanted to? What am I gonna do, sweet-talk some woman in a bar? Go to a massage parlor, pay some cross-eyed Korean girl to get me off? Go out on fucking *dates,* take some woman to a movie, make conversation with her? I try to picture myself doing that and I figure I'd rather stay home and jerk off, only I won't do that either because even *that* seems like it would be disloyal." He sat back abruptly, embarrassed. "I'm sorry," he said. "I didn't mean to spout all this crap at you. I hadn't planned on saying any of that. I don't know where it came from."

I called my art historian when I got back to the hotel. She'd had her class that night and wasn't back yet. I left a message on her machine and wondered if she would call.

We'd had a bad time of it a few nights before. After dinner we'd rented a movie that she wanted to see and I didn't, and maybe I was bitter about that, I don't know. Whatever it was, there was something wrong between us. After the movie ended she made an off-color remark and I suggested she might make an effort to sound a little less like a whore. That would have been an acceptable rejoinder under ordinary circumstances, but I said it like I meant it and she said something suitably stinging in return.

I apologized and so did she and we agreed it was nothing, but it didn't feel that way, and when it got to be time to go to bed we did so on opposite sides of town. When we spoke the next day we didn't say anything about it, and we still hadn't, and it hung in the air between us whenever we talked, and even when we didn't.

She called me back around eleven-thirty. "I just got in," she said. "A couple of us went out for a drink after class. How was your day?"

"All right," I said, and we talked about it for a few minutes. Then I asked if it was too late for me to drop over.

"Oh, gee," she said. "I'd like to see you, too."

"But it's too late."

"I think so, hon. I'm wiped out and I just want to take a quick shower and pass out. Is that okay?"

"Sure."

"Talk to you tomorrow?"

"Uh-huh. Sleep well."

I hung up and said, "I love you," speaking to the empty room, hearing the words bounce off the walls. We had become quite adept at purging the phrase from our speech when we were together, and I listened to myself saying it now and wondered if it was true.

I felt something but couldn't work out what it was. I took a shower and got out and dried off, and standing there looking at my face in the mirror over the bathroom sink I realized what it was I felt.

There are two midnight meetings every night. The closest one was on West Forty-sixth Street and I got there just as they were beginning the meeting. I helped myself to a cup of coffee and sat down, and minutes later I was hearing a voice I recognized say, "My name is Peter and I'm an alcoholic and a drug addict." Good, I thought. "And I have one day back," he said.

Not so good. Tuesday he'd had two days, today he had one. I thought about how difficult it must be, trying to get back in the lifeboat and not being able to get a grip on it. And then I stopped thinking about Peter Khoury because I was there for my own benefit, not for his.

I listened intently to the qualification, although I couldn't tell you what I heard, and when the speaker finished up and opened the meeting I got my hand up right away. I got called on and said, "My name's Matt and I'm an alcoholic. I've been sober a couple of years and I've come a long way since I walked in the door and sometimes I forget that I'm still pretty fucked up. I'm going through a difficult phase in my relationship and I didn't even realize it until a little while ago. Before I came over here I felt uncomfortable and I had to stand under a shower for five minutes to dope out what it was I felt. And then I saw that it was fear, that I was afraid.

"I don't even know what I'm afraid of. I have a feeling if I let myself go I'll find out I'm afraid of every goddamned thing in the world. I'm afraid to be in a relationship and I'm afraid to be out of it. I'm afraid I'll wake up one of these days and look in the mirror and see an old man staring back at me. That I'll die alone in that room some day and nobody'll find me until the smell starts coming through the walls.

"So I got dressed and came over here because I don't want to drink and I don't want to feel like this, and after all these years I still don't know why it helps to run off at the mouth like this, but it does. Thank you."

I figured I probably sounded like an emotional basket case, but you learn not to give a rat's ass what you sound like, and I didn't. It was particularly easy to spew it all in that room because I didn't know anybody there other than Peter Khoury, and if he only had a day he probably couldn't track complete sentences yet, let alone remember them five minutes later.

And maybe I didn't sound that bad after all. At the end we stood and said the Serenity Prayer, and afterward a man two rows in front of me came up to me and asked for my phone number. I gave him one of my cards. "I'm out a lot," I said, "but you can leave a message."

We chatted for a minute, and then I went looking for Peter Khoury, but he was gone. I didn't know if he'd left before the meeting ended or ducked out immediately after, but either way he was gone.

I had a hunch he didn't want to see me, and I could understand that. I remembered the difficulties I'd had at the beginning, putting a few days together, then drinking, then starting all over again. He had the added disadvantage of having been sober for a stretch, and the humiliation of having lost what he'd had. With all of that going for him, it would probably take a while before he could work his way up to low self-esteem.

In the meantime he was sober. He only had a day, but in a sense that's all you've ever got.

Saturday afternoon I took a break from TV sports and called a telephone operator. I told her I'd lost the card telling me how to engage and disengage Call Forwarding. I envisioned her checking the records, determining that I'd never signed up for the service, and calling 911 to order the hotel ringed by squad cars. "Put that phone down, Scudder, and come out with your hands up!"

Before I could even finish the thought she had cued a recording, and a computer-generated voice was explaining what I had to do. I couldn't write it all down as fast as it came at me, so I had to call a second time and repeat the procedure.

Just before I left the house to go over to Elaine's, I followed the directions, arranging things so that any calls to my phone would be automatically transferred to her line. Or at least that was the theory. I didn't have a great deal of faith in the process.

She'd bought tickets to a play at the Manhattan Theatre Club, a murky and moody play by a Yugoslavian playwright. I had the feeling that some of it was lost in translation, but what came over the footlights still retained a lot of brooding intensity. It took me through dark passages in the self without troubling to turn the lights on.

The experience was even more of an ordeal than it might otherwise have been because they staged it without an intermission. That got us out of there by a quarter of ten, which was not a moment too soon, but it put us through the wringer in the process. The actors took their curtain calls, the house lights came up, and we shuffled out of there like zombies.

"Strong medicine," I said.

"Or strong poison. I'm sorry, I've been picking a lot of winners lately, haven't I? That movie that you hated and now this."

"I didn't hate this," I said. "I just feel as though I went ten rounds with it, and I got hit in the face a lot."

"What do you figure the message was?"

"It probably comes through best in Serbo-Croatian. The message? I don't know. That the world's a rotten place, I guess."

"You don't need to go to a play for that," she said. "You can just read the paper."

"Ah," I said. "Maybe it's different in Yugoslavia."

We had dinner near the theater, and the mood of the play cloaked us. Halfway through I said, "I want to say something. I want to apologize for the other night."

"That's over, honey."

"I don't know if it is. I've been in a strange mood lately. Some of it has to be this case. We had a couple breaks, I felt as though I was making progress, and now everything's stuck again and I feel stuck myself. But I don't want it to affect us. You're important to me, our relationship is important to me."

"To me, too."

We talked a little and things seemed to lighten up, although the play's mood was not easily set aside. Then we went back to her place and she checked her messages while I used the bathroom. When I came out she had a curious expression on her face.

She said, "Who's Walter?"

"Walter."

"Just calling to say hello, nothing important, wanted to let you know he was alive, and he'll probably give you a call later."

"Oh," I said. "Fellow I met at a meeting the night before last. He's fairly newly sober."

"And you gave him this number?"

"No," I said. "Why would I do that?"

"That's what I was wondering."

"Oh," I said, as it dawned on me. "Well, I guess it works."

"You guess what works?"

"Call Forwarding. I told you the Kongs gave me Call Forwarding when they were playing games with the phone company. I put it on this afternoon."

"So your calls would come here."

"That's right. I didn't have a lot of faith that it would work, but evidently it does. What's the matter?"

"Nothing."

"Are you sure?"

"Of course. Do you want to hear the message? I can play it back again."

"Not if that's all it said."

"It's all right to erase it, then?"

"Go ahead."

She did, then said, "I wonder what he thought when he dialed your number and there was an answering machine with a woman's voice."

"Well, he evidently didn't think he had the wrong number, or he wouldn't have left a message."

"I wonder who he thinks I am."

"A mysterious woman with a sexy voice."

"He probably thinks we're living together. Unless he knows you live alone."

"All he knows about me is I'm sober and crazy."

"Why crazy?"

"Because I was dumping a lot of garbage at the meeting I met him at. For all he knows I'm a priest and you're the housekeeper at the rectory."

"That's a game we haven't tried. Priest and housekeeper. 'Bless me, Father, for I have been a very naughty girl and I probably need a good spanking.'"

"I wouldn't be surprised."

She grinned, and I reached for her, and the phone picked that moment to ring. "You answer it," she said. "It's probably Walter."

I picked up the phone and a man with a deep voice asked to speak to Miss Mardell. I handed her the receiver without a word and walked into the other room. I stood at the window and looked at the lights on the other side of the East River. After a couple of minutes she came and stood beside me. She didn't allude to the call, nor did I. Then ten minutes later the phone rang again and she answered it and it was for me. It was Walter, just using the phone a lot the way they encourage newcomers to do. I didn't stay on with him long, and when I got off I said, "I'm sorry. It was a bad idea."

"Well, you're here a lot. People ought to be able to reach you." A few minutes later she said, "Take it off the hook. Nobody has to reach either of us tonight."

In the morning I dropped in on Joe Durkin and wound up going out for lunch with him and two friends of his from the Major Crimes Squad. I went back to my hotel and stopped at the desk for my messages, but there weren't any. I went upstairs and picked up a book, and at twenty after three the phone rang.

Elaine said, "You forgot to take off Call Forwarding."

"Oh, for Christ's sake," I said. "No wonder there weren't any messages. I just got home, I was out all morning, it slipped my mind completely. I was going to come straight home and fix it and I forgot. It must have been driving you crazy all day."

"No, but—"

"But how did you get through? Wouldn't it just bounce your call back and give you a busy signal if you called here?"

"It did the first time I tried. I called the desk downstairs and they patched the call through."

"Oh."

"Evidently it doesn't forward calls through the switchboard downstairs."

"Evidently not."

"TJ called earlier. But that's not important. Matt, Kenan Khoury just called. You have to call him right away. He said it's really urgent."

"He did?"

"He said life or death, and probably death. I don't know what that means, but he sounded serious."

I called right away, and Kenan said, "Matt, thank God.

Don't go nowhere, I got my brother on the other line. You're at home, right? Okay, stay on the line, I'll be with you in a second." There was a click, and then a minute or so later there was another click and he was back. "He's on his way," he said. "He's coming over to your hotel, he'll be right out in front."

"What's the matter with him?"

"With Petey? Nothing, he's fine. He's gonna bring you out to Brighton Beach. Nobody's got time to dick around with the subway today."

"What's in Brighton Beach?"

"A whole lot of Russians," he said. "How do I put this? One of 'em just called to say he's going through business difficulties similar to what I went through."

That could only mean one thing, but I wanted to make sure.

"His wife?"

"Worse. I gotta go, I'll meet you there."

18

Late in September Elaine and I had spent an idyllic afternoon in Brighton Beach. We rode the Q train to the end of the line and walked along Brighton Beach Avenue, browsing in the produce markets, window-shopping, then exploring the side streets with their modest frame houses and a network of back streets, little walks and alleys and paths and ways. The bulk of the population consisted of Russian Jews, many of them very recent arrivals, and the neighborhood had felt extremely foreign while remaining quintessentially New York. We ate at a Georgian restaurant, then walked on the boardwalk clear to Coney Island, watching people hardier than ourselves bobbing in the ocean. Then we spent an hour at the Aquarium, and then we went home.

If we had passed Yuri Landau in the street that day I don't suppose we'd have looked at him twice. He would have looked at home there, as he must have once looked in the streets of Kiev or Odessa. He was a big man, broad in the chest, with a face that might have served as the model for an idealized worker in one of those murals from the days of Socialist Realism. A broad forehead, high cheekbones, sharply angled facial planes, and a prominent jaw. His hair was a medium brown, and lank; he was given to tossing his head to get his hair out of his face.

He was in his late forties, and he had been in America for ten years. He'd come over with his wife and his four-year-old daughter, Ludmilla. He'd done some sort of black-market trading in the Soviet Union, and in Brooklyn he gravitated easily into various marginal enterprises, and before long began trafficking in narcotics. He had done well, but then it is a business in which nobody breaks even. If you don't get killed or imprisoned, you generally do very well.

Four years ago his wife had been diagnosed with metastasized ovarian cancer. Chemotherapy had kept her alive for two and a half years. She had hoped to live to see her daughter graduate from intermediate school, but she died in the fall. Ludmilla, who now called herself Lucia, had graduated in the spring, and was now a member of the freshman class of Chichester Academy, a small private high school for girls located in Brooklyn Heights. The tuition was high, but so were the academic requirements, and Chichester had an excellent record at placing its graduates in Ivy League colleges, as well as women's colleges like Bryn Mawr and Smith.

When he'd started calling people in the business to warn them about the possibility of kidnapping, Kenan had very nearly not called Yuri Landau. They were not close, they barely knew each other, but more to the point Kenan saw Landau as invulnerable. The man's wife was already dead.

He hadn't even thought about the daughter. Still, he'd made the call, and Landau had taken it as confirmation of a course of action he had adopted when he'd first sent Lucia off to Chichester. Instead of letting her take subways or buses, he'd arranged to have a car service pick her up every morning at seven-thirty and collect her in front of Chichester every afternoon at a quarter to three. If she wanted to go to a friend's house the car service would take her there, and she was instructed to call them when she wanted to come home. If she wanted to go anywhere in the neighborhood, she usually took the dog with her. The dog was a Rhodesian Ridgeback, and actually very gentle, but looked ferocious enough to constitute a powerful deterrent.

Early that afternoon, the telephone rang in the office of Chichester Academy. A well-spoken gentleman explained that he was an assistant to Mr. Landau and was requesting that the school dismiss Ludmilla half an hour early because of a family emergency. "I've made arrangements with the car service," he assured the woman to whom he spoke, "and they'll have a vehicle waiting in front of the school at two-fifteen, although it probably will not be the car and driver she had this morning." And, he added, if there were any questions she was not to call Mr. Landau's residence; instead she could reach him, Mr. Pettibone, at a number he would give her now.

She didn't have to call the number, because there was no problem following his request. She summoned Lucia (no one at school knew her as Ludmilla) to the office and told her she would be dismissed early. At ten minutes after two the woman looked out the window and saw that a dark green truck or van was parked directly in front of the school's entrance on Pineapple Street. It was quite unlike the late-model GM sedans that normally brought the girl in the morning and took her away in the afternoon, but it was clearly the right vehicle. The car service's name and address was plainly visible in white letters on its side. Chaverim Livery Service, with an address on Ocean Avenue. And the driver, who walked around the truck so that he could hold the door for Lucia, wore a blue blazer the way they always did, and had one of those caps.

For her part, Lucia got into the van without hesitation. The driver closed the door, walked around the vehicle, got behind the wheel, and drove to the corner of Willow Street, at which point the woman stopped watching.

At a quarter to three the rest of the school was dismissed, and a few minutes later Lucia's regular driver showed up in the gray Oldsmobile Regency Brougham in which he had driven Lucia to school that morning. He waited patiently at the curb, knowing that Lucia was routinely as much as fifteen minutes late leaving the building. He would have waited that long and longer without complaint, but one of Lucia's classmates recognized him and told him he must have made a mistake. "Because she was dismissed early," she said. "She got picked up like half an hour ago."

"Come on," he said, thinking she was playing a joke on him.

"It's true! Her father called the office and one of your cars already came and picked her up. Ask Miss Severance if you don't believe me."

The driver did not go in and confirm this with Miss Severance; if he had, that woman would almost certainly have called the Landau residence, and, quite possibly, the police. Instead he used his own car radio to call his dispatcher on Ocean Avenue and ask him what the hell was going on. "If she needed an early pickup," he said, "then you coulda sent me. Or if you can't get me, at least tell me to skip my regular pickup."

The dispatcher, of course, didn't know what the driver was talking about. When she got the gist of it she figured out the only thing that made sense to her, that for some reason Landau had called another car service. She might have let it go at that. Maybe all their lines had been busy, maybe he'd been in a rush, maybe he'd picked the child up himself and hadn't been able to call off the scheduled car. But something evidently bothered her, because she looked up Yuri Landau's number and called him.

At first Yuri didn't get what all the fuss was about. So somebody at Chaverim made a mistake, and two cars went instead of one, and the second driver made the trip for nothing. How was that something to call him about? Then he began to realize that something out of the ordinary was going on. He got as much information as he could from the dispatcher, said he was sorry if there had been any inconvenience, and got her off the line.

Next he called the school, and when he spoke with Miss Severance and heard about the call from his assistant, Mr. Pettibone, there was really no question about it. Someone had managed to lure his daughter out of the school and into a van. Someone had kidnapped her.

At this point the Severance woman also figured it out, but Landau dissuaded her from calling the police. It would be best

232

handled privately, he said, improvising as he went along. "Relatives on her mother's side, extremely Orthodox, you could call them religious fanatics. They've been after me to pull her out of Chichester and send her to some crazy kosher school in Borough Park. Don't worry about a thing, I'm sure she'll be back in your school tomorrow."

Then he hung up the phone and started to tremble.

They had his daughter. What did they want? He'd give them what they wanted, the bastards, he'd give them anything he had. But who were they? And what in God's name did they want?

Hadn't someone said something just a few weeks ago about a kidnapping?

He remembered, then, and called Kenan. Who called me.

Yuri Landau had the penthouse apartment in a twelve-story brick co-op on Brightwater Court. In the tiled lobby, two thick-bodied young Russians in tweed jackets and caps braced us as we entered. Peter ignored the uniformed doorman and told the others that his name was Khoury and Mr. Landau was expecting us. One of them rode up with us in the elevator.

By the time we got there, around four-thirty, Yuri had just received his first call from the kidnappers. He was still reacting to it. "A million dollars," he cried. "Where am I going to get a million dollars? Who's doing this, Kenan? Is it niggers? Is it those crazies from Jamaica?"

"It's white guys," Kenan said.

"My Luschka," he said. "How could this happen? What kind of a country is this?" He broke off when he saw us. "You're the brother," he said to Peter. "And you?"

"Matthew Scudder."

"You been working for Kenan. Good. Thanks to both of you for coming. But how did you get in? You walked right in? I had two men in the lobby, they were supposed to—" He caught sight of the man who had come up with us. "Oh, there you are, Dani, that's a good boy. Go back down to the lobby and keep an eye out." To no one in particular he said, "Now I post guards. The horse is stolen so I lock the barn. For what? What can they take from me now? God took my wife, the dirty bastard, and these other bastards take my Luddy, my Luschka." He turned to Kenan. "And if I post men downstairs from the time you called me, what good does it do? They get her out of school, they steal her away under everybody's nose. I wish I did what you did. You sent her out of the country, yes?"

Kenan and I looked at each other.

"What's this? You told me you sent your wife out of the country."

Kenan said, "That was the story we settled on, Yuri."

"Story? Why did you need a story? What happened?"

"She was kidnapped."

"Your wife."

"Yes."

"How much did they hit you for?"

"They asked a million. We negotiated, we settled on a lower figure."

"How much?"

"Four hundred thousand."

"And you paid the money? You got her back?"

"I paid."

"Kenan," he said. He took him by the shoulders. "Tell me, please. You got her back, yes?"

"Dead," Kenan said.

"Oh, no," Yuri said. He reeled as if from a blow, threw up an arm to shield his face. "No," he said. "Don't tell me that."

"Mr. Landau—"

He ignored me, took Kenan by the arm. "But you paid," he said. "You gave them an honest count? You didn't try to chisel them?"

"I paid, Yuri. They killed her anyway."

His shoulders sagged. "Why?" he demanded, not of us but of that dirty bastard God who took his wife. *"Why?"*

I stepped in and said, "Mr. Landau, these are very dangerous men, vicious and unpredictable. They've killed at least two women in addition to Mrs. Khoury. As things stand, they haven't got the slightest intention of releasing your daughter alive. I'm afraid there's a strong possibility that she's already dead."

"No."

"If she's alive we have a chance. But you have to decide how you want to handle this."

"What do you mean?"

"You could call the police."

"They said no cops."

"Naturally they'd say that."

"The last thing I want is cops here, poking into my life. As soon as I come up with the ransom money they'll want to know where it came from. But if it gets my daughter back ... What do you think? We have a better chance if we call the cops?"

"You might have a better chance of catching the men who took her."

"To hell with that. What about getting her back?"

She's dead, I thought, but told myself that I didn't know it, and that he didn't have to hear it. I said, "I don't think police involvement at this stage would increase the chance of recovering your daughter alive. I think it might have the opposite effect. If the cops come in and the kidnappers know about it, they'll cut their losses and run. And they won't leave the girl alive."

"So fuck the cops. We'll do it ourselves. Now what?"

"Now I have to make a phone call."

"Go ahead. Wait, I want to keep the line open. They called, I talked with him, I had a million questions and he hung up on me. 'Stay off the line. We'll get back to you.' Use my daughter's phone, it's through that door. Kids, on the phone all the time, you could never reach the house. I had that other thing, Call Waiting, drove everybody crazy. All the time clicking in your ear, telling this one to hold on, you have to take a call. Terrible. I got rid of it, got her her own phone, she could stay on it all she wanted. God, take anything I got, just give her back to me!"

I called TJ's beeper and punched in the number on the Landau girl's Snoopy figural phone. Snoopy and Michael Jackson both seemed to play key roles in her personal mythology, judging from the room's decor. I paced, waiting for my call, and found a family photo on the white enamel dressing table, Yuri and a dark-haired woman and a girl with dark hair that fell past her shoulders in cascading ringlets. Lucia looked to be about ten in the photo. Another photo showed her alone, older, and looked to have been taken last June at graduation. Her hair was shorter in the more recent photo and her face looked serious and mature for her years.

The phone rang. I picked it up and he said, "Yo, who wants TJ?"

"It's Matt," I said.

"Hey, my man! What's goin', Owen?"

"Serious business," I said. "It's an emergency, and I need your help."

"You got it."

"Can you get hold of the Kongs?"

"You mean right away? They sometimes hard to reach. Jimmy Hong got a beeper, but he don't always have it with him."

"See if you can get him and give him this number."

"Sure. That's it?"

"No," I said. "Do you remember the laundromat we went to last week?"

"Sure."

"Do you know how to get there?"

"R train to Forty-fifth, a block to Fifth Avenue, four, five blocks to the wishee-washee."

"I didn't realize you were paying attention."

"Shit," he said. "Man, I allus payin' attention. I's attentive."

"Not just resourceful?"

"Attentive *an'* resourceful."

"Can you get out there right away?"

"Right now? Or call the Kongs first?"

"Call them, then go. Are you near the subway?"

"Man, I always be near the subway. I talkin' to you on the phone the Kongs liberated, Forty-third an' Eighth."

"Call me as soon as you get out there."

"'Kay. Somethin' big goin' down, huh?"

"Very big," I said.

I left the bedroom door open so that I could hear the phone if it rang and went back into the living room. Peter Khoury was at the window looking out at the ocean. We hadn't talked much on the drive, but he'd volunteered the information that he hadn't had a drink or a drug since the meeting I'd seen him at. "So I got five days," he said.

"That's great."

"That's the party line, isn't it? One day or twenty years, you tell somebody your time and they tell you it's great. 'You're sober today and that's what counts.' Fucked if I know what counts anymore."

I went over to Kenan and Yuri and we talked. The bedroom phone didn't ring, but after perhaps fifteen minutes the one in the living room sounded and Yuri answered it. He said, "Yeah, this is Landau," and glanced significantly at me, then tossed his head to get the hair out of his eyes. "I want to talk to my daughter," he said. "You got to let me talk to my daughter."

I went over and he handed me the phone. I said, "I hope the girl's alive."

There was a silence, then, "Who the fuck are you?"

"I'm the best chance you've got of making a nice clean exchange, the girl for the money. But you'd better not hurt her, and if you're playing any games they better get called right now on account of rain. Because she has to be alive and well for the deal to happen."

"Fuck this shit," he said. There was a pause and I thought he was going to say more, but he hung up.

I reported the conversation to Yuri and Kenan. Yuri was agitated, concerned that I was going to screw things up by taking a hard line. Kenan told him I knew what I was doing. I wasn't sure he was right, but I was glad for the support.

"The important thing right now is to keep her alive," I said. "They have to know that they won't be able to rig the exchange on their terms, without even demonstrating that they've got a living hostage for us to ransom."

"But if you make them mad—"

"They're already madder than hatters. I know what you're saying, you don't want to give them an excuse to kill her, but they don't need an excuse. It's already on their agenda. They have to have a reason to keep her alive."

Kenan backed me up. "I did everything their way," he said. "Everything they wanted. They sent her back—" He hesitated, and I finished the sentence mentally: "in pieces." But he hadn't shared that aspect of Francine's death with Yuri and didn't do so now. "—sent her back dead," he said.

"We're going to need cash," I said. "What do you have? What can you raise?"

"God, I don't know," he said. "Cash I got damn little of. Do the bastards want cocaine? I got fifteen kilos of slab ten minutes from here." He looked at Kenan. "You want to buy it? Tell me what you want to pay me."

Kenan shook his head. "I'll lend you what I got in the safe, Yuri. I'm in the bucket already waiting for a hash deal to fall apart. I fronted some money and I think it was a mistake."

"What kind of hash?"

"Out of Turkey via Cyprus. Opiated hash. What's the difference, it ain't gonna happen. I got maybe one hundred large in the safe. Time comes I'll run back to the house and get it. You're welcome to it."

"You know I'm good for it."

"Don't worry about it."

Landau blinked away tears, and when he tried to speak his voice was choked up. He could barely get the words out. He said, "Listen to this man. I hardly know him, this fucking Arab here, he's giving me a hundred thousand dollars." He took Kenan in his arms and hugged him, sobbing.

The phone rang in Lucia's room. I went to answer it.

TJ, calling from Brooklyn. "At the laundromat," he said. "What I do? Wait for some white dude to come in an' use the phone?"

"That's right. He should get there sooner or later. If you could park yourself at the restaurant across the street and keep an eye on the laundromat entrance—"

"Do better than that, man. I be right here in the laundromat, just another cat waitin' on his clothes. Neighborhood here's enough different colors so's I don't stick out too much. Kongs ever call you?"

"No. Did you reach them?"

"Beeped 'em and put your number in, but if Jimmy don't have the beeper with him, it's like it ain't beepin'."

"Like that tree in the forest."

"Say what?"

"Never mind."

"I be in touch," he said.

When the next call came in Yuri answered it, said "Just a minute," and passed it to me. The voice I heard was different this time, softer, more cultured. There was a nastiness in it but less of the obvious anger of the previous speaker.

"I understand we have a new player in the game," he said. "I don't believe we've been introduced."

"I'm a friend of Mr. Landau's. My name's not important."

"One likes to know who's on the other side."

"In a sense," I said, "we're on the same side, aren't we? We both want the exchange to go through."

"Then all you have to do is follow instructions."

"No, it's not that simple."

"Of course it is. We tell you what to do and you do it. If you ever want to see the girl again."

"You have to convince me that she's alive."

"You have my word on it."

"I'm sorry," I said.

"It's not good enough?"

"You lost a lot of credibility when you returned Mrs. Khoury in poor condition."

There was a pause. Then, "How interesting. You don't sound very Russian, you know. Nor do the tones of Brooklyn echo in your speech. There were special circumstances with Mrs. Khoury. Her husband tried to haggle, in the nature of his race. He sliced the price, and we in turn—well, you can finish that thought yourself, can't you?"

And Pam Cassidy, I thought. What did she do that provoked you? But what I said was, "We won't argue the price."

"You'll pay the million."

"For the girl, alive and well."

"I assure you she's both."

"And I still need more than your word. Put her on the phone, let her father talk to her."

"I'm afraid that won't—" he began, and the recorded voice of a NYNEX announcer cut in to ask for more money. "I'll call you back," he said.

"Out of quarters? Give me your number, I'll call you."

He laughed and broke the connection.

I was alone in the apartment with Yuri when the next call came. Kenan and Peter were out with one of the two guards from downstairs, looking to raise what cash they could. Yuri had given them a list of names and phone numbers, and they had some sources of their own. It would have been simpler if we could have made the calls from the penthouse, but we only had the two phone lines and I wanted to keep both of them open.

"You're not in the business," Yuri said. "You're some kind of cop, yes?"

"Private."

"Private, so you been working for Kenan. Now you're working for me, right?"

"I'm just working. I'm not looking to be on the payroll, if that's what you mean."

He waved the issue aside. "This is a good business," he said, "but also it's no good. You know?"

"I think so."

"I want to be out of it. That's one reason I got no cash. I make lots of money, but I don't want it in cash and I don't want it in goods. I own parking lots, I own a restaurant, I spread it out, you know? In a little while I'm out of the dope business altogether. A lot of Americans start out as gangsters, yes? And wind up legitimate businessmen."

"Sometimes."

"Some are gangsters forever. But not all. Wasn't for Devorah, I'd be out of it already."

"Your wife?"

"The hospital bills, the doctors, my God, what it cost. No insurance. We were greenhorns, what did we know from Blue Cross? Doesn't matter. Whatever it cost I paid. I was glad to pay it. I would have paid more to keep her alive, I would have paid anything. I would have sold the fillings out of my teeth if I could have bought her another day. I paid hundreds of thousands of dollars and she had every day the doctors could give her, and what days they were, the poor woman, what she suffered through. But she wanted all the life she could get, you know?" He wiped a broad hand across his forehead. He was about to say something else but the phone rang. Wordless, he pointed at it.

I picked it up.

The same man said, "Shall we try again? I'm afraid the girl cannot come to the phone. That's out of the question. How else can we reassure you of her well-being?"

I covered the mouthpiece. "Something your daughter would know."

He shrugged. "The dog's name?"

Into the phone I said, "Have her tell you—no, wait a minute." I covered the phone and said, "They could know that. They've been shadowing her for a week or more, they know your schedule, they've undoubtedly seen her walking the dog, heard her call him by name. Think of something else."

"We had a dog before this one," he said. "A little black-and-white one, it got hit by a car. She was just a small thing herself when we had that dog."

"But she would remember it?"

"Who could forget? She loved the dog."

"The dog's name," I said into the phone, "and the name of the dog before this one. Have her describe both dogs and furnish their names."

He was amused. "One dog won't do. It has to be two."

"Yes."

"So that you may be doubly reassured. I'll humor you, my friend."

I wondered what he would do.

He'd have called from a pay phone. I was certain of that. He hadn't stayed on the line long enough for his quarter to run out, but he wasn't going to change the pattern now, not when it had worked so well for him. He was at a pay phone, and now he had to find out the name and description of two dogs, and then he would have to call me back.

Assume for the moment that he wasn't calling from the laundromat phone. Assume he was at some phone on the street, far enough from his house that he'd taken a car. Now he would drive back to the house, park, go inside, and ask Lucia Landau the names of her dogs. And then he would drive around to still another phone and relay the information back to me.

Was that how I would do it?

Well, maybe. But maybe not. Maybe I'd spend a quarter and save a little time and running around, and call the house where my partner was guarding the girl. Let him take the gag out of her mouth for a minute and come back with the answers.

If only we had the Kongs.

Not for the first time, I thought how much easier it would be if Jimmy and David were set up in Lucia's bedroom, with their modem plugged into her Snoopy phone and the computer set up on her dressing table. They could sit on Lucia's phone and monitor her father's, and whenever anyone called we'd have an instant trace.

If Ray called home to find out the names of the dogs, we'd be perching on that line, and before he knew what to call the dogs we'd know where they were keeping the girl. Before he had relayed the information to me we could have cars at both locations, to pick him up when he got off the phone and to lay siege to the house.

But I didn't have the Kongs. All I had was TJ, sitting in a laundromat in Sunset Park and waiting for someone to use the phone. And if he hadn't been profligate enough to squander half his funds on a beeper, I wouldn't even have that.

"Makes a person crazy," Yuri said. "Sitting, staring at the phone, waiting for it to ring."

And it was taking its time. Evidently Ray—that was how I was thinking of him, and I had come alarmingly close once already to calling him by name—evidently he had not called home, for whatever reason. Figure ten minutes to drive home, ten minutes to get the answers from the girl, ten minutes to get back to a phone and call us. Less if he hurried. More if he stopped to buy a pack of cigarettes, or if she was unconscious and they had to bring her around.

Say half an hour. Maybe more, maybe less, but say half an hour.

If she was dead it could take a little longer. Suppose she was. Suppose they'd killed her right off the bat, killed her before their first call to her father. That, certainly, was the simplest way to do it. No danger of escape. No concern about keeping her quiet.

And if she was dead?

They couldn't admit it. Once they did there was no ransom. They were far from destitute, they'd taken four hundred thousand from Kenan less than a month ago, but that didn't mean they didn't want more. Money was something people always wanted more of, and if they hadn't there would have been no first call, and probably no kidnapping. It was easy enough to pick a woman off the street at random if all you wanted was the thrill of it. You didn't need to get cute.

So what would they do?

I figured they would probably try to brazen it out. Say she was out of it, say she'd been drugged and couldn't focus enough to respond to questions. Or make up some name and insist that was what she'd told them.

We would know they were lying and would be about ninety percent certain Lucia was dead. But you believe what you want to believe, and we would want to believe in the slender possibility that she was alive, and that might lead us to pay the ransom anyway because if we didn't pay there was no chance, no chance at all.

243

The phone rang. I snatched it up, and it was some jerk with a wrong number. I got rid of him and thirty seconds later he called back again. I asked him what number he was calling, and he had it right, but it turned out he was trying to call someone in Manhattan. I reminded him he had to dial the area code first. "Oh, God," he said, "I'm always doing that. I'm so stupid."

"I got calls like that this morning," Yuri said. "Wrong numbers. A nuisance."

I nodded. Had he called while I was getting rid of that idiot? If so, why didn't he call back? The line was clear now. What the hell was he waiting for?

Maybe I had made a mistake, asking for proof. If she was dead all along I was only forcing it all out into the open. Instead of trying to bluff it through, he might decide to write the operation off and scramble for cover.

In which case I could wait forever for the phone to ring, because we wouldn't be hearing from him again.

Yuri was right. It made a person crazy, sitting, staring at the phone. Waiting for it to ring.

Actually it took only twelve minutes over the thirty minutes I'd figured as an average. The phone rang and I grabbed it. I said hello, and Ray said, "I'd still like to know how you figure in this. You'd have to be a dealer. Are you a major trafficker?"

"You were going to answer some questions," I reminded him.

"I wish you'd tell me your name," he said. "I might recognize it."

"I might recognize yours."

He laughed. "Oh, I don't think so. Why are you in such a rush, my friend? Are you afraid I'll trace the call?"

In my mind I could hear him taunting Pam. "Pick one, Pam-mee. One's for you and one's for me, so which'll it be, Pam-mee?"

I said, "It's your quarter."

"So it is. Ah, well. The dog's name, eh? Let's see, what are the old standbys? Fido, Towser, King. Rover, that's always a popular favorite, isn't it?"

I thought, shit, she's dead.

"How about Spot? 'Run, Spot, run!' That's not a bad name for a Rhodesian Ridgeback."

But he would have known that much from the weeks of stalking her.

"The dog's name is Watson."

"Watson," I said.

Across the room, the big dog shifted position, pricked up its ears. Yuri was nodding.

"And the other dog?"

"You want so much," he said. "How many dogs do you need?"

I waited.

"She couldn't tell me what breed the other dog was. She was young when it died. They had to put it to sleep, she said. Silly term for it, don't you think? When you kill something you ought to have the courage to call it that. You're not saying anything. Are you still there?"

"I'm still here."

"I gather it was a mongrel. So many of us are. Now the name's a bit of a problem. It's a Russian word and I may not have it right. How's your Russian, my friend?"

"A little rusty."

"Rusty's a good name for a dog. Maybe it was Rusty. You're a tough audience, my friend. It's hard to get a laugh out of you."

"I'm a captive audience," I said.

"Ah, would that it were so. We could have a very interesting conversation under those circumstances, you and I. Ah, well. Some other time, perhaps."

"We'll see."

"Indeed we will. But you want the dog's name, don't you? The dog's dead, my friend. What good is his name? Give a dog a dead name, give a dead dog a bad name—"

I waited.

"I may be saying this wrong. Balalaika."

"Balalaika," I said.

"It's supposed to be the name of a musical instrument, or so she tells me. What do you say? Does it strike a chord?"

I looked at Yuri Landau. His nod was unequivocal. On the phone, Ray was saying something or other but the words weren't getting through to me. I felt light-headed, and had to lean against the kitchen counter or I might have fallen.

The girl was alive.

19

As soon as I got off the phone with Ray, Yuri fell on me and wrapped me up in a bear hug. "Balalaika," he said, invoking the name as if it were a magic spell. "She's alive, my Luschka is alive!"

I was still in his embrace when the door opened and the Khourys came in, trailed by Landau's man Dani. Kenan was carrying an old-fashioned leather satchel with a zipper top, Peter a white plastic shopping bag from Kroger's. "She's alive," Yuri told them.

"You spoke with her?"

He shook his head. "They told me the dog's name. She remembered Balalaika. She's alive."

I don't know how much sense this made to the Khourys, who had been out on a fund-raising mission when the recognition signals were arranged, but they got the gist of it.

"Now all you need is a million dollars," Kenan told him.

"Money you can always get."

"You're right," Kenan said. "People don't realize that but it's absolutely true." He opened the leather satchel and began

247

taking out stacks of wrapped bills, arranging them in rows on top of the mahogany table. "You got some good friends, Yuri. Good thing, too, is most of 'em don't believe in banks. People don't realize how much of the country's economy runs on cash. You hear cash, you think drugs, you think gambling."

"Tip of the iceberg," Peter said.

"You got it. Don't just think of the rackets. Think dry cleaners, think barber shops, beauty parlors. Any place that handles a lot of cash, so they can keep an extra set of books and skim half the take out from under the IRS."

"Think coffee shops," Peter said. "Yuri, you shoulda been a Greek."

"A Greek? Why should I be a Greek?"

"Every corner there's a coffee shop, right? Man, I worked for one of them. Ten employees on my shift, six of us were off the books, paid in cash. Why? Because they got all this cash they're not declaring, got to keep the expenses in proportion. If they report thirty cents of every dollar goes through the register, that's a lot. And you know the frosting on the cake? Eight and a quarter percent sales tax on every sale, law says they have to collect it. But the seventy percent of sales they don't report, they can't exactly hand over the tax on that, can they? So it gets skimmed, too. Pure tax-free profit, every penny of it."

"Not just Greeks," Yuri said.

"No, but they got it down to a science. You were Greek, all you gotta do is hit twenty coffee shops. You don't think they all got fifty grand in the safe, or stuffed in the mattress, or under a loose board in the clothes closet? Hit twenty and you got your million."

"But I am not a Greek," Yuri said.

Kenan asked him if he knew any diamond merchants. "They have a lot of cash," he said. Peter said a lot of the jewelry business was markers, IOUs that passed back and forth. Kenan said there was still some cash in it somewhere, and Yuri said it didn't matter because he didn't know anyone in diamonds.

I went into the other room and left them at it.

248

* * *

I wanted to call TJ and I got out the piece of paper with all the calls the Kongs had logged to Kenan's phone. I found the number of the laundromat pay phone but hesitated. Would TJ know to answer it? And would it compromise him if the place was crowded? And suppose Ray picked up the phone? That seemed unlikely, but—

Then I remembered there was a simpler way. I could beep him and let him call me. I seemed to be having trouble adjusting to this new technology. I still automatically thought in more primitive terms.

I found his beeper number in my notebook, but before I could dial it the phone rang, and it was TJ.

"Man was just here," he said. He sounded excited. "Just on this phone."

"It must have been someone else."

"No chance, Vance. Mean dude, you look at him an' you know you seein' evil. Wasn't you just talkin' to him? I got this flash, said my man Matt is talkin' to this dude."

"I was, but I got off the phone with him at least ten minutes ago. Maybe closer to fifteen."

"Yeah, be about right."

"I thought you'd call right away."

"I couldn't, man. I had to follow the dude."

"You followed him?"

"What you think I do, run away when I see him comin'? I don't walk out arm in arm with the man, but he walk out an' I give him a minute an' I slip out after him."

"That's dangerous, TJ. The man's a killer."

"Man, am I supposed to be impressed? I'm on the Deuce 'bout every day of my life. Can't walk down that street without you're followin' some killer or other."

"Where did he go?"

"Turned left, walked to the corner."

"Forty-ninth Street."

"Then walked across to the deli on the other side of the avenue. Went inside, stayed a minute or two, came out again.

Don't guess he had them make him a sandwich on account of he wasn't in there that long. Could of picked up a six-pack. Package he carried was about that size."

"Then where did he go?"

"Back the way he came. Sucker walked right past me, crossed Fifth again, and he's headin' straight back for the laundry. I thought, shit, can't follow him back in there, have to hang around outside until he makes his call."

"He didn't call here again."

"Didn't call nowhere, 'cause he didn't go inside the laundry. Got in his car an' drove off. Didn't even know he had a car until he got into it. It was parked just the other side of the laundry, where you couldn't see it if you were sittin' where I was."

"A car or a truck?"

"Said a car. I tried to stay with it but there wasn't no way. I was layin' half a block back, not wantin' to tag him too close on his way back to the laundry, and he was in the car an' outta there before I could do nothin'. Time I could get to the corner he was around it an' out of sight."

"But you got a good look at him."

"Him? Yeah, I saw him."

"You could recognize him again?"

"Man, could you recognize yo' mama? Kind of a question is that? Man is five-eleven, one hundred-seventy pounds, real light brown hair, has eyeglasses with brown plastic frames. Wearin' black leather lace-up shoes an' navy pants and a blue zip-up jacket. An' about the lamest sport shirt you ever saw. Blue an' white checks. Could I recognize him? Man, if I could draw I'da drawed him. You put me with that artist you was tellin' me about, we'd wind up with somethin' looked more like him than a photograph."

"I'm impressed."

"Yeah? Car was a Honda Civic, sort of a blue-gray, a little beat up. Up until he got into it I figured I'd follow him right back to where he's stayin'. He snatched somebody, right?"

"Yes."

"Who?"

"A fourteen-year-old girl."

"Motherfucker," he said. "I knowed that, maybe I tag him a little closer, run a little faster."

"You did fine."

"What I think I do now, I check out the neighborhood some. Maybe I see where he park his car."

"If you're sure you'd recognize it."

"Well, I got the plate number. Be a lot of Hondas, but not too many got the same license plate."

He read it out to me and I jotted it down and started to tell him how pleased I was with his performance.

He didn't let me finish. "Man," he said, exasperated, "how long we gonna go on this way, with you bein' stone amazed every time I do somethin' right?"

"It's going to take us a few hours to get the money together," I told him when he called again. "It's more than he has and it's going to be difficult to raise it at this hour."

"You're not trying to lower the price, are you?"

"No, but if you want the whole amount you'll have to be patient."

"How much do you have now?"

"I don't have a count."

"I'll call in an hour," he said.

"You can use this phone," I told Yuri. "He won't be calling for the next hour. How much have we got?"

"A little over four," Kenan said. "Less than half."

"Not enough."

"I don't know," he said. "One way to look at it, who else are they gonna sell her to? If you tell him this is all we got, take it or leave it, what's he gonna do?"

"The trouble is you don't know what he's likely to do."

"Yeah, I keep forgetting he's a lunatic."

"He wants a reason to kill the girl." I didn't want to stress this in front of Yuri, but it had to be said. "That's what got them started in the first place. They like killing. She's alive, and he'll keep her alive as long as she's their ticket to the money,

251

but he'll kill her the minute he thinks he can get away with it, or that he's lost his shot at the money. I don't want to tell him we've only got half a mil. I'd rather show up with half a mil and tell him it's the whole thing, and hope he doesn't count it until we've got the girl back."

Kenan thought about this. "The trouble is," he said, "the cocksucker already knows what four hundred thousand looks like."

"See if you can raise some more," I said, and went off to use the Snoopy phone.

There used to be a number you called at the Department of Motor Vehicles. You gave your shield number and told them the plate you wanted to trace and somebody looked it up and read it off to you. I no longer knew that special number, and had a feeling it had long since been phased out. Nobody answered the listed number for DMV.

I called Durkin but he wasn't at the station house. Kelly wasn't at his desk, either, and there was no point in paging him, because he couldn't do what I wanted him to do from a distance. I remembered when I'd been in to pick up the Gotteskind file from Durkin and pictured Bellamy at the adjacent desk, having a one-sided conversation with his computer terminal.

I called Midtown North and got him. "Matt Scudder," I said.

"Oh, hey," he said. "How you doing? Joe's not around, I'm afraid."

"That's okay," I said. "Maybe you can do me a favor. I was riding around with a friend of mine and some son of a bitch in a Honda Civic clipped her fender and just plain took off. Most flagrant thing you ever saw."

"Damn. And you were in the car when it happened? Man's a fool, leaving the scene of an accident. Most likely drunk or on drugs."

"I wouldn't be surprised. The thing is—"

"You got the plate? I'll run it for you."

"I'd really appreciate it."

"Hey, nothing to it. I just ask the computer. Hang on."

I waited.

"Damn," he said.

"Something the matter?"

"Well, they changed the damn password for getting into the DMV data bank. I enter like you're supposed to and it won't let me in. Keeps saying back 'Invalid Password.' If you call tomorrow I'm sure—"

"I'd love to move on this tonight. Before he gets a chance to sober up, if you follow me."

"Oh, definitely. If I could help you—"

"Isn't there someone you can call?"

"Yeah," he said with feeling. "That bitch down in Records, but she'll tell me she can't give it out. I get that crap from her all the time."

"Tell her it's a Code Five emergency."

"Say that again?"

"Just tell her it's a Code Five emergency," I said, "and she'd better give you the password before you wind up with circuits backed up all the way to Cleveland."

"Never heard that before," he said. "Hang on, I'll give it a shot."

He put me on Hold. Across the room, Michael Jackson peeked at me through the fingers of his white glove. Bellamy came back on the line and said, "Damn if it didn't work. 'Code Five emergency.' Cut right through the bullshit. She came up with the password. Lemme enter it. There you go. Now what was that license number?"

I gave it to him.

"Let's just see what we get. Okay, didn't take long. Vehicle is a Eighty-eight Honda Civic two-door, color is pewter . . . Pewter? Man, why can't they say gray? But you don't care about that. Owner is—you got a pencil? Callander, Raymond Joseph." He spelled the last name. "Address is Thirty-four Penelope Avenue. That's in Queens, but where in Queens? You ever hear of Penelope Avenue?"

"I don't think so."

"Man, I live in Queens, and it's a new one on me. Wait, here's the zip. One-one-three-seven-nine. That's Middle Village, innit? Never heard of no Penelope Avenue."

"I'll find it."

"Yeah, well, I guess you're motivated, aren't you? Hope nobody in the car was hurt."

"No, just a little body damage."

"Nail him good, leaving the scene like that. Other hand, you report it and your friend's insurance rates go up. Best thing might be if you and him can work something out private, but that's probably what you got in mind, huh?" He chuckled. "Code Five," he said. "Man, that really lit a fire under that girl. I owe you for that."

"My pleasure."

"No, I really mean it. I run into problems with this thing all that time. That's gonna save me a lot of major headaches."

"Well, if you really figure you owe me—"

"Go ahead."

"I just wondered if he had a sheet, our Mr. Callander."

"Now that's easy to check. Don't have to call a Code Five 'cause I happen to know that entry code. Hang on now. Nope."

"Nothing?"

"Far as the state of New York is concerned, he's a Boy Scout. Code Five. What's it mean, anyway?"

"Let's just say it's high level."

"I guess."

"If you get a hard time," I heard myself say, "just tell them they're supposed to know that a Code Five supersedes and countermands their standing instructions."

"Supersedes and countermands?"

"That's it."

"Supersedes and countermands their standing instructions."

"You got it. But don't use it on routine matters."

"God no," he said. "Wouldn't want to wear it out."

For a moment there I'd thought we had a bead on him. I had a name now, and an address, but it wasn't the address I wanted. They were somewhere in Sunset Park, in Brooklyn. The address was somewhere in Middle Village, in Queens.

I called Queens Information and dialed the number given to me. The phone made that sound they've developed, somewhere between a tone and a squawk, and a recording told me the number I had reached was no longer in service. I called Information again and reported this, and the operator checked and told me that the termination of service was recent and the listing had not been deleted yet. I asked if there was a new number. She said there was not. I asked if she could tell me when service had been terminated and she said she couldn't.

I called Brooklyn Information and tried to find a listing for a Raymond Callander, or an R or RJ Callander. The operator pointed out that there were other ways to spell that last name, and checked more possibilities than would have occurred to me. Spelled one way or another, there were a couple of listings for R and one RJ, but the addresses were way off, one on Meserole in Greenpoint, another way over in Brownsville, none of them anywhere near Sunset Park.

Maddening, but then the whole case had been like that from the beginning. I kept getting teased, making major breakthroughs that didn't really lead anywhere. Turning up Pam Cassidy had been the best example. From out of nowhere we'd managed to produce a living witness, and the bottom-line result of that was that the cops had taken three dead cases and shoved them all into a single open file.

Pam had provided a first name. Now I had a last name to go with it, and even a middle name, all thanks to TJ with an assist from Bellamy. I had an address, too, but it had probably stopped being valid at about the time the phone was disconnected.

He wouldn't be all that hard to find. It's easier when you know who you're looking for. I had enough now to find him, if I was able to wait until daytime, and if I could allow a few days for the search.

But that wasn't good enough. I wanted to find him now.

In the living room, Kenan was on the phone, Peter at the window. I didn't see Yuri. I joined Peter, and he told me that Yuri had gone out to look for more money.

"I couldn't look at the money," he said. "I was getting an anxiety attack. Rapid heartbeat, cold damp hands, the whole bit."

"What was the fear?"

"Fear? I don't know. It just made me want to do some dope, that's all. You gave me a word-association test right now, every response'd be heroin. A Rorschach, every inkblot'd look like some dope fiend bangin' himself in a vein."

"But you're not doing it, Pete."

"What's the difference, man? I know I'm gonna. All it is is a question of when. Beautiful out there, isn't it?"

"The ocean?"

He nodded. "Only you can't really see it anymore. Must be nice living where you can look out at water. I had a girlfriend once, she was into astrology, told me that's my element, water. You believe in that stuff?"

"I don't know much about it."

"She was right that it's my element. I don't like the others too much. Air, I never liked to fly. Wouldn't want to burn up in a fire or be buried in the earth. But the sea, that's the mother of us all, isn't that what they say?"

"I guess."

"That's the ocean out there, too. Not a river or a bay. That's just nothing but water, straight on out, farther than you can see. Makes me feel clean just to look at it."

I clapped him on the shoulder and left him looking at the ocean. Kenan was off the phone, and I went to ask him how the count stood.

"We got a shade under half of it," he said. "I been calling in every favor I got coming and Yuri's been doing the same. I got to tell you, I don't think we're going to find a whole lot more."

"The only person I can think of is in Ireland. I hope this looks like a million, that's all. All it has to do is get past whatever rough count they give it on the spot."

"Suppose we shoot some air into it. If every pack of hundreds is short five bills, you got a tenth again more packs."

"Which is fine unless they pick one pack at random and spot-count it."

"Good point," he said. "First glance, this is going to look like a good deal more than what I handed over to them. That was all hundreds. This has about twenty-five percent of the total in fifties. You know there's a way to make it look like a lot more than it is."

"Bulk it up with cut paper."

"I was thinking with singles. The paper's right, the color, everything but the denomination. Say you got a stack, supposed to be fifty hundred-dollar bills, total of five grand. You dummy it up with ten hundreds on top and ten on the bottom and fill in with thirty singles. 'Stead of five grand you have a little over two grand looking like five. Fan it, all you see is green."

"Same problem. It works unless you take a good look at one of the dummied-up packets. Then you see it's not what it's supposed to be, and you know right away, no argument, that it was phonied up that way to fool you. And if you're a nut case to begin with, and you've been looking for an excuse to murder all night long—"

"You kill the girl, bang, and it's over."

"That's the trouble with anything flagrant. If it looks as though we're trying to screw them—"

"They'll take it personally." He nodded. "Maybe they won't count the stacks. You got fifties and hundreds mixed, five thousand to a stack, half that in a stack of fifties, how many stacks are we talking if we come in at half a mil? A hundred if it's all hundreds, so call it a hundred and twenty, thirty, something like that?"

"Sounds right."

"I don't know, would you count it? You count in a dope deal, but you've got time, you sit back, you count the money and inspect the product. Different story. Even so, you know how the big traffickers count? The guys who turn upwards of a mil in each transaction?"

"I know the banks have machines that can count a stack of bills as quickly as you can riffle through it."

"Sometimes they use those," he said, "but mostly it's weight. You know how much money weighs, so you just load it on the scale."

"Is that what they did at the family enterprise in Togo?"

He smiled at the thought. "No, that was different," he said. "They counted every bill. But nobody was in a hurry."

The phone rang. We looked at each other. I picked it up, and it was Yuri on the car phone, saying he was on his way. When I hung up Kenan said, "Every time the phone rings—"

"I know. I think it's him. When you were out before we had a wrong number, some guy who called twice because he kept forgetting to dial two-one-two for Manhattan."

"Pain in the ass," he said. "When I was a kid we had a number that was one digit off from a pizzeria on Prospect and Flatbush. You can imagine the wrong numbers we got."

"Must have been a nuisance."

"For my parents. Me and Petey, we loved it. We'd take the fucking order. 'Half cheese and half pepperoni? No anchovies? Yessir, we'll have it ready for you.' And fuck 'em, let 'em go hungry. We were terrible."

"Poor bastard in the pizza place."

"Yeah, I know. I don't get many wrong numbers these days. You know when I got a couple? The day Francey was kidnapped. That morning, like God was sending me a message, trying to give me some kind of a warning. God, when I think what she must have gone through. And what that kid's going through now."

I said, "I know his name, Kenan."

"Whose name?"

"The one on the phone. Not the rough half of their rough-and-smooth act. The other one, the one who does most of the talking."

"You told me. Ray."

"Ray Callander. I know his old address in Queens. I know the license plate on his Honda."

"I thought he had a truck."

"He's got a two-door Civic, too. We're going to get him,

Kenan. Maybe not tonight, but we're going to get him."

"That's good," he said slowly. "But I have to tell you something. You know, I got in on this because of what happened to my wife. That's why I hired you, that's why I'm here to begin with. But right now none of that means shit. Right now the only thing matters to me is this kid, Lucia, Luschka, Ludmilla, she's got all these different names and I don't know what to call her and I never met her in my life. But all I care about now is getting her back."

Thank you, I thought.

Because, as it says on the T-shirts, when you're up to your ass in alligators you can forget that your primary purpose is to drain the swamp. It didn't matter right now where the two of them were holed up in Sunset Park, didn't matter if I found out tonight or tomorrow or never. In the morning I could hand everything I had to John Kelly and let him take it from there. It didn't matter who brought Callander in, and it didn't matter if he did fifteen years or twenty-five years or life, or if he died in some side street at Kenan Khoury's hands or at mine. Or if he got away scot-free, with or without the money. That might matter tomorrow. It might not. But it didn't matter tonight.

It was very clear suddenly, as it really should have been all along. The only thing of importance was getting the girl back. Nothing else mattered at all.

Yuri and Dani came back a few minutes before eight. Yuri had a flight bag in either hand, both bearing the logo of an airline that had vanished in mergers. Dani was carrying a shopping bag.

"Hey, we're in business," Kenan said, and his brother beat his hands together in applause. I didn't start clapping, but I felt the same excitement. You'd have thought the money was for us.

Yuri said, "Kenan, come here a minute. Look at this."

He opened one of the flight bags and spilled out its contents, banded stacks of hundreds, each wrapper bearing the imprint of the Chase Manhattan Bank.

"Beautiful," he said. "Wha'd you do, Yuri, make an unauthorized withdrawal? How'd you find a bank to rob this hour of the night?"

Yuri handed him a stack of bills. Kenan slipped them from their wrapper, looked at the top one, and said, "I don't have to look, do I? You wouldn't ask me if everything was kosher. This is schlock, right?" He looked closely, thumbed the bill aside and looked at the next one. "Schlock," he confirmed. "But very nice. All the same serial number? No, this one's different."

"Three different numbers," Yuri said.

"Wouldn't pass banks," Kenan said. "They got scanners, pick up something electronically. Aside from that, they look good to me." He crumpled a bill, smoothed it out, held it to the light and squinted at it. "Paper's good. Ink looks right. Nice used bills, must have soaked 'em with coffee grounds and then ran 'em through the Maytag. No bleach, hold the fabric softener. Matt?"

I took a real bill—or what I assumed was a real bill—from my own wallet and held it next to the one Kenan handed me. It seemed to me that Franklin looked a little less serene on the counterfeit specimen, a little more rakish. But I would never have given the bill a second glance in the ordinary course of things.

"Very nice," Kenan said. "What's the discount?"

"Sixty percent in quantity. You pay forty cents on the dollar."

"High."

"Good stuff don't come cheap," Yuri said.

"That's true. It's a cleaner business than dope, too. Because who gets hurt, you stop and think about it?"

"Debases the currency," Peter said.

"Does it really? It's such a drop in the bucket. One savings-and-loan goes belly-up and it debases the currency more than twenty years' worth of counterfeiting."

Yuri said, "This is on loan. No charge if we recover it and I bring it back. Otherwise I owe for it. Forty cents on the dollar."

"That's very decent."

"He's doing me a favor. What I want to know, will they spot it? And if they do—"

"They won't," I said. "They'll be looking quickly in bad light, and I don't think they'll be thinking of counterfeit. The bank wrappers are a nice touch. He print them, too?"

"Yes."

"We'll repackage them slightly," I said. "We'll use the Chase wrappers, but we'll take six bills out of each stack and replace them with real ones, three on the top and three on the bottom. How much have you got here, Yuri?"

"Two hundred fifty thousand in the schlock. And Dani's got sixty thousand, a little over. From four different people."

I did the arithmetic. "That should put us right around eight hundred thousand. That's close enough. I think we're in business."

"Thank God," Yuri said.

Peter eased the wrapper off a bundle of counterfeit bills, fanned them, stood looking at them and shaking his head. Kenan pulled up a chair and began removing six bills from each packet.

The phone rang.

20

"This is tiresome," he said.

"For me too."

"Maybe it's more trouble than it's worth. You know, there are plenty of dope dealers around, and most of them have wives or daughters. Maybe we should just cut and run, maybe our next client will prove more cooperative."

It was our third conversation since Yuri had come back with the two flight bags full of counterfeit money. He had called at half-hour intervals, first to suggest his own agenda for making the transfer, then to find something wrong with every suggestion I made.

"Especially if he hears how we cut before we run," he said. "I'll carve young Lucia into bite-size pieces, my friend. And go looking for other game tomorrow."

"I want to cooperate," I said.

"Your actions don't show it."

"We have to meet face-to-face," I said. "You have to have an opportunity to inspect the money and we have to be able to assure ourselves that the girl is all right."

"And then you people come down on us. You can have the whole area staked out, God knows how many armed men you can put together. Our resources are limited."

"But you can still create a standoff," I said. "You'll have the girl covered."

"A knife at her throat," he said.

"If you want."

"The edge of the blade right up against her skin."

"Then we give you the money," I went on. "One of you holds on to the girl while the other makes sure the money's all there. Then one of you takes the money to your vehicle while the other still holds the girl. Meanwhile your third man is posted where we can't see him, covering us with a rifle."

"Someone could get behind him."

"How?" I demanded. "You'll be in place first. You'll see us arrive, all of us at the same time. You'll have the drop on us, that's to offset the numerical edge we've got. Your man with the rifle will be able to cover your withdrawal, and you'd be safe anyway because we'd have the girl back by this point and the money would be in the car with your partner, and out of our reach."

"I don't like the face-to-face business," he said.

Nor, I thought, could he rely too strongly on the third man, the one covering his retreat with the rifle. Because I was virtually certain there were only two of them, so there wouldn't be any third man. But if I let him think we figured their strength at three, maybe it would make him feel a little more secure. The value of the third man lay not in the covering fire he could lay down but in our belief that he was there.

"Say we set up fifty yards apart. You bring the money halfway and then return to your lines. Then we bring the girl halfway and one of us stays there, knife at her throat, as you said—"

As *you* said, I thought.

"—while the other withdraws with the money. Then I release the girl and she runs to you while I back off."

"No good. You have the money and the girl at the same time and we're on the other side of the field."

Around and around and around. The operator's recorded voice cut in, asking for more money, and he dropped a quarter in without missing a beat. He wasn't worried about having calls traced, not at this stage. His calls were lasting longer and longer.

If I'd been able to reach the Kongs early on, we could pick him up while he was still on the phone.

I said, "All right, try it like this. We set up fifty yards apart, just as you said. You'll be in place first, you'll see us arrive. You'll show the girl so we can see you've brought her. Then I'll approach your position carrying the money."

"By yourself?"

"Yes. Unarmed."

"You could have a gun concealed."

"I'll have a suitcase full of dough in each hand. A hidden gun's not going to do me much good."

"Keep talking."

"You check the money. When you're satisfied, you let the girl go. She joins her father and the rest of our people. Your man takes off with the money. You and I wait. Then you take off and I go home."

"You could grab me."

"I'm unarmed and you've got a knife, a gun, too, if you want. And your sharpshooter is behind a tree covering everybody with the rifle. It's all going your way. I don't see how you can have a problem with it."

"You'll see my face."

"Wear a mask."

"Cuts the visibility. And you'd still be able to describe me even if you didn't get that good a look at my face."

I thought, fuck it, let's throw the dice.

I said, "I already know what you look like, Ray."

I heard his intake of breath, then a stretch of silence, and for a minute there I was afraid I'd lost him.

Then he said, "What do you know?"

"I know your name. I know what you look like. I know about some of the women you killed. And one you almost killed."

"The little whore," he said. "She heard my first name."

"I know your last name, too."

"Prove it."

"Why should I? Look it up for yourself, it's right there on the calendar."

"Who are you?"

"Can't you figure that out for yourself?"

"You sound like a cop."

"If I'm a cop, why isn't there a pack of blue-and-whites lined up in front of your house?"

"Because you don't know where it is."

"Try Middle Village. Penelope Avenue."

I could almost feel him relax. "I'm impressed," he said.

"What kind of cop plays it this way, Ray?"

"You're in Landau's pocket."

"Close. We're in bed together, we're partners. I'm married to his cousin."

"No wonder we couldn't—"

"Couldn't what?"

"Nothing. I should bail out now, cut the bitch's throat and get the hell out."

"Then you're dead," I said. "An all-points goes out nation-wide in a matter of hours, with you on the hook for Gotteskind and Alvarez, too. Do the deal and I guarantee I'll sit on it for a week, longer if I can. Maybe forever."

"Why?"

"Because I won't want it to come out, will I? You can go set up shop on the other side of the country. Plenty of dope dealers in L.A. Plenty of fine-looking women out there, too. They love to go for a ride in a pretty new truck."

He was silent for a long moment. Then he said, "Go over it again. The whole scenario, from the time we arrive."

I went through it. He interrupted with a question from time to time and I answered them all. Finally he said, "I wish I could trust you."

"Jesus Christ," I said. "I'm the one who has to do the trusting. I'll be walking up to you unarmed with a bag of money in each hand. If you decide you don't trust me you can always kill me."

"Yes, I could," he said.

"But it's better for you if you don't. It's better for both of us if the whole transaction goes off just the way it's scheduled to. We both come out winners."

"You're out a million dollars."

"Maybe that fits in with my plans, too."

"Oh?"

"You figure it out," I said, leaving him to puzzle out my own interfamilial secret agenda, some strategy I must have for getting the upper hand on my partner.

"Interesting," he said. "Where do you want to do the switch?"

I was ready for the question. I had proposed enough other sites in earlier phone calls, and I'd been saving this one. "Green-Wood Cemetery," I said.

"I think I know where that is."

"You ought to. That's where you dumped Leila Alvarez. It's a distance from Middle Village, but you found your way there once before. It's nine-twenty. There are two entrances on the Fifth Avenue side, one around Twenty-fifth Street, the other ten blocks south of there. Take the Twenty-fifth Street entrance and head south about twenty yards inside the fence. We'll enter at Thirty-fifth and approach you from the south."

I laid it all out for him, like a war-games tactician re-creating the Battle of Gettysburg. "Ten-thirty," I said. "That gives you over an hour to get there. No traffic at this hour, so that shouldn't be a problem. Or do you need more time?"

He didn't need anything like an hour. He was in Sunset Park, a five-minute drive from the cemetery. But he didn't need to know that I knew that.

"That should be time enough."

"And you'll have plenty of time to set up. We'll enter ten blocks south of you at ten-forty. That gives you ten minutes lead time, plus the ten minutes it'll take us to walk up to meet you."

"And they'll stay fifty yards back," he said.

"Right."

266

"And you'll come the rest of the way alone. With the money."

"Right."

"I liked it better with Khoury," he said. "Where I said 'Frog' and he jumped."

"I can see where you would. Twice as much money this time, though."

"That's true," he said. "Leila Alvarez. Haven't thought of her in a while." His voice took on an almost dreamy quality. "She was really nice. Choice."

I didn't say anything.

"Lord, she was frightened," he said. "Poor little bitch. She was really terrified."

When I finally got off the phone I had to sit down. Kenan asked me if I was all right. I said I was.

"You don't look so hot," he said. "You look like you need a drink, but I guess that's the one thing you don't need."

"You're right."

"Yuri just made some coffee. I'll get you a cup."

When he brought it I said, "I'm okay. It takes it out of you, talking to that son of a bitch."

"I know."

"I tipped my hand some, let him know some of what I know. It started to look as though that was the only way to get him off the dime. He wasn't going to move unless he could control the situation completely. I decided to show him he was in a little weaker position than he realized."

Yuri said, "You know who he is?"

"I know his name. I know what he looks like and the license number of the car he's driving." I closed my eyes for a moment, feeling his presence on the other end of the telephone line, sensing the workings of his mind. "I know who he is," I said.

I explained what I'd worked out with Callander, started to sketch out a diagram of the terrain, then realized that what we needed was a map. Yuri said there was a street map of Brooklyn somewhere in the apartment but didn't know where. Kenan said Francine had kept one in the glove box of the Toyota, and Peter went downstairs for it.

We had cleared off the table. All of the money, repackaged to hide the counterfeit bills, was packed into two suitcases. I spread the map on the table and traced a route to the cemetery, indicating the two entrances on the graveyard's western border. I explained how it would work, where we'd set up, how the exchange would be made.

"Puts you right out in front," Kenan observed.

"I'll be all right."

"If he tries anything—"

"I don't think he will."

You can always kill me, I'd told him. Yes I could, he'd said.

"I am the one who should carry the bags," Yuri said.

"They're not that heavy," I said. "I can manage them."

"You make a joke, but I am serious. It is my daughter. I should be out in front."

I shook my head. If he ever got that close to Callander, I couldn't trust him not to lose it and go for him. But I had a better reason to offer him. "I want Lucia to run to safety. If you're there she'll want to stay with you. I need you here," I said, pointing to the map, "so you can call to her."

"You'll tuck a gun in your belt," Kenan said.

"I probably will, but I don't know what good it'll do. If he tries anything I won't have time to get it out. If he doesn't I won't have any use for it. What I wish I had is a Kevlar vest."

"That's the bulletproof mesh? I heard it won't stop a knife."

"Sometimes yes, sometimes no. It won't always stop a bullet, either, but it gives you a sporting chance."

"You know where you can get one?"

"Not at this hour. Forget it, it's not important."

"No? It sounds pretty important to me."

"I don't even know that they've got guns."

"Are you kidding? I didn't think there was anybody in this town doesn't have a gun. What about the third man, the sharpshooter, guy hiding behind a tombstone covering everybody. What do you figure he's doing the job with, a fucking Wham-O slingshot?"

"That's if there is a third man. I was the one who mentioned him, and Callander was bright enough to follow my lead."

"You think they're doing this with two guys?"

"They only had two when they kidnapped the girl on Park Avenue. I can't see going out and recruiting an extra person for an operation like this. This is lust murder that developed a commercial hook to it, not an ordinary professional criminal operation where you can go out and put a string of men together. There are some witnesses who would seem to indicate the existence of a third man in the two abductions that were witnessed, but they may just have assumed there was a driver, because that's the way you would expect people to do it. But if you only had two people to start with, one of them would double as the driver. And that's what I think happened."

"So we can forget the third man."

"No," I said. "That's the aggravating thing about it. We have to assume he's there."

I went into the kitchen for more coffee. When I came back Yuri asked how many men I wanted. He said, "We have you, me, Kenan, Peter, Dani, and Pavel. Pavel is downstairs, you met him coming into the building. I got three more men ready to come, all I got to do is tell them."

"I can think of a dozen," Kenan said. "People I talked to, whether they had money to kick in or not, everybody said the same thing. 'You can use a hand, tell me, be right there.'" He leaned over the map. "We can let them get in position, then bring in a dozen more men in three or four cars. Seal up both exits, plus the rest of them, here and here. You're shaking your head. Why not?"

"I want to let them get away with the money."

"You don't even want to try for it? After we've got the girl back?"

"No."

"Why not?"

"Because it's crazy to get into a firefight in a graveyard at night, or shoot at each other from cars careening around Park Slope. An operation like that's no good unless you can control it, and there are too many ways this one can slip out of control.

Look, I sold this by setting it up as a standoff, and I did a good job designing it that way. It is a standoff. We get the girl, they get the money, and everybody goes home alive. A few minutes ago that was all we wanted out of the deal. Is that still how we feel?"

Yuri said it was. Kenan said, "Yeah, sure, it's all I ever wanted. I just hate to see them get away with anything."

"They won't. Callander thinks he's got a week to pack his valise and get out of town. He hasn't got a week. It won't take me that long to find him. Meanwhile, how many men do we need? I think we're fine with the people we've already got. Say three cars. Dani and Yuri in one, Peter and ... is it Pavel in the lobby downstairs? Peter and Pavel in the Toyota, and I'll ride with Kenan in the Buick. That's all we need. Six men."

The phone rang in Lucia's room. I answered it and spoke to TJ, who was back at the laundromat after having no luck looking in driveways and at curbs for the Honda.

I went back to the living room. "Make that seven," I said.

21

In the car Kenan said, "I figure the Shore Parkway and the Gowanus. That sound okay to you?" I told him he knew more about it than I did. He said, "This kid we're picking up. How's he fit into the picture?"

"He's a kid from the ghetto who hangs out in Times Square. God knows where he lives. He goes by his initials, assuming they're his initials and he didn't find them in a bowl of alphabet soup. He's been a big help, believe it or not. He put me on to the computer wizards, and he saw Callander tonight and got the license number."

"You think he's gonna do anything for us at the cemetery?"

"I hope he doesn't try," I said. "We're picking him up because I don't want him wandering around Sunset Park being resourceful when Callander and his friends are on their way home. I'd like to keep him out of harm's way."

"You say he's a kid?"

I nodded. "Fifteen, sixteen."

"What's he want to be when he grows up? A detective like you?"

"That's what he wants to be now. He doesn't want to wait until he grows up. I can't say I blame him. So many of them don't."

"Don't what?"

"Grow up. A black teenager living on the streets? They've got the average life expectancy of a fruit fly. TJ's a good kid. I hope he makes it."

"And you really don't know his last name."

"No."

"You know what's funny? Between AA and the streets, you know a hell of a lot of people without last names."

A little later he said, "You get any sense of Dani? He a relative of Yuri's or what?"

"No idea. Why?"

"I was just thinking, the two of them riding around in that Lincoln with a million dollars in the backseat. We know Dani's got a gun. Say he pops Yuri and takes off. We wouldn't even know who to look for, just a Russian guy with a jacket that don't fit him too good. He's another guy with no last name. Must be a friend of yours, huh?"

"I think Yuri trusts him."

"He's probably family. Who else you gonna trust like that?"

"Anyway, it's not a million."

"Eight hundred thousand. You gonna make me a liar for a lousy two hundred thousand?"

"And almost a third of it's counterfeit."

"You're right, it's hardly worth stealing. We're lucky if these two jokers we're meeting are willing to haul it away. If not it goes in the basement, save it for the next Boy Scout paper drive. You want to do me a favor? When you're up there with a suitcase in each hand, you want to ask our friends a question?"

"What?"

"Ask 'em how the hell they picked me, will you? Because it's still driving me nuts."

"Oh," I said. "I think I know."

"Seriously?"

"Uh-huh. My first thought was that he was in the dope business on some level or other."

"Makes sense, but—"

"But he's not, I'm almost certain, because I had somebody run a check and he hasn't got a criminal record."

"Neither have I."

"You're an exception."

"That's true. How about Yuri?"

"Several arrests in the Soviet Union, no serious jail time. One bust here for receiving stolen goods but the charges were dropped."

"But nothing involving narcotics."

"No."

"All right, Callander's got a clean slate. So he's not in the dope business, so—"

"The DEA was trying to make a case against you a while ago."

"Yeah, but it didn't get anywheres."

"I was talking to Yuri before. He said he backed out of a deal last year because he sensed that some agency was trying to trap him with a sting. He had the sense it was federal."

He turned to look at me, then forced his eyes front and swung out to pass a car. "Jesus Christ," he said. "This a new national law-enforcement policy? They can't make a case against us so they kill our wives and daughters?"

"I think Callander worked for the DEA," I said. "Probably not for very long, and almost certainly not as an accredited agent. Maybe they used him once or twice as a confidential informant, maybe he was strictly office help. He wouldn't have gone very far and he wouldn't have lasted very long."

"Why not?"

"Because he's crazy. He probably got into it because of a low-grade obsession about dope dealers. That's an asset in that line of work, but not when it's out of proportion. Look, I'm just going on a hunch. There was something he said on the phone when I told him I was Yuri's partner. It was as if he was starting to say that explained why they hadn't been able to rope Yuri in."

"Jesus."

"It's something I can find out tomorrow or the next day,

if I can get a hook into the DEA and see if his name rings a bell with them. Or take an unauthorized dip into their files, if my computer geniuses can swing it."

Kenan looked thoughtful. "He didn't sound like a cop."

"No, he didn't."

"But the guy you described wouldn't really be a cop, would he?"

"More like a buff. But a buff with the Feds, and fixated on the subject of narcotics."

"He knew the wholesale price of a kilo of cocaine," Kenan said, "but I don't know what that proves. Your friend TJ probably knows the wholesale price of a key."

"I wouldn't be surprised."

"Lucia's classmates at this girls' school, they probably know it, too. Kind of world we live in."

"You should have been a doctor."

"Like my old man wanted. No, I don't think so. But maybe I should have been a counterfeiter. You meet a nicer class of people. At least I wouldn't have the fucking DEA on my back."

"Counterfeiting? You'd have the Secret Service."

"Jesus," he said. "If it's not one goddamn thing it's another."

"That the laundromat? There on the right?" I said it was, and Kenan pulled up in front but kept the motor running. He said, "How are we on time?," then glanced at his watch and the dashboard clock and answered his own question. "We're fine. Running a little early."

I was watching the laundromat, but TJ emerged instead from a doorway on the other side of the avenue and crossed over, getting in the back. I introduced them, and each claimed to be pleased to meet the other. TJ shrank back against the seat and Kenan put the car in gear.

He said, "They get there at ten-thirty, right? And we're due ten minutes later, and then we work our way up to where they're waiting. Is that about right?"

I said it was.

"So we'll be face-to-face across no-man's-land about ten

274

minutes of eleven, is that about how you figure it?"

"Something like that."

"And how long to make the trade and get out? Half an hour?"

"Probably a lot less than that, if nothing goes wrong. If the shit hits the fan, well, it's another story."

"Yeah, so let's hope it doesn't. I was just wondering about getting back out again, but I guess they don't lock the gates until midnight."

"Lock the gates?"

"Yeah, I woulda guessed it'd be earlier, but I guess not or you would have picked someplace else."

"Jesus," I said.

"What's the matter?"

"I never even thought of that," I said. "Why didn't you say something earlier?"

"Then what would you do, call him back?"

"No, I guess not. It never occurred to me that they might lock the gates. Don't cemeteries stay open all night? Why would you have to lock them up?"

"To keep people out."

"Because everybody's dying to get in? Jesus, I must have heard that one in the fourth grade. 'Why do they have a fence around the cemetery?' "

"I guess they get vandals," Kenan said. "Kids who tip over the gravestones, take a shit in the floral urns."

"You think the kids can't climb fences?"

"Hey, man," he said. "I'm not setting the policy here. It's up to me, all the graveyards in town'll be open admission. How's that?"

"I just hope I didn't screw up. If they get there and the gates are locked—"

"Yeah? What are they gonna do, sell her to white slave traders in Argentina? They'll climb the fence, same as we'll do. Matter of fact, they probably don't lock it before midnight. People might want to go after work, pay a late call on the dear departed."

"At eleven o'clock?"

He shrugged. "People work late. They got office jobs in Manhattan, stop for a couple of drinks after work, they have dinner, then they got to wait half an hour for the subway because they're like some people I know, they're too cheap to take a cab—"

"Jesus," I said.

"—and it's late by the time they get back to Brooklyn and they say, 'Hey, I think I'll go over to Green-Wood, see if I can find where Uncle Vic is planted, I never liked him, I think I'll go piss on his grave.'"

"You nervous, Kenan?"

"Yeah, I'm nervous. What do you fucking think? You're the one's gotta walk up to a couple of stone killers armed with nothing but money. You must be starting to sweat."

"Maybe a little bit. Slow down, that's the entrance coming up. I think it's open."

"Yeah, it looks like it. You know, even if they're supposed to lock up, they probably don't get around to it."

"Maybe not. Let's drive once around the entire cemetery, all right? And then we'll find a place to park near our entrance."

We circled the cemetery in silence. There was no traffic to speak of, and there was a stillness to the night, as if the deep silence within the cemetery fence could reach out and suppress all sound in the vicinity.

When we were just about back where we'd started TJ said, "We goin' in a cemetery?"

Kenan turned aside to hide a grin. I said, "You can stay in the car if you'd rather."

"What for?"

"If you'd be more comfortable."

"Man," he said, "I ain't scared of no dead people. That what you think? That I scared?"

"My mistake."

"Your mistake is right, Dwight. Dead folks don't bother me."

Dead people didn't bother me much, either. It was some of the live ones that worried me.

We met at the Thirty-fifth Street gate and slipped inside right away, not wanting to draw attention on the street. For now, Yuri and Pavel were carrying the money. We had two flashlights among the seven of us. Kenan took one of them. I had the other, and I led the way.

I didn't use the light much, just flicked it quickly on and off when I needed to see where I was going. This wasn't necessary most of the time. There was a waxing moon overhead, and a certain amount of light from the streetlamps on the avenue. The tombstones were mostly of white marble and they showed up well once your eyes were accustomed to the dimness. I threaded my way among them and wondered whose bones I was walking over. One of the papers had run a story within the past year or so on where the bodies were buried, an inventory of gravesites of the rich and famous throughout the five boroughs. I hadn't paid too much attention to it, but I seemed to recall that a fair number of prominent New Yorkers were interred at Green-Wood.

Some enthusiasts, I'd read, make a hobby of visiting graves. Some take photographs, others make rubbings of tombstone inscriptions. I couldn't imagine what they got out of it, but it doesn't sound that much nuttier than some of the things I do. Their pursuit only brought them out in the daytime. They weren't stumbling around in the dark, trying to keep from tripping over a chunk of granite.

I soldiered on. I stayed close enough to the fence to see the street signs, and I slowed down when I got to Twenty-seventh Street. The others drew closer, and I gestured for them to fan out a ways without advancing any farther north. Then I turned toward where Raymond Callander was supposed to be and pointed my flashlight out in front of me, triggering the trio of flashes we'd agreed on.

For a long moment the only answer was darkness and silence. Then three flashes of light blinked back at me, coming from a little right of dead ahead. They were, I calculated, something like a hundred yards from us, maybe more. It didn't seem that far when someone was running with a football under his arm. Now, though, it looked much too distant.

"Stay where you are," I called out. "We're going to approach a little closer."

"Not too close!"

"About fifty yards," I said. "The way we arranged."

Flanked by Kenan and one of Yuri's men, with the rest of our party not far behind, I covered about half the distance separating us. "That's far enough," Callander called out at one point, but it wasn't far enough and I ignored him and kept on walking. We had to be close enough so that someone could cover the transfer. We had one rifle, and Peter had been entrusted with it, having proved a good marksman during a six-month hitch a while back in the National Guard. Of course that was before a lengthy apprenticeship as a drunk and a dope addict, but he still figured to be the best shot in the group. He had a decent rifle with a scope sight, but the scope wasn't infrared so he'd be aiming by moonlight. I wanted to keep the distance down so that he could make his shots count if he had to.

Although I wondered what difference it made to me. The only reason he'd start shooting would be if the players on the other side tried a cross, and if they did they'd take me out in the first minute of the opening round. If Peter started firing back at them, I wouldn't be around to know where the bullets went.

Cheering thoughts.

When we'd cut the distance in half I signaled to Peter, and he moved off to the side and selected a shooting stand for himself, propping the rifle barrel on a low marble grave marker. I looked for Ray and his partner and could only see shapes. They had drawn back into the darkness.

I said, "Come out where we can see you. And show the girl."

They moved into view. Two forms, and then as the light got better you could see that one form was made up of two persons, that one of the men had the girl in front of him. I heard Yuri's intake of breath and just hoped he'd keep his cool.

"I've got a knife to her throat," Callander called. "If my hand slips—"

"It better not."

"Then you'd better bring the money. And not try anything cute."

I turned, hefted the suitcases, checked our troops. I didn't see TJ and asked Kenan what had happened to him. He said he thought he might have gone back to the car. "'Feet, do yo' stuff,'" he said. "I don't think he's crazy about graveyards at night."

"Neither am I."

"Listen," he said, "whyntcha tell them we're changing the rules, the money's too heavy for one person to carry, and I'll walk up there with you."

"No."

"Gotta be the hero, huh?"

I can't say I felt terribly heroic. The weight of the suitcases kept me from being particularly jaunty. It looked as though one of the men had a gun, not the one holding the girl, and it looked as though the gun was pointed at me, but I didn't feel in danger of being shot, not unless someone on our side panicked and got off a round and everybody just let fly. If they were going to kill me, they'd at least wait until I'd brought them the money. They might be crazy but they weren't stupid.

"Don't try a thing," Ray said. "I don't know if you can see it, but the knife's right at her throat."

"I can see."

"That's close enough. Put the bags down."

It was Ray holding the girl, holding the knife. I knew his voice but I would have made him from TJ's description, which was right on the money. His jacket was zipped so I couldn't see the lame sport shirt, but I was willing to take TJ's word for it.

The other man was taller, with unkempt dark hair and eyes that looked in the half-light like a pair of holes burned in a bedsheet. He wore no jacket, just a flannel shirt and jeans. I couldn't see his eyes but I could feel the anger in his stare and I wondered what the hell he thought I'd done to provoke it. I was bringing him a million dollars and he was itching to kill me.

"Open the bags."

"First let the girl go."

"No, first show the money."

The pistol Kenan had insisted on giving me was in the small of my back, its barrel wedged under my belt, its bulk concealed by my sport jacket. There is no terribly adroit way to draw it quickly from that position, but I had my hands free now and could go for it.

Instead I knelt and unfastened the snaps on one of the cases, lifting the lid to show the money. I straightened up. The man with the gun started forward and I held up a hand.

"Now let her go," I said. "Then you can examine it. Don't try to change the ground rules now, Ray."

"Ah, sweet Lucy," he said. "I hate to see you go, child."

He let go of her. I'd barely had a chance to look at her, half-shadowed by his body. Even in the darkness she looked pale and drawn. Her hands were clutched together at her waist, her arms tight against her sides, her shoulders hunched. She looked as though she was trying to present the smallest possible target to the world.

I said, "Come here, Lucia." She didn't move. I said, "Your father's over there, darling. Go to your father. Go ahead."

She took a step, then stopped. She looked very unsteady on her feet, and she was gripping one hand tightly with the other.

"Go on," Callander told her. "Run!"

She looked at him, then at me. It was hard to tell what she was seeing because her gaze was unfocused, vacant. I wanted to pick her up, toss her over my shoulder, run back to where her father was waiting.

Or tug my jacket aside with one hand, draw the gun with the other, and drop both of the bastards where they stood. But the dark man's gun was pointing at me, and Callander also had a gun in his hand now, a companion piece for the long knife he was still holding.

I called out to Yuri, told him to call her. "Luschka!" he cried. "Luschka, it's Papa. Come to Papa!"

She recognized the voice. Her brow contracted in concentration, as if she was struggling to make sense out of the syllables.

I said, "In Russian, Yuri!"

He replied with something that I certainly couldn't understand, but it evidently got through to Lucia. Her hands unclasped and she took a step, then another.

I said, "What's the matter with her hand?"

"Nothing."

As she drew alongside me I reached for her hand. She snatched it away from me.

There were two fingers missing.

I stared at Callander. He looked almost apologetic. "Before we set the terms," he said, by way of explanation.

There was another burst of Russian from Yuri, and now she was moving faster, but hardly running. She couldn't seem to manage more than an awkward shuffle, and I wasn't sure how long she could sustain even that much.

But she stayed on her feet and kept going, and I stayed on mine and looked into the barrels of two handguns. The dark man stared silently at me, still a study in rage, while Callander watched the girl. He kept the gun pointed at me but he couldn't keep his eyes from turning to her, and I could feel how much he wanted to swing the gun, too, in her direction.

"I liked her," he said. "She was nice."

The rest of it was easy. I opened the second suitcase and stepped back a few paces. Ray came forward to inspect the contents of both cases while his partner kept me covered. The bills got only a cursory examination. He flipped through half a dozen packs, but he didn't count any of them, or make a rough count of the number of packets. Nor did he spot the counterfeits, but I don't think anybody on earth would have.

He closed the cases and fastened their clasps, then drew his gun again and stood aside while the dark-haired man came to pick up both of them, grunting with the effort. It was the first sound he had made in my presence.

"Take one at a time," Callander said.

"They ain't heavy."

"Take one at a time."

"Don't tell me what to do, Ray," he said, but he put down

one of the suitcases and went off with the other.

He wasn't gone long, and neither Ray nor I spoke in his absence. When he got back he hefted the second case and pronounced it lighter than its fellow, as if this meant we'd cheated him on the count.

"Then it should be easier to carry," Callander said patiently. "Go ahead now."

"We oughta plug this cocksucker, Ray."

"Another time."

"Fucking dope-dealing cop. Oughta blow his head off."

When he had gone Callander said, "You promised us a week. Will you keep your word on that?"

"Longer, if I can."

"I'm sorry about the finger."

"Fingers."

"As you prefer. He's difficult to control."

I thought, But you were the one who used the wire on Pam.

"I appreciate the week's lead time," he went on. "I think it's time to try a change of climate. I don't think Albert will want to come with me."

"You'll leave him here in New York?"

"In a manner of speaking."

"How did you find him?"

He smiled faintly at the question. "Oh," he said, "we found each other. People with specialized tastes often find each other like that."

It was an odd moment. I had the sense that I was talking to the person behind the mask, that our circumstances had provided a rare window of opportunity. I said, "May I ask you something?"

"Go ahead."

"Why the women?"

"Oh, my. Take a psychiatrist to answer that, wouldn't it? Something buried in my childhood, I suppose. Isn't that what it always turns out to be? Weaned too early or too late?"

"That's not what I meant."

"Oh?"

282

"I don't care how you got that way. I just want to know why you do it."

"You think I have a choice?"

"I don't know. Do you?"

"Hmmm. That's not so easy to answer. Excitement, power, just sheer intensity—words fail me. Do you know what I mean?"

"No."

"Have you ever been on a roller coaster? Now I hate roller coasters, I haven't been on one in years, I get sick to my stomach. But if I didn't hate roller coasters, if I loved them, then that's what it would be like." He shrugged. "I told you. Words fail me."

"You don't sound like a monster."

"Why should I?"

"What you do is monstrous. But you sound like a human being. How can you—"

"Yes?"

"How can you do it?"

"Oh," he said. "They're not real."

"What?"

"They're not real," he said. "The women. They aren't real. They're toys, that's all. When you have a hamburger are you eating a cow? Of course not. You're eating a hamburger." A slight smile. "Walking down the street she's a woman. But once she gets in the truck that's over. She's just body parts."

A chill ran the length of my spine. When that happened my late aunt Peg used to say a goose must have just walked over my grave. A funny expression, that. I wonder where it came from.

"But do I have a choice? I *think* I do. It's not as though I'm driven to act out every time the moon is full. I always have a choice, and I can choose not to do anything, and I do choose not to, and then one day I choose the other way.

"So what kind of choice is it, really? I can postpone it, but then the time comes when I don't want to postpone it any longer. And postponing just makes it sweeter, anyway. Maybe that's why I do it. I read that maturity consists of the ability to defer gratification, but I don't know if this is what they had in mind."

He looked to be on the point of further revelation, and then something shifted within him and the window of opportunity slammed shut. Whatever real self I'd been talking to ducked back behind its protective body armor. "Why aren't you afraid?" he asked, petulant. "I've got a gun on you and you act like it's a water pistol."

"There's a high-powered rifle trained on you. You wouldn't get a step."

"No, but what good would it do you? You'd think you would be scared. Are you a brave man?"

"No."

"Well, I'm not going to shoot. And let Albert keep everything? No, I don't think so. But I think it's time for me to melt into the shadows. Turn around, start walking back toward your friends."

"All right."

"There's no third man with a rifle. Did you think there was?"

"I wasn't sure."

"You knew there wasn't. That's all right. You got the girl and we got the money. It all worked out."

"Yes."

"Don't try to follow me."

"I won't."

"No, I know you won't."

He didn't say anything more, and I thought he had slipped away. I kept walking, and when I'd gone a dozen steps he called after me.

"I'm sorry about the fingers," he said. "It was an accident."

22

"You quiet," TJ said.

I was driving Kenan's Buick. As soon as Lucia Landau had reached her father's side, he had scooped her up in his arms and slung her over his shoulder and hurried back to his car, with Dani and Pavel taking off after him. "I told him not to wait around," Kenan had said. "Kid needed a doctor. He's got somebody lives in the neighborhood, guy'll come to the house."

So that had left two cars for the four of us, and when we reached them Kenan tossed me the Buick's keys and said he would ride with his brother. "Come on out to Bay Ridge," he said. "We'll send out for pizza or something. Then I'll run you two home."

We were stopped at a traffic light when TJ told me I was quiet, and I couldn't argue with that. Neither of us had said a word since we got in the car. I still hadn't shaken off the effect of the conversation with Callander. I said something to the effect that our activities had taken a lot out of me.

"You was cool, though," he said. "Standin' up there with those dudes."

"Where were you? We thought you were back at the car."

He shook his head. "I circled around 'em. Thought maybe I could see this third man, one with the rifle."

"There wasn't any third man."

"Sure made him hard to see. What I did, I made a big circle around 'em and slipped out the place they came in. I found their car."

"How did you manage that?"

"Wasn't hard. I seen it before, it was the same Honda again. I backed up against a pole an' kept an eye on it an' the dude without no jacket came hurrying out of the graveyard an' threw a suitcase in the trunk. Then he turned around an' ran back in again."

"He was going back for the other suitcase."

"I know, an' I thought while he's gettin' the second suitcase, I could just take the first one off his hands. Trunk was locked, but I could open it same way he did, pressin' the release button in the glove compartment. 'Cause the car doors wasn't locked."

"I'm glad you didn't try."

"Well, I coulda done it, but say he come back and the suitcase ain't there, what he gonna do? Go back and shoot you, most likely. So I figured that wasn't too cool."

"Good thinking."

"Then I thought, if this here's a movie, what I do is slip in the back an' hunker down 'tween the front an' back seats. They be puttin' the money in the trunk an' sittin' up front, so they ain't even gone look in the back. Figured they go back to their house, or wherever they gone go, an' when we got there I just slip out an' call you up an' tell you where I'm at. But then I thought, TJ, this ain't no movie, an' you too young to die."

"I'm glad you figured that out."

"'Sides, maybe you don't be at that same number, an' then what do I do? So I wait, and he come back with the second suitcase, throw it in the trunk, an' get in the car. An' the other one, one who made the phone call, he come an' get behind the wheel. And they drive off, an' I slip back into the cemetery an' catch up with everybody. Cemetery's weird, man. I can see havin' a stone, tells who's underneath it, but some of 'em has

286

these little houses an' all, fancier than they had when they alive. Would you want somethin' like that?"

"No."

"Me neither. Just a little stone, don't say nothin' on it but TJ."

"No dates? No full name?"

He shook his head. "Just TJ," he said. "An' maybe my beeper number."

Back on Colonial Road, Kenan got on the phone and tried to find a pizza place that was still open. He couldn't, but it didn't matter. Nobody was hungry.

"We ought to be celebrating," he said. "We got the kid back, she's alive. Some celebration we got here."

"It's a draw," Peter said. "You don't celebrate a tie score. Nobody wins and nobody shoots off firecrackers. Game ends in a tie, it feels worse than losing."

"It'd feel a lot worse if the girl was dead," Kenan said.

"That's because this isn't a football game, it's real. But you still can't celebrate, babe. The bad guys got away with the money. Does that make you want to toss your hat in the air?"

"They're not in the clear," I put in. "It'll take a day or two, that's all. But they're not going anywhere."

Still, I didn't feel like celebrating any more than anybody else did. Like any game that ended in a tie, this one left an aftertaste of missed opportunities. TJ thought he should have stowed away in the back of the Honda, or found some way to follow the car back to where it lived. Peter had had a couple of chances to drop Callander with a rifle shot, times when there would have been no danger to me or to the girl. And I could think of a dozen ways we could have made a try for the money. We'd done what we set out to do, but there should have been a way to do more.

"I want to call Yuri," Kenan said. "Kid was a mess, she could barely walk. I think she lost more than her fingers."

"I'm afraid you're probably right."

"They must have really done a number on her." He jabbed at the buttons on the phone. "I don't like to think about that

because then I start thinking of Francey, and—" He broke off
to say, "Uh, hello, is Yuri there? I'm sorry. I got the wrong
number, I'm really sorry to disturb you."

He broke the connection and sighed. "Hispanic woman,
sounded like I woke her out of a sound sleep. God, I hate when
that happens."

I said, "Wrong numbers."

"Yeah, I don't know which is worse, to give or to receive.
I feel like such an asshole disturbing somebody like that."

"You had a couple of wrong numbers the day your wife
was kidnapped."

"Yeah, right. Like an omen, except that they didn't seem
particularly ominous at the time. Just a nuisance."

"Yuri had a couple of wrong numbers this morning, too."

"So?" He frowned, then nodded. "Them, you think? Calling to make sure if somebody was home? I suppose, but so
what?"

"Would you use a pay phone?" They looked at me, lost.
"Say you were going to make a call that would just play as a
wrong number. You weren't going to say anything and nobody
would take any notice of the call. Would you bother to drive
half a dozen blocks and spend a quarter in a pay phone? Or
would you use your own phone?"

"I suppose I'd use my own, but—"

"So would I," I said. I grabbed my notebook, looking for
the sheet of paper Jimmy Hong had given me, the list of calls
to the Khoury house. He had copied out all the calls starting
at midnight, even though I had only needed the ones from the
time of the initial ransom demand. I'd had the slip earlier that
day, I'd looked for the laundromat phone number with the
intention of calling TJ there, but where the hell had I put it?

I found it, unfolded it. "Here we are," I said. "Two calls,
both under a minute. One at nine-forty-four in the morning,
the other at two-thirty in the afternoon. Calling phone is 243-
7436."

"Man," Kenan said, "I just remember there were a couple
of wrong numbers. I don't know what time they came in."

"But do you recognize the number?"

"Read it again." He shook his head. "Doesn't sound familiar. Why don't we call it, see what we get?"

He reached for the phone. I covered his hand with mine. "Wait," I said. "Let's not give them any warning."

"Warning of what?"

"That we know where they are."

"Do we? All we got's a number."

TJ said, "Kongs might be home now. Want me to see?"

I shook my head. "I think I can manage this one by myself." I took the phone, dialed Information. When the operator came on I said, "Policeman requiring directory assistance. My name is Police Officer Alton Simak, my shield number is 2491-1907. What I have is a telephone number and what I need is the name and address that goes with it. Yes, that's right. 243-7436. Yes. Thank you."

I cradled the phone and wrote down the address before it could slip my mind. I said, "The phone's in the name of an A. H. Wallens. He a friend of yours?" Kenan shook his head. "I think the A stands for Albert. That's what Callander called his partner." I read off the address I'd written down. "Six-ninety-two Fifty-first Street."

"Sunset Park," Kenan said.

"Sunset Park. Two, three blocks from the laundromat."

"That's the tiebreaker," Kenan said. "Let's go."

It was a frame house, and even in the moonlight you could see that it had been neglected. The clapboard badly needed painting and the shrubbery was overgrown. A half-flight of steps in front led up to a screened-in porch that sagged perceptibly in its middle. A driveway, concrete patched here and there with blacktop, ran along the right-hand side of the house to a two-car detached garage. There was a side door about halfway back, and a third door at the rear of the house.

We had all come in the Buick, which was parked around the corner on Seventh Avenue. We all had handguns. I must have registered surprise when Kenan handed a revolver to TJ, because he looked at me and said, "If he comes he carries. I say he's a stand-up guy, let him come. You know how this works, TJ? Just point and shoot, like a Jap camera."

The overhead garage door was locked, the lock solid. There was a narrow wooden door alongside it, and it too was locked. My credit card wouldn't slip the bolt. I was trying to figure out the quietest way to break a pane of glass when Peter handed me a flashlight, and for a second I thought he wanted me to smack the glass with it, and I couldn't think why. Then it dawned on me, and I pressed the business end of the flashlight up against the window and switched it on. The Honda Civic was right there, and I recognized the plate number. On the other side, harder to see even when I angled the flashlight, was a dark van. The plate was not where we could see it and the color was impossible to determine in that light, but that was really as much as we had to see. We were in the right place.

Lights were on throughout the house. There were signs that the house was a one-family dwelling—a single doorbell at the side door, a single mailbox alongside the door to the porch—and they could be anywhere inside it. We worked our way around the house. In back, I interlaced my fingers and gave Kenan a boost. He caught hold of the windowsill and inched his head above it, hung there for a moment, then dropped to the ground.

"The kitchen," he whispered. "The blond's in there counting money. He's opening each stack and counting the bills, writing numbers on a sheet of paper. Waste of time. It's a done deal, why's he care how much he's got?"

"And the other one?"

"Didn't see him."

We repeated the procedure at other windows, tried the side door as we passed it. It was locked, but a child could have kicked it in. The door in back, leading to the kitchen, hadn't looked much more formidable.

But I didn't want to crash in until I knew where they both were.

In front, Peter risked drawing attention from someone passing by and used the blade of a pocketknife to snick back the bolt of the porch door. The door leading from the porch into the front of the house was equipped with a sturdier lock, but it also had a large window which could be broken for quick access. He didn't break it, but looked through it and established that Albert wasn't in the living room.

He came back to report this, and I decided that Albert was either upstairs or out having a beer. I was trying to figure out a way for us to take Callander silently and then figure out Phase Two later on, when TJ got my attention with a fingersnap. I looked, and he was crouched at a basement window.

I went over, stooped, and looked in. He had the flashlight and played it around the interior of a large basement room. There was a large sink in one corner, with a washer and dryer next to it. A workbench stood in the opposite corner, flanked by a couple of power tools. There was a pegboard on the wall above the workbench, with dozens of tools hanging on it.

In the foreground was a Ping-Pong table, its net sagging. One of the suitcases was on the table, open, empty. Albert Wallens, still wearing the clothes he'd worn to the cemetery, was sitting at the Ping-Pong table on a ladderback chair. He might have been counting the money in the suitcase except that there wasn't any money in the suitcase and it was a curious activity to conduct in the dark. But for TJ's flashlight, there was no light in the basement.

I couldn't see it, but I could tell there was a length of piano wire wrapped around Albert's neck, and it was very likely the same piece of wire that had been used to perform a mastectomy upon Pam Cassidy, and perhaps upon Leila Alvarez as well. In the present instance it had not been as surgically precise, having encountered bone and cartilage instead of the unresisting flesh it had met before. Still, it had done its work. Albert's head had swelled grotesquely, as blood had been able to flow in but not out again. His face was a moon face turned the color of a bruise, and his eyes were bulging out of their sockets. I had seen a garrote victim before so I knew right away what I was looking at, but nothing really prepares you for it. It was as awful a sight as I had ever seen in my life.

But it did lower the odds.

* * *

Kenan had another look through the kitchen window and couldn't see a gun anywhere. I had a feeling Callander had put it away. He hadn't brandished a gun in any of the abductions, had used it in the cemetery only to back up the knife at Lucia's throat, and had rejected it in favor of the garrote when he dissolved his partnership with Albert.

The logistical problem lay in the time it took to get from any of the doors to where Callander was counting his money. If you went in the back or side door, you had to rush up half a flight of stairs to the kitchen. If you went in in front, from the porch, you had to go all the way to the rear of the house.

Kenan suggested we go in quietly through the front. There'd be no creaking stairs that way, and the front door was the farthest from where he was sitting; as engrossed as he was in his counting, he might not hear the glass break.

"Tape it," Peter said. "It breaks but it doesn't fall on the floor. Lot less noise."

"Things you learn bein' a junkie," Kenan said.

But we didn't have any tape, and any stores in the neighborhood that would carry it had long since closed. TJ pointed out that there was sure to be suitable tape on the workbench or hanging above it, but we'd have had to break a window to get to it, so that limited its usefulness. Peter made another trip to the porch and reported that the floor in the living room was carpeted. We looked at each other and shrugged. "What the hell," somebody said.

I boosted TJ up, and he watched through the kitchen window while Peter broke the glass in the front door. We couldn't hear it from where we stood, and apparently Callander couldn't hear it, either. We all went around to the front and in the door, stepping carefully over the broken glass, waiting, listening, then moving slowly and quietly through the still house.

I was in the lead when we got to the kitchen door, with Kenan right at my side. We both had guns in our hands. Raymond Callander was seated so that we were seeing him in profile. He had a stack of bills in one hand, a pencil in the other. Lethal weapons in the hands of a good accountant, I understand, but a lot less intimidating than guns or knives.

I don't know how long I waited. Probably no more than fifteen or twenty seconds, if that, but it seemed longer. I waited until something changed in the set of his shoulders, showing that an awareness of our presence had somehow reached him. I said, "Police. Don't move."

He didn't move, didn't even turn his eyes toward the sound of my voice. He just sat there as one phase of his life ended and another began. Then he did turn to look at me, and his expression showed neither fear nor anger, just profound disappointment.

"You said a week," he said. "You promised."

The money all seemed to be there. We filled one suitcase. The other was in the basement, and nobody much wanted to go get it. "I'd say for TJ to go," Kenan said, "but I know how he got in the cemetery, so I guess it'd spook him too much to go down there with a dead body."

"You just sayin' that so I'll go. Tryin' to psych me out."

"Yeah," Kenan said. "I figured you'd say something like that."

TJ rolled his eyes, then went for the suitcase. He came back with it and said, "Man, it stinks pretty powerful down there. Dead people always smell that bad? I ever kill somebody, remind me to do it from a distance."

It was curious. We worked around Callander, treating him as if he weren't there, and he made such treatment easier than it might have been by staying put and keeping his mouth shut. He looked smaller sitting there, and weak and ineffectual. I knew him to be none of those things, but his blank passivity gave that impression.

"All packed up," Kenan said, fastening the hasps of the second suitcase. "Can go right back to Yuri."

Peter said, "All Yuri wanted was to get his kid back."

"Well, tonight's his lucky night. He gets the money, too."

"Said he didn't care about the money," Peter said dreamily. "The money didn't matter."

"Petey, are you saying something without saying it?"

"He don't know we came here."

"No."

"Just a thought."

"No."

"Whole lot of money, babe. And you been takin' a bath lately. That hash deal's gonna go down the tubes, isn't it?"

"So?"

"God gives you a chance to get even, you don't want to spit in His eye."

"Awww, Petey," Kenan said. "Don't you remember what the old man told us?"

"He told us all kinds of shit. When did we ever listen?"

"He said never to steal unless you can steal a million dollars, Petey. Remember?"

"Well, now's our chance."

Kenan shook his head. "No. Wrong. That's eight hundred thousand, and a quarter of a mil is counterfeit and another hundred and thirty thousand is mine to start with. So what's that leave? Four-something. Four-twenty? Something like that."

"Which gets you even, babe. Four hundred this asshole took off of you, plus ten you gave Matt, plus expenses, comes to what? Four-twenty? Goddamn close to it."

"I don't want to get even."

"Huh?"

He stared hard at his brother. "I don't want to get even," he said. "I paid blood money for Francey and you want me to steal blood money from Yuri. Man, you got that fucking junkie mind, steal his wallet and help him look for it."

"Yeah, you're right."

"I mean for Christ's sake, Petey—"

"No, you're right. You're absolutely right."

Callander said, "You paid me with counterfeit money?"

"You simple shit," Kenan said, "I was beginning to forget you were here. What are you, afraid you'll get picked up trying to spend it? I got news for you. You ain't gonna spend it."

"You're the Arab. The husband."

"So?"

"I was just wondering."

294

I said, "Ray, where's the money you got from Mr. Khoury? The four hundred thousand."

"We divided it."

"And what happened to it?"

"I don't know what Albert did with his half. I know it's not in the house."

"And your half?"

"Safe-deposit box. Brooklyn First Mercantile, New Utrecht and Fort Hamilton Parkway. I'll go there in the morning on my way out of town."

Kenan said, "You will, huh?"

"I can't decide whether to take the Honda or the van," he went on.

"He's kind of spaced, isn't he? Matt, I think he's telling the truth about the dough. The half in the bank we can forget about. Albert's half, I don't know, we could turn the house upside down but I don't think we're gonna find it, do you?"

"No."

"He probably buried it in the yard. Or in the fucking cemetery or someplace. Fuck it. I'm not supposed to have that money. I knew that all along. Let's do what we gotta do and get outta here."

I said, "You have a choice to make, Kenan."

"How's that?"

"I can take him in. There's a lot of hard evidence against him now. He's got his dead partner in the basement, and the van in the garage is going to be full of fibers and blood traces and God knows what else. Pam Cassidy can ID him as the man who maimed her. Other evidence will tie him to Leila Alvarez and Marie Gotteskind. He ought to be looking at three life sentences, plus an extra twenty or thirty years tacked on as a bonus."

"Can you guarantee he'll do life?"

"No," I said. "Nobody can guarantee anything when it comes to the criminal justice system. My best guess is that he'll wind up at the State Hospital for the Criminally Insane at Matteawan, and that he'll never leave the place alive. But anything could happen. You know that. I can't see him skating, but I've said that about other people and they never did a day."

He thought it over. "Going back to our deal," he said. "Our deal wasn't about you taking him in."

"I know. That's why I'm saying it's your choice. But if you make the other choice I have to walk first."

"You don't want to be here for it."

"No."

"'Cause you don't approve?"

"I don't approve or disapprove."

"But it's not the kind of thing you would ever do."

"No," I said, "that's not it at all. Because I *have* done it, I've appointed myself executioner. It's not a role I'd want to make a habit of."

"No."

"And there's no reason why I should in this case. I could turn him over to Brooklyn Homicide and sleep fine."

He thought about it. "I don't think I could," he said.

"That's why I said it has to be your decision."

"Yeah, well, I guess I just made it. I have to take care of it myself."

"Then I guess I'll be going."

"Yeah, you and everybody else," he said. "Here's what we'll do. It's a shame we didn't bring two cars. Matt, you and TJ and Petey'll take the money to Yuri."

"Some of it's yours. Do you want to take out the money you lent him?"

"Separate it out at his place, will you? I don't want to wind up with any of the counterfeit."

"It's all in the packages with the Chase wrappers," Peter said.

"Yeah, except it all got mixed around when this dickhead here counted it, so check it out at Yuri's, okay? And then you'll pick me up. Figure what? Twenty minutes to Yuri's and twenty minutes back, twenty minutes there, figure an hour. You'll come back here and pick me up on the corner an hour and fifteen minutes from now."

"All right."

He grabbed a bag. "C'mon," he said. "We'll take these out to the car. Matt, watch him, huh?"

They left, and TJ and I stood looking down at Raymond Callander. We both had guns, but either of us could have guarded him with a flyswatter at this point. He seemed barely present.

I looked at him and remembered our conversation in the cemetery, that minute or two when something human had been talking. I wanted to talk to him again and see what would come out this time.

I said, "Were you just going to leave Albert there?"

"Albert?" He had to think about it. "No," he said at length. "I was going to tidy up before I left."

"What would you do with him?"

"Cut him up. Wrap him. There's plenty of Hefty bags in the cupboard."

"And then what? Deliver him to somebody in the trunk of the car?"

"Oh," he said, remembering. "No, that was for the Arab's benefit. But it's easy. You spread them around, put them in dumpsters, trash cans. No one ever notices. Put them in with restaurant garbage and they just pass as meat scraps."

"You've done this before."

"Oh, yes," he said. "There were more women than you know about." He looked at TJ. "One black one I remember. She was just about your color." He heaved a sigh. "I'm tired," he said.

"It won't be long."

"You're going to leave me with him," he said, "and he's going to kill me. That Arab."

Phoenician, I thought.

"You and I know each other," he said. "I know you lied to me, I know you broke your promise, that was what you had to do. But you and I had a conversation. How can you just let him kill me?"

Whining, querulous. It was impossible not to think of Eichmann in the dock in Israel. How could we do this to him?

And I thought, too, of a question I had asked him in the graveyard, and I fed his own remarkable answer back to him.

"You got in the truck," I said.

"I don't understand."

"Once you get in the truck," I said, "you're just body parts."

We picked up Kenan as arranged at a quarter to three in the morning in front of a credit jeweler on Eighth Avenue, just around the corner from Albert Wallens's house. He saw me behind the wheel and asked where his brother was. I said we'd dropped him off a few minutes ago at the house on Colonial Road. He was going to pick up the Toyota, but changed his mind and said he'd go straight to sleep.

"Yeah? Me, I'm so wired you'd have to hit me over the head with a mallet to put me out. No, stay there, Matt. You drive." He walked around the car, looked in back at TJ, sprawled across the rear seat like a rag doll. "Past his bedtime," he said. "That flight bag looks familiar, but I hope it's not full of counterfeit money this time."

"It's your hundred and thirty thousand. We did our best. I don't think there's any schlock mixed in."

"If there is it's no big deal. It's just about as good as the real stuff. Your best bet's the Gowanus. You know how to get back on it?"

"I think so."

"And then the bridge or the tunnel, up to you. My brother offer to take my money into the house with him, keep an eye on it for me?"

"I felt it was part of my job to deliver it personally."

"Yeah, well, that's a diplomatic way to put it. I wish I could take back one thing I said to him, telling him he had a junkie mind. That's a hell of a thing to say to a person."

"He agreed with you."

"That's the worst thing about it, we both of us know it's true. Yuri surprised to see the money?"

"Astonished."

He laughed. "I'll bet. How's his kid?"

"The doctor says she'll be all right."

"They hurt her bad, didn't they?"

"I gather it's hard to separate the physical damage from the emotional trauma. They raped her repeatedly and I understand she sustained some internal injuries besides losing the two fingers. She was sedated, of course. And I think the doctor gave Yuri something."

"He should give us all something."

"Yuri tried to, as a matter of fact. He wanted to give me some money."

"I hope you took it."

"No."

"Why not?"

"I don't know why not. It's uncharacteristic behavior on my part, I'll tell you that much."

"Not the way they taught you at the Seventy-eighth Precinct?"

"Not at all what they taught me at the Seven-Eight. I told him I already had a client and I'd been paid in full. Maybe what you said about blood money struck some kind of chord."

"Man, that makes no sense. You were working and you did good work. He wants to give you something, you ought to take it."

"That's okay. I told him he could give TJ something."

"What did he give him?"

"I don't know. A couple of bucks."

"Two hundred," TJ said.

"Oh, you awake, TJ? I thought you were asleep."

"No, just closed my eyes is all."

"You stick with Matt here. I think he's a good influence."

"He be lost without me."

"Is that right, Matt? Would you be lost without him?"

"Absolutely," I said. "We all would."

I took the BQE and the bridge, and when we came off it on the Manhattan side I asked TJ where I could drop him.

"Deuce be fine," he said.

"It's three in the morning."

"Ain't no gate around the Deuce, Bruce. They don't close it up."

"Have you got a place to sleep?"

"Hey, I got money in my pocket," he said. "Maybe I see if they got my old room at the Frontenac. Take me three or four showers, call down for room service. I got a place to sleep, man. You don't need to be worryin' about me."

"Anyway, you're resourceful."

"You think you jokin' but you know it be true."

"And attentive."

"Both them things."

We dropped him at the corner of Eighth Avenue and Forty-second Street and caught a light at Forty-fourth. I looked both ways and there was no one around, but neither was I in a hurry. I waited until it changed.

I said, "I didn't think you could do it."

"What? Callander?"

I nodded.

"I didn't think I could either. I never killed anybody. I've been angry enough to kill, one time or another, but anger passes."

"Yes."

"He was like nothing, you know? A completely insignificant man. And I thought, how am I going to kill this worm? But I knew I had to do it. So I figured out what I had to do."

"What was that?"

"I got him talking," he said. "I asked him a few questions, and he gave little two-word replies, but I kept at it and I got him talking. He told me what they did to Yuri's kid."

"Oh."

"What they did to her and how scared she was and all. Once he got into it he really wanted to talk. Like it was a way for him to have the experience again. See, it's not like hunting, where after you shoot the deer you get to stuff the head and hang it on the wall. Once he was done with a woman he was left with nothing but memories, so he welcomed the chance to take them out and dust them off and look at how pretty they are."

"Did he talk about your wife?"

"Yeah, he did. He liked that he was telling it to me, too. Same as he liked giving her back to me in pieces, rubbing my nose in it. I wanted to shut him up, I didn't want to hear that, but fuck it, you know? I mean, she's gone, I fed her to the fucking flames, man. It can't hurt her no more. So I let him talk all he fucking wanted, and then I could do what I had to do."

"And then you killed him."

"No."

I looked at him.

"I never killed nobody. I'm not a killer. I looked at him and I thought, no, you son of a bitch, I am not gonna kill you."

"And?"

"How could I be a killer? I was supposed to be a doctor. I told you about that, right?"

"Your father's idea."

"I was supposed to be a doctor. Petey'd be an architect because he was a dreamer, but I was the practical one, so I'd be a doctor. 'Best thing in the world to be,' he told me. 'You do some good in the world and you make a decent living.' He even decided what kind of a doctor I should be. 'Be a surgeon,' he told me. 'That's where the money is. That's the elite, top of the heap. Be a surgeon.'" He was silent for a long moment. "So all right," he said. "I was a surgeon tonight. I operated."

It had started to rain, but it wasn't coming down hard. I didn't switch on the windshield wipers.

"I took him downstairs," Kenan said. "In the basement, where his friend was, and TJ was right, it stank something awful down there. I guess the bowels let go when you die like that. I thought I was gonna gag, but I didn't, and I guess I got used to it.

"I didn't have any anesthetic, but that was okay because he passed out right away. I had his knife, big jackknife with a blade about six inches long, and there were all sorts of tools on the workbench, anything you could possibly need."

"You don't have to tell me, Kenan."

"No," he said, "you're wrong, that's exactly what I have to do is tell you. If you don't want to listen that's something else, but I gotta tell you."

"All right."

"I cut his eyes out," he said, "so he'd never look at another woman. And I cut his hands off so he'll never touch one. I used tourniquets so he wouldn't bleed out, I made 'em out of wire. I took his hands off with a cleaver, wicked fucking thing. I suppose it's what they used to, uh—"

He breathed deeply, in and out, in and out.

"To dismember the bodies," he went on. "I opened his pants. I didn't want to touch him but I forced myself, and I cut off his works 'cause he wasn't gonna have any further use for 'em. And then his feet, I chopped his fucking feet off, because where's he got to go? And his ears, because what does he have to listen to? And his tongue, part of his tongue, I couldn't get it all, but I gripped it with a pliers and pulled it out of his mouth and cut off what I could, because who wants to hear him talk? Who wants to listen to that shit? *Stop the car.*"

I braked and pulled over, and he opened the car door and vomited in the gutter. I gave him a handkerchief and he wiped his mouth and dropped it in the street. "Sorry," he said, pulling the door shut. "I thought I was done doing that. Thought the tank was empty."

"Are you all right, Kenan?"

"Yeah, I think I am. I believe so. You know, I said I didn't kill him but I don't know if that's true. He was alive when I left but he could be dead by now. And if he isn't dead, shit, what's he got left? It was fucking butchery, what I did to him. Why couldn't I just shoot him in the head? Bang and it's over."

"Why didn't you?"

"I don't know. Maybe I was thinking eye for eye, tooth for tooth. He gave her back to me in pieces so I'll show him piece-work. Some of that, maybe. I don't know." He shrugged. "Fuck it, it's done. He lives or he dies, so what, it's over."

I parked in front of my hotel and we both got out of the

car and stood awkwardly on the curb. He pointed to the flight bag and asked if I wanted some of the money. I told him his retainer more than covered my time. Was I sure? Yes, I said. I was sure.

"Well," he said. "If you're sure. Give me a call some night, we'll have dinner. Will you do that?"

"Sure."

"Take care now," he said. "Go get some sleep."

23

But I couldn't sleep.

I took a shower and got in bed, but I couldn't even find a position I was able to stay in for more than ten seconds. I was too restless even to think about sleeping.

I got up and shaved and put on fresh clothes, and I turned on the TV and made a circuit of the channels and switched the set off again. I went outside and walked around until I found a place where I could have a cup of coffee. It was past four and the bars were closed. I didn't feel like drinking, I hadn't even thought of a drink all night long, but I was just as happy the bars were closed.

I finished my coffee and walked around some more. I had a lot on my mind and it was easier to think it through if I was walking. Eventually I went back to my hotel, and then a little after seven I caught a cab downtown and went to the seven-thirty meeting on Perry Street. It broke at eight-thirty, and I had breakfast at a Greek coffee shop on Greenwich Avenue and wondered if the owner would skim the sales tax, as Peter Khoury had said. I took a cab back to the hotel. Kenan would have been proud of me, I was taking cabs left and right.

I called Elaine when I got back to my room. Her machine picked up and I left a message and sat there waiting for her to call back. It was around ten-thirty when she did.

She said, "I was hoping you would call. I've been wondering what happened. After that phone call—"

"A lot happened," I said. "I want to tell you about it. Can I come over?"

"Now?"

"Unless you have something planned."

"Not a thing."

I went downstairs and took my third cab of the morning. When she let me in her eyes searched my face and she looked troubled by what she found there. "Come in," she said. "Sit down, I made coffee. Are you all right?"

"I'm fine," I said. "I didn't get to sleep last night, that's all."

"Again? You're not going to make a habit of this, are you?"

"I don't think so," I said.

She brought me a cup of coffee and we sat in her living room, she on the couch and I in a chair, and I started with my first conversation the previous day with Kenan Khoury and went all the way through to our last talk, when he dropped me at the Northwestern. She didn't interrupt, nor did her attention wander. I took a long time telling it, not leaving anything out, and reporting occasional conversations essentially verbatim. She hung on every word.

When I was done she said, "I'm overwhelmed, I think. That's quite a story."

"Just another night in Brooklyn."

"Uh-huh. I'm surprised you told me all of it."

"I am, too, in a way. It's not what I came here to tell you."

"Oh?"

"But I didn't want to leave it untold," I said, "because I don't want to have things I don't tell you. And that *is* what I came here to tell you. I've been going to meetings and saying things to a roomful of strangers that I don't let myself say to you, and that doesn't make sense to me."

"I think I'm scared."

"You're not the only one."

"Do you want more coffee? I can—"

"No. I watched Kenan drive off this morning and I went upstairs and went to bed, and all I could think about was things I haven't said to you. You'd think what Kenan told me might keep a person awake, but it didn't even enter my mind. There was no room for it, it was too full of a conversation with you, except it was a very one-sided conversation because you weren't there."

"Sometimes it's easier that way. You can write the other person's lines for them." She frowned. "For him. For her. For me?"

"Somebody had better write your lines, if that's how they come out when you make them up yourself. Oh, Jesus, the only way to say it is to say it. I don't like what you do for a living."

"Oh."

"I didn't know it bothered me," I said, "and early on it probably didn't, I probably got a kick out of it, if you go all the way back to the beginning. Our beginning. And then there was a period when I didn't think it bothered me, and then a stage where I knew it did but tried to tell myself it didn't.

"Besides, what right did I have to say anything? It's not as though I didn't know what I was getting into. Your occupation was part of the package. Where did I get off telling you to keep this and change that?"

I went to her window and looked across at Queens. Queens is the borough of cemeteries, it overflows with them, while Brooklyn has only Green-Wood.

I turned to face her and said, "Besides, I was scared to say anything. Maybe it would lead to an ultimatum, choose one or the other, quit turning tricks or I'm out of here. And suppose you didn't pick me?

"Or suppose you did? Then what does that commit me to? Does it give you the right to tell me what you don't like about the way I live my life?

"If you stop going to bed with clients, does that mean I can't go to bed with other women? As it happens I haven't been with anybody else since we started keeping company again, but I've always felt I had the right. It hasn't happened, and once or twice I made a conscious choice to keep it from happening, but I didn't feel committed to that course. Or if I did it was a secret commitment. I wasn't about to let either of us know about it.

"What happens to our relationship? Does it mean we have to get married? I don't know that I want to. I was married once and I didn't much like it. I wasn't very good at it, either.

"Does it mean we have to live together? I don't know that I want that, either. I haven't lived with anybody since I left Anita and the boys, and that was a long time ago. There are things I like about living alone. I don't know that I want to give it up.

"But it eats at me, knowing you're with other guys. I know there's no love in it, I know there's precious little sex in it, I know it has more in common with massage than with lovemaking. Knowing this doesn't seem to matter.

"And it gets in the way. I called you this morning and you called back an hour later. And I wondered where you were when I called, but I didn't ask because you might say you were with a john. Or you might not say it, and I'd wonder what you weren't saying."

"I was getting my hair done," she said.

"Oh. It looks nice."

"Thanks."

"It's different, isn't it? It does look nice. I didn't notice, I never notice, but I like it."

"Thank you."

"I don't know where I'm going with this," I said. "But I figured I had to tell you how I felt, and what's been going on with me. I love you. I know that's a word we don't speak, and one reason I have trouble with it is I don't know what the hell it means. But whatever it means, it's how I feel about you. Our relationship is important to me. In fact its importance is part of the problem, because I've been so afraid it would change into something I won't like that I've been withholding myself from you." I stopped for breath. "I guess that's it. I didn't know I was going to say that much and I don't know if it came out right, but I guess that's it."

She was looking at me. It was hard to meet her gaze.

"You're a very brave man," she said.

"Oh, please."

"'Oh, please.' You weren't scared? *I* was scared, and I wasn't even talking."

"Yes, I was scared."

"That's what brave is, doing what scares you. Walking into those guns at the cemetery must have been a piece of cake in comparison."

"The funny thing is," I said, "I wasn't that fearful at the cemetery. One thought that came to me was that I've lived long enough so that I don't have to worry about dying young."

"That must have been comforting."

"Well, it was, oddly enough. My biggest fear was that something would happen to the girl and that it would be my fault, for doing something wrong or not taking some useful action. Once she was back with her father I relaxed. I guess I didn't really believe anything was going to happen to me."

"Thank God you're all right."

"What's the matter?"

"Just a few tears."

"I didn't mean to—"

"To what, to reach me emotionally? Don't apologize."

"All right."

"So my mascara runs. So what." She dabbed at her eyes with a tissue. "Oh, God," she said. "This is so embarrassing. I feel so stupid."

"Because of a few tears?"

"No, because of what I have to say next. My turn now, okay?"

"Okay."

"Don't interrupt, huh? There's something I haven't told you, and I feel really stupid about it, and I don't know where to start. All right, I'll blurt it out. I quit."

"Huh?"

"I quit. I quit fucking, all right? My God, the look on your face. Other men, silly. I quit."

"You don't have to make that decision," I said. "I just wanted to say how I felt, and—"

"You weren't going to interrupt."

"I'm sorry, but—"

"I'm not saying I quit now. I quit three months ago. More than three months ago. Sometime before the first of the year. Maybe it was even before Christmas. No, I think there was one guy after Christmas. I could look it up.

"But it doesn't matter. I could look it up if I ever want to celebrate my anniversary, the way you celebrate the date of your last drink, but maybe not. I don't know."

It was hard not saying anything. I had things to say, questions to ask, but I let her go on.

"I don't know if I ever told you this," she said, "but a few years ago I realized that prostitution saved my life. I'm serious about that. The childhood I had, my crazy mother, the kind of teenager I turned out to be, I think I probably would have killed myself, or found somebody to do it for me. Instead I started selling my ass, and it made me aware of my worth as a human being. It destroys a lot of girls, it really does, but it saved me. Go figure.

"I made a nice life for myself. I saved my money, I invested, I bought this apartment. Everything worked.

"But sometime last summer I started to realize that it wasn't working anymore. Because of what we have. You and I. I told myself that was meshugga, what you and I have is in one compartment and what I do for money is way over there, but it got harder to keep the doors of the compartments shut tight. I felt disloyal, which was strange, and I felt dirty, which was something I never really felt hooking, or if I did I was never aware of it.

"So I thought, well, Elaine, you had a longer run than most of them, and you're a little old for the game anyway. And they've got all these new diseases, and you've had a scaled-down practice the past few years anyway, and just how many executives do you figure would throw themselves out of windows if you hung it up?

"But I was afraid to tell you. For one thing, how did I know I wouldn't want to change my mind? I figured I ought to keep my options open. And then, after I'd told all my regulars I was retired, after I sold my book and did everything but change my number, I was afraid to tell you because I didn't know what it would do. Maybe you wouldn't want me anymore. Maybe I'd stop being interesting, I'd just be this aging broad running around taking college courses. Maybe you'd feel trapped, like I was pressuring you into marriage. Maybe *you'd* want to get married, or live together, and I haven't ever been married but then again I haven't ever wanted to be. And I've lived alone ever since I got out of my mother's house, and I'm good at it and I'm used to it. And if one of us wants to get married and the other doesn't, then where are we?

"So that's my dirty little secret, if you want to call it that, and I wish to God I could stop crying because I'd like to look presentable, if not glamorous. Do I look like a raccoon?"

"Only the face."

"Well," she said. "That's something. You're just an old bear. Did you know that?"

"So you've said."

"Well, it's true. You're my bear and I love you."

"I love you."

"The whole thing's very fucking Gift-of-the-Magi, isn't it? It's a beautiful story and who can we tell?"

"Nobody diabetic."

"Send 'em right into sugar shock, wouldn't it?"

"I'm afraid so. Where do you go when you slip away for mysterious appointments? I assumed, you know—"

"That I was going to blow some guy in a hotel room. Well, sometimes I was getting my hair done."

"Like this morning."

"Right. And sometimes I was going to my shrink appointment, and—"

"I didn't know you were seeing a shrink."

"Uh-huh, twice a week since mid-February. A lot of my identity is bound up in what I've been doing all these years, and all of a sudden I've got a lot of crap to deal with. I guess it helps to talk to her." She shrugged. "And I've gone to a couple of Al-Anon meetings, too."

"I didn't know that."

"Well, how would you know? I didn't tell you. I figured they could give me tips on how to deal with you. Instead their program is all about dealing with myself. I call that sneaky."

"Yeah, they're devious bastards."

"Anyway," she said, "I feel stupid for keeping it all to myself, but I was a whore for a lot of years, and candor's not part of the job description."

"As opposed to police work."

"Right. You poor bear, up all night, running around Brooklyn with crazy people. And it's going to be hours before you get a chance to sleep."

"Oh?"

"Uh-huh. You're my only sexual outlet now, do you realize what that means? I'm likely to prove insatiable."

"Let's see," I said.

And, later, she said, "You really haven't been with anybody else since we've been together?"

"No."

"Well, you probably will. Most men do. I speak as one with professional knowledge of the subject."

"Maybe," I said. "Not today, though."

"No, not today. But if you do it's not the end of the world. Just so you come home where you belong."

"Whatever you say, dear."

"'Whatever you say, dear.' You just want to go to sleep. Listen, as far as the other's concerned, we can get married or not get married, and we can live together or not live together. We could live together without getting married. Could we get married without living together?"

"If we wanted."

"You think so? You know what it sounds like, it sounds like a Polish joke. But maybe it would work for us. You could keep your squalid hotel room, and several nights a week you'd put on Call Forwarding and spend the night with *moi*. And we could ... you know what?"

"What?"

"I think this is all something we're going to have to take a day at a time."

"That's a good phrase," I said. "I'll have to remember that."

24

A day or so later, an anonymous tip led officers of Brooklyn's Seventy-second Precinct to the house Albert Wallens had inherited upon his mother's death three years before. There they found Wallens, a twenty-eight-year-old unemployed construction worker with a record of sexual offenses and minor assault charges. Wallens was dead, with a length of piano wire fastened around his neck. In the same basement room they also found what appeared to be the mutilated corpse of another man, but thirty-six-year-old Raymond Joseph Callander, whose employment history included a seven-month hitch as a civilian employee with the New York office of the Drug Enforcement Administration, was still alive. He was removed to Maimonides Medical Center where he regained consciousness but was unable to communicate, making simple cawing sounds until his death two days later.

Evidence discovered in the Wallens house, and in two vehicles found in the adjacent garage, strongly implicated both men in several homicides which police at Brooklyn Homicide had recently determined to be linked, and to be the work of a team of serial killers. Several theories sprang up to explain the death scene, the most persuasive of which suggested that there had been a third man on the team and that he had slain his two partners and made his escape. Another conjecture, given less credence by anyone who had seen Callander or read his injury report at all closely, held that Callander had gone completely out of control, first killing his partner with a garrote, then indulging in a fitful orgy of self-mutilation. Considering that he'd somehow managed to divest himself of hands, feet, ears, eyes, and genitalia, "fitful" would barely begin to describe it.

Drew Kaplan represented Pam Cassidy in her negotiations with a national tabloid. They ran her story, "I Lost a Breast to the Sunset Park Choppers," and paid her what Kaplan called "a high five-figure price." In a conversation conducted without her attorney present, I was able to assure Pam that Albert and Ray were indeed the men who had abducted her, and that there was no third man. "You mean Ray really did himself like that?" she wondered. Elaine told her there are some things we aren't meant to know.

About a week after Callander's death, which would have made it sometime around the end of the week following our trip to the cemetery, Kenan Khoury called me from downstairs to say that he was double-parked out front. Could I come down and have a cup of coffee or something?

We went around the corner to the Flame and got a table by the window. "I was in the neighborhood," he said. "Thought I'd stop by, say hello. It's good to see you."

It was good to see him, too. He was looking well, and I told him so.

"Well, I made a decision," he said. "I'm taking a little trip."

"Oh?"

"More accurately, I'm leaving the country. I cleaned up a lot of loose ends the past few days. I sold the house."

"That quickly?"

"I owned it outright and I sold it for cash. I sold very cheap. The new owners are Korean, and the old guy came to the closing with his two sons and a shopping bag full of money. Remember

Petey saying it was a shame Yuri wasn't a Greek, he coulda raised so much cash that way? Man, he shoulda been Korean. They're in a business don't know from checks, credit cards, payrolls, taxes, nothing. The whole business is conducted in green. I got the cash, they got clear title, and they damn near gave birth when I showed 'em how to use the burglar alarm. They loved that. State of the art, man. They oughta love it."

"Where are you going?"

"Belize first, to see some relatives. Then Togo."

"To go in the family business?"

"We'll see. For a little while, anyway. See if I like it, see if I can stand living there. I'm a Brooklyn boy, you know. Born and raised. I don't know if I can hack it that far from the old neighborhood. I might be bored to death in a month."

"Or you might love it."

"No way to know unless you try, right? I can always come back."

"Sure."

"It's not a bad idea to leave now, though," he said. "I told you about that hash deal, right?"

"You said you didn't have much faith in it."

"Yeah, well, I walked away from it. I had a lot of money in it, too, and I walked. I didn't walk, you'd have to talk to me through bars."

"There was a bust?"

"There was indeed, and they had an invitation with my name on it, but this way even if the guys they caught roll over, which I'm sure they will, they still got no real case against me. But what do I need with the bullshit of subpoenas and all that, you know? I've never been arrested, so why don't I get the hell out of the country while I'm still a virgin?"

"When do you leave?"

"Plane leaves from JFK in what, six hours? From here I drive out to a Buick dealer on Rockaway Boulevard and take whatever he'll give me for the car. 'Sold,' I'll say, 'provided you throw in a ride to the airport,' which is like five minutes from there. Unless you want a car, man. You can have it for like half of Blue Book just to save me the aggravation."

"I can't use it."

"Well, I tried. Did my part to try to keep you out of the subways. Would you take it as a gift? I'm serious. Run me out to Kennedy and you can have it. The hell, if you don't want it you can take it straight over to the car lot yourself, make a few dollars on the deal."

"I wouldn't do that and you know it."

"Well, you could. You don't want the car, huh? It's my only remaining loose end. Past few days I saw some of Francine's relatives, told 'em more or less what happened. I tried to leave out some of the horror of it, you know? But you can only sweeten it up so much and you're still left with the fact that a good and gentle and beautiful woman is dead for no fucking reason at all." He put his head in his hand. "Jesus," he said, "you think you're over it and it comes and takes you by the throat. Point is I told her folks she had died. I said it was a terrorist thing, it happened overseas, we were in Beirut, it was political, crazy people, you know, and they bought it, or at least I think they bought it. Way I told it, it was quick and painless, the terrorists were killed themselves by the Christian militia, and the service was private and unpublicized because the whole incident had to be hushed up. Some of it's more or less parallel with the truth. Some I wish was true. The quick and painless part."

"It may have been quick. You don't know."

"I was there at the end, Matt. Remember? He told me what they did to her." He closed his eyes, breathed deeply. "A change of subject," he said. "You seen my brother at any of your meetings lately? What's the matter, that a delicate subject?"

"In a manner of speaking," I said. "See, AA's an anonymous program, and one of the traditions is that you don't tell someone not in the program what gets said at a meeting, or who does or doesn't attend. I stretched a point before because we were all involved in a case together, but as a general thing that's probably not a question I can answer."

"It wasn't really a question," he said.

"What do you mean?"

"I guess I just wanted to feel things out, see what you knew or didn't know. Fuck it, there's no way to ease into this. I got a call from the police the night before last. See, the Toyota was registered in my name, so who else would they call?"

"What happened?"

"They found the car abandoned in the middle of the Brooklyn Bridge."

"Oh, Jesus, Kenan."

"Yeah."

"I'm very sorry."

"I know you are, Matt. It's so fucking sad, isn't it?"

"Yes, it is."

"He was a beautiful guy, he really was. He had his weaknesses but who the fuck doesn't, you know?"

"They're sure that—"

"Nobody specifically saw him go over, and they didn't recover a body, but they told me the body might never be recovered. I hope it never is. Do you know why?"

"I think so."

"Yeah, I bet you do. He told you he wanted to be buried at sea, right?"

"Not in so many words. He told me how water was his element, though, and how he wouldn't want to burn up or be buried in the earth. The implication was clear, and the way he talked about it—"

"Like he was looking forward to it."

"Yes," I said. "Like he longed for it."

"Ah, Jesus. He called me, I don't know, a day, two days before he did it. If anything happened to him would I make sure he was buried at sea. I said yeah, sure, Petey. I'll book a stateroom on the QE Fucking Two and slip you out the porthole. And we both laughed, and I hung up and forgot about it, and then they call me up and they found his car on the bridge. He loved bridges."

"He told me."

"Yeah? When he was a kid he loved 'em. He was always after our father to drive over bridges. Couldn't get enough of 'em, thought they were the most beautiful thing in the world. One he jumped off, the Brooklyn, that does happen to be a beautiful bridge."

"Yes."

"Same water under it as all the others, though. Ah, he's at peace, the poor guy. I guess it's what he always wanted, you come right down to it. The only peace he had in his life was when he had smack in his veins, and aside from the rush the sweetest thing about heroin is it's just like death. Only it's temporary. That's what's good about it. Or what's wrong with it, I guess, depending on your point of view."

And a couple of days after that I was getting ready for bed when the phone rang. It was Mick.

"You're up early," I said.

"Am I then?"

"It must be six in the morning there. It's one o'clock here."

"Is it," he said. "My watch stopped, don't you know, and I called in the hope that you could tell me the time."

"Well, this must be a good time to call," I said, "because we've got a perfect connection."

"Clear, is it?"

"As if you were in the next room."

"Well, I should fucking well hope so," he said, "as I'm at Grogan's. Rosenstein got everything cleared up for me. My flight was delayed or I'd have been in hours ago."

"I'm glad you're back."

"No more than I. She's a grand old country, but you wouldn't want to live there. But how are you keeping? Burke says you haven't been around the saloon much."

"No, not much at all."

"So why don't you get yourself down here now?"

"Why not?"

"Good man," he said. "I'll put up a pot of coffee for you and crack the seal on a bottle of Jameson. I've a great store of tales to tell."

"I have a few of my own."

"Ah, we'll make a night of it, won't we now? And go to the butchers' mass in the morning."

"We might do that," I said. "It wouldn't surprise me."

All Orion/Phoenix titles are available at your local bookshop or from the following address:

Littlehampton Book Services
Cash Sales Department L
14 Eldon Way, Lineside Industrial Estate
Littlehampton
West Sussex BN17 7HE
telephone 01903 721596, *facsimile* 01903 730914

Payment can either be made by credit card (Visa and Mastercard accepted) or by sending a cheque or postal order made payable to *Littlehampton Book Services.*
DO NOT SEND CASH OR CURRENCY.

Please add the following to cover postage and packing

UK and BFPO:
£1.50 for the first book, and 50P for each additional book to a maximum of £3.50

Overseas and Eire:
£2.50 for the first book plus £1.00 for the second book and 50p for each additional book ordered

----

BLOCK CAPITALS PLEASE

name of cardholder ....   *delivery address*
....   *(if different from cardholder)*

address of cardholder ....
....
....
....
postcode ....   *postcode* ....

☐ I enclose my remittance for £..............................

☐ please debit my Mastercard/Visa (delete as appropriate)

card number ☐☐☐☐☐☐☐☐☐☐☐☐☐☐☐☐

expiry date ☐☐☐☐

signature ....

prices and availability are subject to change without notice